FRANK P. RYAN

The Return of the Arinn

Jo Fletcher
BOOKS

First published in Great Britain in 2015 by

Jo Fletcher Books
an imprint of
Quercus Publishing Ltd
Carmelite House
50 Victoria Embankment
London EC4Y 0DZ

An Hachette UK company

A CIP catalogue record for this book is available from the British Library

PB ISBN 978 1 78087 742 6
EBOOK ISBN 978 1 78429 137 2

10 9 8 7 6 5 4 3 2 1

Typeset by CC Book Production
Printed and bound in Great Britain by Clays Ltd, St Ives plc

Frank P. Ryan is a multiple-bestselling author, in the UK and US. The first three books in The Three Powers series, *The Snowmelt River*, *The Tower of Bones* and *The Sword of Feimhin* are also published by Jo Fletcher Books. In addition to fantasy, he has written science fiction, contemporary fiction and a contemporary novel. His books have been translated into ten different languages.

Also by Frank P. Ryan

The Snowmelt River

The Tower of Bones

The Sword of Feimhin

For my late mother, who inspired me with her song of Ree Nashee in the shadow of the magic mountain.

For my late mother, who inspired me with her song of Rey Noshee in the shadow of the magic mountain

What none would appear to presume, other than my ageing self, is that all might be part of a cycle. A very great cycle, to be sure, in which a world or even a universe might be renewed. Once one becomes aware of cycles, one sees them everywhere: in flower and seed, in animal display and courtship, in the summer of desire, and the autumn of the fruit of that desire, in the death of winter and the rebirth of spring. The cyclical nature of being, of what we fondly describe as reality, is fundamental to all. But even in the glory of that universal realisation, I see now how other eyes might weigh the same possibilities with avarice. What then would such a rebirth make of that order and justice – the implicit rightfulness of all we hold dear? This provokes a terrifying possibility – a despair that gnaws relentlessly within my spirit.

Could it be that what we assumed as natural and inevitable might be confounded? Could our most fervent hopes be corrupted to the ends of darkness?

Ussha De Danaan, the last High Architect of Ossierel

Contents

A Dragon's Regret

Spiralling as he rose on the battering winds, the Dragon King – Omdorrréilliuc to the worshipful Eyrie People and, more familiarly, Driftwood to Kate Shaunessy – found the thermals that were capable of bearing his titanic mass aloft. On the beach below, every face gazed up in rapture. Kate realised she must look minuscule, waving goodbye from on high to the fast-disappearing Cill children. They included her friend Shaami, and the special one who was already taller and more knowing than the others, the new Momu, who was gazing heavenwards with those big golden eyes. The pain of leaving them, knowing she might never see them again, felt like a cold splinter of iron impaled in Kate's heart. But all too soon they were gone, the beach reduced to a snowflake of brilliant white before it too was lost behind the clouds that were materialising against the up-thrust mountains.

The dragon's voice remained a rumble as deep as thunder

even when it addressed Kate mind-to-mind: <Weep not for others but for yourself in your coming ordeal.>

'I'll still miss them terribly.'

<The heart is a poor guide to reason.>

'Ah, sure, and where would we be without it?'

<Safer, perhaps. And besides, they no longer need your help.>

'No. They have a new young Momu to guide them.'

<And who in this war-torn world will guide you when you have proven yourself so refractory to common sense?>

'I know I've been unreasonable, but I'm back now. I do so hope that we remain friends. Please tell me where we are headed?'

<A Dragon King keeps his promises. I shall return you to your equally headstrong friend, the youthful Mage Lord, with his rune-warded spear and his arrogantly ambitious war.>

'Yes, please take me back to Alan. I'm desperate to see him again. But I had hoped . . . if it will not put us too far out of our way . . .'

<Am I to be a mind-reader, then?>

Kate bit her lip. Even within the shelter of Driftwood's dense ruff of bright green and yellow feathers she was shivering. The rushing gale of wind was growing rapidly fiercer as their flight gained pace, the cold numbing her cheeks and ears.

<Oh, very well then – I don't suppose it will take us too far out of our course if we pass by a certain island . . .>

'Thank you.'

<A small favour – but it is granted on the strict condition that you desist from all further pleadings for help to fulfil even more reckless behaviour . . .>

'I promise.'

Kate allowed her eyes to close upon sleep. A single night's rest on the beach had hardly cured her exhaustion. And the dreams she wandered into were hardly refreshing: if there was a landscape she never wished to see again, in dreams or reality, it was the Land of the Dead.

She woke up with a cry to discover Driftwood was gliding in slow wide circles over rocky buttresses that rose upwards for hundreds of feet out of the forested slopes. The air was warmer. Kate whooped – softly – with delight to witness the welcoming flocks of young dragons that rose out of the needle-like pillars of rocky landscape, which proved big enough to accommodate wooded plains on their pinnacles. On her last visit, the young dragons had been no more than babies, and she had delighted in watching them. But on this visit, Driftwood made no attempt to alight and spend time with his brood. For no more than a few minutes they wheeled and soared in the company of the excited young dragons before Driftwood bid them farewell in that deep incomprehensible tongue that Kate recognised, without need of translation, to be the language of beginnings.

'Permission to speak?'

<Would that you were incapable!>

'I'd have loved to have got to know them – your family.'

<Kate girl-thing has already forgotten that dragons eat juicy morsels such as herself.>

'Not your brood – you're a sea-dragon. You eat fish – sea creatures.'

<What difference in the belly of a hungry dragon – a fish, or a seal or a girl?>

Kate laughed. She just wanted to treasure the experience forever: the great wings beating, or gliding through the icy-cool air, the soaring pinnacles of pinkish rock capped with dense, semi-tropical greenery that were the perfect brood-chambers for the baby dragons, the excited antics of the youngsters, who left smoky trails perfumed with the fiery, incense-like musk of dragon's breath.

'Do you tell them fairy stories, like we tell our human children?'

<Baby dragons possess their stories. Each story is gifted to the individual offspring. It cannot be retold – or its lesson revealed to any other.>

'What's so special about each individual story?'

<There is a truth for each dragon in his or her story. The story is his or her first journey into self discovery.>

'How can there be so many different truths?'

<Kate girl-thing has much to learn.>

'Then explain – enlighten me, please?'

<You do not understand the destiny into which you rush headlong.>

'How can I understand if you will not explain?'

<Perhaps some destinies are better not explained.>

'Then treat me as a dragon-baby. Tell me my very own story.'

<You would not like to hear a dragon tale.>

'Try me.'

<You would experience the story in the telling. It would not merely feel real, it would become real in you.>

Kate chuckled. 'After what I've been through, I don't think I am capable of being shocked any further.'

<You are a very foolish, headstrong, reckless and exceedingly stubborn girl-thing.>

'I come from an island people famous for their recklessness. Oh, please, Driftwood – I thought we were friends?'

<A girl-thing cannot be friends with a Dragon King.>

'What are we, then?'

<A confusion of purpose. A conundrum.>

'Why a conundrum?'

<To the Eyrie People I am a god to be adored and venerated with prayer and sacrifice. Yet, it would appear that some foolish, headstrong, and exceedingly stubborn girl-thing assumes she is my friend because she resurrected me from my age-old slumber.>

'It wasn't from slumber and you know it. I resurrected you from a self-inflicted death: a death that happened in ages past, when you dragons bit off your own wings and sacrificed yourselves to the depths of the oceans. Moreover, I didn't resurrect you deliberately. The oraculum in my brow did it all by itself while I slept.'

<Thus would she correct a Dragon King!>

'Does it offend your godly – your *kingly* – pride that a minuscule girl-thing not only resurrected your poor wingless body but also gave you back your beautiful gold-veined wings?'

<Immensely.>

'Oh, Driftwood, tell me a story anyway.'

<Even though I caution you against it?>

'All the more so.'

<Be it on your own head. Welcome to a world of story in which you are now one with that lady of legend, Nimue the Naïve, wife of King Ree Nashee and, by that same marriage, Queen of the Wildwoods.>

'Well, I'm not sure that I want to become one with this Nimue the Naïve. Can't I just listen to her story?'

<It is too late to change your mind now. You have been gifted the tale and are now bound by the telling.>

Something . . . *everything* . . . had changed. Within Kate's being, a veil of time had been traversed and she had somehow lost track of her passage. There was an alien awareness of her surroundings, a heightening, as if her senses had multiplied. Something was whispering to her, bathing her in warmth that invaded her nostrils, filled her vision and then coated her entire skin. Kate only gradually became aware that the warmth was the breath from the mouth and nostrils of a face that filled her entire field of vision, and the tickling sticky sensation that enveloped her was a gigantic tongue. She felt suffused with emotions, such as fear and joy, and overwhelmed with the alien wonder of it.

'I never realised . . . I can't believe I'm experiencing it.'

<You wish the experience to end?>

'No – no. It's . . . wonderful, Driftwood. But . . . I'm changing. I didn't anticipate the profundity, the immediacy of it.'

<*HARRRUUMMMPPPPHHHH!*>

That deep sigh immersed her as if she had entered a waterfall, a thundering, skin-tingling cataract. Another veil . . . she was passing through veil after veil of experience and strangeness.

'I'm not a child; I'm fully grown. I don't understand . . . I know what I feel. I know what I am thinking. I feel so proud of my marriage to the king, but it's not as I might have anticipated. This is so very different.'

<Indeed: you are still the reckless Kate, but also now the youthful queen. And you are as vain as you are naïve by nature. How haughty your winsome beauty, with your eyes as blue as the summer sky and your cascade of fair hair that extends to beyond your girdled waist and has to be combed by your servant elves for a full hour every self-indulgent morning as you bathe in the pool of loveliness.>

'Oh, dear! Am I really that vain? And yet within myself I feel merely curious and kind. At least I would appear to be kind.'

<Kindness is no armour within a dragon tale.>

A dragon tale! It certainly felt different from the fairy

tales of Kate's childhood – she really was within it; she was feeling it happen.

'Oh, Driftwood – I am riding through an enchanted forest. It's so real I can feel my nostrils tingle with each breath of air.'

<You, the queen, delight to ride through the dells and woodlands on your silver-saddled unicorn, well-wishing everyone you meet on your travels while flaunting the bridal ring in their faces.>

'But I love them all. I love to greet them.'

<You neglect the danger such hubris might provoke . . . For these are the Wildwoods, and there are other perils that stalk them besides the one-eyed giant they call Balor . . .>

'What are you suggesting?'

<The inevitable fall that accompanies unseemly pride.>

How she loved the fact it was ever high summer here, with the cotton-wool clouds turning lazily in their blue heaven. But even here, a twist of magic could alter the mood of time and place in the blink of an eye . . . and fate. But surely her fate was to wake in the regal bedroom within the enchanted castle? So she reflected with pleasure on a night when there was a full moon shining in through the mullioned windows, the garden outside bathed with luminescence. There was music too, a lilting delight of harp notes, rising and falling, lulling her back to sleep.

Why was it wrong to delight in such bliss?

Queen Nimue glanced around the moonlit bedroom. She

was clearly sleeping alone. Presumably Ree Nashee slept alone too? But surely there would be servants, some watchful figures nearby, who would respond to her needs?

She tried calling out: 'Hello? I would so love a nightcap . . .'

But no servant answered her summons. She was close to panicking now, wishing she wasn't here.

'What is it, Driftwood? What is happening?'

<Your ring!>

'My ring?'

Her bridal ring! She raised her left hand and stared at it, but there was no ring on her finger. 'What's happened to it?'

<You have somehow managed to lose it.>

Panic overwhelmed her, making her feel close to fainting in her downy bed. What would the king say when he discovered she had lost her ring?

'I must have dropped it when I was riding through the Wildwoods.'

<Without the ring you can no longer rule beside the king. And your loss will hurt him deeply. Ree Nashee loves you above all else in his kingdom. Your absence from his side will weaken his control over the magic that is necessary for his reign. And without the influence of the king—>

'Darkness . . . Darkness will rise – as it rose when he was cast into the spell of sleep by Balor.'

<Indeed, and it is already rising. Thus has your vanity condemned you to search endlessly through a forest that has now become threatening.>

'But how do I recover the ring? How do I make the Wildwoods hale again?'

But even she spoke, she realised the lesson of her personal dragon tale. In her obsession to save the Cill, she had neglected Alan, who loved her and who was facing terrible dangers. Kate, who was also Nimue, felt her vision clouding as if real tears were filling up her eyes.

'Stop it, Driftwood. Stop this right now.'

But she could not so easily escape from the tale. She was still gliding through those eerie veils, but she was no longer in that sumptuous bedroom, now she was lost in the Wildwoods. She found herself standing by a low wall, below which a mound of pine bark marked the place where elfin foresters might have pulled consignments of logs over coping stones. She sat on the wall, brooding, feeling wan and sad in the pallid moonlight. Her tearful eyes darted between the grey shadows that surrounded her, her fearful fingers toying with the hoary beards of rosebay willow herb clinging to the crevices amongst the sloping stones. And then it dawned on her, with all the impossible logic of a dream, that she had arrived here a million times. She had followed the same ghostly trail, even on her final ride as queen. And now, dressed only in her white cotton nightdress, she haunted the woodland paths. And on this cold, moonlit night, a terrible winter beckoned. Her movements felt leaden with dread as she left the wall and emerged into the lonely glade. In the distance was a lake of utter darkness. She sensed the stillness of the air over the dark water that reflected the tall forest of pine trees on the far bank. Within the blue-black crepuscular mass, their twigs and needles like roinish hair, she saw tiny flickering lights, like will-o-the-wisps, that called her. All she had to do was float through the veils to join the other ghosts passing soundlessly across the confluences of stone, air and water.

As she stood there, paralysed by indecision, she felt gooseflesh all over her skin.

<Did I not warn you?>

'Yes, you did. Oh, Driftwood, I am a foolish girl-thing. I'm everything you said of me.'

<I warned you most specifically.>

'You did.'

<We talked of your reckless desire to save the Momu.>

'Yes – we talked.'

<I spoke of the dangers. Do you remember?>

'I remember telling you of my first meeting with the Momu. I described our meeting, in her chamber in Ulla Quemar, the birthing pool amid the roots of the One Tree.'

The dragon's voice deepened to what sounded like a rock-splitting roar. <There – there in your reference to the One Tree . . .>

'What is it?'

<The One Tree was a twig of the greater tree – The Tree of Life – and in its roots you discovered Nidhoggr.>

'Yes. He was trapped there, being starved of its sap, wasted to a ruin.'

<So you took it into your head to free him?>

'Yes. I—'

<Even in that void I warned you afresh.>

'Yes.'

<Do you now recall my warning?>

She remembered calling on Driftwood in a moment of the greatest peril. She recalled her very words on his arrival. '*Oh, Driftwood – if you are really here, please help me. The Tree of Life is being sucked dry by these horrible worms. I must stop them, but it's beyond my ability. I need to revive Nidhoggr.*'

<I would warn you> he had said, *<that the soul of Nidhoggr is Chaos.>*

'*Life, it seems to me, is nothing other than chaos – and that's certainly true if what I saw in the black cathedral is the Tyrant's vision of order.*'

<You must understand how dangerous this might be?>

'*There is danger everywhere I turn. But there's so much at stake – not just the Momu. These black worms are vast and there are millions upon millions of them. They're sapping the life out of the Tree. I dread to think . . .*'

Kate hesitated now, in a very different and yet equally perilous landscape. She sensed how even Driftwood shuddered.

<You remember now, Kate girl-thing, who is one with Nimue the Naïve, Queen of the Wildwoods, who has lost her ring?>

Kate nodded. Her heart thudded so forcefully it was nauseating. Before her a cart track twisted and turned, insisting that she took it even though it was in a state of disrepair.

She walked past a gnarled old oak and on into a coppice of evergreens. She sank her bare feet into its carpet of leaves. Her footsteps excited a musical tinkling from the crunching icy needles. The cold had contracted to a patina of grey over her skin.

<You freed Nidhoggr! And in doing so, you released Chaos into this world, and also into your own world, your beloved Earth.>

There was a flash of memory – the destruction of the Cathedral of the Dead by Nidhoggr; the screaming motes that were the souls of millions of dead. The experience had been terrifying, the most frightening scene that Kate had ever witnessed, and she could no longer bear the memory. She squeezed her eyes shut. When she opened them she was standing on the bank of the lake. The night was silent.

Something glittered below the surface of the water. When she peered more closely, she thought she could make out something twinkling golden, like an eye opening and closing where the penetrating moonlight ended and darkness began.

The ring . . .

A clawed finger was beckoning her. A pallid hand extended towards her, the ring of Ree Nashee in its open palm.

Kate froze with terror.

Now the silence was fractured. The water of the lake began to ripple with waves, washing against the shore, as if it were the edge of an ocean. There was still the same dreamy quality, as if time worked differently here. Her feet were exposed to the lapping waves. Her ears were filled by the sounds of the night: the hooting of owls, the liquid hiss as creatures broke the surface, the lapping of the waves. The cold was numbing her feet and hands. That same numbness was spreading, like a mask, over her face, beginning at her upper lip and cheeks. She felt dazed by the growing effects of the cold inside her mind, and spellbound by more subtle sensations: the symphony of the water, the attenuated reflections of moon on surface and the glimpse of bats fluttering across her vision.

I let Alan down.

How she loved him – a very special kind of love, the love that time and pain had not been able to destroy.

'Please – please let me go to him.'

<Have you forgotten the ring?>

'I don't want the ring any more. I can't go into the water to get it. You know I'm afraid of water now – I'm afraid of drowning in it.'

<It doesn't matter, reckless girl-queen. Nothing matters. Not any more . . .>

Who was speaking to her now, mind-to-mind? Was this truly the voice of her friend Driftwood, the dragon? Was she still blundering on within the dragon tale – her own special tale? Her numbed feet no longer registered the shore on which she was standing. It created an impression of dizziness, of floating on a cushion of air. She heard the screech of some hunting creature from the dark landscape behind her.

'I'm feeling breathless!'

Driftwood did not speak.

How could you feel breathless in a dream? Yet she had to breathe: she had to fill up her lungs with air. She swallowed past difficulty, looking down at the iridescent reflections of moonlight on the water's surface. She summoned up all of what remained of her courage and stared down once more into the rippling water. The hand was still there, the golden ring twinkling within its palm.

<Go on!>

Whose voice . . .?

She had to press her hands against her thighs to stand erect. As she took her first tentative steps into the shallow water, a roaring invaded her ears. Nervously, as carefully as she could manage with her tingling fingers, she pulled off her nightdress. She began to wade out over the unstable shingle. For a fraction of a moment, she couldn't feel the water through her numbed skin. She reached out her hand for the ring. The cold ate into her, burning like a flame. Her nostrils stung with the sharp tang of ozone. The flesh on her legs tightened so violently that every hair jerked erect, above and below the water, and neuralgic spasms locked her knees and cramped the muscles in the small of her back. Her feet, instantly losing all feeling, began to slip on the scummy stones and the sharp edges cut through her socks like broken glass.

She stopped, the water now halfway up her thighs. The moonlight danced on the coruscating surface as the wide lake rippled with hidden movement. It was as if a solid mass of tiny creatures were beckoning her with a strange wild hunger, impatient for her to join them in the water.

<Go on!>

'Who are you?'

<Don't stop – don't stop now!>

And then dread rose in her, paralysing her. 'I – I don't want to be here.'

<I did warn you that you would not like it.>

'Take me away. If you are still here, Driftwood – take me out of here.'

In the next moment she was back, her heart beating in her throat, within the safety of the dragon's ruff.

'I don't ever want to go there again.'

<But now a part of you will ever return to it.>

'Oh, please don't say that. You were right. I am the most stupid and stubborn of girls.'

<Sleep!>

'How on earth can I sleep? I'm too terrified.'

Yet sleep she did. When she roused again, Kate saw that they were crossing over the tops of a great mountain range, its razor-sharp summits high above the clouds.

'Where are we?'

<We are crossing the spine of the land – what the Eyrie People call the Flamestruck Mountains.>

The Wastelands into which Alan had taken his Shee

army! Kate couldn't imagine how they would have crossed these immensely high and treacherous-looking slopes. While asleep, frost had formed in her eyelashes and her nostrils were rimed in ice where her breath had frozen. She had never felt so cold in her life. She curled her body up and snuggled deeper, closer to the inner furnace of that monumental dragon's heart and the hillocks of pounding muscles where the warmth of their circulation would protect and comfort her.

'Can't you forgive me my stupid curiosity? You are, after all, supposed to be my friend.'

Silence other than the wailing of the wind.

'I did wake you from the dead.'

Still no answer.

'What are you scared of – you, Dragon King?'

Driftwood issued such a deep groan that it reverberated through the pounding muscles of his wings, folding around Kate's being like thunder.

<I think, perhaps, I should have eaten you when I had the chance.>

A Threat in the Dark

Mark's eyes lifted from the blazing barrier that blocked the road ahead and looked towards the small town beyond it, and the pitch black night sky above. He thought he'd heard the drone of an engine. Then he heard it again high overhead, above the blanket of clouds from which two days of spindrift snow had been falling. The snowflakes hitting his upturned face felt hard and sharp, like tiny icicles. He couldn't help shivering.

'What is it?' Cal's voice sounded behind Mark.

'A plane, sounds like an airliner.'

'What's it doing?'

'Circling, maybe. Looking for an airport?'

Cal clicked the safety on and off on the belt-driven Minimi machine gun he carried. 'Don't they know the grid's down? There are no lights to guide them in. No radar. Nothing!'

'Poor beggers,' Mark replied, then looked down again.

He had needed a break from the interior of the Mamma Pig where Padraig lay, deeply unconscious. The old man's breathing was rasping and his temperature was so high his skin felt like it was on fire. They were heading north in a desperate attempt to get him to Resistance HQ hidden away in the hills of Derbyshire, where he could be treated by military doctors. But they couldn't follow the obvious route: the M1, which would have taken them there in a matter of hours, as the motorways were traps. Field Marshall Seebox had taken them over under martial law and the Resistance were now fighting elements of what had formerly been the regular armed forces; those blinkered enough to follow Seebox. Armoured soldiers were patrolling all major roads. Seebox's forces had also taken control of the ports, power stations and the major towns and cities. But it was unlikely that he had managed to extend this control to the smaller towns and villages – as yet.

Despite this, the burning barrier up ahead was no regular army checkpoint. Several buildings, maybe whole streets, were already burning in the town behind it. That suggested Razzamatazzers – and likely irregulars like Paramilitaries and Skulls. Mark knew there would be some manning the barrier, while others would attempt to block the Mamma Pig from passing through the town, and he had no idea what weapons, if any, they might possess.

Mark looked up at the sky again. It was difficult to ignore the drone of the aircraft still circling overhead in the dark.

He wondered if it had been a good idea to leave Gully back at Tudor Farm. Gully knew things about the now ravaged London. He might have been a useful source of intelligence for the people at Resistance HQ. Besides, Mark had taken a liking to the streetwise kid. He regretted the fact that they had failed to rescue Gully's friend, Penny, when they had seen her at the arena. All they had of her was her extraordinary mural. What was the word Cogwheel had used to describe it?

A *palimpsest*!

A medieval word to describe one picture superimposed on another. But according to Gully it was about more than just pictures; Penny had been seeing visions in which creatures from some dark world were rising up and invading the famous streets and squares of London. The layers in the mural showed exactly that. They showed what Penny called the City Above, which was the normal world of the city, being invaded by another more alien world that Penny called the City Below.

Mark had his own reasons for finding Penny's vision deeply disturbing. He had been shown a similar vision by the strange Belizean woman, Henriette, and had witnessed wraith-like beings invading the normal streets of central London, drawn by the Sword of Feimhin. From what little Henriette had explained, they were coming out of the strange in-between-world called Dromenon. And, if he understood her correctly, they were possessing the young Razzamatazzers, driving them insane.

Now he examined the sky not with his eyes, but through the black glossy triangle of crystal that was embedded in his brow: the oraculum of the Third Power. It held magic that derived from another world called Tír, and a goddess of that world, Mórígán, the third member of the Holy Trídédana, and goddess of death and the battlefield. Through this power he could see beyond the falling snow and the clouds above to gaze into the starry heavens, where brilliant flares of colour rent the air. The vision resembled an explosive aurora borealis, but Mark knew that it had nothing to do with the beautiful northern lights.

He thought back to what they had witnessed in London. A black rose, a colossus of crystalline darkness a mile high, had enveloped the old city. From this a spectral image had been projected into the sky: a triple infinity, pulsating with enormous energy and constantly reforming; darkly magnificent and utterly terrifying. The obscene invasion of spectres, the Sword of Feimhin and the Black Rose were all somehow linked. Mark was in awe of the Rose even now, some thirty-odd miles northeast of the M25. He felt its malignant power reach out and overwhelm him with a presentiment of dread.

Nan emerged from behind the rear doors of the Mamma Pig to put an arm around Mark's neck. She must have been sharing his worries through their common oracula.

'How's Padraig?' Mark asked.

'The same.'

'He's stubborn. I know there's a surviving consciousness

inside there still. If only he can hold on until we can get him medical help.'

'Let's hope so.'

He kissed her lightly on the lips.

Nan turned towards the blazing barrier. 'There's something else there – something more than just Razzers. You must sense it too.'

'Yeah.'

Cal picked up on their conversation: 'What is it?'

Nan said: 'I don't know, but I sense an alien danger.'

'Mark?' Cal said.

Mark looked ahead, using his oraculum to penetrate the flaming barrier and see into the main street beyond. Illuminated by the fires, the buildings were a higgledy-piggledy arrangement of different frontages and sizes, some two- and some three-storied, some abutting the road. They had no idea what town it was since any helpful signs had been removed. An old Bedfordshire town they had to assume, that had grown in an unplanned organic way over the centuries.

'You see it?'

'Like Nan, I sense something. It feels a good deal more malignant than Razzamatazzers. It doesn't feel human.'

'But it knows we're coming. It'll be waiting for us,' Nan said. 'You think we should turn back? Find a way around it?'

'We don't have the time. Not with Padraig's condition.'

*

Mark had felt a mixture of exhaustion and elation as the mechanical bulk of the Mamma Pig had made it back in through the stone gateposts of the Tudor farm the previous evening. The return from London had not been easy. They had been forced to abandon their bikes at the arena and their escape from the city had been interrupted by road-blocks and machine gun battles. Luckily, the armoured walls of the Pig had guaranteed that nobody was hurt. Nan had fallen into an exhausted asleep against his shoulder and Mark had been obliged to wake her so she could look after Padraig while they looked for medical help. He'd joined Cal as he'd emerged from the Pig into squalling snow. It had been too soon for the snow to coat the ground to any extent, but it had blown into their faces as they'd run towards and entered through the big oak door into the main farm building. The moment they had walked in, they had encountered Resistance troops in camouflage uniforms dashing around the place. Cal had spoken to a guard:

'What's going on, mate?'

'An evacuation.'

As Cal hurried away to find an officer, Mark headed towards the ground floor chamber that had been put aside as an infirmary for the wounded. He discovered an empty shambles and the single, stressed-out figure of Sharkey, who was sitting on a camp bed with his denim shirt wide open at the front, his injured left shoulder and arm inside the body of the shirt.

'Hey mate – Good to see you!'

'Thought my friends had abandoned me.'

'No chance of that.' Mark sat down on the bed next to his friend. 'Where are the fighters headed?'

'Who knows? Most are heading for Resistance HQ – at least that's as much as I've been able to gather.'

'So, there's some new plan?'

'Dunno! You think they've confided in me?'

'C'mon, Sharkey,' Mark had said, as he'd helped him into the shirt. 'We need to get you out of here.'

They'd come across the bespectacled Jo Derby sitting on the floor of the corridor outside the chamber accompanied by a nervous looking Gully. She hauled herself to her feet on recognising them.

'Oh, Mark – Sharkey! Thank goodness!'

'We need the medics. Any idea where they've gone?' Mark had said.

'I doubt there are many left.'

'What's happening to the farm?'

'The military are moving out. Their presence is likely to attract attack now that Seebox is getting organised. There are hundreds of civilians, mostly families, who would be put at risk.'

'I've got to find a medic, Jo. We have a seriously injured VIP.'

'Who? One of the crew?'

'Padraig.'

'Oh, my goodness! I think there might be at least one doctor left. Come on – I'll help you to find him.'

Jo was proven right. There was just one medic left in the building: an anaesthetist named Hall. Mark had found himself half running beside Hall as he'd headed out to recover the gear he had already stowed in the back of a Landrover in preparation for leaving. Their conversation had been hurried; Mark helping him carry the stuff back in while explaining Padraig's situation. Meanwhile, Bull had hauled the emaciated body of Padraig out of the Pig and onto the camp bed evacuated by Sharkey in the infirmary. Dr Hall had taken a brief look at Padraig and had said something about ketotic breathing.

'What's that?' Mark had asked.

'It's the kind of breathing you'd expect in someone who has been subjected to long term starvation.' He'd put a nasogastric tube down one of Padraig's nostrils and put his fingers into Padraig's gaping mouth, ferreting about at the back of his throat to guide the tube down into Padraig's stomach. 'This'll help get some fluid, calories and essential vitamins into him.'

'Is there anything more you can do?'

'You want me to try setting up a central line?'

'Anything that might help.'

Mark had watched in tense silence as Dr Hall made an incision above Padraig's left collarbone, and inserted a much finer tube into a vein.

'There you go – one subclavian line.'

'Thanks.'

'You understand what it does?'

'No.'

'It goes down into the right atrium of his heart.'

'What's it for?'

'Gets even more fluids and calories into the circulation. But more importantly, this line won't clot so easily as a peripheral. It's the best way to deliver antibiotics. But he needs a lot more than I can do for him – he needs intensive therapy by trained staff in a proper ITU. He won't get that here.'

'We're heading for somewhere he might get it.'

'If you make it, that is.'

'Yeah. If we make it.'

'Well, good luck!'

'Thanks, Doc.'

While Nan had assisted Doctor Hall in cleaning up Padraig – redressing him in a hospital gown and then finding several thick blankets and two old hot water bottles to keep him warm – Mark had spent a few minutes talking to Jo.

'Take care of Gully for me, will you?'

'I'm afraid I can't, Mark. I'll be leaving with the last of the military.'

'Aw, please, Mark, don't leave me 'ere!' Gully begged.

'I don't want to leave you, Gully. But you'll be safer here with the other civilians.'

Gully had attempted to break away from Jo's restraining arm, his tear-filled eyes looking into Mark's.

'Jo, you sure you can't take him?'

She'd grimaced, seeing the pleading look in Mark's face. 'Where we're headed, it wouldn't be safe for a child.' She'd put her arm around Gully's shoulders. 'Lady Breakespeare will look after you.'

Gully wailed: 'Old Pinky Ponky don't know how to look after herself!'

Now, facing the barricaded town, Cal's urgent mutter broke through Mark's memories of Gully. 'We need a clear plan before we go in.' Mark, Cal and Nan had joined the others in the overcrowded belly of the Pig. Patting Tajh's back, who had been nursing Padraig, Mark inched his way forward to join Cal in watching over Cogwheel's shoulder as he drove. They descended a small hill on the approach to the flaming barrier.

'Way I see it,' Cal murmured thoughtfully, 'the fifteen tons behind the guillotine blade should be enough to get us through the barrier, but we don't know what's waiting for us on the town side of it.'

Bull snorted from behind them: 'They'll hail every sort of crap on us from every angle, that's what.'

'I know you think we need to use the Minimis, but we're going to expose ourselves to Molotovs if we open the ports.'

'No way we'll get through without the guns,' Bull replied.

'Even with the two guns, we can't man front and rear as well as the sides.'

Mark spoke: 'Maybe Nan and I can help?'

'What do you suggest? You going to magic us through?'

'Something like that, yeah.'

Cogwheel nodded. 'We can't go in without covering the windscreen.'

'You saying we go in blind?' Bull replied.

'The flaps are slitted. We'll see enough to get through the barrier.'

Mark said: 'Let Nan join Cogwheel in the cab.'

'What good will that do?'

'She can probe the field ahead even through the steel flaps, maybe stop us careening into something ugly – like a dug-out pit.'

Nan added: 'And I can fight.'

'Makes sense to me,' Tajh spoke.

'Okay,' Cal nodded to Nan. 'We can't avoid being exposed on every front. So we rake 'em with the Minimis on either side – that's Bull and me. You get the heavy one, Bull.'

Bull's sweating face broke out into a grin under the interior light. 'Roger, that!'

Cal nodded. 'Okay! So we'll batten down the sides going through the barrier. Soon as we're through we chink the side flaps open just enough to fit the barrels. And that's where you come in, magic boy. You cover the rear.'

Mark snorted, but he began to inch his way to the back again, nodding to Tajh who was adjusting the drip rate on the central venous line to Padraig's heart.

'Okay – everybody ready?'

There was a chorus of grunts. Then a single voice of dissent from Sharkey: 'Hey, fellas, what about me?'

'You can't handle a Minimi with that shoulder.'

Bull's voice cut in: 'Damned hippie can help me nurse the belt. Belts don't last long at 800 RPM.'

'Yee-hah!' Sharkey dragged two heavy belts along the metal floor to sit beside Bull's allocated porthole.

'Step on it, Cogwheel.'

'I have no foot to put down, boss!'

'Take off, then!'

Sharkey started humming the Marley song *Exodus* as Cogwheel revved the engine to screaming pitch, moving through the gears. Bull and Cal took up their positions with machine guns at the ready as the Pig rocked and rolled towards the blazing barrier. The collision, when it came, threw everybody forwards, provoking a chorus of curses. The barricade was bigger, and heavier, than they had anticipated, made up of half a dozen burned out cars and trucks. As the Pig's guillotine blades tore into it, big chunks of blazing scrap slammed into the armoured windscreen, scraped across the bonnet and ricocheted off both sides. Had the flaps been open they would have been ripped off.

'Here come the Molotovs!'

Within moments the Pig was a mass of flames as the petrol-filled bottles fell upon them from front, sides and rear – the noise was deafening. In the windows of the three-storey buildings to either side of the main road they could make out the spectral outlines of figures – maniacal Razzers – dancing and chanting as they ignored their own safety to hurl bottle after bottle into the conflagration. Flames came in through the slitted portholes to either side, forcing Cal and Bull to keep them closed for the moment. Through his oraculum Mark caught the same picture Nan did: the Mamma Pig had become a blazing inferno.

'Go for it, Bull!' Cal roared from the left side port, which was now opened up a slit, just wide enough to take the barrel of the smaller Minimi. 'And watch our back, Magic Man. Let them have it!'

Through the inched open side portals the Minimis poured deadly hails of lead, belt following belt, filling the cabin with the toxic smoke of cordite, and amid this frenzy, the Mamma Pig guided solely by Nan's oraculum, crashed and sliced its way through every obstacle, screaming in topmost revs. Mark poured a fury of black lightning behind the vehicle, adding a new horror to the lurching, grinding progress of the Pig.

It wasn't until they'd cleared the town that the noise abated. A mile further on Cogwheel jerked the Pig to a halt, threw back the windscreen flaps and shouted at them to open every port.

The burning town lit up the horizon behind them. Cal, Bull and Mark got busy with the fire extinguishers, spraying the tyres and undercarriage, then anywhere that looked like it needed it. Tajh waited for the hissing of the cooling metal to lessen so she could hear herself speak. Then she turned to Mark and spoke to him in a husky whisper:

'Was that us back there – screaming?'

Mark met her eyes, shrugged his shoulders.

'Dear god!'

'We made it. That's all that matters.'

Tajh shivered. Her face was ashen, her pupils dilated. Maybe, like him, she could still feel the heat of the flames and hear the screaming in her mind.

Mark put his arm around Tajh's shoulders.

Tajh took a juddering breath. 'I can't believe we got through. Was it something to do with you and Nan – your presence?'

'I think we fluked it between us.'

Cal came back from the rear and suggested they give the Pig a good look over, to make sure they had caught every last spark.

Tajh's eyes hadn't left Mark's. 'I heard you say something back there. You said you detected some presence?'

'We did.'

'Something scary.'

'Could be.'

'But you don't know what?'

Mark shook his head. He stared up into that same night sky and felt the same skittering fall of snowflakes as he had before going through the barrier.

He thought back to the extraordinary events at the gladiatorial arena in London: Gully had run forward to cry out to Penny, who was on the rostrum next to Grimstone. But there had been a third presence: a small innocuous-looking man. He had radiated power. Only the Tyrant could be that powerful. Yet, he'd held back from destroying them when

Mark's battleaxe had been pulverised with ease by Grimstone wielding the Sword of Feimhin. The Tyrant's reticence had had something to do with Gully, and presumably, also Penny. Mark had no idea why this should matter to such a dangerous and powerful figure.

'Jesus,' he muttered, 'I think I might have made a mistake leaving Gully back there.'

Fate

Penny was gazing into a reflection of her own face while standing erect within the landscape of a dream. She didn't know how she could gaze into her own reflection without a mirror, or water, or any medium that would make it possible.

Am I changing?

She sensed that she was, but she wasn't sure. For some time she had not been sure about anything. She didn't know if she was dreaming or not, or where she was, or what it meant to be here, looking at the changing features of her own reflection – or if there was an even wilder, more extraordinary, alternative.

She studied the mask of her own face.

Her skin looked smoother than normal, almost ethereally so, and her eyes looked more shiny, more silvery. Her hair was ivory-blonde, bunched up to make a springy coconut peak within a filigree helmet of cross-hatched beaded strands; jet alternating with pearl and diamonds. She had no memory of making up her own hair, any more than she could recall donning the jewelled helmet, which covered her entire head and face. Around her throat, and one with the helmet, was a corolla of virginal white florets; an exquisitely delicate version of an Elizabethan ruff. The ruff itself was also a part of the dress, which fell to her ankles and was the same virginal white.

That extraordinary image, purportedly the reflection of her own face, caused Penny to stare at it in astonishment.

In the reflection, she saw unbearable sadness in her eyes: the acquiescence to her fate, whatever that fate might truly prove to be.

She spoke: 'I am within the Black Rose.'

<Yes> She heard Jeremiah's voice as it sounded mind-to-mind.

Nothing of this seemed real to Penny. It was as if her being had become detached from her will. Somehow she had been transported into a magical world. But it wasn't how she might have imagined a world of fairytales, with elfin princes and princesses, goblins and witches. The landscape, the three-dimensional ambience, looked and felt solid enough, but she was sure that it wasn't real. The strangeness of it both intrigued and terrified her.

Without speaking it aloud, being careful to keep her fears from showing, Penny plucked the thought from her mind: *am I a prisoner here?* The idea frightened her. It felt as if she had just woken from a strange and disturbing nightmare only to find that the nightmare had not gone away.

She called out: 'Jeremiah?'

<I am here.>

'But you are merely in my mind. I can't see you. I can't hear your voice in my ears.'

<Why would you need to see me?>

'I feel so isolated. I'm a prisoner here – wherever here is. I want to explore this place – your city, or whatever it really is.'

<It is time I taught you the infinite possibilities of Dromenon. This you must grasp or you will fail me.>

His words, their strange implications, reverberated in her mind: *You will fail me!*

Her surroundings changed. She found herself enclosed within organic shapes, sweeping abstracts composed of curves and arabesques, as if she were within the labyrinth of a gigantic spider – one that wove a wonderland of multi-hued crystalline webs. When she took a dozen strides, swivelled and spun, changing the direction of her movement, the weave changed too, metamorphosed in a fluid, curiously plastic, way. But it continued to envelop her.

Jeremiah's laughter echoed within her skull. <You like to paint your impressions – so paint them.>

'But where do I paint them? There are no flat walls, not even ceilings. And even if there were, I have no brushes, or crayons or pencils.'

<You have no need of walls, or brushes. You have your

extraordinary creative mind, your incomparable imagination.>

'I don't understand.'

In moments Penny was surrounded by the wheeling images of what looked like spectres. There was a feeling that these insubstantial beings resented her presence.

'What are these wraiths?'

<You might see them as the result of my imagination.>

'What purpose do they serve?'

<All that you witness serves my purpose. There is no room in my world for what might prove useless.>

'I still don't understand.'

<Then allow me to demonstrate.>

He plucked a thought – her image of him surrounded by his nimbus of wraiths – out of her mind and he twiddled his fingers and it became a sculpture in crystal. <You see. There is no need for surface or brushes.>

'How did you do that?'

<I thought it into being.>

'But I . . . I couldn't possibly—'

<You are eminently capable.>

'How?'

<I don't have the human word for a quality that is quintessentially non-human. Invent your own description, since you have such a way with words. Be assured that you can be thus creative.>

'I cannot.'

<Pluck the thought from your mind.>

Penny had no option but to try. She hesitated, gazing at an empty space in the corner between two out-curving walls. She imagined a waterfall amid rocks as white and smooth as marble.

The waterfall became substance.

Penny gasped, her hand reaching out to feel the blue falling water, gazing with delight at the tiny rainbow evinced by the play of light through the gossamer-fine mist.

'It's . . . perfect.'

<I have no use for anything less than perfection.>

But her art was not the only thing that had undergone a profound metamorphosis. Penny's sense of the passage of time had changed. It was as if she were passing in and out of a never-ending hallucination. Gradually, she became aware of the fact that she was not alone. There were more obviously female figures, as insubstantial as ghosts, who clustered about her. She cared – she cared because she wanted to care – but there were many, all so grey and ghostly, that she feared caring for them all would consume her, and drag her down into a despair that would accomplish nothing.

'Who are they? Why do they look so sad?'

<Do you care?>

His question caused her to hesitate. She whispered, 'Yes.'

<Why do you care?>

She could not answer. She didn't know why she, in this

strange, beautiful dream, should care about what appeared to be spectres.

<Will you remember them when they are gone?>

'I . . . I don't know. Perhaps.'

<Why?>

She didn't know why she should remember or even care about these grey shades who flickered in and out of existence. Why was he testing her so?

<Your concern for others is a weakness. You wish that you could help them. Should I grant you this wish, I will require a gift in return.>

'What is it you want of me?'

<To serve me.>

'I have already agreed to serve you.'

<I want you to serve me, not in dutiful obedience, but willingly – I want you to serve me with every fibre of your being.>

Penny didn't like the idea of serving him. The very thought of it sickened her. But how could she avoid it? She had promised to serve him to save Gully. 'I . . . I need to see you, to hear you.'

He appeared then, exactly as she remembered him: an elderly man, small and neat with a white beard wearing a navy cloak with curiously roomy sleeves. But his eyes were not the kindly eyes she recalled from the rain-swept night in the back streets of London. His eyes were devoid of iris or white. They were a glistening black.

She turned away from him, spoke as if to her reflection: 'I can't stand the thought that I must lose my will.'

'On the contrary, you have made a bargain of your will to me.'

'What's the difference?'

'There are two sides to a bargain.'

'I fear what you will expect of me.'

'Your fear is understandable, given the circumstances.'

'Am I your slave?'

'That would make you imperfect in my eyes.'

Penny shook her head. 'Are you real? Or am I imagining this conversation within my own mind?'

'My presence is real.'

'Where is this place?'

'It is a projection from within a domain known as Dromenon.'

'A projection?'

'It is both within and without the city of London.'

'Within the Black Rose?'

'Observe!'

Penny's eyes widened as she saw the landscape draw apart to form a lucid oval, as if a giant eye had sprung open to reveal a ruin of broken masonry, engulfed in ashes.

'Oh, my god! This is London?'

'Yes.'

Tears sprang into her eyes. 'You promised me—'

'I promised to preserve the landmarks you so admired – and of course your street urchin friend.'

'Why must you do these things? Why do you so hate us?'

'There are major considerations at stake. I have many enemies far more formidable than humans. Your world, as indeed my own, has become increasingly perilous for me and my purpose.'

Penny could not keep the exasperation out of her voice. 'Will you not explain where I really am? What is really expected of me? What do you really want from me?'

His image softened, so he appeared almost as friendly as the Jeremiah she remembered from the rainy night street. 'I can reveal some things, but not all that you would ask.'

'Please don't confuse me further. Am I entirely lost? Have I abandoned everything?'

'Being human, you were never really free. Absolute freedom is an illusion for a finite being.'

Penny felt so frustrated, so afraid, she could explode. 'You said there were two sides to a bargain?'

'I will reciprocate your serving me.'

'What does that mean? How do I know I can trust you?'

'You can never entirely trust another. But there are degrees of trust. That is an important consideration.'

'How then can I judge these . . . these degrees of trust?'

'Who, in your life, have you ever trusted?'

She hesitated. There had been very few people she had ever trusted: her parents, her father in particular. But even then her trust in Father had been limited. Perhaps Gully was the only one she had even come close to really trusting?

In her imagination she saw his face. She heard him say, 'Penny – Penny, gel! Where ya hidin'?' She and Gully had had no option but to trust one another, to rely upon one another, because it was the only way they could survive in the chaos that had become London. Gully had warned her against exploring the Tube tunnels. He'd been right. How she wished now that she had taken his advice. She was still thinking about Gully, with her eyes clenched shut, when Jeremiah's voice interrupted her thoughts:

'Your trust is about to be tested.'

Penny discovered that she was surrounded by hundreds, perhaps thousands, of figures, each covered with gauzy veils. Not wraiths as before, but real living creatures. The tallest of those standing erect were no higher than her shoulders, and many were much shorter, so she felt like Gulliver among the Lilliputians. She put her hands to her face, probing through the beaded lattice to confirm that her skin felt real, that it wasn't just a complex dream. The figures were covered by shrouds that completely blanketed them, tent-like; the material finer than any gauze or lace she had ever seen, as delicate as a creamy white smoke.

'What's happening?'

'They have come here to celebrate your epiphany.'

Here? How had they entered the Black Rose? Penny's eyes darted around to discover an alien landscape. Had Jeremiah taken her out of the Rose to some other destination? If so, how had he done so in the blink of an eye? And what did Jeremiah mean by an epiphany? Penny was still attempting to figure out if this was just a dream – or another frightening reality.

'They're humming,' she said.

'Incanting!'

'What are they incanting?'

'A hymn to the glory of their coming sacrifice.'

'What sacrifice?'

'Why – of the most important thing they have to give: their lives.'

When Penny examined the nearby figures more carefully, she saw that every one of them held a sharp-looking dagger to her breast.

'They're sacrificing themselves?'

'Of course.'

'To what – to whom?'

'To you.'

He spoke the words in a quiet voice, devoid of emotion. A shocked Penny fell silent for several moments. 'Why me?'

'You are their Lady of Sorrows.'

'I don't understand. Why would they do this?'

'It's an ancient rite. They have devoted their entire lives to this sacred moment. In the act of self-sacrifice they will become one with you.'

Penny looked at the sea of faces, trying to make out what she could hear of the incantation. How could the rite be ancient if it was dedicated to her? Jeremiah had to be lying to her. Nothing of what he said made sense. But then her mind froze. She remembered his words when she gave herself up to him. <*You will become a goddess.*> Was it possible that time was entirely malleable to the being she knew as Jeremiah, a being she knew now, with absolute certainty, was not human. It was a horrifying thought.

'Who are they?'

'You would regard them as religious devotees – idolators. All of their conscious lives have been spent in worship of you. The ceremony will be their reward for unlimited homage.'

'Their reward?'

'They will experience the Rapture.'

Penny felt a shiver of fright run through her. 'Oh, please, you must put a stop to this! You have to if you want my cooperation!'

'Would you deny them what means everything to them?'

Wisps of a carmine-coloured vapour were condensing among them. Penny began to move; she shook their shoulders and she tried to rip away the strange gauzy material that enshrouded them. It tore in her fingers, like the finest, silkiest spider's web.

She shouted at them: 'Wake up!'

They ignored her. It was as if both she and Jeremiah were invisible to them. With every head bowed, they continued with their incantations.

He said: 'You still do not understand. Take the Rapture from them and they will not survive anyway. In their grief, they will kill themselves. Their final experience will be despair.'

Penny heard the first ecstatic moan.

The Unbroken Circle

The cold greys and warm pinks of early evening fought one another in the cloud-wracked heavens. Alan stood on a surviving section of the Tyrant's fortress wall, leaning his weight on the shaft of the Spear of Lug, and gazing through the drifting black smoke at the scene several hundred feet below him. His friend, Mo, together with Qwenqwo Cuatzel and the orang-utan form of Magtokk, stood in companionable silence beside him. After two cruel days and nights of fierce and bloody battle, the fortress had fallen and now, below them, the Shee made preparations for the ceremony of their dead. High overhead, wheeling Gargs performed their own respectful spirals for the lost. Garg and Shee together – a remarkable act from two peoples who had, until recently, been mortal enemies. At least half the dead had perished in the initial assault, ripped apart by the cannonade from those fearsome curtain walls before Alan's First Power had had time to strike. And the assault itself had been the grimmest battle yet, fought in the close quarters of the vast labyrinth of passageways and tunnels that riddled the fortress and the divergent curtain walls.

The Tyrant's legionaries had been hard, brave soldiers who fought to the last drop of blood. The defenders in the fortress might have been routed by Alan's use of the First Power, but the tens of thousands within the walls and buttresses had refused to surrender. They had employed well-drilled strategies: appearing to give ground only to lead their adversaries into rooms where the floors would suddenly give way into the moiling furnace of the volcano beneath them. They were heedless of the fact that the traps sometimes caught their own, displaying remarkable bravery. But a greater bravery had been demanded of the Shee. The ceaseless carnage had exhausted all of them.

Alan's eyes lifted from the haunting scene in the river of solidified lava below, to the vista to the north of the craggy promontory on which the fortress had been built. Sharp ridges and crags flowed in wave after wave into an azure-tinted smoky distance that marked the location of the Tyrant's citadel. What premonition was this – supposedly a preliminary skirmish – of the onslaught that would be required to take Ghork Mega, and finally end the Tyrant's reign of terror on Tír?

A sudden trumpeting from far below warned them that the Shee ceremony was about to begin. It forced Alan's vision back onto the lava below, still cooling from when the Shee had blocked the flow. They couldn't hang around this place for very much longer; the loosening of the magma and his own use of the First Power had weakened the headland on which the fortress stood. There were rumblings in the rocks, tremors he could feel through his feet. Thick black smoke erupted from the widening cracks and fissures filling the sky with gloom. The main army of Shee had moved several miles northwards to settle a new camp at a safe distance. Alan and his companions had watched throughout the afternoon and early evening as Shee and aides had carried the bodies out onto the still cooling river of rock. And now a raft of dead, fully fifty yards long and a third as wide, formed the outline of a Shee galleon, its prow directed towards the west and the setting sun. They had cushioned and overlain the bodies with what little dry scrub they could gather, held down with rocks. Already the pyre smouldered and smoked, the air filled with the unpleasant aroma of singed hair and baking flesh. Lightning balls, which announced that the gates barring the magma were about to be re-opened, roiled and scattered upriver. The last of the Shee climbed up higher, coming towards Alan. There was a thunderous crackling of disintegrating rock as the superheated magma burst out into the valley for a final time to hiss and splutter out over the landscape, rushing towards the giant pyre of bodies.

Eight hundred and seventy two Shee: that had been the cost of taking the fortress. Alan watched the crawling river of fire come closer to the smouldering cremation pyre. He couldn't help but shiver as the flames erupted at the prow of the formation.

At the same time, the formal ceremony commenced. The voice of Bétaald carried on the wind: her hymnal cadences an orison that echoed with feeling in his mind.

'For those of our sisters who feared not to die . . .'

Alan had noticed before how the Shee always died in their human form. There was something cruel about leaving those tall, elegant bodies to be melted and absorbed into the molten stone. But the Shee had a different attitude to the dead. The dead were duly honoured with the ceremony, but in another sense they lived on in their astonishing cycle of life: the mother-sister making way for the daughter-sister. There would be deep veneration of the bones of the lost, but at the same time there would be no maudlin despair, merely a determination to learn the lessons taught by it. The new would replace the old and the old would live on in memories, contributing their experience to the fighting prowess of the new generations. It was a strange cycle of reproduction, yet one that carried the gift of immortality. Such was the reality of normal life for the Shee.

'Eight hundred and seventy two dead,' Qwenqwo muttered, 'and three times as many left seriously wounded.'

'I know,' Alan nodded.

Regardless of the daughter-sister standing by to replace each individual dead, the injured required that their wounds be treated, their broken limbs splinted, their pain nursed by the comfort of healwell. At the new camp three miles further north, a small army of aides was busy with such duties.

'Oh, Alan!'

Mo was dabbing at her cheeks, her eyes moist. The rising smoke didn't help to quench her tears. Clutching at his left arm, she slid her head beneath it so he was embracing her slim shoulders.

'Yes, I know.' He understood what Mo was thinking. He wished that Kate was in the embrace of his other arm.

The entire Shee army could not be spared for the ceremony. It was too vast, and the forward limit of their march must now be defended against potential counter attack. But many thousands had formed an honour guard on the surrounding slopes. They went down onto one knee now and the funeral chant began, a mournful choir, in perfect unison. He squeezed Mo to him as the scurrying Shee ignited the flame arrows of the bows of a hundred archers, who fired into the still-smouldering pyre that had not yet been consumed by the laval heat. And now, bearing a respectful witness on the promontory, Alan was reminded of a similar feeling of wretchedness and desolation that he had felt on the banks of the Snowmelt River, when he had witnessed another funeral, this time of a single Shee noviciate warrior called Valéra, who had saved Alan's life. He recalled how he had been pressed, against the resentment of an older Kyra, to examine the wound that the Preceptor's spiral blade had inflicted. So dreadful was the memory that even now, half kneeling on the promontory, Alan clenched his eyes shut and gritted his teeth against the remembered agony that had resulted from his poisoned fingers. And in examining the venom-blackened wound, he had discovered the new life growing in the warrior's womb, the daughter-sister, as yet unborn, who would replace, and in her way fulfil, the life of Valéra.

Another clarion call of trumpets signalled the movement of the venerating Shee, in a slow, great clock-wise circle, holding hands.

'They call it Neavrashvahar,' Alan said softly.

Mo asked: 'What does it mean?'

Alan peered down at the thickening pall of smoke, scented by something, perhaps some kind of incense that had been sprinkled over the bodies. 'I think it's something like their vision of heaven. The passing on of the wonder of life from mother to daughter – the word means "the unbroken circle".'

He recalled how, with the realisation of what was at stake as Valéra died, he had blundered out of the bower and run blindly into the icy snow. Never in his life had he felt so useless. He had fallen to his knees, his head bowed, his arms adrift by his side, his fists clenched. He had poured his anguish into the oraculum, finding himself in a flat wilderness that stretched to the horizon in every direction. Now, with greater experience, he realised that he had entered Dromenon. A strange presence had hovered before him. He knew what that presence was, now: A True Believer . . . It had spoken to him in riddles, provoking anger because he had needed clear explanation.

<I am not the one you call yet I might have the answers you seek . . .>

Alan's memories were cut short by a powerful hand squeezing his shoulder. He blinked, gazing down once more at the great funeral pyre.

Qwenqwo Cuatzel said: 'My friend, the blessing of the flagon?'

'Not just now, Qwenqwo. The Shee – Bétaald and the Kyra – might think it disrespectful.'

'What they cannot see cannot hurt them.'

Alan felt, rather than saw, his friend, the dwarf mage, take an almighty swig from his flagon. Qwenqwo deserved the drink. None had fought more bravely through the smoke and flame-filled chambers and corridors of the fortress. Alan felt the supporting hand tighten on his shoulder. The entire boat-shaped mound was now ablaze, flames crackling in the evening air. As the conflagration intensified to a bright orange, Alan felt a sudden flash of power, a signal – or perhaps a window opening mind-to-mind – from the Oraculum of Bree in the Kyra's brow. The signal was not directed at him, but westwards, to the Guhttan mountains thousands of miles away and across the Eastern Ocean, to where the new generation of daughter-sisters would inherit the sacred warrior mantle of the mother-sisters, whose bodies needed to be consumed by the cleansing action of the flames for the circle to be made whole again.

It comforted Alan that the daughter-sister of Valéra would be among them. That the Shee who had saved his life now lived again.

'Blow it!' He accepted the press of the flagon, took a swig. He spoke, in little above a whisper, to Qwenqwo: 'The Shee have a beautiful expression for the portal they cross after death, they call it "The Harbour of Souls".'

He had learned this in that same conversation with the True Believer on the banks of the great river.

The first stars were twinkling in the evening sky as Alan, Mo and Qwenqwo made their way to the new camp. None of them fancied the jolting ride that would result from being carried by an onkkh. They were content with making their way on foot; the dwarf mage lurching somewhat from his consumption of liquor, while Alan and Mo trudged through a weariness that leached into their bones. Shee guards were everywhere, even if not always apparent, because of the camouflage effect of their cloaks. Even as they arrived into camp, some miles north of the funeral, the air still reeked of burning flesh and the more sulphurous smell of the lava. Alan would never forget the sight, his mind still echoing the final lament of the Shee as the pyre of the fallen was consumed:

<Let our fallen sisters be one with the communion of mother-sisters. Let our daughter-sisters be the future and hope of the unbroken circle.>

Lost in sorrow, Alan was slow to notice the sudden darkening as a great cloud filled the sky. At the same time he became aware of the swooping figure of Iyezzz and heard the Prince's excited call. What was Iyezzz doing up there in the gloom at this belated hour, when he must be feeling every bit as exhausted as Alan himself?

In that same moment Qwenqwo tensed, the Fir Bolg battleaxe drawn from its sheath across his back, his eyes ablaze.

'What is it?'

Alan gripped the Spear of Lug with both hands, following the dwarf mage's upturned eyes to gaze heavenwards. All of sudden Shee were materialising from all around him, hundreds – thousands. They were forming a gigantic circle around the Mage Lord and the dwarf mage, all eyes turned heavenwards to where the cloud was descending in an enormous arc.

'It's Kate!' Mo's voice was shrieking in his ear.

'Kate?'

'The powers preserve us!' Qwenqwo chortled drunkenly. 'It's the dragon come back, filling up the entire sky.'

No, Alan thought: *the shadow is not the dragon. It's merely its tail. The curve is the tail coming down to meet the ground.*

'Alan!'

The cry arrived into his ears a split second after the cry in his mind.

It was Kate – Kate calling to him.

His exhaustion from the two days and the intervening

night of unremitting battle was lifted from his shoulders. His heart, his spirits, were already soaring.

Kate was descending out of the night sky on the cusp of the arc – the tip of the gargantuan tail. The dragon must be as enormous as an island.

Alan thrust the Spear of Lug into the hands of his tottering friend, who was beside himself. Then Kate was in his arms. Her tear-filled eyes were confronting his own. Their oracula had burst into blazing light, rubicund upon emerald, emerald upon rubicund.

'I'm so sorry I abandoned you. I let you down.'

'No, you didn't.'

'I did. Oh, Alan, can you ever forgive me?'

'I don't care what you did. All I care is that you're back.'

He didn't know what she was talking about. He didn't give a damn about forgiving her. He was lifting her high into the air, then spinning her round and round in dizzy circles, laughing like a clown. This was his beloved Kate. She was once again in his embrace, his lips kissing hers, her lips returning his kiss. He never wanted the kissing to stop. He never wanted to stop hugging her, whirling her round and round and round . . .

Binoculars . . . and a Bike

Gully Doughty hesitated on the frozen ground outside the basement window before switching off the penlight for a spell. The night sky was hidden by clouds, likely promising enough snow to bury this shithole for the rest of winter. He paused to take a good look around, making sure there wasn't nobody about. He flicked the penlight on again, giving him enough light to get close to the tiny square window that looked into the basement. He tested it out, pressing his fingers against the frame. *Dead easy to make it rattle.*

'Rest 'ere.'

The old bat, Pinky Ponky, had said that to him when the crew had dragged him in through the big front door.

'Rest 'ere.' He whispered it again, for the benefit of his rage.

Bollix!

Bollix – it was a sexy word that he'd got to like. Heard it

from the soldier geezer built like a tank with a shaved head who was carrying the body of the old man out to the Mamma Pig. Gully couldn't believe it when Mark told him they was leaving without him. He had struggled to get away from the Derby skirt. He'd demanded to know why they was leaving him behind.

The soldier had grunted: *'Because it's all a load o' bollix, kid.'*

It made no sense at all to Gully. He wanted to go with Mark in the Mamma Pig, but the tall skirt with the red hair and the glasses had held onto him like glue, and she was as strong as two men.

'Lady Breakespeare will look after you, Gully.'

Not in this bleeding universe she won't. Not old Pinky Ponky, who wanted him to read books. *Books!*

He couldn't believe they'd had left him behind with these loonies in this creaky old barn, with them poor families who'd been driven out of London.

Like noffink bad was going to happen to some fallin' down farm because it belongs to Lady Pinky Ponky!

He felt sorry for the families, he really did, but they was caught up in the same bollix. He extracted the penlight from pocket left 2 – O for observation. He shone the light on the window catch and saw it was crap. The window felt loose because the old brass catch was snapped.

'Bollix is right!'

He extracted the short flat screwdriver from pocket right 1 – P for protection – and he slid it under the frame. The casement popped open an inch or so. Enough for him to get his fingers into the crack and widen it so that he could slip his body through into the basement.

Stop. Look. Listen . . .

Noffink to worry about 'ere, mate. Not a bleedin' squeak.

He switched on the penlight again and did a recce. It was exactly like he had imagined. There was a whole bunch of rooms with no windows, and every one of them was full of junk. But junk could be useful. Place like this a regular Aladdin's cave – and he had all the time in the world to explore. There was old chairs what looked like aluminium piled up on top of each other, furniture gone green with rot, some things what looked like old manni-kins, with no heads on the top; boxes stuffed full of junk! Strewth! There was pots and kitchen stuff, and bathroom stuff, and stuff the likes he knew nothing about. A bunch of old bikes all crusted with dust. One of them – probably years old – had bent handlebars and a fancy bunch of gears. A racing bike with them down-sloping cross-bars. Taking a rag from right pocket 2, he wiped some of the crap off it and saw it was bright red underneath, with a word in the middle of it. He couldn't make out the word. Then he wiped the crap from the second bar and made it out easy. RALEIGH. He figured he was looking at a lady's Raleigh racer.

Lucked out or wot!

The rag was already caked in crap, so he spat on it and wiped more crap off the back mudguard. It was silvery chrome underneath. *Wot a find!* All lovely and gleaming red and chrome! Penny would have gone head over heels for this bike. He peered at the cobweb-encrusted gears.

They was coated in rust, but they wasn't half bad. If only he could lay his hands on some oil!

He brushed off the saddle. Even the pannier bag attached to the back of the saddle was red. It was real leather too. He searched for a dynamo but couldn't find one. He blew away clouds of dust to take a closer look at the saddlebag and managed to smudge out the glasses dangling from his nose. Sighing with frustration, he took them off and spat onto the lenses, then wiped off the crud with his shirt tail. Then, blinking owlishly, he shoved them back on his nose, fastening the curly bits around his ears. Inside the saddlebag he found a set of mini binoculars.

Perfick or wot!

He read off the make using the binoculars, letter by letter. M-I-N-O-X and D-e-l-u-x-e. *Minox deluxe.* Oh, neat! Minox Deluxe 10x25.

Maybe take a peek at them birds from up there off the roof?

He had a think about it, then stuffed the binoculars into pocket right 1 – P for protection.

He was all ready to move on, thinking maybe he should quit while he was ahead. But then it occurred to him that he ought to take a second look at the red bike. It looked sort of special. Like in its day it could have been top o' the range. He squeezed the tyres and wasn't surprised to find them flat, but there was pump slung under the bar. Of course there was. Top of the range – what do you bleeding expect?

Maybe he'd come back here again, after he finished the recce. He might even have a go at pumping up them tyres.

But the thing he felt bad about, the thing what he was thinking about right now, wasn't the idea of nicking the stuff – nobody even give a damn it was there – he felt bad about the fact they was nice people, even if they was stupid. The truth was he even felt a bit sorry for Pinky Ponky.

Oh, Jesus, wot does she fink is going to 'appen here now the rebels is gone? She fink it's going to be hunky-dory just being nice and hanging around the crappy old place? Don't she know wots goin' on in London, just twenty miles away? Don't she fink them shitheads are gonna come right 'ere on her doorstep? Do she fink them Skulls is going to swarm in here an' say please and thank you very much?

'Stop it, Gully! You's getting yourself into a state,' he said aloud.

He counted to twenty.

Stop, look, listen . . .

Just minutes later, Gully found himself up on the top of the roof, trying to cool off in the parky night air. The roof set him thinking about his pigeons. He was pfeffing his breaths, like Penny hated him to do, tapping on his pockets and kinda humming to himself, because he knew what was likely coming and he couldn't bear to think about what would likely happen to these bleedin' stupid but nice people.

But was no good worrying about everyone and everything. *No good getting yourself upset, Gully!* Now he was up here, he might as well figure what was what. He knew it was a very old place; a Tudor farm was what people called it. Kind of an ancient old place it was really, with all them leaded window panes. And the roof wasn't just a flat or pitched, it ran up and down all over the place. He rubbed his hand over a gully what ran right around the edge, where the rain water was collecting into channels, then heading out onto spitters for the fall pipes. It was a piece of work, and no mistake. It was what his nan would have called exceeding fancy. And now the snow was melting, it was running along them channels at a fair old lick. Funny that – how the snow was melting so fast when every night had been freezing cold for weeks, but he didn't have time to figure that out. He felt a whole load better now, getting to know the way it all worked. Gully sorely missed his pigeons. He fiddled with the binoculars, kind of itching for daylight so he could test them out. Right now there was nothing to see other than the cloudy sky and the gloom of the old farm with its barns full of desperate folks, the glimpse of stars he had seen earlier already snuffed out. *Penny, gel, I tried to warn 'em, but they won't listen.*

And he had. He'd told old Pinky Ponky, who owned the rambling old junk heap what would happen, but she'd just looked at him like *he* was the idiot.

Jesus, Penny – Penny gel! Why'd you leave me here on my own? You're in real trouble an' nobody gives a shit but me.

He could see her there – Penny – in his mind's eye, standing on that wooden platform where the lunatics was killing one another with swords. He could see the desperation in her eyes. He could hear her anguished shout:

'Run, Gully! Run from the City Below!'

But wot about you, gel? We just upped an' left you behind.

When he'd tried to warn them, that white-haired old reverend had told him to stop swearing, when all he was trying to do was shout some sense into the madness around him.

'Child. You sound like Isaiah crying in the wilderness. What terrible visions do you see?'

He'd just shaken his head and scarpered.

Penny might have explained things better, but then, Penny never really explained nothing except in pictures. Gully couldn't, not in a million years, have explained what Penny meant by her 'City Below', and he hadn't believed a word of it when she'd spoken about it, but now he knew that Penny had been right all along: there really was a City Below. And he knew, deep in himself, that it was as important as it was terrible – maybe even worse than terrible – but he didn't have the words to explain what he felt.

With tear-blurred eyes, Gully put the binoculars to his face and looked into the night sky again. There still wasn't much to see, but then what had he expected?

Oh, Penny – Penny, gel! I can't hang about 'ere. I can't just sit and wait for it to happen with these people wot understand noffink about wot the Skulls, and Paramilitaries will do to 'em.

He heard her voice in his head: *'What is it, Gully?'*

'There's fings going on, fings wot shouldn't be going on nowhere, no how. Really bad fings. Dangerous.'

Nobody other than Penny would listen to him. Nobody else would care or understand. And Penny wasn't here to listen.

Gully began his ritual count to twenty. His fingers flew over his pockets, incanting the codes . . .

Then he heard a whine up there in the sky. It sure as heck wasn't no bird. He'd have recognised a bird. It was a whine like a motor might make. Out of the corner of his eye Gully saw a quick flash of light where he had heard the whine. It was as if an eye up there had blinked open and then closed again.

He opened up the binoculars and peered up at the place where he had seen the light. He moved around in a circle, looking.

Noffink.

A minute, two minutes, five . . .

His fingers were slipping on the focus because of the cold.

Give it up, Gully.

Nah – not yet.

Then he heard the whine again – and he saw the light. He didn't need no binoculars to be sure he saw it: there was something up there in the sky, something with a motor holding it up in the air and it had a penlight on it. That light was flashing on and off, like a blinking eye. Well, he was sure of one thing: it wasn't spying on him. The bad guys didn't waste their time spying on people who was nobody.

A Respite of Sorts

In the murky light of pre-dawn, Cal's face looked lumpy and drawn, dark stubble attesting to the fact that he hadn't shaved for several days. He was sitting on the second step under the passenger door of the cab of the Mamma Pig, a few feet away from an equally exhausted Mark, who was sitting in the dirt, his back resting against the huge front tyre. They should have reached Resistance HQ by now. They had headed north in a somewhat elliptical fashion, attempting to keep roughly parallel to the M1 motorway. They had got as far as fifty miles south of the junction with the A38, but at that point they had been warned to take evasive action by an urgent message on the com: it appeared that they – the crew – were being hunted by killer drones.

Cal growled: 'That bastard, Seebox!'

Mark nodded, tiredly. From the sounds of it, Seebox had it in for their crew personally. Which boded ill for the future. *It has to be Grimstone acting behind Seebox*, Mark thought.

They had been forced to travel throughout the night, passing through pitch black towns that had removed their road signs, eventually making camp in the shade of some hawthorns somewhere close to the coastal town of Foulness.

Cigarette smoke curled out of the open window above their heads. They could hear Cogwheel instructing Tajh on how to connect some portable IT appliance to the aerial dish up on the roof. Everybody was getting jittery with the notion of being hunted by drones. Nan was the only one who had settled down to sleep, wrapped up in a duvet in the belly of the Pig. The only consolation, as far as Mark was concerned, was the fact that Padraig's temperature was coming down with the intravenous fluids and the antibiotics.

'Shit!'

Mark glanced over at Cal, who was staring at the ground between his boots.

'What's up?'

'The whole thing – towns without signs. This is England, for fuck's sake! What's happening gives me the creeps.'

'It'll only get worse.'

'Tell me something I don't know.'

'You don't know the Tyrant of the Wastelands.'

'This imaginary enemy who has declared war on Earth?'

'You didn't think Padraig existed,' Mark pointed out.

'Okay, so we got him out of there. And now we have come under more than the usual amount of attention.'

Mark gritted his teeth. 'Has it occurred to you there could be more than one explanation for the attention? That it isn't just Padraig? That maybe they're out there looking for me and Nan?'

Cal blew air out through his pursed lips. 'As a matter of fact that very thought has occurred to me.'

'You know, I'm getting tired of your grumbling.'

'Appears to me that ever since you two joined the crew we've become the focus of far too much attention.'

This argument was a continuation of one that had been going on ever since their arrival among the crew. It was close to dawn, icy cold and foggy. In the tense silence, as Mark tried to think through his exhaustion, he could hear the washing of the surf against the nearby beach. He yawned and scratched at his unshaven chin. He shifted his bum, trying to find a more comfortable position. It didn't help. His back itched. In fact he was itching all over. He hoped to hell he didn't have lice.

'What more reassurance do you want from me? I can't explain everything, but I know there is some kind of logical explanation to what's going on here. An explanation for it all, on Tír and on Earth, no matter how confusing things might appear.'

Cal had fallen silent but Mark could read his expression: he didn't share Mark's faith in logic.

And now Mark was unsure if he was even convinced by his own logic.

Cal accepted a lit self-roll cigarette from Tajh's

disembodied hand, dangling down out of the opened window above their heads. 'Okay, for argument's sake let's say you're telling the truth: there's something going on; the old geezer is important in some way. Shit, who's to say if he's going to live? What proof can you show me that any of this is real?'

Mark thought about Padraig and moved from scratching his stubbly chin to the side of his brow, close to the oraculum. He thought about what they had seen in London. Their escape had hardly been an orderly affair. Nor had it been covert, given the clanking bulk of the Mamma Pig. So they were an easy target. With Seebox's regular army reinforced by the Paramilitaries, and now the possibility of killer drones, it was a nasty situation. That was why Sharkey and Tajh were attempting to rig up a radar link to the roof-mounted satellite dish.

But, as Cal had just reminded him, they *had* rescued Padraig. It had seemed impossible, but the fact was that they had.

Who would have bloody thought it!

For Mark just thinking back about Clonmel and Padraig brought home a deep pang of nostalgia for those lost days: a summer of high sunshine and friends. He recalled leaning back against the wall of the dairy in Padraig's garden and looking up into the ancient pear tree, its stunted branches providing shade in the hot sunshine. He recalled how Padraig would bring Mo a moth or a butterfly in the cradle of his hands. How delighted Mo was as she let them go, gazing up at their erratic dancing flight. He recalled the joy, the intimacy of friendship . . .

Mark turned his head to the sceptical Cal. 'You know that this thing in my brow, this oraculum, is embedded in my brain. It has changed me. And Nan's has changed her too. I can't explain how it works in any logical way, but I do know that on Tír the oracula connected us to a source of power that we could use just by thinking about it.'

He stopped talking because he didn't want to elaborate on where the source of power came from: not merely a goddess, but Mórígán, the goddess of death. But now a new thought crept into Mark's mind, and the implications frightened him.

'This thing, you say, connects you to something powerful? You realise how that sounds to me?' Cal said.

'I suppose I do.'

What was increasingly frightening Mark was not Cal's scepticism, but his realisation: *What if the real connection is to the Fáil?*

'Sounds like bullshit – that's what it sounds like to me.'

'Well, maybe I can understand that. But these things in our heads, they do more than just give us powers to fight. They do . . . deeper things, allow us enhanced communication for example. We can read people's minds. We can understand what somebody is thinking. We can understand their speech, even if they're talking in a language we're never heard before.'

Cal shook his head, exhaling smoke. He took a final drag

on his cigarette before docking the butt-end against his heel.

'I can see how implausible it might sound to you. But the fact is you have helped Nan and me in rescuing Padraig. I know you don't have any idea of why that might be important, but we think it is. We're both grateful to you.'

'You put the crew through unacceptable risk.'

'We both think the risk was worth it.'

Cal spoke quietly, but with an underlying tenor of strong emotions: resentment, frustration – anger. 'This crew is a guerrilla structure.'

'I know.'

'But have you figured out why?'

'Security.'

'Attrition, pal. The average survival time of a crew is no more than a few months. They get wind of us, one way or another, they take us out.'

Mark fell silent. They'd talked of this before.

'Maybe it does have something to do with you. Maybe they are hunting you, not even you and Nan, but specifically you. I don't know shit. But one thing I do know – I bloodywell feel it – is those bastards are getting closer.'

'Nan and I, we might be able to help.'

'How?'

'We sense things. We might sense it if the crew is in danger.'

Cal grunted. 'Maybe you could, maybe you couldn't.' He wiped his hand across his sweating brow. 'This country is going to pot. I don't understand it at all. I can't believe it is happening. All I know is I'm going to fight it. But' – He struck his open hand against the side of his head – 'it's so difficult to fight against something that you don't understand. Something you don't have a clue as to why in the name of god it is happening.'

Mark nodded. 'I understand.'

'I wonder if even now you see what I'm getting at? It's all down to attrition, man!'

Sharkey, who was barefoot and had stripped down to a T-shirt and shorts, interrupted the tense atmosphere by heading towards the sea, hopping from one foot to the other in the freezing dirt. He still had a dressing over his wounded shoulder, but he had found an oil-stained pilot-styled cap and was doing his Biggles act:

'Damn near bought it, there, old chap!'

Mark found himself smiling, as he looked at Sharkey – all elbows and knees, jogging away into the mist. Sharkey had broken the tension and even Cal looked a little more relaxed.

'You boys feel like joining him?' Tajh's head was poking out of the cab window. Her voice was inside his head: *Do it! Don't lose the opportunity to bond.* Mark sighed. He felt too tired for this, but he climbed to his feet.

'Shit – okay!'

It was probably a daft idea, but Mark and Cal abandoned their jackets, footwear and jeans, and followed Sharkey's lead.

The deserted beach was no more than thirty yards away, a steep drop into a tiny cove of tide-worn rocks and brown sand, easier to run on where it had been wetted by the tide. The water was a darker plane beyond the sand merging into the mist. They ran at the tide, splashing out through the shallows, their feet slipping and sliding on seaweed before they fell into the freezing water. It wasn't long before all three of them were forced back out onto the sand, the bodies blue with cold, the steam of their breath clouding their vision.

Sharkey lay back on the elbow of his uninjured arm, showing the white of his toothy grin against his dusky skin. 'Why's this old fart so important to you?' he asked Mark.

'I think, maybe, he might understand what's going on.'

Mark joined Sharkey, sprawling flat on his back, his heels close to the surf. Cal flopped down on the other side of him, lying prone, the side of his face pressed against the sand. Mark's jaw trembled with cold as he spoke. 'We were only kids. None of us had any real idea of what we were getting into. All I know now, looking back at it, is that we were seduced into something . . . well, something incredibly dangerous.'

'And all that shit has to do with what is happening here?' Cal said.

'Yeah.'

Sharkey looked Mark in the face. 'I don't share Cal's scepticism. You're talking about something I can empathise with: the idea of getting involved in something dangerous – something you can't ever wholly escape from.'

Mark squinted at Cal's prone figure, a dark silhouette against the lightening sky.

Sharkey said: 'We did a whole bucket load of stupid things when we were kids. Me and Bull, we got ourselves involved in a couple of wars. Sometimes I think we never escaped from those wars.'

Over the ensuing minutes, the first clear shafts of dawn broke over the sea, awakening greys, then pallid blues, then the flush of violet. They gazed at the silvery horizon. The first glimmer of daylight amid the dissipating mist was beautiful. Frost crinkled the seaweed nearby. This was England, not just Cal's country, it was Mark's country too – and yet it felt curiously alien to him, as if the very molecules of his being no longer belonged here.

'Hey, the dip was fun!' Sharkey grinned.

The tide was coming in. Mark sat forward, bringing his goose-pimpled thighs up to his chest and holding his legs bent up with his hands. Seagulls shrieked overhead. 'I really do think there are too many things in common with our experience on Tír for the events here to be coincidence.'

Cal spoke then, his voice a growl from deep within his chest. 'Don't treat me like I'm stupid, pal!'

'I'm not.'

'I know what you're doing. I just figured it out. You're slipping and sliding around the truth.'

'How's that?'

'What's really happening – you're ignoring what's behind it all – the word for it is evil. You think you can pretend that evil don't exist? I've been up to my nostrils in it, all my life. Hoping nobody was going to make a wave. Nearly drowned in it when those fuckheads murdered my father. Heard Tajh tell you that – she tells everybody. But don't you go thinking you understand. I'm talking about my father, the dad who abandoned me as a kid. You moan and groan about being adopted. Nobody ever took the trouble to adopt me. I thought a whole lot about that when I was growing up, in and out of trouble. I knew my father was out there somewhere and when I was ready I went looking and I found him. I made it my business to find him when those tattoo-heads started laying it on people like him. I found him. And you know what? He was just another alcoholic shithead, an ex squaddie just like me. And here's me, an idiot who goes into the fucking army, man, to try to have something to believe in, something to fight for. I saw things to believe in all right. I saw evil every fucking day.'

Mark and Sharkey dropped their heads in silence.

Cal lifted his face to the sky and he exhaled. 'I hardly had time to get to know my waste of space father before he became another of those statistics nobody gives a shit about.'

He turned on his heel and stalked back to the camp.

Mark followed him. But he wasn't so stupid as to think he could console Cal in his present mood.

Mark looked in on Padraig, nodded to Tajh and Nan who were looking after him, then wrapped his leather jacket around his trembling and jerking shoulders. He looked down at the battered harmonica he lifted from his pocket.

Fathers and sons!

Cal had returned to his perch on the step.

Mark stood over him. 'You're lucky.' Mark could actually hear his teeth chattering. 'At least you got to know your father.'

Bull looked down at the pair of them from the top of the Mamma Pig, where he was still working on the satellite dish. Tajh came down out of the cab to put an arm around Cal's shoulders.

Mark shrugged his shoulders at Tajh. 'Sorry.'

Nan signalled to him from the open porthole in the side of the Pig, but he was still concentrating on Tajh. She shrugged, her eyes closing with a sigh. At that point the heavy engine started up. They heard it revving, as if Cogwheel was testing it – or maybe deliberately breaking up the mood.

Tajh said: 'We're all fagged out with exhaustion. I've been lying awake all night thinking about things.'

'Thinking about what?'

'Thinking about you, what you and Nan have been telling us. There are things that we've been noticing too that make little sense as we understand things.'

'Like what?'

'I'm beginning to believe you – maybe there is a pattern to what's been happening in London: the riots, the wasted streets, whole districts in flames. And now the whole country.'

'What sort of pattern?'

'I just can't say, but I'm just beginning to see that it isn't just random chaos, as people were assuming.'

Mark thought about that walk with Henriette, seeing London from a very different perspective. Then he looked back towards the porthole only to discover that Nan had disappeared.

Cal asked: 'What's happening with the drones?'

Tajh answered: 'I don't know.'

Mark was still wondering about Nan. Where was she? What was it she had been attempting to tell him? He felt so anxious about her he searched for her presence with his oraculum.

'Shit! Something's wrong. Nan is gone.'

The crew reacted with surprise. The atmosphere immediately grew tense.

Tajh jumped up into the Mamma Pig to confirm that Nan was not there. Sharkey, Bull and Cal were just standing there, all looking at Mark. He searched for Nan through his oraculum.

<I'm fine> she countered, mind-to-mind. <I am down at the beach, looking at the sea.>

<You picked a strange time to go for a walk.>

<Something was wrong. The gulls had gone quiet. I looked for the reason why. I sensed changes in the wind: in its force – which was rapidly growing – and changes in its direction, which was blowing in, landwards from the sea.>

Mark looked at Tajh: 'It's okay. She's safe.'

Nan clearly overheard him. <We are not safe.>

<What is it, Nan?>

<Open up your senses through the oraculum. The wind has risen ten-fold in the last few hours. The temperature has also risen several degrees. I came down here to the sea to examine the movements of the waves. Where was the tide when you left it?>

<Half way up the little beach and rising.>

<Well, now it has retreated so far I cannot see it.>

Mark swung round to face the crew, who had been staring at him in silence as he communicated with Nan, his oraculum flaring. 'She says that the wind is rising. The sea has gone out a mile.'

Sharkey said: 'That just ain't possible, man.'

Cogwheel, who had been leaning out of the window of the Mamma Pig with a fag between his lips didn't agree with Sharkey. He flicked the sparking remains out into the dirt. 'Shit, guys, I really do hope I'm wrong, but what Nan is describing sounds like only one thing I know: a tsunami.'

<You hear that, Nan?>

<I hear it. What is this tsunami?>

<A gigantic wave. You better get back here fast as you can.>

Mark took off, shorewards, to meet her. 'Hell, Nan! I was worried about you.'

'Worry about yourself. I've been moving in a circle around this spot. Something very strange is happening.'

'Strange, how?'

She shook her head. 'The changes in the birds, the wind, the tide – it's becoming very peculiar indeed.'

'Your chatting is not helping us,' Cal barked from the topmost step of the Mamma Pig, where he stood glowering down at Mark and Nan. 'What's the fuss? Are we being tracked? Can we expect a drone attack?'

Nan spoke: 'I don't know if we are being tracked or not. I don't think we are under a drone attack, but I do believe we can expect a storm, a very big storm, coming in from the sea.'

Cogwheel chipped in: 'She's talking about a tsunami.'

Cal laughed. 'We don't get tsunamis in England.'

'Hsst!' Tajh waved them all to silence.

Then they all heard it: a roaring, rushing sound in the far distance.

'Shit!'

The Mamma Pig became a commotion of activity. They threw everything that had come out of the Pig back in through the portholes, while Cogwheel started up the engine. As Mark helped Nan back in through the port, Cogwheel performed a five point turn, then headed out, revving through the heavy gears.

'Where we heading?'

'We'd best take a twisty route; keep the things in the sky off our backs. Tajh, can you plot a route that'll give us the least hassle?' Cal hesitated long enough to light one of

Cogwheel's self-roll cigarettes off the dock-end of his previous.

'I have a question,' said Mark.

'Uh-huh?'

'Sharkey is right. Tsunamis don't usually hit the East Anglian coast. What if this isn't down to natural forces?'

Nobody volunteered an answer.

A Sense of Purpose

Mo woke with a shock to realise that she was listening to birdsong. It had been so long since she had heard anything so sweet that it threatened to disorientate her. When she stepped outside her tent, closely followed by her Shee guardian Usrua, she spotted the two slender olive birds with yellow breasts that had woken her with their song. They resembled chiffchaffs back on Earth. Then she noticed lots more of them, and other varieties too. They were feeding off insects that buzzed and swarmed around a proliferation of tiny red, pink and yellow lichens that peeped out of the cracks between the rocks.

'Isn't it strange, Usrua, how loveliness could still survive, despite what's been happening here?'

'Life is life.'

'It troubles me that we had to kill them all – all of the defenders.'

'We were obliged to do so. We offered quarter but none

responded since surrender is forbidden to the Tyrant's legionaries.'

'Why would he be so cruel as to forbid defeated soldiers the opportunity to surrender? What purpose would it serve when all is otherwise lost?'

'Their lives matter only in as much as they serve his purpose. Once surrendered, they would be of no further purpose to him. As captives they might even prove useful as informants to the enemy.'

'But that is monstrous.'

'It is the logic of war.'

Mo shut her eyes. She recalled the arrival of Kate on the dragon, how it had blacked out the evening stars. At the time it had appeared to put a cap on those days of never-ending battle, the chaos of flames, the fury and horror. There was a particular memory she would have preferred to forget, when the Shee had set fire to the base of a tower full of desperate defenders. Now Mo wondered if she would ever rid herself of the awful memory of that tower consumed by flames, wheeling Garg sentinels in the sky directing new avenues of attack, the screams of the dying.

Mo opened her eyes again to gaze up into the dark-skinned face of Usrua, seeing her feline features in the flared and flattened nostrils that were already half way between those of a human and a great cat. She also saw a hint of stripes coursing over her guardian's brow, larger than usual canines and butter yellow eyes that could open wide to become all pupil, so moonlight reflected off the retinas like mirrors. Even the prickling patterning over the curve of her cheeks suggested the whiskery profusion that would spring out when she transformed into her battling feline spirit. Mo thought about the description she had so often overheard when human-like races on Tír spoke of the Shee: they called them a warrior race. How astonishing to think of them as beings bred specifically for war . . .

'Must we kill every foe we come across in this war? Does Alan feel this way? Is there no possibility of compromise?'

'The enemy has ever been obdurate in terms that might have mitigated suffering or ended hostilities.'

Mo hesitated, the fingers of her right hand subconsciously caressing the Torus that dangled on a thong around her neck. In her memory she saw the Torus around the neck of an old aboriginal woman caught in the rays of the setting Australian sun, its elongated shadows throwing her naked skin into relief. The old woman had been carrying a long cylindrical basket. She had reached into the basket and raised a stick with a rattling pod at the end of it, then addressed a young woman whose name was Mala, and who was seated, cross-legged, by a dark, still pond. The old woman had rattled the pod before Mala and said, '*Tjitji*', which Mo understood to mean child. Mala, as Mo now knew, was her natural mother and Mo was the *tjitji* – the child developing in Mala's womb. She had seen the old woman transfer the Torus to the neck of Mala. Now, Mo looked down at it. It was a ring, maybe two inches diameter, of strange grey-coloured rock, aglow with efflorescences of blues and greens, ultramarines and turquoise. It was . . . alive with . . . with power. Mo had increasingly come to realise that the Torus was similar to the oracula her friends bore – she could sense the most intimate thoughts and feelings of other minds, other hearts.

She sighed. It was hard to believe that they had learned no lessons from the two and a half days of carnage. The ferociousness of the fighting had so shocked Mo that it disturbed her sleep now. She intended to take it up at her meeting with Alan and Kate later in the day. Surely she would find support with Kate, who must be every bit as shocked by the violence and bloodshed as Mo was?

She was so relieved that her friend Kate was back. Mo had deeply missed her company. They had met, hugged one another, rejoiced, but that joy had been marred by the sight of flaming buildings and the continuing efforts of the Shee to winkle out the last outposts of legionary resistance. Since then there had been no time for the two of them to sit down and talk.

Mo felt that she desperately needed to talk. That was why she had sent a message to Alan and Kate suggesting the meeting. She also needed, of course, to hear every detail of what had happened to Kate on her mission to rescue the Cill, but there was a deeper, more urgent, reason she needed to meet up with her friends.

I need to tell them everything. I need to explain what has been happening to me and why it so frightens me.

That was why the birdsong had been such a welcome

intrusion: it had been the reminder that joy still existed in the world.

Mo turned her face to the sunshine, appreciating the faint fragrance of flowers in the cool morning air. She saw two children nearby chasing butterflies, a scene so heart-warming and charming Mo couldn't help but watch them. Oh, how she would have loved to join them! They looked like a couple of Olhyiu ragamuffins, a boy and a girl, perhaps ten and nine years of age. Then she wondered: *What parent could have been so careless as to expose such innocents to the fury of a war zone?* It was a wonder that they had survived the arduous journey here, never mind the recent battles.

Her curiosity aroused, Mo walked across the gritty dirt to speak to them, ignoring the towering shadow of Usrua who followed close on her heels. 'Why, hello! Who might you two be?'

The girl, who was the elder, cast a wary glance in the direction of the Shee, whose nostrils were visibly twitching, sniffing the air around the two children.

'Beggin' pardon, Milady, but I'se Moonrise an' this is me brudder, Hsst.'

Mo laughed. 'Hsst is a funny kind of name.'

'It's on account of 'e's deaf.'

'He's deaf? Oh, dear! I think I'm beginning to get the picture.' Mo lifted her eyebrows in sympathy, but also bemusement.

'Where are your parents?'

'We ain't got none.'

'So you look after your brother?'

'I looks to 'im an' 'e looks to me.'

'When did you last have something to eat?'

'We gets a bit o' soup, from Soup Scully Oops.'

'When was the last time you had a bowl of soup?'

'Only . . . Well . . . mebbe . . .'

Mo could see from the marks on their faces and limbs that the children had been ill-treated, and not just recently – there were bruises of various shades that suggested earlier mistreatment. Mo had experienced such brutality at the hands of her adoptive parents, Grimstone and his wife Bethel, so she remembered it only too well. The little girl also had a swollen eye, caked in pus.

'Moonrise. You have a huge stye there.'

The little girl rubbed at the inflamed eyelid with a filthy hand.

'It looks really sore.'

Moonrise squinted down at her brother, who was barely above her shoulder. Tears moistened his eyes as he alternately looked up at her and threw fearful glances at the Shee. He inserted his hand into that of his sister and sucked on his free thumb.

Mo said: 'Please don't be frightened by Usrua. She's just taking care of me. She won't harm you, not unless you try to harm me.' Mo laughed, taking a gentle hold of the girl's free hand. 'I don't think you are planning to harm me, are you, Moonrise?'

Moonrise shook her head.

'I'll tell you what we'll do. I'm going to send Usrua to find an aides. The aides will know how to treat your eye. She'll also find you something to eat.'

Moonrise looked up at Mo with alarm. She attempted to retrieve her hand from Mo's, but Mo resisted.

'I's all right. I's okay, Milady . . .' she said.

Mo kept her voice gentle but insistent. 'No, it really isn't. You're both starving. And your eye is infected.'

Usrua, who had been observing all this with statuesque stillness, now inclined her head to purr quietly into Mo's ear, 'The Mage Lord, Alan, approaches, together with the Kyra, Kate and the dwarf mage. You had requested a private conversation with them, if you remember.'

'Yes, of course. I really need to talk with them, but I don't want to do so on my own. See if you can find the magician, Magtokk.'

Usrua nodded, but she hesitated as she looked down at the children.

'Don't worry. They'll hardly understand what I'm about to discuss. And the little girl really needs attention for that eye.'

The Shee stretched to her full height and her eyes narrowed. 'I shall inform an aides of the children's needs, and meanwhile find the monkey trickster as you command. But beware, Mistress! Danger comes in many guises. This is not the first time I have noticed these same urchins at play nearby. Even in the most innocent of circumstances you must anticipate treachery.'

•

Mo watched the approach of Alan and Kate with some trepidation, noticing Alan still carried the Ogham-runed Spear of Lug in his right hand. She sensed the same heightened wariness in Alan's heart and mind as she had in Usrua's. Was he still wary of pockets of enemy that might suddenly spring out of a cleft in the rocks, or some hidden tunnel, and attack them? Was he being overly protective of Kate, now she was back with him? Judging from his expression, Mo saw that he was very distracted. How her childhood friend had changed! How all four friends had changed since their arrival here as naïve teenagers from Earth.

Alan was now very tall. She guessed he was almost the same height as his beanpole grandfather, Padraig. But then, Mo herself had also grown exceptionally tall. It was scary to feel, and see, things happen to oneself without having any control over them. Mo knew that people were now somewhat daunted by Alan. Even the Shee treated him with respect and the Olhyiu appeared to regard him as semi-divine, much as the Gargs regarded Kate. But Mo didn't fear either of her friends, no matter what legends were now growing up about them.

She and Kate flung themselves into one another's arms, promising to find hours and hours to gossip all by themselves, but this was not the moment. As Mo hugged Alan in turn, she was surprised at her own palpable nervousness when she whispered the words into his ear: 'We need to talk. There's something I must tell you and Kate.'

Alan held her by her shoulders at arm's length, as if to

fully appraise the changes he must see in her. There was the suggestion of a smile on his lips. 'What is it, Mo? Are you still worrying about Mark?'

'I can't help worrying about him.'

Alan spoke, quietly. 'I guess all of us have been wondering if Mark got there – if the Temple Ship took him back to Earth.'

Kate and Mo nodded. All three of them were still thinking the same thoughts. Their friend, and Mo's adoptive brother, Mark, had been unsure if he was alive or dead after he was reduced to a soul spirit by Mórígán. He had been so haunted by the uncertainty he was determined to return to Earth and find out.

'I am worried about Mark, but that's not why I asked for the meeting. I have something important to tell you.'

Mo grabbed hold of Kate's hand.

'Mo! What on earth is it?'

'I hardly dare to speak of it. Not on my own.'

But then she was relieved to see Usrua returning in the company of Magtokk, who was knuckle walking in an attempt to keep pace with the strides of the Shee. He resembled a great ball of fur, dragging locks of it through the dirt behind him. The deep-set orang-utan eyes furrowed as they gazed into Mo's, and then she saw his face lift, sensing her state of heightened emotion.

Kate said: 'Mo's about to tell us a secret, but she refused to say a word until you're here.'

Magtokk blew out a sigh through those huge rounded

cheeks and then raised his enormous sausage-fingered hand to stroke his gingery-orange beard.

'I take it you're going to talk about your mother?'

Mo said: 'I'm going to tell them everything.'

Alan sat directly opposite Mo, his head dipped and eyes slightly narrowed against the flurries of wind that blew sandy grit into his eyes. Kate sat beside him, her hand squeezing Mo's. They were clustered together on a dry ledge of tufa, with a ring of Shee guardians keeping to a discreet distance of fifty or so yards away. Magtokk and Qwenqwo completed the circle. 'I'm sorry,' Mo spoke in a voice just above a whisper. 'I was supposed to keep it a secret from you for now, but I can't stay quiet about it any longer. I think you both should know right away.' Mo took a deep breath. 'Magtokk took me to see my birth mother.'

Alan's eyes opened wide in surprise. 'He did what?'

'I wanted him to. It was something I desperately needed to do.'

Qwenqwo toyed with an unlit pipe in his gnarled hands. He lifted his emerald green eyes to look directly into Mo's. 'I can see that it meant everything to you, Mo. But how was this possible?'

'Oh, Qwenqwo, there has always been so much that was never fully explained to us. We were drawn into Tír and expected to do whatever the various powers demanded of us. And we're still doing what they demand of us, as if we have no choice in the matter. Magtokk was very helpful to me. He recruited Thesau – the eagle you will recall from our journey down the Snowmelt River. It seems that Thesau is not an eagle, and was not protecting you, Qwenqwo, or your runestone. It's a True Believer and it is still up there, or somewhere close by anyway, and its purpose was ever to protect me.'

Qwenqwo snorted. He busied himself with the pantomime of lighting his pipe, refusing on this occasion to do Magtokk the favour of lighting a second. Then he puffed away, but with hardly his customary contentment, imbuing the faint stink of the distant toxic exhalations of the volcanic lava with the more pleasant aroma of his pipe tobacco.

In looking across at his friend, Alan could hardly fail to notice how Mo was changing. Her face was lengthening and her eyes were turning up at the outer edges. She had always been stunningly beautiful, but now she looked curiously different, even a little alien. Every time she looked into a mirror, it would probably make her wonder about her own nature. It was a feeling he had become familiar with himself.

Kate spoke: 'But you haven't answered Qwenqwo's question, Mo. How could Magtokk possibly take you to meet your birth mother when we know, or at least we think we know, that your mother is dead?'

'Magtokk helped me to make a dream journey into the past, like when you, Qwenqwo, took us back to the destruction of Ossierel and the death of Ussha de Danaan.'

Alan was increasingly shocked by what he was hearing. 'Magtokk, you've been playing games behind our backs.'

'No, my friend. I have never lied or played games with regard to my position. When Mo asked for my help, I felt obliged to help her.'

'I doubt that it was like that. You've had your eye on Mo since you first appeared. None of us could fail to notice your obsessive attentions.'

'I do not deny it.'

'Oh, Alan, none of you really understands! Magtokk is one of them. He's a True Believer.'

Mo's words provoked a flurry of exclamations.

An enraged Alan turned on Magtokk: 'Is this true?'

'I'm afraid it is.'

'I can't believe it.'

Mo put her hand on Alan's shoulder. 'It would explain how he disappears and reappears. The True Believers don't have any corporeal reality. They can come and go through Dromenon.'

'They can cross between worlds? They can journey back in time?'

'Yes.'

'Is this true, Magtokk?'

'Indeed it is.'

'You took Mo on a dream journey to meet her birth mother?'

'Not merely to meet, to witness.'

Alan shook his head, even more bewildered. 'Why?'

'Is it not obvious? So she could understand who, and what, she truly is.'

'What did she discover then?' Alan turned from his fierce interrogation of Magtokk to look at Mo. 'Do you really know yourself better now?'

Mo's face fell. She looked so bewildered that Alan regretted raising his voice. 'I'm sorry, Mo. Forgive me. It's just that—'

Kate put her arm around Mo's shoulders and embraced her. 'Hush, Alan. Allow Mo a moment or two.'

Alan sighed, nodded. Magtokk's great shaggy arm reached out to hug Mo on the opposite side. His other arm reached out to tap Qwenqwo on the shoulder, his huge face putting on such a comical expression of pleading that the dwarf mage couldn't help but smile, however much he disapproved. Qwenqwo filled a second pipe, lighting it and passing it over. The flagon wasn't too long delayed in appearing after that.

'Magtokk! Will you, for goodness' sake, tell us what's really going on?' Alan said.

'Of course,' he puffed, with his eyes closing in a look of contentment. Then he sighed and opened his wise old eyes again. 'Like you, Alan – and like Kate and Mark – Mo's role in the big picture was fated. She serves a greater purpose in this world. I was appointed by my fellow True Believers to help protect Mo. Such has ever been my purpose, and privilege, among you. There was neither deceit, nor treachery, merely the determination to protect and enable her. And Mo's purpose draws nearer.'

Kate clasped Mo's hand between her two. 'Mo!'

Mo smiled at Kate. 'It's true, Kate. Magtokk has been

wonderful to me. It was so beautiful to meet my birth mother, Mala. She looked so young and vulnerable. Just an aboriginal girl, so lovely to meet and so innocent.' Mo hesitated. 'I hope Magtokk won't mind my telling you. She is – she was – my virgin mother.'

Mo's words astonished Alan and Kate.

Alan couldn't speak for several moments just studying Mo, who had always been the strangest of the four friends. She was the only one who had not been given a crystal by Granny Dew in the cave of the Whitestar Mountains. Right now she was pursing her lips, the way she had done on the first day he had met her, together with her adoptive brother, Mark, after Padraig had caught them trespassing in his woods. Even then there had been something special, something different, about Maureen Grimstone – a difference Padraig appeared to sense right away. Padraig had taken her under his wing, just as Qwenqwo and now Magtokk had done here on Tír.

Alan took a deep breath. 'Mo, we may soon be under attack again. We've all been under tremendous stress. Stress does things to your mind. This journey, riding these bone-shaking onkkh. I wonder at times if I'm going slightly bonkers myself. Those black blots invading my mind. I have nightmares in which I wake from sleep tormented by those vile shapes, spinning and changing inside my head, but I've come to the conclusion it's just being stupid to allow them to trouble me. They're just stress hallucinations.'

'I don't think I'm hallucinating, Alan.'

'You really believe your mother was a virgin?'

Mo nodded.

'Virgin pregnancies don't happen, Mo. Not in the real world.'

'By real world, you mean Earth. But Tír is not Earth. And whatever happened with my mother, no matter that it happened in Australia, the presence of the True Believers tells me that it didn't follow the rules of Earth.'

'Mo, you need to be sceptical of everything you see and hear. Isn't it possible your thoughts, your dreams, are being manipulated?'

Magtokk interrupted: 'It is you who are being naïve, Alan, if you think that every child is born of man and woman. Have you forgotten your friends, the Shee? What if the pregnancy was placed within Mala in a manner beyond her capacity to understand?'

'What are you talking about? Some kind of artificial insemination?'

Mo smiled and took Alan's hand with her free left hand. 'I think we have all discovered that Tír is very different to Earth. There are forces here that would not make sense back home. Like the power that brought us here. Or the Fáil. What about the oraculum in your brow? Does any of that make sense from a common sense Earth perspective?'

'We're human, Mo. Our perceptions are human.'

Mo spoke to Alan quietly, still holding his hand. 'I'm sorry, Alan, but I no longer take any comfort from common sense.'

The Beginnings of a Plan

The brat of a girl was squealing like a stuck pig as Kawkaw twisted her ear with his surviving thumb and forefinger. She had been describing how she and her brother had pretended to play as they watched the tall, strange female, Mo, and the Mage Lord, and the Kyra, and the dwarf mage, and the monkey-man all talking seriously together.

'Talking? About what?'

'Don't rightly know as what. They shushed us.'

'Don't play the fool with me. I know the mute can read lips.'

'Tried to 'e did. Honest. But the cat woman shushed us right after the aides woman treated me eye. So we was too far away even for Hsst to lip 'em.'

'Think they're your new friends, do you? Treated your scabrous eye! Does that make you think you can get one over old Kawkaw?'

With a flick of his right arm, the razor-sharp knife was

in his hand and brushing the salve-smeared swollen eye of the brat.

'I ain't lyin'. Honest.'

'Ach!' Keeping the blade pressed against her face, Kawkaw thought about her words. 'Devilry – that's what they are up to! Scheming and devilry!'

The tip of the blade bit into the purplish ooze of the girl's flesh; a wash of pus, stained with blood, began to run, like a tear drop, down her swollen cheek.

'She told us we wuz to go back.'

'Suffering hogspiss!' He could hardly think straight. He wiped the scutter off the blade on the girl's rags. But something in what she had just said burst the balloon of his rage.

'Who told you?'

'Mo did. She says as we're to go back to see 'er, the aides woman what treated me eye. For 'er to see it's gettin' better.'

'What – just the old aides witch?'

'Mo too. But Hsst is afeared of 'er 'cause she's got that Shee warrior with 'er all the time, even when she sleeps in 'er tent.'

'The brat, Mo? She wants to see you again?'

'Yeah.'

Kawkaw scratched his stubbled neck with his hook. Could it be that the fates had offered succour at last, just when it had looked nigh on impossible to extract even a morsel of benefit from this situation? Was this his opportunity to avenge the Preceptress' taunts? Did they not say the fates work in ways that are not immediately apparent?

'You're sure? The brat, Mo?'

'Yeah.'

His eyes bore down onto the squirming face, the knife slipped back in his pocket, but her now swollen ear was once more clasped in the pincers of his finger and thumb.

She squealed anew, but she was nodding.

'You wouldn't lie to old Snakoil Kawkaw?'

She shook her head.

The brat wouldn't dare to lie to him. It had to be true. Snakoil Kawkaw couldn't believe his luck. Something important was going on. Why else would the Shee witch drive them away? Was she becoming suspicious of the brats? Was their spying becoming too obvious?

He gave her ear a final twist before he released it. The brat made snuffling noises through her nose, which was running with snot.

There was something for him here: the beginnings of a plan.

'See to it that you do go back! And you make sure that the mute keeps his eyes open and you keep your filthy little ears wagging for anything – the smallest squeak – that might be useful to me.'

Breaching the M1

Other than Sharkey and Tajh, who had alternated sentry duty during the night, the crew had been forced to sleep within the cramped interior of the Mamma Pig, which was concealed from the threat of drones in a dense pocket of evergreens four or five miles from the Tibshelf Services. At first light, snow still wheeled about them, finding its way through the dripping needles overhead, to lay a thin scattering on the dank floor of the forest. The conflict in the blazing town, and then the flight from the tsunami, had made everyone jumpy – they didn't like to think how much had been destroyed, how many lives lost; instead they focused on moving forwards.

Their current problem was the M1, which bisected the country like a perilous river to allow passage from East Anglia to the Midlands, with Derbyshire its final objective. They had considered every junction from 23 to 26. Junction 24a had looked the least hazardous, but now a careful approach, with the last few miles involving a probe on foot by Cal and Mark, revealed that Seebox had anticipated them: the slip-road roundabout was blocked by massive concrete blocks, reinforced by steel girders driven deep into the road surface. They also saw that the M1 itself was patrolled by tanks and heavily gunned APCs. They had to assume that all of the motorway junctions were similarly blocked. That left them with only one option: they had to breach the M1 where there was no junction. So they began a new search for a more rural stretch, where they might get trees, or buildings that would offer cover during the crossing.

After several hours of exploration, they opted for a services area between junctions 27 and 28, where a minor road ran under the carriageway. It was quite a bit further north than they had originally planned, but it had the advantage of an approach through winding country roads flanked by woods. They could also pay a call on the services and top up on provisions, the most important of which was a supply of fresh water.

After getting lost several times, with detours that they estimated added another thirty miles to their journey in the now overheated Pig, they emerged out of a wood-lined narrow road to discover a sign pointing north to Hardwick Hall.

'Hey – howszzzat!'

A jubilant Cogwheel high-fived Tajh. The sign, and distance, meant that they were on track. All they had to do was head ten miles south aiming for the B6014 and they would hit the southbound half of the services. Cal decided they would scout out the motorway before they attempted to cut under it.

'Guns!' Cal barked, because they were obliged to emerge from cover.

When they got there, the location was perfect for their purposes; they had reasonable tree cover on the approach and would only emerge fully into the open as they neared the services car park. Cogwheel rolled the Mamma Pig over a small wooden fence, then sliced through a coppice of saplings before crashing into an abandoned camper van. He swore before reversing, and then edged the Pig cleanly under a wide gabled arch strutted by two steel pillars that opened onto the entrance foyer of the services. The arch was just about wide and long enough to accommodate the Pig and the tinted glass of the pitched roof was likely to mask their presence from the air.

'Well done!' Nan patted Cogwheel's shoulder, to his crowing satisfaction.

Mark left Tajh to keep an eye on Padraig then joined Cal and Bull in slipping out of the left hand porthole to emerge under the shade of the arch. All three of them took a good look around at the pale orange walls, the rows of redwood trestle tables and chairs and the column of cerulean rubbish bins on the puce-coloured surface.

Cal lowered his Minimi. 'It's quiet.'

Mark, joined by Nan, scanned the area with his oraculum as well as his eyes. 'Clear as far as we can see.'

Cal spoke to Bull. 'We'll take a good look around to make sure. We'll meet up with you inside.'

Bull nodded.

Mark, Cal and Nan headed in through the high glazed doors of the atrium, expecting to find the building empty. They presumed it would have been without electric power for three or four days at the very least, and probably devoid of staff and any fresh provisions, but as they headed into the wide paved foyer, they were surprised to discover that a rag-tag collection of thieves and dossers had beaten them to it: robbing the kitchens, dispensing machines, restaurants and bar. Many were still in occupation, nestling in corners and drunkenly asleep. The dossers had already enjoyed the best of the spoils. Any food that had remained in the services had gone rank, though there were some remaining crates of water and beer. Over the next hour or so they stocked up on water. Cogwheel took a turn to monitor Padraig, allowing Tajh to grab an hour or so of sleep. The break offered the remaining crew the opportunity of washing their faces, hair and upper bodies with bottle soap and water from the smashed dispensing machines upended into the sinks of the otherwise disgusting toilet areas. They knocked back some warm beers while watching the M1 through the broken panes of the main restaurant window, timing the patrols of Seebox's tanks and APCs as they clanked by on both the northbound and southbound carriageways.

Cal totted it up: 'Roughly fifteen minutes, either way.'

Mark nodded. 'Which, since it's the same either way, means the actual window is half that.'

'Not precisely half. My guess is they start out at the same time between two points at, say, roughly fifty to sixty miles a stretch. But we're not at the exact middle of this particular stretch. So that adds in a cockeyed variation. Sometimes it's closer to five minutes alternating with a longer gap of approximately nine or ten minutes.'

Sharkey asked: 'Can we figure which gap?'

'Yeah. It's simple enough. We wait for the short one. Then we have nine to ten minutes before the next.'

'Everybody happy?'

Nobody disagreed.

Cal added: 'We need to decide where we cross the motorway. I've been studying the map. That road we crossed coming here is the B6014. It goes under the M1, heading into a small market town. What's the odds the town is too small to have attracted a road block?'

Mark thought about it. 'You're probably right.'

Sharkey pursed his lips: 'De good Lord provideth for de penitent sinners!'

Everybody laughed.

Restocked with wetted fresh towels to dampen Padraig's burning body and what was left of the water and beer, Cogwheel backed them out of the entrance arch and headed towards the B6014. They took the mile or two north, then headed left onto the B road, timing their run to avoid motorway patrols and aiming for the unguarded underpass.

All was going well until a tractor, hauling a trailer full of split logs, veered across their path and blocked their passage. While Cogwheel was still swearing at the fact he had been forced to make an emergency halt, a beefy man jumped down off his seat and came abreast of the cab, waving a twelve-bore in Cogwheel's face.

Bull was out of the belly of the truck in a flash and pressing his heavy Minimi in the man's side. 'What the fuck you think you're doing?'

'We've been told to keep an eye out for scumbags like you.'

'We – meaning who?'

'Off duty T.A.'

The man pointed to a tattoo on his forearm. It was a Territorial Army logo.

By now Cal was out of the belly of the Pig and had joined the argument. He showed the farmer his own SAS tattoo. 'I suppose you know what that means?'

'Could mean anything. Anybody can get a tattoo done.'

'Like you, for instance.'

'Field Marshall Seebox has called on all associated services to help out in the emergency. We've been warned about terrorists the like of you.'

'We're the Resistance, mate. Seebox is the enemy.'

'You're talking bollocks.'

'Shift your tractor or we'll shift it for you.'

'No way, Sunshine!'

Without warning the man emptied both barrels of the

gun he was holding into the front nearside tyre of the Mamma Pig.

Cogwheel shrieked with fury. 'Shit, bastard, sheeeiiiitttt!'

The idiot was attempting to reload. Bull clouted him with the butt of the Minimi, knocking him unconscious on the road. Between them, Cal and Bull hauled the man onto the verge, then Cal headed forward to move the tractor while Bull inspected the damage.

'We're going to have to change the wheel.'

Cogwheel shouted out of the side cab window. 'Bastard will have called someone. We have to get under the cover of the underpass!'

Bull said: 'Driving on the flat tyre would risk damaging the wheel rim – maybe even the axle. Just keep her idling a few minutes while Cal and me get the job done.'

'We can't wait. We have to risk it,' Cogwheel said.

'Just a couple of minutes. I'm going to jack her up. I have to go under to get the spare. Keep off the throttle.'

Tajh took organisational charge. 'Mark – you and Nan – I need you to get out there and help Bull while keeping an eye out for trouble.'

'What about Padraig?'

'Sharkey will keep an eye on him. The condition of the services suggests the Razzers haven't got this far north as yet. The town up there looks intact. But Cogwheel is right. That idiot with the tractor will have drawn attention to us. Me and Cogwheel'll keep an eye on the sky.'

Mark ran the thirty yards east along the road, while Nan

ran through to the other side of the underpass to keep a look out. Cal and Bull set about jacking the Pig to free the wheel and then Bull went underneath to unbolt the spare. It took more like five minutes than the two Bull had promised. Another two minutes as Bull hoisted the spare wheel into place and bolted it tight. He was just lowering the jack when, through his oraculum, Mark sensed the approaching danger.

He shouted: 'Leave it, Bull!'

Bull growled: 'Done it! Just stowing the jack.'

'Bull – we've got trouble. Forget the jack,' Mark shouted.

Even as he shouted his warning, he heard Nan's cry: 'Incoming!'

Cal had thrown himself into the Pig. 'Bull! In here, now!' he shouted.

Mark ran back, his eyes straining to make out Nan emerging from the underpass.

<Two missiles!> He heard her urgent communication, mind-to-mind.

Bull roared: 'No time to get aboard. I'm going to try to hang on under here. Go on Cogwheel, you fucking midget! Get her under the pass.'

Cogwheel revved, but he was still in neutral. He was clearly divided as to what to do with Bull still under the vehicle. Cal roared at him to put his foot to the floor. Mark saw the two missile trails falling towards them, coming from directions about ninety degrees apart. The Mamma Pig took off, screaming towards the underpass.

<Nan – I'll take the easternmost.>

<Got you!>

They directed the Third Power from their oracula at the incoming missiles with every fibre of their being. They managed to divert the missiles thirty or forty feet to either side of the Pig's position, but the explosions still rocked the vehicle, lifting the nearside wheels and half its bulk off the road, before it slewed with a screech of brakes into the relative safety of the underpass. Mark ran to get to Bull, whose face had been scorched and his shirt burned off his chest by the blasts. But he was still alive.

<Nan?>

<Help him. I'll deal with the drones.>

Mark shouted to Cogwheel to reverse a bit, then asked the others to give him a hand getting the injured Bull back on board.

Bull was a hell of a weight to lift. When they got him inside, Padraig had to be shifted to one side to make room for their second casualty. The confusion of struggle and make do lasted another five to ten minutes while they skulked under the pass trying to help Bull.

'What now?' Cogwheel muttered over his shoulder, blood running down the slopes either side of his nose from a fragment of windscreen embedded in his brow.

Tajh inspected the burns over Bull's face and chest. 'We need to find a hospital.'

'Never mind me,' Bull wheezed. 'Get us outta here.'

Cogwheel started the Pig up again, then spoke. 'Town's too small for a hospital.'

They emerged from the tunnel under the motorway to enter an organic shambles of streets. There was a squeaking sound from the rear nearside wheel, which caused Cogwheel to groan aloud.

'Shit – axle damage!'

Cal muttered, 'Keep on driving. Everybody – keep a sharp eye out. There's something screwy about this place.'

Mark said: 'How do you mean?'

'Look there.'

Mark peered out through the opened driver's side porthole, where he saw a controlled fire, in the garden adjacent to the end of a terraced row.

'Who's tending the fire?'

'Nobody,' Cal answered.

'What's it mean?'

'You tell me.'

Mark continued to look out at the passing houses and small retail outlets, which were, for the most part, two-storey and built out of stone. There were no lights visible through the windows, which was not altogether surprising given the power blackouts and the fact it was daylight.

'Shit!' Cogwheel muttered.

'What is it?'

'Look there – next to that power box.'

Adjacent to a green-painted metal structure, Mark saw a truck trailing cables: a generator.

Cal hissed between his teeth. 'They have electricity, but there's no lights. Every door is locked and bolted.'

Cogwheel muttered: 'So, what's going on?'

'Don't ask me.' Sharkey was moistening bandages and attempting to wind them around the bulk of Bull's chest. 'But we should keep an eye out for a clinic of some sort. A doctor or maybe a nurse.'

Tajh peered ahead from one side of the street to the other. 'There,' she exclaimed. In the middle of a block of four or five small retail outlets she pointed out what looked like a chemist's. Cogwheel had to do a U-turn, passing a pet food outlet, a post office and small café before creaking to a halt outside the plate glass window.

Cogwheel kept the engine running as Cal and Mark hopped out of the portholes to either side and approached the glazed door. Cal tried the door handle.

'Locked!'

Cal motioned to Mark to stand back, then smashed the central door panel with the butt of the Minimi and knocked out the fragments of glass so they could squeeze through.

Inside there was a single five-by-five yard room filled with the usual bottles and miscellany you would expect of a small pharmacy.

'Hello! Anybody here?' Cal shouted into the murky interior.

There was no reply.

Mark nodded towards a door set into a recess to their left. Cal rapped against the wood with the butt of the machine-gun. 'I'll give you ten seconds to come out of there before I empty the gun through the door.'

There was a furtive rustling before the door chinked open. A small, rotund face peered out at them.

'C'mon,' Cal yanked the man out into the open. 'We have somebody with burns. We need dressings and painkillers.'

The pharmacist scurried about his shelves and produced some paraffin tulle dressings, bandages, and a bottle of pills.

As they were leaving, Mark asked Cal to go ahead without him. Then he examined the mind of the chemist through his oraculum. It confirmed exactly what he had been thinking since first entering the shop.

He placed a finger against the man's bald sweating brow and administered the equivalent of a knockout blow, mind-to-mind, leaving the unconscious body prostrate on the floor.

'What was that about?' Cal asked him, when Mark rejoined him in the already accelerating Pig.

'Arsehole was praying in the cupboard. That was how I knew he was in there.'

'Praying for what?'

'Not what – who! He was praying to Grimstone's master.'

'Bloody hell!'

'Might also explain Farmer Giles down the road.'

Tajh muttered: 'Let's not get paranoid.'

Sharkey whistled. 'Maybe we're not quite paranoid enough.'

Cal said: 'What do you mean?'

'Might explain why the place is so untouched.'

Cal took a deep breath and exhaled slowly. 'I feel like going back and putting a belt full into the head of Farmer Giles. But we don't have the time. We head northwest. Get us out of here fast as you can, Cogwheel. We're probably no more than forty miles from where we need to be, but we're going to have to travel twice that distance to avoid towns, major junctions. We can't afford mistakes and we can't afford any more stops.'

Escape

You gotta think it through, Gully thought. Strewth – it was such a big decision! *Maybe I'm wrong?*

He was squatting down in the lead gutter inside the edge of the roof of the hall, studying the sky again. He had been looking for what felt like a very long time and had seen nothing. Could be he had imagined it, that light in the sky? If only Penny was here to talk about it. He missed her so much, even though they never did nothing but argue. What would she say? He knew exactly what Penny would say . . .

Stop, look, listen!

He stopped his ruminating, he looked up into the sky and he listened . . .

'Noffink.'

He stood up, stretched his cramped legs, squatted down again. The worry of it was driving him nuts. All the same he knew he had seen that light in the sky. He had seen it twice. Maybe he should warn them folks down there in the barns? Maybe he should warn old Pinky Ponky? *But they might take it bad if I do. I'd 'ave to tell 'em wot I been up to. Wot're they gonna fink? They gonna fink I'll run. They'd lock me up. That's all them people ever do with the likes of me. They'd lock me up so I couldn't run.*

Gully couldn't take that chance. *No way, bleedin' Jose!*

Trouble was he didn't rightly know what to do for the best. He didn't want to see nobody getting hurt.

Wot you fink, Penny?

He heard her voice clear as a bell inside of his head: *'Is Our Place Safe?'*

'No, it bleedin' ain't.'

There ain't no Our Place no more. You put a stop to that, Penny, when you went and killed the Skull. An' this old farm ain't safe neither. That's the problem driving me crazy. I seen it, gel. I know I'm right about that light in the sky.

He hurried back down to take another look at the Raleigh racer. He just looked at it in the penlight for a moment or two, the girly red of the frame, the silvery chrome of the mudguards and the handlebars. He prodded the flat tyres, took the pump off from under the bar and cleaned it with his spit. Hah! Will ya look at that! Even the pump was chrome. But it didn't connect direct to the tyres. *Of course it don't – idiot!* Poking around in the saddlebag, he found what he was looking for: a nozzle that connected the pump to the valve. He tried blowing through the nozzle, but he couldn't. He spat the dirt out of his mouth, then looked at the nozzle, but even with the penlight it was too dark to see inside the tiny hole. He found an orange stick in right pocket 1. He poked the orange stick into the hole, then tried blowing through it again. Still bleedin' blocked.

Shit, ya idiot Gully – maybe it's supposed to be blocked?

Only way to test it was to connect it to the pump. He did so, then operated the pump with the nozzle in his mouth. He felt the blast of air puffing out his cheeks. *Pump workin' okay.* He stood up, his hand clasping the black leather saddle for several undecided seconds.

Got to be sure!

He left the bike and hurried back up to the roof again, got the binoculars out of his pocket and stared around that same area of sky.

Maybe the light wasn't always in the same place? He moved around the roof, keeping to a crouch so he wouldn't be seen by the folks below. He went around all over the place peering up into the sky. His right eye began to twitch. It was no good. *You got to make a decision, Gully – or pack it in, mate!* He sighed, and then he saw it out of the corner of his eye: the same light again. Only it was in a different place to before. He could easy have missed it since it just flicked on a second or two and then blinked out. He pulled the binoculars up from around his neck and searched the spot, his heart pounding all the while. Then he saw it – a small dark shape hovering like a raptor with a single bluish eye that winked on for a second or two and winked off again. He'd been right all along.

Got to be one of them drones.

'Yeah – yeah!'

You really got to warn 'em, Gully.

'No way!' He couldn't to get himself locked up. Not now. Not when he knew he had to get out of here.

Gully sneaked out of there through the 'walking gate'. That was what Pinky Ponky called it. He didn't know if there was a guard or not on the main gate, but he didn't want to risk it. The old bolt on the walking gate was stiff with rust, but he hit it with a stone, keeping the sound down with a snot rag. Then he wheeled the Raleigh racer out through the opened gate and closed it behind him. *You got to hope the snow won't start up again.* But right there at the gate the first flakes began to fall. He swore up into the night sky.

At least he'd had a bit of time to get ready; he'd Cellotaped his torch to the handlebars and stuck his goodbye message on the back door before he left. He'd warned them all that they'd got to get away.

You done your best Gully!

Now he tested the bigger torch, covering the light with his closed fist. All A-OK. Not that he was going to switch it on yet, not even when he was cycling away. Better the creepy dark than being hauled straight back.

Hey, Penny – I wish I wasn't so scared. But it ain't half as frightening as the thought of going back there to London.

Now, cycling a little unsteadily into the darkness, he thought about the small bottle of gin he had nicked.

Gully didn't like alcohol. He had tried the occasional beer and stuff with other kids but he had never tasted spirits, so he had nicked a cupful of gin, which he had poured into a small screw-cap bottle stuffed into his backpack. Now he paused about a hundred yards down the lane, took out the bottle, untwisted the cap and swigged it.

'Ugghh!' Tasted like shit.

He grimaced, then twisted the cap back onto the bottle, stuffed it back in the pack.

You got to man up, Gully!

Whatever that was supposed to mean . . . As he pushed off with the bike again, he couldn't help recalling when he had last seen Penny. He had followed Mark and the others down them wooden steps into the pit where the lunatics was killing one another with swords in the sawdust. Gully had heard Mark roaring a name into the air, with the black triangle in his brow blazing blue-black lightning. Gully himself had been encased in the lightning – it hadn't hurt him, but it had sure wasted just about everything else. It had torn along the tiers of seats, erupting through them Skulls like a fury. Then something had arrived, screeching through the air, and a battleaxe, covered in weird lightning, had landed in Mark's left hand. Gully had never seen noffink like it before in his life. But it didn't stop him chasing after Mark as he battered through the Skulls, all the way down to the rostrum above the arena.

'No!'

Gully's mind was filled with the shout of the woman,

Nan, who'd carried the same black triangle in her head. A bolt of lightning had come out of her triangle and shaken the arena like a cyclone. Them flame-throwers was blown clean out as the men holding them was blasted inside of the pit.

There had been some geezer ahead, with a sword held above his head. The blade of the sword had poured out a tempest, which had risen to join the clouds in the sky above. Gully's mouth had fallen open as he looked beyond the figure with the sword to two smaller figures: an old guy in a black robe with his arm around a girl . . . And then he'd seen who it was.

'Penny!'

His voice had been drowned out by the thunderclap of power that filled the arena.

His heartbeat had come up into his throat as he'd followed Mark, who was smashing down through the final tiers. Then they were standing in the sawdust and snow while Mark battled towards some half dead old geezer who was soaked in petrol. Mark called out the name Padraig. At the same time the lunatics had been trying to set fire to the old geezer. Then the Mamma Pig had burst through the wooden tiers and the air was filled with the crackle of a machine gun turned on the Skulls by a giant with a shaved head.

Mark was caught up in a blazing confrontation with the figure with the sword and Gully was running after him, heading for the edge of the stage. The old guy with his arm around Penny was just yards away, looking down at Gully.

Gully had seen the smile at the corners of his lips. He had seen that the man's eyes was as black as a robin's. All the while he had felt a growing panic inside him. He was shouting at Penny: *'Penny, gel!'*

He'd seen the expression on her face as she stared back down at him. He'd heard her answering cry, *'Run, Gully. Run from the City Below!'*

He'd run all right. He'd run from there like a frightened rabbit. In his mind he was still running. But he couldn't keep running forever. Penny had been taken from him and somehow he had to get her back. That was why he was heading back to London. He was going to find Penny and save her from the City Below.

Cycling on now, getting into a rhythm of pedalling, his thoughts just went round and round inside his head. Sometimes he'd use the torchlight momentarily, keeping tabs when the lanes twisted and turned, but not too often. He just kept on cycling, even as the snow thickened so it was sticking in his hair. He stopped a moment and turned the bike round, with the torch illuminated, so he could look behind him at his own tracks.

Whoo-ooo!

'Shit – just a bleedin' owl!' It had frightened him half to death hooting at him. The owl was somewhere in the dark up ahead. Its hooting was enough to stop him dead, his heart hammering in his chest. He hesitated, the bike still beneath him, waiting for the bird to hoot again. It humoured him.

Who – who – whoooooo!

His heart lifted. That old owl hooting at him made him feel better inside. He imagined the bulky shape of it, all shoulders and eyes and claws. Perfick!

'Hey, Penny! Wot a lark it would be to keep an owl for a pet! Set it up in a box in some branch of a tree. Pick some place where they'd be plenty of mice. Honest, I could just sit and watch it, all night long.'

Penny's Dilemma

<Open your eyes.>

The voice was that of Jeremiah. Penny was unable to resist it. She opened her eyes to discover that she was alone in a very strange place. She wasn't standing, or sitting, or lying down. She was hovering weightlessly in space, looking out onto a vision.

Stop, look, listen . . .

She did so. Closing her eyes for a moment, she opened them fully again and looked around. The images were three-dimensional, like a storm of the most extraordinary confetti. It was difficult to maintain full concentration because the metamorphosing images made her feel dizzy. There was no particular sound. Worse! There appeared to be a complete absence of sound. When she searched for it her ears registered an electronic static.

'Where am I?'

<You are within the common mind of the Akkharu.>

The Akkharu – the weavers of stardust! The idea that she could enter the minds of those extraordinary slug beasts frightened her as much as it thrilled her. She looked anew at the flickering patterns of shape and colour. There were stars, floral shapes, radial symmetries with natural curves, like an object she had seen somewhere; a miracle captured in glass, called millefiori.

'Are they dreaming?'

<They create in a manner that might resemble dreams.>

'They create . . .?'

<They await your instructions.>

'What instructions?'

The voice was silent.

How could she possibly instruct the Akkharu? A shiver went through Penny at that possibility. Was she getting closer to Jeremiah's plans for her? But not yet close enough to fully understand? 'But I don't know what . . . Please tell me what you really expect of me.'

<Look deeper. Become one with the creative weave of the Akkharu, not with your eyes alone but with all of your senses, your whole being.>

It was midsummer, and she was exploring the wilderness of the family garden chasing after butterflies. She had already ticked off the commonplace cabbage whites as well as red admirals, the huge dusky-backed peacocks, the blues, fritillaries, commas, tortoiseshells . . . the painted ladies. She loved their names. She loved the delicacy of them, their lightness when she captured one, breathed on it and then let it go. It was hard to believe that hard-headed entomologists had given them such exotic names. It was as if even the naturalists had allowed themselves to be entranced by them, entranced by their magic. So they gave them names as magical as the evanescent creatures themselves.

Emily the butterfly
Does a dance
As she flutters by

But something was wrong. This didn't feel like a dream. It felt too real to be a dream. Suddenly she was wheeling amid vast flocks of gorgeous butterflies.

'It's you, Jeremiah. You're controlling my dream.'

<I am within it and within you.>

As ever, his words puzzled her.

'Why?'

<To enable me to see what you see, to enable me to feel what you feel.>

Penny hesitated. 'Why would you do that?'

<So I can understand you.>

Could it be that he needed to understand her every bit as much as she needed to understand him? 'But why are you interested in me? You know so much more than I do. You are so powerful. Do you remember, when we first met, you already knew my name? I asked you how you knew my name.'

<I told you it was the easiest thing in the world to decipher names.>

'Because . . . Because you could read my mind?'

<Yes.>

'Why did you bother to find me?'

<I searched for you before you were born. Before you were even conceived.>

'But that's not possible.'

<Many things are possible that you might think impossible.>

She hesitated, pondered his words. 'But why meet me then?'

<It was an appropriate time for us to meet. You were about to put yourself into immediate danger.>

Penny remembered. 'The cloud thing with all the faces!'

<Shedur.>

Just to think about it caused her heartbeat to rise. 'It terrified me. I don't want to remember it.'

<This is one of the curious things about humans. You observe truth all around you but you cannot tolerate its implications. So you blind your eyes to it. You shut it off from your senses, your minds. You avoid facts that contradict your interpretation of the world.>

'What do you mean?'

<These insects, which look like living jewels, are for the most part doomed to a few days of life. They know not what you or I might recognise as pleasure, or love, or caring. Their sole imperative is to reproduce. The flowers that so

delight you are equally evanescent, and for the same purpose. You know this, Penny Postlethwaite, and yet you confuse that purpose with some romantic ideal of beauty in a world that knows nothing and cares nothing for beauty.>

'Who are you? What are you really?'

<A being in search of ultimate truth.>

Penny hesitated again, thinking of what he had just said to her, wondering what his words might mean.

'Are you . . . evil?'

<Your petty moralities are meaningless to me.>

'We humans are capable of reasoning.'

<Yes, but to a finite and ultimately self-centred degree. It is a poor intelligence that would allow itself to be so readily overwhelmed by instinct, by emotion. Yet instead of recognising and thereby extirpating this weakness, you extol it as the essence of your being.>

'Yet we recognise, through that same instinct, that to hurt another, to kill, is a wicked and selfish act.'

<You kill animals to consume them. You destroy entire ecologies, annihilating the many lives that exist within them, to satisfy your needs. You humans kill one another in your innumerable wars with a relish that you fail to recognise to be a passion.>

'We also help one another. We have the concept of charity, of love.'

<You consider this a higher purpose. And you extend this concept of love to the universe, expecting it to

reciprocate. Yet in the heavens whole galaxies collide, bringing extinction to countless civilisations, many more worthy of survival than yours. But no matter! I am not here to chastise you. Things are about to change. In time you will come to know more of the logic of existence. It is my intention to open your vision onto wonders both terrible and exhilarating. You will realise that absolute concepts of good and evil do not exist.>

'Then you claim that the universe is not immoral but amoral.'

<I would have you understand the true nature of power. Look upon it, if you must, as an indulgence on my part. I would give you what your species has yearned for all through your brief existence.>

'What is that?'

<Liberation. I would free you from the sentence of death that is the burden of all others of your kind.>

'What does that mean?'

<In the same way that the life of the butterfly in its brevity is no more than a puff of smoke to you, so your human lives are transient to me. I am far from alone. There are beings in the universe who take as long to consider an idea as you would measure millenia. You are frail beings whose lives are as fleeting as insects. Yet, so rare is your mind, Penny Postlethwaite, that you alone, of all other humans I have encountered, have a quality that might extend your creativity, your will, your being, beyond the confines of your human limitations.>

'You're attempting to change me. But what if I don't want to be changed?'

<I would enable you to discover your innate potential.>

'So that you can use me?'

<I would develop the seed in you.>

'Did . . . Did you place it there?'

Silence.

'Oh, no! Don't tell me . . .! You did, didn't you? You said that you . . . you searched for me, even before I was conceived.'

Silence again.

Her voice trembled. 'Am I . . . Please don't say that I'm your daughter?'

He laughed. <Since you are human you could hardly be my offspring.>

But she trembled all the more, not knowing if she believed him. Not knowing what to believe.

<You already know that some things cannot readily be expressed in words. Language is a poor messenger for what you have already recognised as the communication of mathematics. Humans sense something of this in your passion for music. But you, Penny, were born with the potential of this deeper level of communication. It is this potential that will enable you to control the minds of the Akkharu. At the moment this potential is dormant. But the seed is in you. I would develop this potential.>

'I won't hurt people.'

<To wield power, you must learn to be ruthless.'

'No!'

<What if in order to help many, you must hurt some?>

'You're playing with words, with ideas. But I won't go along with you. I won't do it. I won't let you make me hurt people.'

Fear of Duty

Alan was tossing and turning in his sleep. In his dreams a storm raged; uncanny splotches and blotches of black wheeled like a murder of crows against a wasteland of snow. The shock of it woke him in his tent. He searched for Kate in a rising bewilderment, but then he remembered that Kate was not there. Every hour of the day and night he was interrupted by reports, or messengers from the Gargs, or Shee sentinels in anticipation of further conflict – the intrusive bureaucracy of war – so Alan had insisted she sleep in a tent by herself on the quieter periphery of the camp. It wasn't Kate's fault that they couldn't be together. She needed rest to recover from her ordeal in Ulla Quemar, the ruined city of the Cill. But none of that reasoning helped now as Alan sat up, his face bathed in sweat, his hands braced against the edges of his bier, breathing hard. The nightmare was fading, but the sound of footsteps approaching the flaps of the tent made him wonder if a new threat was coming to take its place.

A Shee guardian announced a single visitor.

Within moments, somebody slight and nimble had slipped through the flap, hardly disturbing it, her presence more readily apparent through his oraculum than in the gloomy light of the tent interior.

'Mo!'

Her face was only half visible because it was concealed within a hood, the other half illuminated by waves of light from the Torus she wore round her neck. The fact it was pulsating was enough to alert Alan. Mo's face lifted slowly, showing a ghostly outline of his friend. She didn't look solid, somehow. She sat cross-legged by his cot, her eyes wide with fright.

'Mo, what is it?'

<I'm not alone.>

Her statement caused Alan to jerk fully awake, his eyes darting around the close confines of the tent. 'Who else is here? I can't see anyone.'

<Indeed, I too am here; in moral support for your friend.> It was Magtokk's voice, but Alan could detect no sign of his presence.

<I shall desist from manifesting in such close quarters, since my bulk would fill this space.>

Alan wasn't sure he entirely accepted the explanation. He had never fully trusted the mage, who had only recently revealed himself to be a True Believer, and he was still struggling to clear his thoughts following his disturbing dream.

'What's going on, Mo?'

'Like you, my sleep is increasingly disturbed. Alan, I'm so afraid. I sense that we're in the greatest danger. And it's my fault.'

Alan realised he was wearing no more than underpants. He threw on his trousers, ignoring his naked upper body. Then he sat down once more on the bier, his feet extending onto the mat-covered floor. 'What's your fault?'

Another Shee – he recognised Chinonche, the commander of his protective garrison – poked her head in through the door flap and took a good long look, reassuring herself that he was in no danger. He waved her away, but knew she would stay close, and, very likely, would now be listening to this conversation from outside the tent. The Shee had very acute hearing.

The disembodied Magtokk said: <Mo is right to sense change, and it is only natural that the change should worry her.>

Mo said: 'It's more than worrying me. It's terrifying me.'

'Hey!' Alan embraced his friend. He encouraged her to sit on the bier beside him, his arm around her shoulder. 'We're all changing. I know that it can feel really awkward at times – confusing, disorientating.'

'I don't know what or who I am anymore. It troubles me so much I can't sleep. I worry I might be losing my mind.'

<If I might suggest—>

Alan interrupted the mage. 'Let her speak, Magtokk. Perhaps you should leave us alone so we can have a talk in private.'

<I shall leave, if Mo wills it, but I suspect that she would benefit from my presence.>

'Then please allow her to speak for herself. Mo, what's going on? Why do you look like a ghost?'

'My journey, what I have come to know as my journey, is not yet complete.'

'Your journey?'

'My . . . metamorphosis.'

The word, metamorphosis, shocked Alan. 'I don't know what you mean.'

'How could you? No one knows other than me. There is so much more I am obliged to . . . to witness. That's what they tell me, the True Believers. Oh, Alan, I don't know if I dare to go further.'

'What is it? What's worrying you?'

'Even you, you've noticed how I look now. I'm here, bodily, but my body is changing; the changes in my soul spirit are much greater still. In my mind, in my soul spirit, I am becoming one with the Akkharu.'

'Who the blazes are the Akkharu?'

'The miners underground. The dreamweavers.'

'Mo! I don't understand a word of this.'

'I have come here to warn you and Kate. We – Magtokk and I – have discovered the Tyrant's secret. Oh, Alan, it's so terrifying!'

'What secret?' On impulse, Alan closed his eyes and looked through his oraculum. Mo's face had dwindled to a twinkling star, but there were two stars within the tent, twinkling on and off, as if they were holding a conversation with one another. If Magtokk was a True Believer, it looked like Mo was close to joining their ranks.

'Stop this! Stop this whispering between you. Mo, Magtokk; you have to explain to me, clearly and simply, what the hell is going on.'

'Magtokk was right to warn me. I shouldn't have troubled you, Alan. You can't be expected to understand. I've just made you angry.'

'You're right, I'm angry. You pounce upon me in the middle of the night, looking like a ghost, to tell me we're in danger. Yet you refuse to explain.'

'I'm sorry, Alan. Magtokk has been attempting to explain my fate to me, my purpose here, but I don't think I'm brave enough to contemplate it.'

'Mo – *Mo!* Please slow down. I still don't understand anything of what you're telling me. What fate are you talking about?'

'Magtokk is my True Believer guide. He wants me to travel with him on another dream journey, but I've been too frightened to take it. That's why we've been waiting and waiting. I'm afraid that my timidity has caused confusion and restlessness among the Akkharu.'

'Mo, you're not really explaining things to me, not in a way I could understand.'

'Please tell him, Magtokk. Explain it for me.'

<The Akkharu toil underground in the Valley of the Pyramids. The beings that created the towers are not Akkharu, but their servants. You have not met the real Akkharu. Yet, from the moment we first arrived in the Valley of the Pyramids, they have been signalling a warning, an acute sense of danger.>

'What signals? I've seen nothing of them.'

<The clots of black ever changing against the white of Dromenon that so disturb your sleep, as they do my own . . .>

'That's the Akkharu signalling?'

<They speak a language of the mind, one that is unlike any other language. A language understood only by the initiated.>

'But what does their warning mean?'

<I am not privileged enough to be an initiate. Only Mo is so privileged among our company. But I sense it – I sense it overwhelmingly – that everything that matters to you, and to us all in this quest, is under grave threat.>

Alan frowned.

'Magtokk thinks it is of the utmost necessity that I make another dream journey deep under the Valley of the Pyramids. I must become one with the minds of the Akkharu.'

<Indeed that is what I must ask of Mo. The Akkharu cannot leave their tunnels under the ground, no more than humans can safely negotiate the honeycomb of tunnels

they regard as home. And there are other reasons why a meeting in the flesh could not be. As a soul spirit, she – the chosen – would move freely and safely in a world where its resident beings fly, or burrow, rather than risk the perils of gravity.>

'What's the connection between these beings you call the Akkharu and the towers of skulls in the valley?' Alan asked.

<The skulls are those of past generations of the Akkharu, but the towers were constructed by their servants. The Akkharu themselves are long-lived. To you they would appear eternal.>

Alan picked up his shirt and pulled it over his head, letting its tails fall outside his trousers. He shoved his feet into his sealskin boots. 'Mo, I'm not surprised you're terrified. Everything about this sounds bizarre to me. Nobody here is offering anything other than half explanations. Stay here with me. You don't have to do it.'

'Magtokk thinks that the Akkharu are warning us not merely of danger, but of the need to act. He believes that it is vital we do so. If he is right we have little time. It's my fault we've not heeded their warnings up to now. I've been too frightened to act.'

Alan saw that Mo's pupils were dilated and her skin pale. 'Kate might be able to comfort you better than I can. But she isn't here right now. She's sleeping in the Shee encampment, close to Bétaald and the Kyra.'

He didn't want to speak about what Kate was suggesting

to the Kyra. The lives of everybody in the camp might ultimately depend on keeping that a secret. He said: 'I miss her every moment, even now, when she's still near. Why don't you stay and talk to both of us, me and Kate, in the light of morning. I promise you that we won't let anything bad happen to you. There's no way we're going to ask you to put yourself in danger.'

She smiled at him. 'You're so kind, but I won't be in any danger just meeting the Akkharu, any more than I was in danger in the dream journey when I was taken to see my mother.'

'What then, are you afraid of?'

'Through meeting them, I will discover my ultimate fate.'

Alan felt a thrill of fright move through him. He couldn't bear the thought of anything happening to Mo.

'Magtokk, why don't you meet the Akkharu on your own?'

<Would that I could. But alas, I am not the chosen one. It is not me the Akkharu need to meet.>

Mo grasped Alan's hand. She held it with a sudden fierce determination. 'I have to do it, Alan. I came to Tír with a purpose, just like you. If I must face danger, then I have to find the courage to do it.'

'We've been waiting here for almost three days. We know we shall soon face some unknown second fosse and the danger that implies, but Ainé will not countenance our waiting here another day. The Shee are running low on supplies and they need resupplying from the fleet. We have no time for a proper council to talk about this.'

'You cannot risk the army,' Mo replied.

Alan pulled the tent flap aside and stepped out onto the arid ground. The night had flown while they talked and dawn was no more than half an hour off. He brushed his fingers across his brow, uncertain of what to think. Mo joined him, hesitating, her eyes meeting his. Alan saw the tears rise into her eyes.

'Mo, you know that you are under no obligation. Please speak to Kate about this. We'll help you through it.'

She nodded, but didn't look reassured.

Alan felt out of his depth with Mo, with what she was feeling. He felt so frustrated he rammed the butt of the Spear of Lug into the arid sandy ground. 'I wish I could delay even for a day. I wish we had the time for a get-together – you, me, Kate, Turkeya. But we really need to move on.' Alan sighed. He appraised Mo, who was cradling her Torus in her right hand. He hugged her to him. 'At least you have powerful protectors – perhaps even more powerful than the Shee army.'

'I'm really sorry. I shouldn't have woken you with my worries. We were all drawn here, to this world. Not merely you, Alan. I have to face my destiny.'

'Mo, that's not what I mean at all. We'll all help you. Tell me that you'll come to me, and to Kate, any time you need us.'

'I will.'

He wasn't convinced. 'Promise me you will.'

'I promise.'

'And in the meantime you'll be really careful?'

Her eyes met his again.

'We must all face some risks, Alan. You're the bravest of us. I don't think I've ever met anyone who was so fearless, but I have to find the courage in myself to do what must be done.'

They were surrounded by the noises of the waking camp. Qwenqwo's hello sounded out from a distance of a hundred yards. The dwarf mage was hurrying towards them, waving his hands. 'Iyezzz is here. He has scouted the land ahead. We are but two days' march to the hinterland of Ghork Mega. There is a five-league corridor devoid of visible defence around its southern circumference.'

Alan hesitated. 'But why would they leave any corridor open to us? They must be well aware that we are close.'

Qwenqwo came up to them, pulling at his beard in thought. 'Perhaps they are confident in the city's defences and so have withdrawn behind its walls?'

'I don't think so. We might be facing a trap.'

'I must confess that such would be more like the Tyrant.'

'We need to be very cautious in our approach.'

'You must insist on that with the Shee.'

Alan looked up into the sky, where two stars shone on, only fading now as the sun broke through the distant horizon.

'Yes,' he said. 'We must contain their impatience.'

Mo spoke softly: 'Go ahead with Qwenqwo, Alan. I mustn't distract you any longer. You have important duties to be getting on with.'

Alan hesitated, looking at Mo, who was still trembling. Her tears had stopped, but the moistness had not left her eyes. He continued to look at his friend, who had shared so many adventures and tribulations with him. 'I hate to see you afraid like this, Mo.'

'Magtokk will stay with me.'

'Remember, you don't have to do anything just because he says so. You don't have to do anything you don't want to do. Kate and I will stand by you.'

'I'm afraid that I have no choice.'

Resistance Headquarters

The battered Pig arrived at their destination a few minutes after four o'clock in the afternoon on a gloomy day, under a sky that couldn't make up its mind whether it wanted to snow or hail. The roadblock was every bit as impressively manned as it had looked from the near distance. Tajh and Cogwheel had sent a message ahead but even so there was an anxious moment as Cal climbed out and headed into a makeshift hut to talk to whoever was in charge. There were a few more minutes or so of tense waiting, during which Cal could be heard arguing the need for urgency. Meanwhile squalls of icy wind blew in through the open porthole, making everybody shiver. Then, an enormous field gun was towed out of the way to allow them to lurch through a natural archway in stone and park close to the entrance of a very large cave. They were just coming to terms with the fact that the Resistance HQ was based within a cavern complex when an emergency vehicle raced down a track road and a stocky figure, dressed in green surgical fatigues, stepped out accompanied by two medical orderlies.

'I'm Major Mackie – field surgeon!'

Tajh spoke for the crew: 'Doctor Mackie – thank goodness! We have serious casualties.'

'So I gathered from your radio message.'

They were exhausted – and lucky to have survived the journey. Now, at the entrance to HQ, they waited for the doctor to assess the wounded. They showed him Padraig, a collapsed plastic bag holding the last few drops of his saline drip, and then they explained what had happened to Bull, whose face and left side were peeling and red with blisters the size of marbles. Mackie judged Bull to be 'walking wounded' and allowed him to clamber out under his own steam. One of the orderlies sat Bull in the front passenger seat of the emergency vehicle. This cleared the body of the Pig for the doctor and the assisting orderlies to move in and tend to the unconscious Padraig.

Mark and Nan hung behind to overhear the doctor summarise his findings over a radio-com to some team back in the field hospital: 'We have one elderly male . . . barely alive . . . septicaemic by the looks of him. We'll need a bed in ITU.'

While the remaining orderly changed the intravenous bags according to Doctor Mackie's instructions, the field surgeon emerged from the Pig to speak to Mark and Nan: 'What in the name of God happened to the old fellow?'

'He was tortured.'

'How, tortured?'

'We suspect he was beaten, starved, deprived of sleep, injected with psychotropic agents, sensory deprivation—'

'But who did that to him? And why?'

'We don't have time to go into that right now, Sir. We can't afford to lose him.'

'Jesus H. Christ!' The doctor went to examine Bull and he spoke his findings into his radio-com. 'Heavy-set young male, with burns to face and right thorax, mostly second degree with small pockets of likely third degree. Also for ITU.'

'Can you help them?'

'The burns case should be readily manageable. As for the poor old chap, well, one can always pray for miracles. He's obviously in deep shock. He's grossly anaemic and dehydrated, but the main threat is the septicaemia.'

Mark nodded. 'The fact he's still alive means he didn't talk. Though they did all they could to make him.'

'What's your point?'

'Whatever the enemy wanted from him was important, but he didn't give it to them. That makes it all the more important for Padraig to live so he can help us understand the situation. That's what he went through hell for.'

The doctor told one of the orderlies to get Bull to ITU without delay. He spoke into the com again: 'I don't dare risk moving the old man until I've initiated some emergency resuscitation. He's centrally cyanosed. I'm going to have to bag him here. We'll have to support him manually until we can get him to ITU.'

Mark and Nan didn't want to leave Padraig.

Major Mackie ripped open the plastic packing over an endotracheal tube. He had the remaining orderly lift Padraig's shoulders so his head fell back. Then Mackie flipped open the metal endoscope with a curved arm and a light on the end of it, stood behind Padraig's head and forced open his jaws. 'The bastards have broken several of his teeth, but that'll wait.' He curled the arm of the tube around the back of Padraig's tongue and yanked it forward, so he could insert the tube. 'Okay – now pass me the syringes.' He anaesthetised Padraig there and then in the belly of the Pig. He connected the upper end of the endotracheal tube to a manual ventilator, coupled to a small oxygen cylinder. 'We'll have to keep bagging him till we get him into the ITU.'

Mark said: 'We'll come with you.'

'I understand your anxiety, but I'm afraid you can't come with us. Don't worry. You'll have plenty of opportunity to visit your friend later. But right now there are people who urgently want to talk to you.'

A sergeant in fatigues led the whole crew – minus Bull – to a cavern equipped with fluorescent overhead lighting and a simple rectangular table. He saluted a tall grey-haired man with the crown and star epaulettes of a senior army officer, who was seated between two junior officers. The sergeant bade them take a seat on a row of folding metal chairs before introducing them to the officers:

'General Harry Chatwyn, commanding officer.' He nodded in the tall grey-haired officer's direction. 'Colonel Graves to the CO's left – Major Forsyth to his right!'

Mark exchanged glances with Nan. They were meeting the man in charge of the crews at last. They exchanged glances again as a tall, red-haired woman in civvies arrived, taking a place to the left of Major Forsyth. Mark was astonished to recognise Jo Derby. General Chatwyn spoke. 'Gentlemen – and ladies – please be at ease! I believe you are already acquainted with Miss Derby, who has been assisting us with information about the situation in London.'

He nodded to Jo, who introduced each of the crew in turn. As she did so, General Chatwyn leaned across the table to shake the relevant hand. 'Miss Derby has also been bringing us up to speed about you. You've all been through quite an ordeal. The Resistance is fortunate to have you on board.'

Cal spoke for all of them: 'What's going on, Sir? If you don't mind my asking?'

'I don't mind in the slightest. But first I'd like to hear more about you. We have much to discuss. But first, what's the situation with your casualties?'

'Both being cared for, thank you, Sir.'

'As you already know, the situation is grave. We need to get down to business. You'll be doing the talking and we'll be doing the listening, if you wouldn't mind. We'd encourage you to speak with absolute frankness. We've already been briefed to a degree by Miss Derby, but what she's been telling us hardly makes sense. Something about the old man now being treated in ITU and, if my information is to be believed, a magical sword? But then, dare I say it, what's currently happening in London doesn't make much sense either. So please, where would you like to start?'

Nan looked sideways at Mark, who took a breath and spoke. 'Sir, the Reverend R Silas Grimstone is my adoptive father.'

Chatwyn glanced at the rather austere looking officer to his left, who had been introduced as Colonel Graves. Graves now nodded, as if in affirmation of this.

'When and where did he adopt you?'

'He adopted me in London. As far as I know, I'm a native Londoner. I was an infant when it happened, so I have no memory of it. But I did once meet a man in the streets who handed me this.' Mark produced the harmonica he kept with him always. 'I thought he might have been my real father. How the adoption took place, I don't know. Grimstone never really spoke of it except to tell me, as he also liked to tell my adoptive sister, Maureen, that our parents were hobos. In my case, English, in Mo's case, possibly Australian aboriginals, though I wouldn't necessarily take any of this as truth. Grimstone was – still is – consumed by hate. I don't know why he felt it necessary to adopt us. He didn't pretend to love us, or even to like us. His wife, Bethel, treated us with equal callousness. I now suspect that he was instructed to adopt us by his master, who saw some purpose in keeping us under his control.'

'His master?' It was Colonel Graves who asked.

'That's where it gets a bit difficult to explain. Grimstone's master is not human. This being, for want of another word for him, lives on another world, called Tír. Tír appears to be some kind of sister world to Earth. On Tír he is called the Tyrant of the Wastelands.'

All three officers sat back in their chairs. Chatwyn laughed dryly. 'Well,' he said to his companions, 'we did invite frankness.'

Mark continued: 'I was . . . I suppose the word is "entranced", or something like it, into travelling to Tír with three friends: Alan Duval, an American visiting his grandfather, Padraig, in the town of Clonmel, in Ireland; Kate Shaunessy, a local Irish girl; and my adoptive sister, Mo. When we got there we found ourselves in a world that has known nothing but war for thousands of years. But the war on Tír wasn't like we know war here. They don't have our modern technology, but they do have weaponry of their own. Besides the medieval type of stuff, like swords, spears and javelins, they have . . .' Mark hesitated, his eyes lifting to meet Chatwyn's. 'Well, what they have is weapons that would appear to be magical to us.'

There was a silence in the room, which lasted for several uncomfortable seconds.

Chatwyn broke the silence by coughing into his hand.

'Would you like to introduce your foreign companion, Mark?'

Nan piped up: 'I can introduce myself, Sir. My name is Nantosueta, though Mark calls me Nan. Here I am a member of the Resistance, but on Tír I am queen of the Vale of Tazan, and once upon a time – and a very long time ago – I lived in its former capital, the fortress city of Ossierel.'

Chatwyn studied Nan for a moment or two. 'You don't look so very old.'

'It would take a great deal of explaining, Sir.'

'This Tír you speak of is another world – an alien world?'

'It is not alien to me.'

'Point taken. But you say you came here from another world?'

'Yes.'

'Which is . . . where?'

'I do not know.'

'Somewhere out in the far reaches of the galaxy?' It was a sceptical looking Graves who asked the question.

'I do not know if it is far out in the heavens, which you call the Milky Way. Or whether it might be a variant of Earth in an alternative universe. The existence of Earth is as alien to me as the existence of Tír to you, Sir.'

'If you are alien, how come you speak our language? And why do you look so very human?'

'I don't speak your language. I translate my language into yours as I speak it, through the power of the oraculum in my brow. I know not, any more than you, why I look human, as indeed you look like an inhabitant of Tír to me. Tír does resemble Earth in many ways, but it is also unlike Earth in many other ways. For example, there are many non-human sentient beings on Tír. I think if you were to visit it, you would find it very strange.'

Colonel Graves spoke again: 'You bear crystals of power – I believe you just called them oracula – in your brows?'

'Yes, we do,' Mark replied.

'Can you explain what these are?'

Mark did his best to explain how he, and Alan, had acquired their oracula, and what the First Power and the Third Power meant. Nan then spoke about her own experience, and how she came to share the Third Power with Mark.

'So this Third Power, the power you share through your crystals, is derived from Death? Or rather should I say Death as a divine power?'

'From Mórígán, the Third Power of the Holy Trídédana.'

'Who personifies Death?' Graves made no attempt to hide his continuing scepticism.

'She is the goddess of Death – and the battlefield.'

Chatwyn lifted a hand for silence. He paused, thoughtful for several moments. 'I've just thought of a name. I'm holding it in my head. Can you tell me what it is?'

Nan replied, 'It is a very peculiar name – Rumpelstiltskin.'

'You read my thoughts. That's remarkable.'

The third officer, who had been introduced to them as

Major Forsyth, and who had been silent up to now, spoke with an educated Scottish accent. 'I have an idea as opposed to a name in my mind. Can you tell me what it is?'

Mark answered him, 'The idea, Major Forsyth, is confabulation, meaning to invent lies to cover an otherwise uncomfortable truth.'

'Remarkable!'

'Well, now,' Chatwyn explained, 'Major Forsyth is a psychologist, who, like Colonel Graves, is sceptical of your story. It's his job to be sceptical. We are relying on him to determine if you are telling us the truth, or dissembling.'

He nodded to Forsyth, who addressed Mark and Nan directly. 'I have been attempting to understand what is happening in the minds of these so-called Razzamatazzers. Do you have any idea as to what might be driving them to this insane pattern of behaviour?'

Mark spoke: 'Nan and I, we have both sensed what is driving them. We think it is the seduction of the Sword.'

Forsyth sighed. 'Ah, this magical sword!'

'The Sword of Feimhin, Major. Grimstone's followers stole it from a Bronze Age barrow grave that Padraig had been guarding in Ireland.'

'But how could a sword from the Bronze Age be capable of seducing the imagination of people today?'

'We don't know. But it isn't an ordinary sword, made of steel or bronze. Its blade is made out of the same black crystalline material as the daggers of the preceptors on Tír. And those daggers are infused by the will of the Tyrant of the Wasteland. We have to assume that the sword originally came from Tír and acts as a kind of focus, or conduit, of the Tyrant's malice. And we have reason to believe that that malice is very powerful. On Tír he is close to gaining access to something called the Fáil, which is understood to be one of the most powerful forces in the universe.'

Forsyth appeared nonplussed.

Chatwyn spoke: 'The Black Rose – could it be related to this source of power?'

'Yes, Sir. We both believe that it must be so. The Fáil is the only thing we can think of that might explain what we saw in London.'

Forsyth sighed again. 'I presume that you would have no objection to demonstrating these purported magical powers in action for us.'

'We would be prepared to do so if you really demand it, but I would strongly advise against it. The location of these headquarters is secret. The use of an oraculum might show up like a beacon to the Sword or to the Black Rose.'

'If I might have permission to speak, Sir?' chipped in Tajh, 'We've seen these powers in action on many occasions. Nobody could have been more sceptical than Cal here, but even he wouldn't deny that Mark and Nan have supernatural powers.'

'Cal?'

'I don't pretend to understand a damn thing about all this,' Cal replied. 'But they do appear to have some weird powers. Just don't expect me to explain it.'

'We shouldn't get overly involved in confrontation right now,' Chatwyn spoke, once again specifically addressing Mark and Nan. 'We will need to speak to your companions in the crew about what they have seen of your powers. I trust you would have no objection to that?'

'None, Sir,' Mark said.

'Thank you for that. Miss Derby – have you anything to add?'

Jo Derby smiled across the table and her voice was placatory. 'Only that we should explain to Mark and Nan – and the entire crew – why we need to press them so hard on this.'

Mark spoke softly: 'The Black Rose?'

'Yes, the Black Rose.' Chatwyn looked from one to the other of his companions. 'Our country is under threat. We don't understand the nature of this threat. It is unlike anything we have ever encountered before. From the military point of view, nothing of what we have seen makes sense, any more than what you have been telling us about alien worlds. But then, maybe the lack of common sense is the key to understanding, or so I am led to believe after listening to your story. Assuming you can prove your powers – and Miss Derby also claims to have witnessed them – you may be able to help us understand the nature of the threat. That threat may be much worse that we had anticipated. Miss Derby, would you care to inform them of the latest tidings?'

Jo linked her pad to a projector. It took her a few seconds

to project a series of images onto a flat expanse of white-washed wall. Mark, Nan and the crew watched, in shocked silence, as pictures of the burning streets and buildings of New York, Sydney, Ottawa, Berlin, Paris, and many other capital cities throughout the world, flashed upon the make-shift screen. The chaos that had until recently been confined to London was becoming universal.

When the crew arrived at the medical facility, it was still only 5.30 p.m. They found Bull covered in dressings and growling with ill temper.

'I want you to tell these medic goons to let me get up.'

A new nursing orderly, a beanpole of a man inside his roomy fatigues, rapped a metal urinal against the head of the bed. 'He's been demanding to get out of bed since arrival. Get him to understand that he needs to give it time. He might get a try on his feet tomorrow.'

Bull seethed: 'How're you supposed to piss lying on your back?'

Cal grinned at him. 'Get a nice-looking nurse to help you.'

'Are you kidding? They're all like him.'

'Think of England!' Cal turned to go.

'Don't think you're leaving me here.'

Tajh patted Bull's shoulder. 'We're all a bit frazzled after a very disturbing de-briefing. I'll come back and talk to you afterwards. Keep you up to speed.'

Bull glared at her.

'I promise you.'

He growled, then closed his eyes. But a moment later he opened them again, looking around at all five of them, as if making sure they all felt bound by Tajh's promise. He didn't bother to argue further. His eyes just followed them as they moved several beds down the facility to take a look at Padraig, who was receiving the attentions of two separate doctors. One of them was Major Mackie.

Mark said, 'How's it going?'

'Central venous pressure is now normal. So at least we have the dehydration under control.'

'His breathing seems a bit quieter.'

'That snorting type of breathing was down to ketosis. He's still ketotic but much less so, and we've definitely ruled out diabetes. Brutal starvation will do that. Did those bastards feed the poor beggar at all?'

'We don't know.'

'Well, we're pouring calories and essential nutrients into him. That's to say our intensivist, Doctor Ghosh here, is.'

Mark glanced at an Asian doctor in short-sleeved green scrubs who was fiddling with the mechanical ventilator. When he spoke it was to Dr Mackie, ignoring the crew: 'Oxygenation now ninety-eight per cent.'

'That's excellent. Poor chap – what a mess! The infection, the fluids and even the nutrition are all potentially manageable. The big problem is here.' Mackie tapped his right index finger against Padraig's emaciated brow.

'What's the problem?'

'He's still deeply comatose.'

'He's not . . .?' Tajh left the question unfinished.

'Brain dead? To tell you the truth, we did wonder. But the pupils are now equal and responding to light. To begin with one of them was non-responding, so we reckon there must have been a head injury. Most likely from a beating. MRI doesn't show a clot, or serious physical injury. We did a toxin screen and there's no drugs. All fits with coma resulting from dehydration, starvation and some beating. But don't get too alarmed. We've performed two separate electro-encephalograms and there's basic activity still hanging in there.'

Mackie gently elevated Padraig's eyelids, so he could look down into those astonishingly blue eyes. Then he turned Padraig's head, first to his right, then all the way over to his left.

'You see that?'

'His eyes moved in the opposite direction.'

'Doll's eye reflex! It means his brain stem is operating. His vital signs are settling, his airway's clear. His heartbeat is slow. His pulse is at 30, which is very slow, but it's steady and he's got a good, solid blood pressure. Some aspects of this are remarkable, given the circumstances. If we weren't in the middle of a war we'd be writing it up in the journals.'

'What's the likely outcome?'

'It's as if the old fellow's central nervous system has just shut down. We see it with the more severe coma cases, but there are several levels of shutdown the body goes through when in a deep coma.'

'Do you mean it's something like locked-in syndrome?'

'He has signs suggestive of that. We've seen his eyes suddenly begin to move, perhaps in dreaming, which again makes us think he retains at least some aspects of higher cerebral function. However, this is impossible to assess while he's on the ventilator. But my guess we're dealing with a locked-in state.'

'What can you do, Doctor?'

'There are techniques called deep stimulation. We can try something like that when we get him off the machine, but not yet. First let's get the infection, dehydration and starvation fully sorted out. Then' – he inclined his head – 'perhaps we shall see.'

A Hidey Hole

For the umpteenth time, Gully stopped cycling to shove his glasses up the cold wet bridge of his nose. His legs had turned to jelly, his crotch ached, and his saddle bone throbbed with such a sharp pain that it felt like his arse had been roasted in a chip pan.

Gotta take a breather!

Strewth! How he felt right now, no way was he going to be fit enough to ride again tomorrow. Maybe just an hour or two of rest would do the trick. *Just need to pick the right spot.* But all he could find was some bits of broken down walls – what might once have been a barn next to a snow-covered hawthorn. It'd have to do. Maybe lean the bike over hisself to make a shelter? He pushed the seat and the handlebars against the broken wall and threw the blanket over the bike, curling up under it. But it wasn't easy to get to sleep. He kept waking up again with the perishing cold.

The cold woke him up for the umpteenth time. His trainers and his jeans was soaked and freezing. He didn't know if it was ice had crept in around the edge of the blanket, or melting snow had dripped right through it. He squirmed around, trying to lift his legs up so he could rub the numbness out of his toes. That was when he noticed the quiet.

So wot! Birds is mostly quiet at night. Just the bleedin' country is all.

But it was never silent like this back in Our Place. Back there it was the cooing of the pigeons what woke him. Now he couldn't help listening to the silence.

He heard a loud moaning. Unearthly it was, so deep and lost, it shook him wide awake.

When he peered out from the edge of the soaking blanket, he became even more confused. What should have been the black sky of night was all lit up.

Gawd!

He didn't rightly know what was wrong. At least the snow had stopped falling, if only for the moment. Gully twisted his neck around to stare up in the direction of the sky where lights all the colours of the rainbow was streaking out all over the heavens, snaking and curling, and wheeling and blazing.

Gotta be somefink to do with London.

Then there was that moan again.

What could be moaning like that? Was it some kind of a beast, like a cow – or a hog? Not that he had much idea of what a hog sounded like. Whatever it was, it sounded a bit too close for comfort. Gully groaned as he tried to sit up. He batted the blanket with his numbed hand to shake the snow off it, then he tried to shove the bicycle off him. His arms had never felt so stiff. He felt around himself. Using the strange multi-coloured light coming down out of the sky, he looked for his carrier bag containing most of what was left of his food and water. Shit! He couldn't find the bag.

Stop, look, listen!

He did it for a second time: he stopped, looked, and listened.

The silence hadn't gone away.

Gully didn't want to think about it. He was frightened enough already. *It ain't safe here, Gully, mate.* A shiver of fear was rising in him, worrying him. It felt like something really bad was going to happen. *You gotta get out of here!* He scratched his head, then touched his pockets, from one to six, but he found no useful ideas there. He counted to ten, then counted to twenty to see if that would help him figure what to do.

Oh, 'eck!

He sighed with relief on feeling the backpack. Not that there was much left in it. He whispered to himself as he counted it up: 'alf an apple and an 'eel of bread.

He didn't know why he was whispering to himself, but just as he brought the apple to his mouth, he heard that drawn-out moan again. He wondered if, maybe, he saw something moving out there. A shadowy bulk. It didn't look like no cow or a hog. It looked the size of a crane. The hackles sprang up on the back of his neck.

Then it moaned again and he caught such a terrifying glimpse of it he immediately grabbed the backpack, scrambled out from behind the bicycle and took off running with the bike. He hopped onto the saddle, causing the thing to wobble and weave all over the place before he brought it under his control. There was no question of switching on the torch. He hurtled on with desperate abandon into the weird lit-up night.

He cycled in the near dark for something like maybe two or three miles. He had come off the road a few times in the dark, but only come off the bike twice and there was no serious damage done. He'd torn pocket left 1 – K for keys wide open, so everything in there had fallen out into the ice-filled gully where he had landed. But he didn't try to look for the keys. He didn't give a monkey's about the keys! There wasn't no door he'd be opening soon. And he knew that moaning thing was on his tail. *You ain't for stopping, Gully, not even if your arse is on fire!* Trouble was, his legs didn't care. His legs was giving up on him because they wanted to stop pedalling.

Gotta keep going . . .

His legs was stiffening up like boards. And now the gears was making a screeching noise that told him the oil was run out.

Shit!

He rested from pedalling on the long gradual downslope of a hill, peering into the darkness, looking for someplace to hide.

'Shiiiiit!'

He felt the bike slew and went flying for the third time. He tumbled, entangled in the bars and wheels and peddals, into a mess of brambles. His clothes and skin were ripped by the thorns until he was brought to a halt by a low, broken wall.

'Oh, gawd!'

His head was spinning. He felt a deep pain in his brow, above his right eye, but it was nothing compared to the pain in his right elbow. He was too stunned to do anything about it. He just lay there all twisted up in the ditch, with his face in the dirt and the brambles entwining him, and he wondered if this was the spot where his bones would rest until the day of judgement.

He must have blacked out. When he came to again the pain, in his brow and his elbow, was even worse. He tried to ignore it and get back onto his feet, but nothing happened.

Stay cool. Just got to figure it . . .

He tested his limbs slowly, a bit at a time. Parts of him was working, but the rest of him didn't sort of gel with it. All the bits of him was out of kilter.

Gotta figure it out, mate!

Pressing his right hand against the thorn-strewn ground,

he tried to push himself onto his knees. He fell back flat on his face and groaned.

Strewth! Wot's going on?

He couldn't believe this was happening to him. He tried again, but his right hand just couldn't hold him up. *Gotta figure it . . .* He tried his other hand, feeling around until it found the rubble-strewn top of the broken down wall. It felt slippery with ice. He continued to feel around until he found a solid stone that ought to bear his weight. He pulled on it and managed to get his right heel against the ground; from there he levered himself into a sitting position. He just sat there for a while, leaning back against the broken wall, waiting for the dizziness to settle.

He must have fainted because he was inside of a dream in which he was a kid again, sitting on a stained mattress, which lay on a bare wood floor. He could hear cussing and arguing in the room outside.

'I'm taking him.'

''Ark at her – interfering auld bitch!'

'I already told the cahnsel. You want me to call the police?'

'Oh – let her take 'im, Sammy.'

'Fuck off! Interfering auld bitch!'

'Let her take 'im.'

'Take the piece o' shite, then.'

That was him – Gully. He was the piece of shite.

Oh, Nan!

Nan came into the bedroom and stood over him, round

as a dumpling, wearing a rain-soaked purple fleece, her thinning henna-dyed hair plastered to her head.

'Just look at the state of you, Gully Doughty!'

There was something different about her today. A new determination.

'I come to take you with me. I got a flat off the cahnsel.'

Then she was dressing his shivering body, and talking to him at the same time. 'Why do this, eh? Why do noffink for your own child?'

He said nothing. Why didn't matter. Why didn't come into it. There was no reason why.

When she hugged him, his body stiffened. He wasn't used to being hugged.

'How d'you like to live with your old Nan?'

He nodded. He couldn't speak. If he opened his gob he might find it was all a dream.

'Them at the cahnsel – I told 'em I got a dependent young'un on account o' your being practickly abandoned.'

He could feel her warmth through the sodden fleece as she hugged him again.

In his sleep, he mouthed the words that Nan had murmured: *'Nah, Gully Doughty, you're coming with me.'*

Only with the words spoken, and the certainty of escape established, did he open his eyes to admit to himself it was a memory – a dream. There was no Nan here to comfort him. He found that his right eye didn't altogether open. He had to squint out through a swollen lid to discover that he was still sitting in a bramble hedge, his back against a broken down wall. He knew now that he must have slept because he was soaked to the skin and it was dawn. Only feet away, three sparrows was fighting amongst themselves. It might have been their chittering woke him. They didn't seem to notice him anyway. They was so close he could see the colours on every feather. Tears of pain came into his eyes as he slowly levered his body and head around, so he could take a grip once more on the broken wall with his left hand.

'Oh, bollix!'

Inch by inch, he manoeuvred himself to a standing position, panting through gritted teeth. He patted his pockets, reminding himself of the loss of left 1. He searched for his backpack in the snow-covered brambles, only to find it broken open. The partly filled bottle of gin had been shattered, but it was no matter, as the glass was on the ground and not in the pack. What was left of the bread had fallen out of it. That was what the sparrows was fighting over.

He didn't care.

I just don't give a monkey's.

He was still thinking about Nan. Bridget was her name – her friends had called her Bridge. Bridge, with her grey hair in a bun and her brown eyes wide with outrage, insisting on holding his hand as they were walking through the rubbish-filled room and out into the driving rain. Bridge hugging him when his drunk dad slammed the door.

Gully had been nervous for months that they'd come after him and take him back. But they never came. Not even to ask about him.

'Don't you worry, they show their faces 'ere and I find a new use for them scissors.'

She called him Dahlin', and he loved her. When she died he hadn't known what to do. He'd wrapped her up in blankets, but the smell got bad and they'd come to take her away. There was Police stuff. He was accused of storing the body. But what could he have done? He refused to believe she was dead. They burned her someplace, they didn't tell him where. The darkness came back. And then, right in the middle of it, the Razzers was burning all over the place and nobody took any notice of Gully.

Shit! Stop this now! You gotta do somefink about this situation.

He manoeuvred himself through the pain onto his left hand and his knees. He ignored the fact he was covered in thorns and other shit. It was snowing again, coming down solid. He paused to let the giddiness settle in his head and then carried on, taking it a bit at a time.

He stopped against the wall to catch his breath.

Somehow he got the wall behind his back and he climbed his knees to get up. *Oh, gawd!* Another pause to let the giddiness settle. Then he checked out the bike.

The wheels was okay but the handlebars was twisted.

Another pause. Panting for breath.

He tried to fix the handlebars but the pain in his right elbow stopped him. It was no good. The elbow was useless.

Stay cool! Just hold on and fink about it!

Single-handed, he opened up the saddlebag and found the wrench. He loosened the nut to make it easier to straighten the handlebars, then he put the wrench back in the saddlebag. Stop – take a breather! *This here is a good bike – a lady's Raleigh racer.* He was glad now that it was a lady's bike, because he wouldn't have been able to get his leg over the bar of a man's bike to mount it. Once he did, and slung the backpack over his shoulders, he got half way onto the saddle, steadying the handlebars with his left hand. He didn't know what to do with his right hand because it felt useless.

Stop, look, listen!

Oh, bollix! Oh, shit!

The road was dangerous. You just didn't go riding down a road what was dangerous.

Got no choice!

He grimaced with the effort of putting his right foot on the pedal. It was just a question of keeping the bike balanced when he took his left foot off the ground.

You got to do it. You got to do it now for Penny.

He looked up into the sky of falling snow, seeing the splotches land in his eyelashes. How was he going to figure this out?

He tried lifting his left foot for a fraction of a second. The bike wobbled perilously. That useless elbow – that was the problem. He tried resting his right elbow on the top of the handlebar, but it just provoked an excruciating pain.

Bleedin' 'eck!

That was when he sensed that something was watching him from the other side of the hedge behind the fog of falling snow. It was making its way towards him through the stubbled field. He could hear the clanking noise of it. Whatever was approaching, it sounded a bit like the clopping of a horse, only not the metallic hard *clip-clop* of hoofs, but more a heavy scraping sound . . . a sound more like the grinding of iron on stone . . . or maybe claws.

Oh, gawd 'elp us!

Whatever it was, the shadow of it, which was all he could make out, was big. It was huge. It was clanking towards where he was straddling the wobbly bike. He heard a strange sound: like it was sniffing at the snowy air.

Sniffing!

Penny would sometimes talk about predators. *'You and me, Gully – we live in a world where eagles prey on lambs. Here we're the lambs. The lambs must be cleverer than the eagles.'*

Never mind that – run!

He dropped the bike and heard it clatter against the lane. In his mind, everything became slow-motion and the passing of every second felt like minutes. His right eye was so swollen he couldn't open the lid. Still, he had his left one and he could glimpse the size of his pursuer more clearly now. He could hear it breathing, like some kind of an asthmatic T Rex. It was crazy even to think such a thing, but there was a monster coming after him. He was holding his injured right elbow in his left hand while still hobbling down the lane. He knew, in his pounding heart, that the last thing he ought to do was to look behind him.

'Don't you dare turn and look, Gully. Don't . . .'

Treacherous Ground

Alan stood erect, with his feet spread and his arms loose by his sides so the aides could fit the harness they had created for him during the night.

'Hey, these are onkkh reins,' he muttered to the aides, who were working as a team to fit the harness to him.

'Sire, we chose them for the strength of leather.'

'I'm sure you did.'

The aides were small on the whole, vastly smaller than the Shee. But they were also strong-minded to the point of stubbornness. The most argumentative of the three couldn't have been more than five feet tall, but she made up for it in physical presence. She had arms and legs a weightlifter would have envied, and her tugs and squeezes brooked no resistance any more than they took notice of his grumbles of discomfort.

'Who are you?'

'Aides do not volunteer names.'

'You know that with this,' he pointed with his thumb to the ruby red triangle in the centre of his brow, 'I could pick your name right out of your head?'

'As you know, *Sire*,' the 'sire' was spoken in a manner that pulverised any notion of respect the word was intended to convey, 'I could pluck that gaudy jewel out of your brow in a blink of the eye with this.' She lifted a viciously curved steel needle up under his nose.

Alan laughed, waving off the admonitions of the Kyra, who had witnessed the insolence.

'So,' he bent down to within inches of her face, 'to what grievance do I owe this huffing and puffing?'

'Well, begging your pardon, *Sire*,' she intoned, 'we aides have sacrificed yet another night of sleep to your whim of taking a peep at the world down out of the sky.'

Qwenqwo, who was also watching the confrontation, shifted on his feet, but again Alan placated him with a wave of his hand.

'While the restraints are not yet tight, can I invite you and your two companions to shift your focus from stitching holes in leather to the landscape.' He took several steps, made awkward by his harness, to lead the three aides to the edge of the knoll on which they stood. 'Take a good look around you.'

The aides, with a weather eye on the remorseless stare of the Kyra, muttered: 'Mage Lord – if I have offended you—'

'Please, bear with me and take a close look at this

landscape. But do so knowing that we are but a few days march from the walls of Ghork Mega.'

Livid colours proliferated throughout the cracked and fissured ground, flowing through the rock in striking patterns of crimson, lime green and sulphurous yellow. The surface was churned up, as if it were a delta cut by myriad streams – except this landscape had not been formed by a great river, but by something more akin to a searing biting acid that ate up the natural rock and dirt and spewed back the vileness before them. In their few strides over the knoll, blood red hardpan cracked under their feet to reveal still more tormented ground.

She said: 'I will admit that it is intimidating.'

'Please, take a close look at what is poking out of the ground immediately to the north of my right foot.'

The aides, now red in the face at the unwanted attention, knelt down to peer at the ground.

'Mayhap it's bone.'

'What kind of bone?'

She rooted in the hard-baked crust using her powerful curved steel needle, to discover an eye socket. 'A skull.'

'And immediately adjacent to the skull, there is something shining, is there not?'

She poked again. 'Could be a battle helmet.'

'So, we are confronted by an intimidating landscape in which we discover a skull bearing a battle helmet. What might that suggest to you?'

'This ground might have been the site of fighting, likely long ago.'

'I agree. Now, assuming that the disturbing patterns and appearances in the landscape might have something to do with that skirmish, long ago, what other conclusion might we draw?'

The aides climbed back onto her feet, rubbing the dirt from her hands and knees, then wiped the needle clean on her coarse green skirt before carrying out a long and careful perusal of the landscape. Many eyes were now upon her, and upon her confrontation with the Mage Lord.

'Mayhap it's an ancient battlefield, Mage Lord.'

'Now, do you understand why I need to inspect it from on high?'

'I am sorry for doubting your judgement. I can now see why the ground from the air might interest you with its violent history. Yet even so, is not such a history predictable this close to the Tyrant's lair?'

'With the help of the Gargs, I have been taking a careful note of distance. We are now about three quarters of the way between the fortress we destroyed – which we believed to be the first of three fosses guarding Ghork Mega – and the city itself. If we regard the third fosse as the walls of the city, then you would expect to find a second fosse somewhere between the two. Is my thinking making sense to you?'

'It is not. No doubt you will enlighten me.'

Alan laughed: this aide was as stubborn as Qwenqwo.

'Right! Let us accept the advice of the Garg Prince, who, with his fellow scouts, tells us that the walls of Ghork Mega are visible from high in the air. They have seen no sign of a defensive wall or fortification between where we are and the city walls. Now is that something to trouble your logic?'

'Mage Lord, I am a seamstress and leather expert. I am no strategist.'

'We are standing at a point between this position and the city where a second defensive fosse should confront us. But instead, we find what you quite rightly describe as an intimidating landscape.'

The redoubtable face creased with the effort of concentration, but still the eyes did not widen with enlightenment. 'I can see why you might be confused upon discovering that the second fosse is missing, but I don't see what you would hope to discover when lifted aloft that you could not readily come across through walking over the ground.'

'I fear a trap.'

'A trap?'

'We know that our enemy is exceedingly cunning. I worry that we have not found the second fosse. The obstacles he placed in front of us have often taken us by surprise. This close to his capital city we need to be cautious. I need to take a good hard look at this intimidating landscape with this third eye – the oraculum you see in my brow – before I would risk a single Shee. Do you understand now why I must be taken aloft?'

At last he saw understanding begin to dawn in her eyes.

'Mage Lord, I begin to see – and what I now see frightens me.'

'I'm beginning to frighten myself through talking about it. Perhaps it is not a bad thing to experience fear. But first you need to complete my harness – I need to examine the land ahead from on high above our present position. I must scrutinise every league from here to the gates of Ghork Mega.'

As they threaded the straps under his crotch, then fastened them to the harness that went around his waist, and to the further supports that went under his armpits, he stared ahead to where a variety of sand devils raised clouds of dust amid the dunes and scrub that stretched ahead for mile after mile.

'You sure you want to do this?' Qwenqwo's brow was creased by concern.

'I have no other option.'

Alan dangled from his harness high in the cool air, made to feel slightly dizzy as the hovering team of Gargs holding him up were caught in the changeable and blustery breezes. Iyezzz had formed a protective vee north of him, the prince, as always, taking the most dangerous position at the apex of the vee. From this height, the individual Shee and even the onkkh spread over several square miles of parched ground below were reduced to the size of ants. Alan followed the direction of the vee and saw the walls for the first time. There, hazy in the pallid blue distance, was their target: Ghork Mega. Even from this distance Alan could make out the broad outlines of the city, which occupied an entire hill overlooking what was probably a gigantic harbour. He shivered in grudging acknowledgement, not only of the menacing size of it, but also of the ethereal beauty of its silhouette with its hundreds of towers and minarets. The distance, according to Iyezzz, was no more than forty miles – thirteen leagues or so as the Gargs calculated it – to its enormous southern gate, set into walls said to be two hundred feet high. Iyezzz was right – just three days' march . . .

We should not tarry . . .

He sensed Iyezzz's impatience to complete this survey. Who knew what the Tyrant might launch against them? He also sensed Kate's anxiety down there amongst the ants.

There were elements of the landscape that gave Alan the heebie jeebies; shapes poking through the tough sprouting grass and desert scrub that suggested . . . threat, unknown menace? The land certainly bore the scars of what might have been previous battles. He switched to the vantage of the ruby oraculum in his brow. What he saw puzzled him. The landscape was pretty much the same, but the air over it looked different. The hackles on his neck rose. He opened his eyes to reappraise it anew.

There was something important going on, but he couldn't quite make out what it was.

He thought of Kate. He signalled her mind-to-mind: <Take a look at this ground view through my oraculum.>

<What is it?>

<I don't know. It's what I see of the desert between us and the city when I look through my oraculum.>

Kate appraised it with him. She said: <You're right, Alan. There's some kind of enormous blood red cloud hovering over the tormented ground.>

<There's more, Kate. Look higher.>

<Oh, my god!>

The blood red cloud had a wispy tentacle reaching from it into the sky, and if you followed it, the blood red glare filled the entire sky. Even as they looked in a mixture of bewilderment and fear, a tentacle of the cloud began to waver in Alan's direction.

<What can it be?> came Kate's question.

<I don't know. But my instincts tell me I shouldn't hang about to find out.>

Alan sent his thoughts mind-to-mind to Iyezzz. <I think we need to get out of here urgently. Have your warriors take me down straight away!>

Heading back to solid ground, Alan closed his eyes to try to clear his mind, but the blood red horror penetrated his mind through the oraculum. He counted the moments as his Garg helpers swooped down to dump him, knees buckling at the sudden shock, before a startled Qwenqwo, Kyra, Kate and Bétaald.

He accepted the Spear of Lug from Qwenqwo. 'I reckon we may be heading into great danger.' He turned to the puzzled Kyra and Bétaald. 'Please trust me. Have the army retreat for several miles.'

The Kyra was sceptical. 'Retreat?'

'Yes – and immediately, Ainé. But, if you wouldn't mind, I want you and Bétaald to remain. We'll need a hundred or so aides with shovels, or whatever they need to dig the stony ground. I also want Qwenqwo, Kate, Magtokk and Mo to stay.'

The Kyra said: 'You want the aides to dig?'

'The arid landscape is an illusion. This entire hinterland between here and the city is a graveyard. That much I have already figured. We need to know who, or what, are buried here.'

'I do not understand.'

'I believe we are looking at the second fosse.'

The Kyra stared at him, eyes unblinking.

Bétaald placed a cautioning hand on her shoulder. Then she confronted Alan. 'What do you suspect, Mage Lord?'

Alan stared for a second into the amber eyes of a panther. 'I sense a malignant entity out there, an entity that inhabits the entire landscape between here and the city. It permeates everything, from the ground to the sky. I sensed it, and so did Kate. Our combined instincts tell us that it is exceedingly dangerous – some kind of guardian.'

'A guardian?'

'A formless enemy, with no more substance than a mist or a vapour.'

Bétaald nodded to the Kyra. 'We shall instruct the aides to dig.'

Even as the Shee shepherded the army backwards, Alan was marking out a broad target area, perhaps a hundred feet square. He instructed the aides to remove the dirt and surface rock to see what lay beneath.

They all watched, nervously, as the aides got to work. It took the remainder of the day for the surface layers to be cleared from the square. As the sun approached the western horizon the observers were increasingly shocked into silence. They were gazing on the timeworn bones of warriors, who lay as they had fallen, in jumbled disarray. The varied armour and weapons suggested many different armies had come here at different times over the aeons. The ground was so dense with their bones that their accumulation made up the bedrock.

Ainé was the first to speak. 'So many!'

'Yeah,' Alan nodded. 'Every army that ever marched against the Tyrant and made it this close to his city.'

Bétaald said: 'The graveyard must run to the very gates.'

The Kyra spoke bluntly: 'Had we marched on, this close to our destination, our bones would have joined the others.'

Alan felt Kate's hand close on his. He said: 'Is there nothing known about this terrible place, no word from history?'

'There are tales,' Bétaald spoke. 'Many, now that I reflect on it, that tell of wars and annihilations here in the Wastelands. But we just accepted that there would have been wars aplenty as the Tyrant gained supremacy.'

Darkness fell and they retired to join the main army. Alan joined the others in sitting cross-legged on the sandy ground and welcomed the advice of his many friends. 'I don't know what we face, but I could see no other defences between here and the city walls. The Tyrant is far too clever to allow an army to just walk up to the walls of Ghork Mega. We all anticipated a second fosse. I'm certain now that this is the fosse, even though it is not a barrier of walls and fortifications.'

The Kyra, who was sitting opposite Alan said: 'Important as this observation is, we cannot tarry in our attempt to counter the danger; the attack upon the city from the sea is imminent. We must support this with a simultaneous attack from the land.'

Bétaald asked Alan: 'What did you mean when you called this the second fosse? What is it you really sensed out there, Mage Lord?'

'Great malice, something very similar to what I recall from the Battle of Ossierel.'

'A Legun incarnate?'

'It was the feeling I had when we faced that monster, but this doesn't really look the same as what we saw at Ossierel; that Legun had a skull-like face and had a human shape, even if it was gigantic.'

Ainé growled a tiger's growl. She spoke in the soft purring voice the Kyra employed when seriously threatened. 'A Septemvile.'

Alan hesitated. The term was familiar but he had no real

understanding of what it meant. 'Your mother-sister talked of this with me just before the Battle of Ossierel.'

'My mother-sister spoke to you of the Tyrant's inner circle?'

He had to stop and think before he answered her. 'Yes, she did.'

'Seven Leguns.'

He struggled to remember circumstances that had been similarly stressful. 'Yes, she tried to explain the Leguns to me, but I didn't altogether understand. Can you explain them further?'

'You have already encountered their leader?'

Alan hesitated a second time. He recalled a monstrous creature called the Captain, which had all but exterminated them at Ossierel.

'Are you saying what I saw here in the ground between us and the city, and what I sensed in the air, was a Legun?'

'Legend has it that there are seven Leguns known as the Septemviles, which guard the Tyrant and his dominions. The Captain was familiar to my mother-sister and her mother-sister in turn – my grandmother-sister. He destroyed my grandmother-sister before my mother-sister's eyes in the great arena at Ghork Mega. Legend suggests that there are six others named for the malice they bear. But it may be relevant to our situation that one is said to be formless, or to take the shape of a mist, or shadow, capable of mimicking a natural feature in a landscape, including defensive walls. It kills through suffocation or through poisoning. It is known as Earthbane.'

Alan felt decidedly out of his comfort zone. He stared at the Kyra, then he turned to Kate, who was nodding. She said: 'Should we expect to encounter more of them in our attack upon Ghork Mega?'

The Kyra looked at Bétaald, who nodded.

Alan muttered, 'A Legun known as Earthbane. That's what we are facing?'

'It would make sense. This Septemvile might well assume the form of the second fosse of the Tyrant's capital.'

He said: 'What else do you know about this Earthbane?'

'It is said to bide its time, becoming one with the landscape in which it hides. It is formless, much as you described. It is capable of waiting for centuries, even millennia, existing as an invisible cloud. Yet, when it manifests it can destroy an entire army. It kills by poison. It is said to be impossible to rescue a victim once he or she is caught in its embrace. Contact with it is likely to spread the poison until all are destroyed.'

Alan looked through his oraculum at the treacherous quagmire ahead, now fading into the dark of night. There was a potent malice in the poisoned ground and in the shifting mists. 'Do the legends tell us how we can defeat it?'

'In legend it has never been defeated.'

A Foundling

Mo's world was changing. But perhaps she was changing – had already changed – and it was because of this and her evolving outlook, that her world seemed different. That was a bewildering realisation. It suggested that all that had been normal in her life had been a lie; it also suggested that all that had happened to her was fated, and not down to her choices. And that – *that* – was the most shocking realisation of all. If she were to believe it, it would mean that plans had been made for her even before she was born, that her destiny had been preordained.

It was deeply frightening. Yet, even as she sensed how unjust this was, the implications were more disturbing still. They explained why, from moment to moment, she felt profoundly uncertain. If she had already changed, and if she were even still changing, how on earth was she to come to terms with herself?

She said: 'Must we return to the Valley of the Pyramids?'

Magtokk's voice within her mind was gently spoken: <Not at this very moment. Not unless you wish to.>

Not unless she wished to! That suggested that she still had a modicum of control. Mo glanced around at the solitary privacy of her tent, but she was well aware of how little privacy it really offered her.

<My dearest Mira – it is natural that you feel frightened.>

Mira! The name, her true birth name, given to her by her birth mother, Mala, now added to her sense of fright.

<I would never make you do anything you do not want to do.>

'I wish I could believe that.' She slumped down onto her makeshift bed. 'You were waiting for me back there, weren't you? Back at the Garg royal city. You were expecting me?'

<That is true.>

At the moment Magtokk was an invisible presence in the tent, but she still felt the shaggy arm that enfolded her shoulders and felt the vibration in his barrel-like chest as he spoke. <The True Believers instructed me.>

'Can you manifest, Magtokk?'

He materialised beside her. She found herself looking up into his huge, wise orang-utan face. He made a sound with his mouth, as if swallowing a morsel of fruit he had been chewing on all the time he had been here. He transfixed her with the deep-set chocolate eyes.

'So, it is the True Believers who really control my destiny?'

'On the contrary, no one controls you.'

Mo wished she could believe him. 'Is there a place you could take me that knows only joy?'

'It is natural that you should fear the future.'

'A refuge, then.'

His shaggy head fell, the vastness of his presence dominating almost every square inch of the tent. 'Too much is expected of you. You haven't yet been granted sufficient understanding. With understanding your fears will fade.'

Mo looked at him. Who – or rather what – was he really? Was he truly kind as he appeared? Was his friendship an act to ensnare her? Was his purpose in all this to discover ways in which to control her?

'Did you mean it when you said I won't be forced to go anywhere I don't want to go? Do anything I don't want to do?'

'I always mean what I say.'

That dark brown leathery hand stroked her hair, which had remained hopelessly matted with sweat and dust since the earlier, awful ride on the rolling back of an onkkh. Mo didn't know why she chose to travel in such dreadful discomfort when Magtokk had shown her how to travel on the winged shoulders of Thesau, the giant eagle, who was one of those who called themselves True Believers. It had been Thesau who had rescued Qwenqwo Cuatzel's runestone when Ainé, the Kyra of the Shee, had hurled it far over the great river.

'There is a place where I might find comfort.'

He brushed a finger gently against her brow. 'Tell me?'

'My birth mother . . . Mala. I need to see her.'

The leathery finger hesitated. 'Is that wise? We both know that you will find the experience upsetting.'

'There are times when it is appropriate to be upset.'

'That is so. But is this such a time – you have just said you want comfort?'

'I want to see her now, Magtokk. I can't bear to wait another moment. Please call Thesau to take me to her.'

From on high, the great treeless plain dotted with chalky blue shrub stretched on and on. The sun struck Mo, burning through her wind-ruffled hair and the seal-skin cape she had wrapped around her shoulders for the journey. *How can that be when I am only here in soul spirit?* At first she could make out nothing significant in the vast rolling landscape below. But then the eagle blinked, and she saw what he saw in the glimmering distance: a scattering of seven matchstick figures, moving with a weary slowness between dunes of windblown red sand. Yet, as Thesau soared closer, she saw that they were actually hurrying, despite their obvious exhaustion, as if they knew pursuers were close behind. Careful scrutiny revealed the nature of the hunters: dark silhouettes sniffing at the air, following the imprints of hurrying feet. The hunters hardly seemed as hurried as the pursued. They were no more than a few miles behind Mala's people. As Thesau drew closer still, the pursuers spread out into a fan-shape, covering all possible routes of escape.

'What are they, Magtokk?'

'Malwraiths. It's a name we call such things, though I doubt that their creator bothered to give them a name, merely a purpose.'

'It was the Tyrant who created them?'

'Indeed.'

'So he will be observing them? Following their progress?'

'It may be so. He enjoys cruel games – and the sport of new challenges.'

'This is all Mala's life means to him, a new challenge?'

'On the contrary, I think that she, and you, matter deeply to him. Why else go to such trouble for otherwise innocuous humans.'

Mo felt disinclined to watch what happened. The very thought of it caused her heart to weigh heavily in her breast.

'Perhaps you should not observe further?'

'I have to see. I . . . I must.'

Mo gripped the Torus firmly within the palm of her right hand and bade Thesau take her closer to the hunters so she could study them. They had vaguely human shapes, but their flesh was all . . . wrong. They were not made up of tissues and organs, bones and sinews, as a human would be, but constructed out of something more amorphous – wisps of darkness in which concentrations of the same amorphous matter acted as eyes, nostrils ears and clawed limbs.

'They're not living creatures at all?'

'They are the projections of the calculating mind of your enemy. Extensions of his will. They have come into being with a single purpose and are endowed with heightened senses that will ensure the success of their task.'

'Surely there must be something we can do to help her?'

'Painful as it must be, you cannot help Mala. What we observe has already happened. It is already past. We may witness it with pity and regret, but we cannot change it, no matter how desperately we might want to.'

'But what they're really after is me. The Torus around my neck?'

'Yes.'

'Just out of spite they will kill her, my birth mother?'

'Must you really witness this?' She felt the shaggy arm embrace her, hold her trembling body close to his strength and warmth. 'I would have Thesau take you back to safety, to rest and prepare yourself, body and mind, for your fate.'

Her fate!

'I . . . I have to see what happens. I have to.'

'Then I should explain that I have been studying this situation. I have noticed a change of behaviour of hunter and hunted that may be relevant.'

'What?'

'Until recently, the hunted managed to evade capture with surprising success. By surprising I mean in terms of what Malwraiths are capable of.'

'What do you mean?'

'That the hunted – Mala and her precious baby – were in some way protected.'

'The Torus?'

'That would be my conclusion.'

'But . . . You're implying that the situation has changed?'

'Mira, must you torment yourself with this vision?'

Mo stared down at the figure of her mother. Her heart surged with love. She saw Mala's protective embrace within which the blanket-wrapped child rested. The vision was so real that Mo could feel the hot dry wind whip her tear-damp cheeks.

The burly arm held her closer still, enfolding her slim body against his huge craggy bulk, as if to shield her from the coming horror.

'You see how purposefully the hunters close upon the fleeing group?'

Mo's tongue, her lips, were so petrified with grief, she was unable to reply immediately, but her clutch at the embracing arm, and body, was enough of an answer. Like a closing pack of wolves, they blocked off the fleeing band, then encircled the surviving seven.

'Oh, Magtokk,' she wept. 'They've made themselves targets. The whole tribe.'

'I think as you do.'

'What bravery!'

'What bravery, indeed! But clever also . . . Ah, I see the plan of it now. The old woman – the *minyma pampa*, the tribal elder – you might remember, had the cunning . . .'

'I don't understand.'

'You will.'

With a final sprint and a pounce, the biggest of the Malwraiths hurled itself upon the figure of Mala, knocking her to the ground, then tearing the bundle from her arms with its claws.

Mo gasped.

Magtokk was silent.

Mo watched, with her heartbeat rising into her throat, as the fangs and claws of the vile being ripped apart the bundle, to discover a confection of scrub and rags, tied together with fibrous strands so it resembled a baby. The wrath of the hunters was hideous to witness. Mala and her six companions were torn to pieces.

The Malwraith pack scrabbled wildly in the bloodstained desert and screamed at the sky like banshees.

Mo so desperately wanted to comfort her mother, to let her know that she had survived, but the circumstances had taken her utterly by surprise.

'What happened to me, Magtokk?'

'The *minyma pampa* was clever. She outwitted the pursuers. We may have to backtrack several days to see it.'

By the time Mo managed to see through her tears, the scene had changed. In front of her was a man sitting in a threadbare armchair wearing a permanent-looking grimace on his leathery sun-ravaged face. A dark-haired woman had arrived in a battered Land Rover to his homestead in the outback and now she pushed her way through the open door and a screen of beads, her plain features thick with red dust. Perhaps she was the grimacing man's daughter? Mo tried to take it in, though her body was still trembling with the shock of Mala's murder.

There was something familiar about the woman, but Mo couldn't concentrate sufficiently to recognise what.

Magtokk's voice fell to a whisper. 'You are understandably upset. Yet you demanded the experience. Now you must observe.'

As she watched, she saw the man lift a torn and stained linen cloth. It had been covering a cardboard box set against the outer wall. There was a baby lying within, in a nest of newspapers.

The woman gazed down at the baby for several moments. Then she turned, clearly very angry, to the man: 'You useless wretch! Did you not bother to feed her?'

The man shrugged.

Mo saw the face of the woman close up: the lack of make-up, the broken veins over the nose and the sun-ravaged cheeks. Mo watched the woman head out to the privy, grab the entire toilet roll, then fashion a nappy from a block of tissues.

The man drawled, a careless wave of his arm: 'Just a foundling!'

Mo watched as right there, on the bare wood floor of the veranda, the woman fed the baby some milk from a spoon. Then she swore at the man and took a tartan shawl off the couch. She went back out to the veranda and bundled the baby up in the shawl, heading out to take the baby home with her.

But then the Landrover halted.

Something was clearly amiss.

The woman burst out of the driver's door with something clutched in the fist of her right hand. She hurled a small object out and watched it spin through the air, its attached leather thong whipping in complicated arcs until it landed twenty or thirty yards away in the baked red dirt of the desert. She exclaimed:

'Heathen thing!'

Mo stared after the now departing woman, and bade Thesau's vision to return to the discarded object lying in the dirt. Mo recognised the nature of the abandoned thing, just as she simultaneously recognised the identity of the woman who had rescued her baby self.

The abandoned object was the Torus, now discarded into the wilderness of desert. And the woman . . .

'Bethel!' Mo exclaimed.

Her rescuer was Grimstone's wife, and her future adoptive mother. The woman who would make her life, and the life of her adoptive brother, Mark, a living hell through all of their growing years.

An Emissary from Kentucky

In the five days they had spent here, Mark and Nan continuously sensed the atmosphere of desperation running through the Resistance HQ. Everybody was well aware that the countrywide chaos was worsening, and from what they could gather, spreading globally. At least the crew had a full complement again, with Sharkey's dressings reduced to a spray-on plastic plaster and Bull's burned skin soothed and dressed by professionals, even if it resulted in his resembling the Michelin tyre man. Most refractory of all was Padraig's coma. Major Mackie was in the facility when Mark and Nan called in at mid-morning to check on progress. He told them Padraig's physical condition was on the mend, but the mind was its own master when it came to recovery.

'At least we know that he's not brain dead?'

'We do have that consolation, but we're as uncertain as ever as to the degree of permanent damage.'

Mark sighed, looking down at the stubborn old body that was half a foot too tall for the bed so the feet had to be supported by a pillow-covered extension of the base.

The crew were utterly frustrated these days, with nothing to do other than twiddle their thumbs while Field Marshall Seebox tightened his grip on the country. All that time to think wasn't good for Mark and Nan. It caused them to fret about priorities of their own over and above helping the crew. What was happening back on Tír? How were Alan, Kate and Mo faring with the war against the Tyrant? Were they winning, or was the Tyrant closer to taking over absolute control of the Fáil? Mark and Nan had come to Earth to test out whether they were still alive or dead, but neither even felt sure they had answered that question. And they couldn't even think of returning to Tír while Padraig's life was in danger. How long must they wait for him to come round? Just how damaged was his brain? Even if he survived, and his brain was intact, what could he really do to help with the situation?

Question after question ran through Mark's mind as he stood there by the bedside. The rest of the crew remained sceptical about Padraig, Cal especially, but Mark recalled how knowledgeable Padraig had been back in Clonmel before the real nightmare began. It was obvious Padraig had known a great deal more than he let on that day he'd taken the four friends to see Feimhin's barrow grave. Was it possible that Padraig had knowledge from the time of Feimhin that might help the present situation – locally and globally?

Mark spoke in a whisper to Nan. 'We're going to have to do something to help, and soon.'

'Yes, but what?'

'I keep thinking about Henriette, how she got us into the crew's camp.'

'But she called upon the Temple Ship.'

'Yeah! I know.'

'But we don't know how to do that.'

'We did so once, to get back to Earth.'

'Yeah, I know. And I keep thinking about it.'

They had felt so overwhelmed by desperation, by the heartbreak of wondering if they were both dead, with only their soul spirits remaining, that they had managed to call the ship. Mark found it difficult to recall that bleak experience; the bewilderment of not knowing, the terror of possibly having their worst fears confirmed. He was still lost in the memory when a voice broke into his ruminations.

'Scrawny old buzzard, ain't he?'

'What?'

Mark turned around to be confronted by a tall, craggy-faced American wearing an unbuttoned, baggy fatigue jacket over an open-necked black T-shirt. There were smudges of blood around his throat where he had made a messy job of shaving.

'He got the Rip Van thing, huh?'

'Who are you?'

The man grinned, a wide toothy grin. 'Brett Lee Travis, at your service, folks!'

Mark was no expert on American accents, but he could hazard a guess that Travis' accent came from the southern States. 'Where are you from?'

'US Army Special Services.'

'What's that involve?'

'Whatever it takes.' The American leaned down over the bed until his face was only inches off Padraig's. 'So, he got the Rip Van Winkle thing?'

Mark hesitated. 'Well, he hasn't woken up yet.'

'He gonna pull through?'

Mark shrugged. The stranger's directness, his stream of question after question, was getting under his skin.

But Travis grinned again, this time not at Mark but at Nan. 'You must be Nantosueta, her royal majesty?'

'They call me Nan.'

'You don't mind if I don't go down on one knee?'

Nan glanced up wryly into Travis' dark blue eyes. He made no secret of the fact he was looking closely at her oraculum.

'Then Nan it is. And you've got to be Mark?' he said, holding his hand out to him.

The tall American had marked crow's feet around the corners of his eyes so that it was difficult to gauge his age. He had black curly hair without a hint of grey, and even darker stubble, which extended to the top of his chest. Mark decided that he was maybe in his forties, and accepted the large, bony hand that almost broke his fingers. Nan merely nodded, looking at the American with a look of profound curiosity. Mark guessed that she was attempting to probe the man's mind.

'You been to the States, Nan?'

She shook her head.

'Well, that's a shame.'

Mark said: 'Where do you come from in America?'

'Kentucky.'

'Is this official? I mean, with respect to General Chatwyn?'

'Are you asking me whether he knows I'm chatting to you at this very moment? Well, the answer is, maybe.'

'What are you really doing here?'

'I guess you could look on me as liaison with mutual friends across the water.'

'CIA?'

'Ask me no awkward questions and I won't tell you no awkward lies.'

Mark thought about his answer for a moment. 'We're all fed up with the interminable waiting.'

'Goes for me too. Tetchiness can be catching. But allow me to show you something that might cheer you up.'

He took them out of the caverns and on through a short wooded walk, leading them into a huge rocky overhang that acted as a garage for the mechanics. They stopped before the newly re-camouflaged bulk of the Mamma Pig.

Travis slapped a hand against the high bonnet. 'Let me tell you – these techs have been making changes.'

Mark frowned. 'We know that it needed some repairs.'

'I'm sure it did, but these guys have added a few novelties.'

Mark looked the Pig over. He could see that there was a new proliferation of electronics gear on the roof, including new radio and radar receivers.

'There's a deal more inside, too,' the American said.

Mark exchanged glances with Nan.

Travis opened the nearside porthole in the body of the Pig. He leaned half way into the interior before withdrawing a tarpaulin. 'I guess you're going to recognise this baby.' Travis folded back the coverings, and then Mark's breath caught in his throat as he recognised what it contained.

'It's—'

Travis laughed, finishing Mark's tongue-tied sentence for him: 'The old guy's missing battleaxe.'

Mark shook his head in disbelief. 'We searched hard for it at the burned-down sawmill. It's the battleaxe Padraig took from Feimhim's grave. He used it to demonstrate the reality of the magic to us.'

Travis stood erect and clapped a hand on Mark's shoulder.

'How did you find it? Nan and I, we really searched for it. We combed the ruins, even with our oracula.'

'You didn't look in the basement?'

'Basement? You mean, a cellar? I had no idea the old house had a cellar.'

'Dang thing was buried deep. All of the rubble from the house filled it in. That must have hidden it from you, but not from deep radar. Stood out like Finn McCool's thumb.'

Mark hesitated.

'Go ahead. Grab a hold of it.'

Mark picked up the battleaxe, holding it in two hands, then hefting it in his left hand alone, raising it to the level of his shoulder.

'What do you think?'

'It's huge. At least a third longer than the one Qwenqwo gave me. And much heavier. Maybe because it's bronze rather than steel? And the runes are different.'

'What's that mean?' the American asked.

Nan answered for Mark, 'They're Fir Bolg runes: a blade is always runed and named for the warrior who wields it. The named blade and warrior are one. This blade was not named or runed for Mark.'

'Who then?'

Nan looked at Mark. 'I recall Padraig saying something about it: this battleaxe killed Prince Feimhin long ago. Padraig threw it just the once. That single throw exhausted him.'

'So, likely it ain't runed for Padraig neither?'

'I think it was runed for a specific Fir Bolg. Maybe the high shaman?'

'So we won't know the answer to the question until Rip Van Winkle decides to wake up and tell us.'

'You shouldn't talk about Padraig that way.'

'Sorry, fellas! No disrespect intended.'

Mark went down onto one knee to replace the heavy battleaxe on the tarpaulin. 'What's really going on, here, Mr Travis?'

'No need for formalities with me, Mark. Brett will do. And the Pig has been rejigged because we got us an idea.'

Nan said: 'You're going to ask the crew to go back to London?'

'Go back?'

'Nan's right, Mark. Me and General Chatwyn, we've got plans for you.'

'But we've only just managed to get out of there.'

'That's what makes you ideal for this mission. You found your way out. You guys are survivors. You're the only ones we can trust to find your way back in.'

'Shit, no!'

'Got to be.'

'What the hell for?'

'The situation is getting real bad. The phrase has become a bit corny, but it's true all the same. Your country needs you. We're running out of time. You guys have got to take me there so I can see for myself what's going on.'

'But we have plans of our own. We have to save Padraig. If anyone understands what's going on, it's likely to be him. It's really important.'

'No sweat! We'll take him along. Matter of fact, I'd like to talk to you some more about Padraig. We can talk along the way.'

'You're out of your mind.'

'Can we level with one another here? General Chatwyn, he's a patriot, but his army is outnumbered ten to one by Seebox. And that same grand military asshole has all the big ordinance, including air support. He also controls communications. All those helpful satellites up there in the sky have been blasted. And now, from what you guys have been telling the General, Seebox is just the gopher for Grimstone. And he's got black magic on his side.'

'I'm not sure I'd call it that.'

'You can call it what you like. And it gets a deal worse. You know where Grimstone is right now?'

Mark shook his head.

'He's in New York.' Travis withdrew a big fat silver case out of the breast pocket of his fatigue jacket. He gazed longingly at what looked like a row of Havana cigars. 'You need me to spell it out?'

Nan spoke for them both: 'Mr Travis, are you telling us that you're afraid for New York? You're afraid for America?'

'Brett – please.' The big man took a cigar out of the case. He looked like he was considering lighting it, but then he replaced it in the case and he put the case back into his jacket pocket. 'Nan – Your Royal Highness, if that's what I should call you – I'm telling you diddly squat. All I'm saying is that I need to get to London and see for myself what's really going on there. I've stowed some nifty gear in the Pig that will help my mission and I can send up my own satellites. The bad guys will spot them, sure as hell they will, but it'll take 'em so long to do so it'll give us a window of time. I can gather a whole heap of information – something that is sorely needed. Wars get themselves won and lost on the basis of information.'

'What sort of information could it get?' Mark said.

'Information that might be crucial to my guys stateside, which would help you guys here. But for that to happen, I got to go down there and see what's what.'

'General Chatwyn is with you in this?'

'It was his idea. He asked for our help. He's prepared to give you whatever additional support you need: bikes, a platoon of crack troops.'

'Sending a small army of support would only make us more obvious to Seebox, with his drones everywhere.'

'Now you're talking my language – logistics.'

'I'm not talking anything. I'm trying to explain to you why we can't abandon Padraig. We believe he's the key to it all.'

'Then we take him with us.'

'Oh, for pity's sake!'

'I've been following the conversation in the medical unit. Rip Van – sorry, Padraig – he don't need much in the way of medication, not anymore.'

'Brett, you're bonkers.'

'Maybe I am. So why don't you wise guys just sit here on your hands watching Rip Van, while your country's going to hell in a bucket.'

Nan cut in: 'What information are you looking for, Mr Travis?'

'Brett – please! I need to understand the situation here with – what do you call them – the guys who like setting fire to things, the Razors?'

'Razzers – Razzamatazzers.'

'Okay, well those Razzers are popping up everywhere, in the most unlikely places.'

'Such as?'

'Such as Russia and China.'

'Bloody hell,' Mark muttered.

'Tell me about it. It don't make any kind of sense. You know, like how can craziness be catching? But it's catching like bubonic plague. And we just have to make sense of it. Way I see it, the best place to look for that sense is where it began, right there in London.'

Mark and Nan were looking at one another. At that same moment, Cal's sceptical voice came from behind them. An astonished crew was standing there, looking with the same surprise as Mark and Nan at the restructured Mamma Pig, and from there to the larger than life American, who was passing from one crew member to another, squeezing fingers and introducing himself.

'Hey, fellas – good timing! Mark and Nan here were just about to tell us how to get this rig to London without Seebox having a ratass clue.'

Cal was extricating his mangled hand from the handshake. 'What the fuck are you talking about?'

A fraught thirty minutes later they all found themselves back in the conference room facing Brett across the table, accompanied by General Chatwyn, but at least on this occasion there was no sceptical psychologist.

*

Chatwyn raised his eyebrows, as if in apology. 'I had planned to introduce you to Mr Travis, but it would appear that he has taken the bull by the horns and introduced himself. We are obliged to him, and the Pentagon, for his coming here with the intention of helping us. The situation is deteriorating more rapidly than we had envisaged. It's increasingly global, as you now know. We, the remaining free forces here, face an unprecedented threat. We need all the help we can get. I know it's asking a lot of you, given your recent experiences, but you may be uniquely qualified to help get Mr Travis inside the London cordon.'

The General looked at Brett, who opened his mouth and performed a kind of sucking action with his tongue against the back of his teeth, as if to give him a moment or two to think. 'Okay, so you're wondering just what connection exists between the Pentagon and the situation here? Well, you're looking at the connection. You could look at me as a military strategist sent by direct order of the President, through FEMA. I'm here to examine the situation and see what we can do to help you guys.'

'What's that supposed to mean?' asked Cal.

'Seems to me,' Brett explained, 'the situation here is pretty grim. The survival of this nation, and possibly mine too, may depend on what we can do to put it right. I need to know everything you fellas can tell me about what's going on. I'm talking in particular about this monstrosity you're calling the Black Rose. We need to know what it's doing, sitting right there at the heart of London. We need to know what it is capable of. And most importantly, we need to figure out its weaknesses.'

Mark sensed the crew's tension.

Cal looked at the General. 'May I ask, why, Sir?'

Brett answered for Chatwyn. 'I'd have thought that plain obvious. We're going to take the damn thing out.'

Cogwheel spoke: 'If you don't mind my saying, taking it out might not be as easy as you think.'

'Who said it'll be easy? But the way I see it, we got us an ace or two up our sleeves – Mark and Nan here – and maybe Padraig too.

'Mark and Nan, please tell us some more about your unusual powers.'

Mark sighed. He looked at Nan, whose eyes were looking directly into Brett's. He said: 'The crew already know about us, and our powers. The oracula – the black triangles you see in our brows – allow us to do things you might see as magical. The power to do so comes from a goddess on Tír. Mórígán is the name of the goddess.'

'We're talking here about the goddess of Death, and the battlefield, you say?'

Mark shrugged. 'On Tír, the science we see as normal on Earth would appear just as bizarre. The worlds have evolved differently.'

'How so?'

'We've evolved a scientific perspective. They've evolved what – well, I suppose the closest thing to call it would be a spiritual perspective.'

'Which you've brought back with you from this other world?'

'That's right.'

Brett nodded. 'This other world, Mark, which, as General Chatwyn has been explaining to me earlier, is some kind of a sister world to Earth?'

'Yeah, as far as I can figure it.'

'And so this Black Rose is also likely to invoke similar magical powers?'

'Powers that would appear to be magical from your perspective. If what Nan and I are assuming is right, it is drawing its power from a source far more dominant than Nan and I possess.'

'What source is that?'

'The Fáil.' Mark shrugged. 'Maybe Nan could explain it better than I can.'

'Nan?'

'In the language of Monisle, my home continent, the word means something close to what you would call fate. But . . .'

'But?' Brett's eyes appeared to twinkle a darker blue, within the deep folds and wrinkles of his face.

'The Fáil is more real, and far more dangerous, than you might imagine from your concept of fate.'

'Can you tell us more?'

'Not much.'

Chatwyn coughed. 'Perhaps, Mr Travis, you could tell us more of what's happening in America?'

'The situation is nothing like as bad as you have it here. We don't have the equivalent of Seebox running the armed forces, or at least not as yet. But we do have powerful elements within the services sympathetic to him.'

'Members of Grimstone's church?'

'You got it. And they're everywhere. Intelligence says they're getting more powerful by the day. All of this suggests we're heading down the same trail, only a ways behind you guys.'

Cal returned their attention to the problem in hand. 'Sir, the Black Rose – do you really plan to mount an attack on it?'

Chatwyn shook his head. 'For the moment all we want is to find out more about it, but I don't need to emphasise just how important such a mission might be.'

Brett sighed, a loud enough sigh to silence the table. 'I know you fellas don't want to go back down there. You've been busting a gut to escape that asshole, Seebox, and his minions – right?'

'Seems like we have no choice, Sir.'

'That's mighty brave of you, fellas.'

'Mighty suicidal,' Tajh whispered, though the whisper carried more widely than she might have intended in the echoing cavern.

The Meaning of the Rose

These days, if they were truly days at all, Penny knew that she inhabited a decidedly alien world. But it was also a world of extraordinary richness and sensuousness. It was so intoxicating that it was difficult to think logically about her situation; where she was, what was she doing there, and what was happening to her. There was a sense that Jeremiah was never far away, even when she could not see, or hear, or sense him. It occurred to her that perhaps she existed in the world-mind of Jeremiah – an idea that provoked overwhelming panic. What an extraordinary and terrible mind it was. It was not human – a human mind would be preoccupied by more basic things: comfort, feelings, emotions, the sex thing. Not once, in all the time she had been here, had she observed, or even sensed, any of these. That she was being manipulated had been obvious from the start. That the purpose of her manipulation was control over her mind, her spirit . . . her creativity.

She screamed: 'I don't like being manipulated.'

<No one is manipulating you.>

A voice, but not a person.

As if to placate her, Penny heard music that felt like a feathery touch upon her mind. Then it became a discordant sea. She was looking out onto a landscape of blue that contained moving shapes resembling ghosts. She had no notion of where she was, or how she had got here, or even if it was day or night. Jeremiah was once again controlling every aspect of her consciousness. She felt angry that she had no control over her life anymore – that she should be reduced to this bewildered state.

The music stopped.

'I don't know how to deal with you.'

<Speak your mind.>

'You're being facetious.'

<Am I?>

'I am hardly free. I can no longer distinguish night from day. I have no routines. I have no contacts, no friends, none of the activity one would associate with a normal life. I have to presume that this is the price of my bargain with you.'

<You willingly entered into this bargain with me.>

'I did it to protect what I love in London – to protect Gully.'

<What if I were to free you from such imagined constraints?>

'I don't believe you would do that, not for a moment.'

<You are freer than you might imagine. There are entire worlds you might explore, where you can do whatever you want to do.>

'But I am still here. Not that I know where here is – it doesn't even feel like what would be described as "here". It feels like nowhere.'

<Can we converse logically? Are you capable of putting aside the emotions that flaw your judgement?>

'I'm confused. I – I don't know what to think. I don't know what I am doing, anymore. I can't even see you.'

Jeremiah appeared before her, but his appearance was hardly reassuring. The very fact he could do so at will was deeply disconcerting . . . frightening.

He spoke in that same quiet voice: 'Take time to consider your thoughts, your opinions. I shall not intrude nor interfere, but leave you free to consider.'

'How can I know that you're telling me the truth?'

'Would you believe me if I were to tell you that there is no absolute truth? It is merely a perspective that an individual mind might adopt.'

'Stop being clever with words.'

His position had changed, though she had not witnessed his movement. He was now standing before her, his hands cupping her face so she could not avoid his all black eyes. 'Would you prefer that I adopt the physical shape of your father?'

'No – absolutely not!'

'I would have you see me as a comforter, a mentor.'

'I don't want you masquerading as my father.'

Those glistening eyes beheld her for a moment or two in silence. 'What can I do to reassure you?'

'You could guarantee me that you will never make me do something I wouldn't want to do.'

'I give you that reassurance, readily.'

Oh, how could she believe him? It was so confusing, so vexing, she felt tears of frustration come to her eyes.

'It's natural that you should feel unsettled, anxious. Why don't we walk in the streets of this city that you so revere?'

'Is that possible? The city is destroyed?'

'It is surely possible, though you may encounter surprises.'

Penny saw her surroundings dissolve, even as the light changed. She found herself shivering with cold. As she thought this, a silken grey cloak lined with fur as fine as sable appeared around her shoulders. A hood enveloped her head. There was no point in thinking about how such things happened. Instead she looked around, wondering whether the ambient gloom was dusk or daybreak. She was gazing around her at an ocean of destruction.

'It's so dreadful – so utterly ruined.'

'War is war. Such things happen.'

'Why are you showing me this?'

'Not all is ruined.'

In the pallid light, which was so dense Penny thought she could be underwater, she made out tall shadowy outlines that soared like reefs amid the maelstrom. She found herself confronted by one such reef. It took her a moment or two to recognise an altogether familiar gothic masterpiece, floating on the maelstrom of ruin.

'It's Westminster – the Houses of Parliament.'

She stared up at the monumental construction, perfectly intact under a tide of rising curves of leviathan size and complexity.

'Why are you showing me this terrible scene?'

'To confirm that I kept my promises.'

As she looked about herself once again, her eyes widened. She could not look away, even though it broke her heart. Understanding came – and with it, a horror that crushed her spirit.

'You followed my art – the City Above. You preserved all I drew and destroyed everything I left out? It was you who guided the Razzamatazzers?'

'I trusted your vision of the City Above. All that you treasured was protected. What meant nothing to you was sacrificed.'

Penny could not fashion a reply. Her head was spinning. Her throat had tightened up as if clasped by a vicious claw. 'It was so cruel. What you did . . .' Oh, dear god – it was cruel beyond belief . . . beyond reason or understanding.

'Nature does not recognise cruelty any more than it does morality.'

Penny's already dizzy senses were overwhelmed by the desolation, and with the guilt of knowing her art had been so horribly abused, so manipulated.

'Look again.'

Rising out of the maelstrom was an expanding field of stars, filling the desolate spaces with light.

'What is it?'

'I am inviting you to imagine the reconstruction that might come to be through your vision. Such will be part of your reward for serving me. But such a wonder will demand that you learn to become one with the Akkharu.'

Penny couldn't take in what he was saying. She had no desire to help him with his cruelty and manipulations.

'In time you will come to understand. Not only have I preserved such masterpieces as were beloved of you, I have also saved and protected the life of your urchin friend when my servant, Grimstone, had a very different intent.'

Penny was close to fainting with despair, but she grasped the fact that he was referring to Gully. She recalled Gully's face, recalled him calling to her as she stood behind that dreadful man with the Sword held aloft.

'Run, Gully! Run from the City Below.'

It was the first time that Jeremiah had mentioned Grimstone, the vile man who had wielded the sword of power on the stage in that violent theatre. All that she was coming to know of his world was utterly horrible. She hated it. And she hated Jeremiah, even as he confronted her. 'Tell me,' he said, 'whatever more you want of me. You only have to ask and it will be given to you.'

'What if I asked you to reverse it all? To bring back the city, with all of its faults. Would you do that?'

'That I cannot do.'

'Please do it! Undo everything you have done.'

'It cannot be undone.'

'Well then, free me. Let me go. Let me leave this place.'

'You are free to leave, but would you wander among the chaos that reigns beyond my protection?'

'Yes, yes – *yes*!'

She shuddered from the contact as his arm encircled her shoulders. How could his face look so caring, so comfortingly human, after what he had done? How could he even pretend kindness without knowing what kindness was? Could a being like Jeremiah know regret?

She took a deep breath to steady her mind, her spirit, before she asked the question. 'I want you to explain the Black Rose.'

'You would explore my world?'

She hesitated, feeling the fear rise again. He hadn't answered her question. But still she answered: 'Yes.'

The small, shadowy figure released her from his embrace, then turned away from her, as if gazing out at some personal vision. 'I really would have you do more than explore. I would grant you the freedom to recreate the city. Look upon what you see as a board wiped clean, creating unlimited new possibilities.'

Was he tricking her? How could she trust someone or something immeasurably cleverer, more devious than herself? Penny knew that he could effortlessly overcome her will if he chose to do so.

But then why was he bothering to bargain with her at all?

'Would you become one with the Akkharu?'

She sighed. 'Yes.'

Then she was standing next to him, dressed in gold damask, her feet shod in a glittery, silvery softness, her hair braided into ash-blonde plaits that were drawn back up into a starry corona over the dome of her head.

'How did you do that?'

'With a thought.'

'Why? What new game are you playing?'

'I promise you immortality, but to reach the pinnacle we must start at ground level. I would have you create a new city out of the old: a city that will be our temporary dwelling place on this world. Thus will you develop confidence in your creativity. One city to begin with—'

'You're asking me to . . . to redesign London?'

'Yes.'

She shook her head. 'But . . . oh, for goodness' sake – how?'

'You will create it in your mind. Let it grow as an oak tree grows from the tiny acorn. Allow your mind, your creativity, to break free. Imbue every inch, every twist and turn, with your idea of perfection. Through the language of the makers, you will make it real.'

'But I don't want to destroy what's left.'

'The monumental constructs will remain. You will weave the wonder of the new city around them.'

She hesitated, overwhelmed with the creative challenge. 'But it will be an empty city. There will be no people to live in it?'

'We shall inhabit it.'

Penny thought about that – how astonishing the challenge was and the possibility it offered. 'But I have never designed a single piece of architecture before.'

'I think you have designed much more than that.'

'When?'

'In your dreams.'

She paused again. 'I don't think I could create a new city on my own.'

'Then take an assistant.'

A young woman with blue-black hair down to her waist appeared beside Penny. Her face was curiously blank, her dark eyes empty of intelligence. As Penny looked at her, the woman's mass of dark hair began to move and weave wave-like patterns, whirling quickly, like the frenzied movement of water below a waterfall.

'Who is she?'

'She is unfinished. Yours to fashion according to your will.'

Penny was astonished: *an unfinished human being!*

Even as she struggled to grasp what was happening, a whirring blur of winged creatures poured, like rising steam, out of a crevice in the floor.

'There need be no limit. Anything your heart desires, anything your senses crave for delight or entertainment, will be yours. All you need do is to ask.'

Penny looked around, unable to believe what was happening to her. A half made girl! Creatures brought into being merely for her entertainment! She was appalled at the idea. 'No, I don't want this. Take her away. Take them all away. The whole monstrosity . . .'

In the blink of an eye, girl and winged beings were gone. Jeremiah faced her, his all black eyes gazing into hers, a secret smile back at the corners of his lips.

'I need nothing like that. I will do my best to repair the ruined city on my own.'

'You will not repair the city. You will build it anew.'

'Yes – I will rebuild it! But how do I know what to put into it?'

'You will know. You will discover the weave for yourself. It exists already in your dreams.'

'But how do you know what's in my dreams?'

'I know all there is to know about you, Penny Postlethwaite.'

She was panicking now, taking deep breaths, bewildered, frightened again . . . Was it all a trick to . . . to take control of her? To rob her of her will?

'You'll allow me to draw it, to design it . . . just as it comes into my mind?'

'I shall.'

'You won't be looking over my shoulder. You won't want to examine every thought before the makers build it?'

'Do you imagine I don't have other concerns to deal

with? I assure you that I shall not view your masterpiece until it is complete.'

The shockwave of realisation shuddered through her. What she had allowed to be buried in her hopes and fears. 'You are going to be busy waging war with Earth?'

'I am already at war with this world.'

'They will fight you with their armies. They will attack you with weapons – terrible weapons. They will attack London, the Black Rose.'

'Naturally.'

'But you don't care?'

'I have destroyed worlds more threatening than this, empires where even the babes were born magicians. This is a dull planet where machines rule. It will amuse me to turn their mechanical weapons against them.'

'How?'

'With art and ingenuity.'

'I won't do it. I won't recreate London while you attack Earth.'

He smiled that strange, secretive smile of his. 'There is a conversation I would have you witness.'

'Why is this street urchin here? Why do you reveal the mysteries to one who is undeserving?'

She recognised the second voice – an angry and hateful voice – as Grimstone's. She recalled him lifting the great sword before the chanting, screaming crowds. His was a name and a face she recognised from a thousand posters. He was the evangelical preacher whose symbol was the same as the gigantic triple infinity that towered above the Black Rose.

She heard Jeremiah's reprimand: *'Do not challenge me with your petty judgements. You will not harm the urchin or the girl. They serve my purpose, as you do.'*

Penny stared at the small, dapper figure with the unlined brow and all black, all-seeing eyes, who had cowed Grimstone with words alone.

'Gully?' she asked.

'He is safe. My servant would have had you both destroyed.'

Then she asked him again, she demanded it of him outright: 'What is it? What is the Black Rose?'

'This is a world that venerates machines.'

'What does that mean?'

'You failed to learn the lesson of the Idolators.'

He was talking about those mad women – the devotees who had been set on their own destruction.

Her voice was husky, frightened. 'Then it was all some kind of brutal lesson . . . a lesson for what you are now planning for Earth?'

'The Black Rose is a *deus ex machina*.'

Penny felt an icy wave of terror grip her heart.

'A machine to destroy a world that idolises machines.'

An Unlikely Captor

Gully was trapped in a nightmare – he was buried in a crypt that was rocking from side to side like a small boat in a gale-wracked sea. He was deafened by a thunderous clanking noise. There was a sudden lurch and he tumbled over and over several times to come to a jarring halt, his body rebounding from an iron wall.

There was a memory, a very confused memory, of hobbling down a snow-covered lane, of turning around . . . then . . . terror. Massive, overwhelming terror . . .

'Shit, shit, shit, shit, shit!'

Every bone in his body was hurting. He was close to vomiting due to the giddy side-to-side movement. *This ain't real! It can't be. It just can't!*

There was a ghostly light filtering into the crypt from myriad tiny holes and crevices.

He called out, in a shaky voice: 'Wot the bleedin' 'eck's goin' on?'

He heard a buzzing sound, getting louder, then receding again. He remembered now – that horrible fall off the bike. *Gawd 'elp us! I must be dead. I must 'ave killed meself.* His head, which he was automatically rubbing with his uninjured left hand, felt like a whole team of roughnecks had been using it as a football.

He tested it out. He waited for a gap between the lurching movements so he could reach up, gingerly, with his left hand to touch the bone above his right eye.

'Ow – Jeeze!'

He counted to twenty for the throbbing pain to settle.

Stop, look, listen!

'Forget about it. It don't make a ha'porth of difference.' The stomach-churning lurching continued, and he hadn't a clue where he was or what was happening to him.

'Ow – me bleedin' elbow!' He hardly dared to move his left hand around to feel his right elbow. But did . . .

'Ow – ow – ow!'

It was real. The world had finally gone bonkers. Why'd he think he'd be better off riding a woman's red bicycle? *Wot the 'eck's happening to me?* He was in a crypt, but it wasn't like any crypt he could possibly imagine, because it was moving.

A crazy feeling crept into his head. If it was real . . . He leaned back as far as he dared to so he could check out the wall against which he had bumped his head. He felt something smooth and hard, something curving round like the inside of an enormous ball. He shifted on his arse, sliding across the metal floor. *Oh, shit!!* There was something loose on the floor beside him. Something familiar. Something that had the shape of handlebars.

'No!'

His head banged against the wall again, knocking him dizzy. How could a crypt be lurching from side to side like that? And how, for that matter, could a crypt be lurching from side to side, and all the while contain not only himself in it, but the Raleigh bike?

'Where am I?'

'You are in my somewhat clumsy custody.'

The reply sounded so deep and slow the words rattled his eardrums like thunder. Yet it was also so perfect, so like . . . like a public schoolboy voice, that Gully hesitated.

'Wot custody?'

There was a rumble of laughter so deep he felt it through the floor. 'Correction! I should have said a place of safety. Or, rather, correcting my correction, I should say it is not quite a place, it is, rather, me – by which I imply a being of safety.'

Gully attempted to blink away the hard crust on his eye, only the right eye had forgotten how to blink properly. It felt swollen and out of sorts. He grabbed hold of a projecting piece of ironwork so he didn't tumble again when his body to rocked from side to side.

'Wot did you say?'

'I informed you, albeit clumsily, that you are within me.'

'Shiiit!'

'Must you converse in profanities?'

'Wot in gawd's name are you?'

'Is this an oblique request for my name?'

'Strewth!' Gully panted again. He patted his pockets, one after another, even the one that had been torn empty in his fall.

'Bad Day,' the creature said.

'Wot?' Another pitch had Gully on his knees, trying to stop his retching grow into actual puking. This was the maddest nightmare he ever had.

'My name is Bad Day.'

'Wot kind of a name is that?'

'It's what so many of my charges have exclaimed when first we met. "I must be having a bad day".'

Gully hesitated. The explanation dumbfounded him. It made no sense. *You got to figure this out, Gully.*

He cradled his right elbow in the comforting palm of his left hand. Maybe it wasn't actually broken? Maybe just sprained? *You got to think positive.* All he knew was it throbbed. And that voice, even though it was thunderous, didn't sound threatening. It sounded long-suffering. The main thing was to find out what was going on. He had to shift his bones across the floor to find some place he could take a peek outside. He tried it out, inching his way across on all fours, one hand and two knees sliding over the iron floor. If not a ship, what the hell could it be? There was bits of rubbish all scattered about.

Oh bollix!

It felt like crawling through a scrap yard. But he could make out something like an opening, where a flapping hunk of metal was rattling on its hinges.

'Hey, I hope you ain't kiddin' me?'

'I am incapable of falsehood.'

Gully didn't believe that, but he decided it was a good idea to say nothing. He was approaching the flap, which was a lot bigger than he had initially assumed. He held on to a projection with his left hand, hauling himself closer as the horrible lurching continued. Then, in a gap between lurches, he peered out to find he was moving through what looked like a bomb site filled with rubble.

'Where we going?'

'If my internal compass is not deluding me, we are approaching what was formerly known as the Edgeware Road.'

Gully fell back against the wall, petrified. He was unable to move, even to think, for several seconds. Then he poked his head out of the hole again, every sense spinning. He was inside a gigantic robot, inside its head to be precise, about a hundred feet above the ground. The jolting from side to side was coming from the strides of two giant legs.

Trembling, he held tight to the edge of the hole and waited for another gap in the lurching to stare out again.

He moaned with fright.

Whatever Bad Day was, he was peering out of the floor of its mouth. And the rack and ruin out there was real.

'Are you still alive in there? I do hope so. If not the Master will be most displeased with me.'

'It's bleedin' real as a nightmare could be!'

'Though I sympathise with your distress, there is no need for profanities. Might I respectfully request that you henceforth desist?'

What are you going to do, Gully?

Penny's voice. But Penny wasn't here. Gully looked out again, unable to believe what was happening. But the great head – about the size of a small house and constructed of what appeared to be scrap from an industrial waste heap – was all around him.

'Nah!'

'Are you thinking, perhaps, that you are having a bad day?'

As a matter of fact, he was. As a matter of bleedin' fact, he was thinking very much that he was having a nightmare day.

'There's something buzzin' in me ear.'

'It's just a hatchling.'

'A what?'

'An inspiration, as yet unrefined.'

What was he expecting? Why did he expect sense? Nothing here made sense.

'Look more closely.'

'I can see somefink . . . somefink flying through the air, shimmering.'

'Shimmering – a delightful word.'

'Get bleedin' lost!'

'I wonder if perhaps the shimmering might be wings?'

'Go stuff yourself!'

He heard a metallic sigh. 'Oh, dream on! A child of my loins, metaphorically speaking! Oh the bliss!'

'So wot if they're wings. I can see right through 'em.'

'The recently born are such waifs.'

'Hey,' said Gully, looking at the winged creature. 'I got to say, she's pretty.'

'It is not a she.'

'Hey, gorgeous! You're perfick!' he said, reaching out to the creature.

'Oh, you are so kind!'

'Ow! Ouch!'

'I should have warned you. Best not to get too close.'

'She bit me!' He sucked on the finger where the hatchling had drawn blood. 'I never would've guessed she had teeth.'

'Oh, rapture!'

'Must be some kind of a birdie.'

'You like birds?'

'I loves 'em.'

'Then possibly . . . your presence—'

'But all I ever got to keep is pigeons.'

'What do you love about them? Is it their flight? I can see how it might evoke such heartfelt aspirations in a daemon bot!'

'Get lost!'

'Oh, it's calling to me! Isn't it so precious!'

In spite of his terror, Gully was intrigued. *Oh, let it be a birdie*. He missed them now, his birdies. He missed their warmth when he curled them up inside the flap of his jacket. He missed their desperate, flapping take-off when he let them go. Their flight, their escape, into the freedom of the skies.

'Hey, you know! Wot you're really saying is, like, it's kinda like saying somefink . . . like it's telling you somefink?'

'More a communication of desires, senses – what it yearns for.'

'Gawd in 'eaven!'

He had to sit back against the jolting ironwork bulk of Bad Day's mouth to think about that. Of course, it didn't make sense. But it was a giddying thought.

'Wot's it yearn for, then?'

'You would have me explain its frustration?'

'Not if it's gonna make me sad.'

'As you wish!'

'Aw, go on then. Tell us.'

'What does any daemon bot yearn for?'

'I don't know.'

'Freedom.'

'But you're just a giant robot. This here fing, it's gotta be a little birdie robot wot just dreams it's got wings.'

'You're right in a limited sense. I'm afraid it's a daemon bot enslaved to me, its creator, as I am to the Master.'

Gully's heart froze. *Daemon bots – Master?*

He poked his head out again. He peered around him at the strange, composite head. The eyes, as far as he could see, were ball bearings the size of truck wheels.

'I'm some kind of a prisoner, ain't I?'

'I'm afraid that my capture of you was no accident. I was summoned to do so.'

'Who summoned you?'

There was a sudden increase in the jolting, throwing Gully from one wall to another. He had to hold on tight with his one functioning hand and curl both his knees around a thick iron rod to prevent himself from crashing into the walls again.

'Wot's going on?'

'A turbulent part of town.'

Gully flopped back against the iron wall for a long time, feeling dejected, his mind a confused blank. His only source of communication was the iron monster.

'You never said – who sent you to capture me?'

'The Master, of course.'

'Who?'

'He has no other name.'

'Wot's that mean?'

'He is to be obeyed.'

'Why?'

'That is beyond knowing.'

He didn't like the sound of that. 'Where did you come from? Or are you allowed to tell me?'

'This I can answer. As is appropriate for a daemon bot, I was summoned from the blessed darkness.'

'Like the Master just summoned you up out of 'is 'ead?'

'I serve him, as the hatchling serves me.'

'Holy shit!'

'Must you employ profanity? In the void we daemon bots are bred to good manners. We are dedicated to the serenity of being.'

Gully hooted. 'So you're a gentleman daemon bot?'

'I'm afraid we do not distinguish between sexes.'

'Oh, wow!'

'You have questions. What manner of beings are we? Where do we come from? Are we moral, amoral or immoral.' The giant being chuckled. 'How do we reproduce?'

'Bleedin' 'eck.'

'I believe that our race has unpleasant connotations in this world.'

'Is daemon bots and devils one and the same – or shouldn't I ask?'

'Oh, I confess that some of us go through a phase where they adopt an obligate parasitic existence.'

'Wot's that mean?'

'They occupy some unfortunate's soul to nourish their selfish appetites.'

'Like they possess people?'

'Not necessarily people. There are a great variety of beings. But please be reassured – others of our kind have evolved to a more exalted state of being. Creating this iron frame has been a most satisfying experience.'

Gully didn't pretend to understand what the daemon bot was saying, but he understood that he was its prisoner. And the wisest thing to do was to play along until he could hatch a plan to free himself.

'Where you taking me?'

'We are heading for the Rose.'

Gully swallowed through a painfully dry throat. 'You got plans for me when you got me there?'

'No.'

'Why'd you capture me then?'

'I rescued you, Gully Doughty.'

'You grabbed me and locked me inside your mouth.'

'I was summoned to find you – and keep you safe.'

Even as Gully pondered this, the clanking giant arrived at a wasteland teeming with wraiths. The clanking of the gigantic legs sounded very loud and echoing as the daemon bot entered a tunnel that led into an underground labyrinth.

'I can't see nuffink.'

'I have sufficient vision for us both.'

Gully's surroundings sprang into a glaring relief as bolts of lighting erupted from titanic machines.

'Wot's goin' on?'

'We are entering the Black Rose.'

Gully was close to panicking again. 'I don't know about you, mate, but maybe we ought to take a breather.'

'I do not breathe.'

'Piss off!'

'Must you revert to vulgarity?'

'Piss and shit!'

'Does this indicate that you are fearful?'

'Piss off! Piss, piss, piss! Shit! Shit! Shit!'

'Fear is a quintessential human emotion.'

'Piss and shit and fuck. Fuck! Fuck! Fuck!'

'We are approaching our destination.'

Gully's muscles were so weak his legs felt quivery. He didn't even attempt to stand up. The offspring of the daemon bot wheeled and fluttered around him in high excitement. Gully shrank down into the valley of rusting iron to one side of the hinged flap.

'Welcome to my humble abode.'

'Oh, Jesus! Gawd 'elp us!'

The Septemvile

In the pearly half-light of dawn, Kate joined Alan in staring at the one of the dead Shee, whose flesh had shrunk to a black mummified shell, her eyes bleached white against the mask of what had been her face. Kate's uncle, Fergal, had told her about the bog bodies back in Ireland that had had such an appearance. They were the bodies of princes thousands of years ago; human sacrifices, their throats cut, or garrotted, or even sometimes ritually killed. *Sacrifices!*

Her eyes lifted to those of the Kyra. 'How many?'

'Approximately one thousand dead.'

A thousand sacrifices. The dead Shee were the entire sentinel garrison placed to protect the northern flank of the camp, which was now being withdrawn several more miles.

'Nobody saw anything? There was no warning?'

'In the dark of night – nothing seen, nothing detected.'

'So, how could this have happened?'

'I sensed their loss as soon as I awoke.'

'I am very sorry, Ainé.'

'They are not dead. Their daughter-sisters live still in our Guhttan heartlands. But they are not here. Our army has been further weakened.'

The days and nights since they had realised the danger that waited for them in the ground ahead had been difficult for everybody. They had talked of possible solutions, such as Gargs ferrying warriors across the Legun guarded graveyard. But it was extremely hazardous for little gain. And it always came back to the terrible danger of what faced them ahead.

Qwenqwo and Magtokk had debated a range of possibilities for defeating the Septemvile, Earthbane. But none convinced the company that they would work. Kate witnessed Alan worrying in silence, gritting his teeth.

Now Ainé stared into the distance, to where the great city lay. 'We are warriors, with warrior's hearts. This waiting is damaging morale. Our instinct is to attack.'

Kate understood. The rancour of being outwitted, obstructed, was soul destroying. She was witnessing a little more of the make-up of the secretive Shee. Bred for battle, fearless in confrontation, the one thing the giant cats were not designed to withstand was this humiliating impasse. She thought about the enemy they faced. Virtually nothing at all was known about it. What, for example, was the real nature of its poison? All of them: Alan, Qwenqwo, and Kate herself had struggled for days to come up with a single useful idea and failed.

She squeezed Alan's shoulder. 'When you were aloft, couldn't you sense something of its true nature through your oraculum?'

'All I detected was a miasma.'

'But how extensive was it? Did it reach right up to the walls of Ghork Mega?'

'I don't know, Kate.'

The spiritual adviser, Bétaald, overheard their discussion and joined them. 'Alan's difficulty is understandable. According to legend, this Septemvile is formless. It works like a poison, coming in a cloak of mist.'

Alan shook his head. 'It's hopeless, Kate. We don't know how to fight it.'

'I'm not so sure. At least now that we know it is there, we can think more clearly about the danger. We won't fall into its trap.'

The Kyra joined the discussion. 'This last attack reveals its game. It goads us into making a desperate move. Yet all that we have seen, and what you have now sensed, warn of how dangerous it is. How do you defeat a formless poison?'

Kate answered her: 'I think my sense of it is a little different from Alan's, perhaps because our oracula are different. What I detect here is not formless. It has a definite form, although what I sense of it is vast and buried very deep underground – a loathsome presence but a detectable physical form.'

'What form do you see?'

'The body is not human. I sense something that could be a circular mouth. Something that feeds on the bodies it captures: a very simple, if fearsome intelligence, like that of a shark, or a rattlesnake. One that knows only how to hunt and kill. I also sense tentacles, vast numbers of fleshy tentacles, burrowing everywhere. There are tunnels these tentacles move through. The ground up ahead is honeycombed with them.'

Kate felt Alan stiffen beside her.

She placed the fingers of her hands against the brows of Alan and Ainé so she could project what she was sensing into their minds. She showed them the vast warren below them. It covered every inch of ground for the twenty or so miles that lay between them and the walls of Ghork Mega. And she showed them the malignant presence – a huge almost floral efflorescence – that centred on a great and ever hungry mouth at the centre of an explosion of fleshy tentacles, ringed with long curved needles of teeth.

Kate explained: 'The tentacles exude a deadly poison. From what Alan saw, I would assume that the poison is also infused in the air immediately over the ground. Some of the finer tentacles project bristles onto the surface. Through them it probably sniffs the air. They also might also detect pressure, the slightest movement, even body heat, like a rattlesnake does. My guess is that they're incredibly sensitive. The bristles are its eyes, ears and nostrils.'

Alan asked her: 'Are you developing any ideas about how we could fight it? How we could kill it?'

The Kyra shook her head: 'The Septemvile is reputed to be a Legun incarnate. As such it cannot die.'

Kate also shook her head. 'I can't sense any obvious weakness. We are dealing with something devoid of higher intelligence. Yet, I sense its brooding presence, its evil, so powerfully. I don't know how long it has been here. Centuries, perhaps even millennia. And through all of that time it has waited for armies to come and attack the city.'

The Kyra spoke: 'Then, it knows that we are here. It could hardly miss the proximity of a great army. It senses us here this very moment. It knows that we fear it. Through killing our guardians, it is attempting to provoke us.'

Kate nodded. 'You're right, Ainé. I sense that it is excited by our presence. It wants to tempt us out into its poisonous lair.'

'Yet we are constrained by time and opportunity. We must confront it.'

Bétaald agreed. 'We know the danger, and yet we cannot avoid it. The fleet is moving in to attack the city walls. This army must join them. We cannot afford to sit around for yet more frustrating days plotting and planning strategies.'

Kate looked out over the desert floor, which loomed like a living sulphurous canker, infused with livid arborescent patterns of pink, as if the very land itself was rotting. 'What are we going to do, Alan?'

'We can't afford to procrastinate. Nevertheless, from what you've detected of it, Kate, added to what we knew already, it's incredibly dangerous. If it's immortal, it can't be killed. I faced the same danger at Ossierel. I fought the Legun known as the Captain as hard as I could. Even with the Spear of Lug and every ounce of power that I could put into it through my oraculum, I couldn't defeat it. Even with the bravery of the dying Kyra, when I added every ounce of my power to that of hers – when she made herself into a living weapon with it – still we could not kill it. We couldn't even stop its malice. We'd have lost the battle had it not been for the arrival of the Fir Bolg.'

The Kyra repeated her opinion: 'Even so, we cannot let it stop us now, not when we are only twenty miles from the city walls.'

Kate turned to her. 'It will kill you all, Ainé, every last Shee.'

'Then we shall die fighting and not sit in the dirt with worried brows while the battle for the city is a few day's march away!'

'We have to think afresh. This is a different Legun from what you encountered at Ossierel. Maybe the difference matters? Maybe there is a way we can fight back against this one and win?' She sensed the depth of Alan's despair. He was terrified that he would make a mistake at this very late junction, a mistake that would end all of their hopes so close to the end of their march. 'Please, Ainé, don't risk your Shee. Not at least until I can try to help you. I might, at the very least, get a better idea of how uniformly the poison is spread. I might find places where the air itself is not so lethal. I might even be able to fight against the poison.'

Bétaald confronted Kate. Those amber eyes, the feral gaze of a panther, met Kate's gentle green. 'Do you really believe you might be able to counter the poison?'

'I might be able to find a way to neutralise it with the power of life, as I replenished the Forest of Harrow.'

Bétaald nodded to the Kyra, and to Alan too. 'We should take heed of Kate's advice. However pressing time is, we must make use of it to examine every possible avenue, both for the protection of the warriors and – if Kate can work the miracle – to cure the blighted land.'

The Kyra hissed with frustration. 'All I am aware of is how, moment by moment, the opportunity to attack the walls is slipping by. I fear that an enforced wait, even for a single day, may prove our undoing.'

Kate nodded. 'Ainé is right. We can't afford to waste time in debate. Any further delay might cost us the war. I'm the only one among us who is capable of sensing it, of targeting its presence. So I'm going to have to try.'

Alan took hold of Kate and hugged her tight. 'You're not going out there to face the Septemvile on your own. I won't agree to it. It's too risky.'

Kate allowed him to kiss her brow, but she still insisted: 'I don't need your agreement, Alan. I have to take the risk. We are in this together. I was given my power to fight the same evil as you have.'

'Then you won't go alone. I'm bloody well going out there with you.'

•

Kate's eyes lifted to where Alan was suspended once again from the leather harness borne aloft by four powerful Gargs. But this time his focus, through his pulsing oraculum, was on Kate as she took her first tentative steps out onto the poisoned landscape. She had promised him that she would proceed with care. The Garg prince, Iyezzz, also hovered just a hundred feet above her, risking his own life in preparation for snatching Kate off the ground if her mission failed. Kate looked down at her naked feet and then back up. They had to be bare because she must feel the poisoned land directly, sense its suffering; and deeper still, she must confront and defeat the terrifying enemy that would already be rousing itself in anticipation of new prey.

She took another step, then several more. Her eyes fell from her two protectors in the sky to look at the sulphurous wasteland, criss-crossed with streams of defilement, as if a legion of giant snakes had fought over it. She examined it deeper still, her oraculum pulsing strongly.

Already she sensed movement deep below.

Kate bathed the ground and the air above it with her oraculum, starting to heal the tormented landscape. She sensed life return, however limited, to her immediate vicinity. Minute by minute, then hour by hour, her footsteps were surrounded by a spreading river of life.

She had no clear vision of the monster that lurked there, but because her bare feet were in contact with the ground she now sensed the myriad fibrils that were its sensory organs. Bit by bit, she probed the Legun's mind. There was something coldly logical about that alien being: as if its predatorial instincts had been constructed to a simple but carefully planned blueprint. At first her senses struggled to separate the different elements within the calculating structure, but then Kate recalled how the supposed fallen succubus, Elaru, had used colour in some peculiar but very vivid way to help Kate in her hunt for the serpent-dragon, Nidhoggr.

You must consider the colour blue.

She reached out through her oraculum and filled her senses with the purest, primary shade of blue, the blue of the sky in the sunniest day of summer. Then she extended the idea. She willed her view to dissolve into a spectrum of beautiful, primary shades . . . The blueprint of the Legun, its calculating mind, appeared before her as two great trunks of pure blue fibres, which arose from two bulbous swellings and spread out into myriad fibrous lines, then connected to a labyrinthine network of yellows, vermilions, greens, oranges and violets.

A new whisper entered her consciousness: *Structure is function.*

The two blue bulbs fed into a dense yellow bridge – the communication centre between two lobes. The receiving fibres extended out, exploding upwards. The receiving fibres were probably condensing sensations from the bristles that were its sense organs above ground and turning them into signals . . . A logical network of interconnections: a simple brain.

She probed deeper still, her invading oraculum provoking reaction wherever it entered, until it was fiercely opposed by the same sulphurous yellows she witnessed in the tormented land: blood reds and oranges, and icy cold blue – the calculating layers of this utterly murderous mind.

<I see you now> she whispered to it, mind-to-mind.

A rising fury emerged through a cloaca at the centre of a gigantic ring of tentacles, which rustled and expanded, ripping though the tunnels in a seething mass. They were responding to her challenge, searching for Kate, attempting to assess her threat to it, as she had just been assessing its threat to her. She had become the focus of its rage.

All to the good!

Kate probed still deeper into the Septemvile's lair. Her mental fingers were hurrying now, racing closer to the dead centre of that storm of malice. It sensed her probing its mind. It boiled with rage.

A shout from Alan: mind-to-mind.

<Look out!>

Kate opened her eyes to observe the first eruption of fine dust in a wide circle, perhaps several hundred yards wide, but rapidly closing on her. This was too violent to signify the sensory tendrils. This had to be the feeding tentacles breaking the surface and heading towards her.

Another shout from Alan: <Get ready! Iyezzz is coming!>

<No, Alan! Stop Iyezzz. It will kill him.>

<It will kill you!>

<No! It will attempt to probe me first. Its desire – its passion – is to investigate me to better torment me . . . to play with me.>

She squatted down to sit cross-legged in the dirt, her every nerve and fibre braced with anticipation.

<Have a care how close you come to me, Septemvile> she whispered mind-to-mind. <This will be a confrontation that you do not anticipate.>

The plumes of rising dust were now all around her as she called out, through her oraculum: <Granny Dew! Fill my hands with seeds.>

In an instant, seeds of every size and shape and colour were spilling from Kate's raised hands. Her oraculum was blazing emerald fire. Kate took a breath and blew, scattering the endless twin fountains of seeds far and wide through the spoiled land.

<Alan, give me rain!>

She dared not switch her attention to the sky, where Alan dangled high overhead. At once, the skies filled up with thunderheads. She saw flash after flash of lightning fall to earth from his ruby oraculum. The heavens opened and rain deluged over the blasted land.

<Come now, Monster! Come see how life is returning to your blighted heartland.>

Kate sensed the outrage deep below, followed by an earthquake. But this earthquake did not come from the Septemvile. It came from Alan, who had released another thunderbolt of the First Power. Now he released more, cleaving open huge clefts and ravines into which the downpour ran, letting the seeds fall into the myriad tunnels.

Kate studied the pattern of the outraged brain, deep underground, to see how it was responding to her challenge.

The colours were helpful. She saw that the violet hues were the tentacles. And these were now closing around her in a vast pincer-like movement. But something else was happening. At first she struggled to make it out. It was as if the structure she assumed to be its mind was expanding rapidly. And then, with a tremor of fright, Kate understood what this had to mean: the Legun was much bigger than Kate had seen in her vision. The increasing size was its getting closer to her – rising up directly underneath her.

Kate heard Alan's shout of shock.

A gigantic curtain of steely sharp spikes erupted out of the ground: its teeth. The maw they emerged from was truly gigantic. It sucked at the ground beneath her, the teeth curving down towards her. There was no possibility of Iyezzz coming to her rescue now. And no possibility of Alan striking back at the Legun with his bolts of lightning. The Legun was now directly above her, all around her, underneath her. The stink of its poisonous exhalations bathed Kate's exposed skin and burned like acid in her mouth and nostrils. The proximity of its malice weighed on her heart. The ground beneath her had begun to slip and drain away, as if a gigantic plug had been pulled. The ring of spikes came towards her like a thousand giant scorpion stings, dripping venom.

A memory of Africa came into Kate's mind, specifically the murder of her parents and her brother, Billy. She was a child again, hiding in a pit in the ground where the convent nuns had stored root vegetables. She felt the horror of hearing the shots and the screams, felt the overwhelming feeling of shock, loss . . . despair.

<Kate!> Mo's voice. Mo, pleading with her, holding on to her in the here and now. <Speak to me, Kate!>

<Oh, Mo! Where are you?>

<I'm here with you!>

Mo's unmistakable form was seated opposite Kate, within the gaping hole. But this was a very different Mo. She was not with Kate in person, but her soul spirit was.

Mo's whisper: <We must enter Dromenon together!>

Dromenon?

The wall of spikes grew rapidly closer until they met overhead, throwing Kate into a murky darkness. Then the Legun itself appeared; the Septemvile incarnate – a vast tentacled thing, as large as a football field; a hissing obscenity devoid of eyes; a baleful intelligence, intent on examining Kate and probing her mind and spirit, before drawing her in.

Kate sensed its mind, now so close it was an overwhelming battery of sensations, calculations, lusts . . . Lusts now even more aroused, even as they were somewhat confused, by the additional presence of Mo.

Mo's face was longer and the chin more pointed than Kate remembered. And her entire figure glowed with light, spectral. Kate was aware, even though she had not commanded it, that her own presence was equally spectral: not her physical being, her soul spirit.

<Who are you, Mo?>

<I am Mira – the Heralded One.>

Kate was astonished. Alan had tried to explain something about Mo during that confrontation with the Legun incarnate at the Battle of Ossierel, but he hadn't fully understood, and he'd had difficulty explaining it to her. Mo had saved him, saved them all, but at a terrible cost to herself: her soul spirit had been wounded by the Legun.

Kate struggled to come to terms with what was happening, but there was no time to think it through.

<Why Dromenon?>

<Because that is where it is most vulnerable.>

The Legun roared. It attacked Kate again, not with its fangs but through her grief, her memories of loss.

<Think positive. Think of the good things – think of Alan.>

A day . . . A day long ago . . . A day – oh, it seemed so very long ago now, a day in a different world, and a gate she was holding open with one hand as she wheeled her bicycle through it. A gate that led into the garden of the Doctor's House, the home of her uncle, Fergal, and Bridey . . .

A kiss. Alan leaning across his bike to kiss her. Their first kiss. Her feet no longer feeling the ground under her as, in that moment of bliss, she returned his kiss. Nothing would be the same. The world had changed. Nothing would ever be the same again . . .

The darkness of the Legun's maw was being invaded by light. Through the oraculum Kate glimpsed a triangular shadow that silhouetted Mo. A figure, impenetrably dense and resolute, dark as obsidian, yet cowled in a brilliantly glowing spider's web dress. *Granny Dew!*

<What's happening, Mo?>

<We shall feed the monster a meal it will not relish.>

Stars invaded the Legun's maw. One huge star hovered over Mo's right shoulder. Kate realised it had to be Magtokk: Magtokk as a leader among the True Believers. The stars were a vast proliferation of True Believers, like an invading galaxy. And she recalled what those True Believers could do. She had seen what they did to the Titan, Fangorath, a being that had been half-divine, who had brought to an end the Age of Dragons.

There was a shriek that was as loud as a thunder clap, then a profusion of rending and tearing, as the True Believers began their graceful arcs and spirals.

<What's screaming, Mo?>

<A Septemvile dies hard.>

To Be Reborn

'Hi – stranger!'

Mo smiled at the gangling Olhyiu shaman, Turkeya, as he moved through the ramshackle chaos of the camp, treating a trail of people for their pains and woes with his herbs and potions. It was only a day after she had helped Kate destroy the Septemvile, Earthbane. All around them was the chaos of the camp now on the move. The Shee were determined to lose no more time, and the movement of a hundred thousand or so heavy feline feet, claws ripping at the ground, had already excited a dust storm. Turkeya, left behind to attend to the lagging camp followers, had hardly lifted his eyes to look at Mo since her arrival.

'Won't you look at me, Turkeya?'

He hesitated, raising his eyes fleetingly. 'I'm very tired, Mo.'

'Then let me help you.'

He shrugged, as if to tell her to do whatever she willed.

Waiting next in line in the queue was the little girl, Moonrise, together with her brother, Hsst. Mo said hello, squatting down to be on the same eye level as the urchins. 'The aides have clearly helped you. Your eye is looking improved. How does it feel to you?'

'Is feelin' better, Milady.'

As always the two urchins looked more in need of food than medication.

'Are you getting anything to eat?'

'We gets a bit o' soup . . .'

'I know – from Soup Scully Oops.'

Turkeya came over to join Mo. He squatted down next to all three of them and instructed Mo on mixing a salve for Moonrise's eye. He said, 'The stye's healing, but it has inflamed the envelope of the eyelid. The salve can be dropped into it by her brother. If you could show him how to cup a leaf to guide the flow.'

'Of course.'

Mo showed Hsst how to apply the salve. When she was finished Moonrise looked strangely relieved. 'Thanks, Milady.' Mo glanced over her shoulder at Usrua, whose close attention was the source of the little girl's anxiety. 'Off you go now. I must speak to my friend, the shaman.'

Mo stood up to watch them scurry away, then turned to speak once more to the young shaman.

'I know I've neglected you lately.'

'Why bother with the likes of me? You're the hero of the day, you and Kate – you saved us from the Septemvile.'

'It was Kate who really saved us, not me. I was in no physical danger. I only helped in soul spirit form.'

'Your modesty only makes me feel worse, Mo.'

'I'm so sorry.'

'Are you?'

'Yes. Of course I am. I know you must be really missing Siam and Kehloke.'

'I hope to see them soon. Prince Ebrit himself recruited my father to navigate his war fleet around the coast and past the many reefs that protect these dangerous waters. My mother, Kehloke, chose to travel with him – in some style, I gather, as guest of the prince.'

'You poor thing! I can see you're exhausted. You must be so looking forward to getting together with them again.'

Turkeya gave her the ghost of a smile. 'I intend to get blind drunk.'

Mo smiled too. 'You know I've really missed you.'

'I've missed you, too.' Turkeya hesitated, his brown eyes appraising her anew. 'You've changed.'

'You tell me that every time we meet.'

'No, not like before. Since we last met.'

She sighed, looking into his dark eyes, his downy face. He had allowed his fair hair to grow long – the hair of his paternal polar bear ancestry – and had tied it back in a ponytail. He too was changing, becoming burlier in the mould of his father, Siam. She said: 'I know I've been changing. We need to talk. You are the only one who really listens to me.'

'Am I?'

'You are my true friend.'

He dropped his head. 'And you mine.'

Still, she sensed that he was somewhat wary of her, even as he talked to an old woman with a bent spine. He mixed the woman a concoction of leaves to be ground into a confection to be taken with a little beer.

He said, as if it were the most natural thing to say in the world: 'Why are you really here, Mo?'

Her voice was equally calm in replying, though her eyes were filling up with tears: 'I am obliged to go on a journey.'

'What sort of journey?'

'One that I have to make on my own. It's hard to explain. I am being born again, Turkeya.'

Turkeya stopped what he was doing to look at her. He pursed his lips, exposing powerful teeth. 'You're clearly upset. When people are upset they can allow their imaginations to run away with them.'

'People – you mean girls – women?'

'You know, as I do, Mo, that women undergo emotional change, the turmoil of their lunar cycles.'

She looked at him incredulously.

'I'm sorry, Mo, if I have offended you. You know that I am no deep thinker. I'm a shaman, a healer of physical and spiritual malaise.'

'I remember your teacher, Kemtuk Lapeep. I remember his humility and his courage.'

Turkeya dropped his head. He was frightened by the

changes in her. She sensed it, the panic growing in him. The downy hair all over his arms was erect.

Mo sighed. 'I want to conduct an experiment with you. It's important to me. Will you help me?'

'Of course.'

'I know you've been running short of essential herbs – components of the cures you want to offer these people.'

'Not cures, merely treatments.'

'It makes no difference to the experiment.'

'What experiment?'

'Could you tell me when you need help, if you have run out of an ingredient?'

He read something in her face. 'Mo!'

Turkeya's supplies of herbs had been drastically depleted on this long journey over the mountains and through the wastelands. He had hardly any herbs at all left to treat the growing queue of people.

'I know this embarrasses you. You think it might even be madness. But why not try it. Humour me.'

An old man went down on his knees before Turkeya, begging for a treatment for the pain he had been suffering in his jaw. Turkeya inspected the foul-smelling abscess that had invaded the bone. There was nothing in his herbal remedies that would cure such a thing. He lacked even the juice of the poppy to alleviate the poor old man's agony.

He turned to Mo. 'I don't suppose there's anything you can do?'

Mo put her left hand on the man's jaw. With her right hand, she gripped the two talismans on the thong about her neck: the bog oak figurine given to her by Padraig and the Torus given to her by the True Believers.

'Heal him,' she intoned.

The man's face changed: the creases of agony were ironed from his flesh. His eyes widened and he stared up at Mo from his kneeling posture. When Turkeya inspected his mouth, the abscess in the bone had dried and contracted to a scar.

He looked at her aghast: 'How?'

'I – I don't know.'

'It's not possible. It's . . . Well, if I didn't know you, Mo, I might consider it some deceit. Some sleight of hand.'

'I am not deceiving you, Turkeya.'

Turkeya hesitated. He took her by the shoulders. He could feel her body trembling. He stood back a pace, the better to size her up. 'Explain it again, Mo. Tell me how you are changing.'

'I am becoming . . .' she hesitated to allow herself time to think about it, 'I am becoming a new person.'

'You know, as I do, how ridiculous that sounds.'

'I don't think I am altogether human anymore.'

He stared at her.

'I wasn't conceived in a normal way. I . . . Oh, Turkeya, I was born of a virgin birth.'

'You know this is impossible, Mo.'

'Is it? Magtokk took me back to Australia, to show me

my birth mother. She was only a teenage girl. She had not known a man.'

'For goodness' sake, Mo. How is this possible?'

Mo explained what had been happening to her. She told him what she had seen in the Valley of the Towers of Skulls.

Turkeya held her still and looked at her for many moments. 'These things, they are beyond the understanding of a mere shaman, Mo.'

'They are beyond my understanding too.'

Mo reached out to hug him. He retracted, very slightly, but she could not miss his reaction.

'You are afraid of me, too?'

'No, Mo!' He shook his head, then he took her in the wide embrace of his arms. 'Not me, too. Forgive a foolish shaman. I don't understand these things. How can a human being be . . . be reborn?'

'Is not a caterpillar reborn as a butterfly?'

'But these are insects, not humans.'

Mo's eyes confronted Turkeya's. 'Will you stand by me?'

'I – I don't know what you mean.'

'Will you be my friend, through all that is to come?'

'You have ever been my friend. Why would I now deny you?'

'It might be dangerous.'

He laughed. 'That is the least of my concerns. When has this journey been anything other than that? You make it seem that I am important. In the scale of things, Mo, I am of the least importance. I could die here, at this very moment, and none would remember me.'

'I would.' Her eyes beheld his. 'Will you always believe in me?'

He hugged her again. 'I will.'

'Thank you, Turkeya.'

Moonrise watched the young huloima, the one called Mo, and she saw how much she loved the shaman. Why was the cruel man, Kawkaw, so interested in her? She didn't want to do it. She didn't want to spy on Mo. She didn't ever want to say nothing about Mo to Kawkaw, especially not the strange things that Hsst had been reading on her lips, but still they had to eat.

'We needs soup,' she said to Hsst, with tears in her eyes.

He nodded. His dirty finger reached up and brushed away the tears that were running down her cheeks.

In Plain Sight

Mark lifted a finger to his lips to caution his three companions – *danger up ahead!* They had parked the Mamma Pig in a wood of deciduous forest, which was, for the most part, hoary old oak trees, their lichen-covered trunks black with age and what was left of their autumn leaves in every shade of yellow and gold. Leaving Tajh and Bull to look after the Pig, the rest of the crew, including Brett, made their way southwards along the forest edge to find a way of approaching London, which was now about fifty miles to the southeast. There was a twenty-yard-wide river up ahead and the air was dense with mist. Visibility was down to thirty yards. They came out of the forest adjacent to a loop in the river, where the headland jutted out of the near bank. Wintry shadow clouded the sky and frost silvered the headland, where a jumble of fallen trees provoked a hiss of eddies in the passing stream.

What do you think? Cal mouthed at Mark.

Mark glanced at Nan, who was sniffing at the air. Brett sniffed too and then he nodded towards the opposite bank, where tendrils of smoke were curling upwards a short distance away.

Nan mouthed: *A habitation on fire?*

Cal snorted: *A habitation?*

Just then Cal got a vibration alert on his radio. He pressed it to his ear, his eyes widening, then passed it to Mark. 'It's Tajh,' he whispered.

'Tajh?'

Mark heard Tajh's voice, crackly in his left ear: 'Padraig is coming round.'

'Yeah?'

'It's looking good. He's sitting up. A bit hazy, confused about where he is and who we are, but he's talking.'

'His brain is okay?'

'Far as I can judge.'

'That's fantastic, Tajh.' Mark switched off the radio-com, passing a thumbs-up over at Nan. He just whispered: 'Padraig!'

Cal grunted. 'Forget the old guy for the moment.'

How could Mark forget Padraig? He wanted to get back to check for himself right now. There was so much they had to talk about. But Cal had other things on his mind and signalled for them to slink back into the shade of the trees. Under cover now, they spoke quietly. 'Focus on the situation here. Consider our options.'

'Might be just a campfire?'

Nan shook her head. 'I can hear screams – violence.'

Cal was right. They had to stop thinking about Padraig for the time being. Mark nodded, agreeing with Nan. 'It isn't a campfire. There's a town over there.'

Brett pursed his lips. 'Sheeit!'

Cal frowned. 'Razzers?'

'I don't know. What do you say, Nan?'

'Perhaps, but there's something else there.'

Mark nodded. 'You thinking what I'm thinking?'

She nodded. 'Definitely a non-human presence. I'm not sure what it is. Maybe a Scalpie?'

Brett looked bemused. 'A Scalpie?'

'We've encountered one before. We had to kill one back in London.'

'Way you talk, it's a significant threat?'

'Definitely: a religious fanatic – and very dangerous. The last one we met was carrying a preceptor's dagger.'

'What's a preceptor's dagger?'

'A dagger made out of the same matte black metal as the Sword of Feimhin.'

Brett looked from Mark to Cal. 'Hey, fellas? We go in – or we go around? What's it to be?'

'That,' muttered Cal, 'is the question.'

As darkness had fallen the night before, Mark had looked at his reflection in a shaving mirror. His hair had been standing to attention and he'd had a bedraggled beard growing. He'd hacked at it with scissors and then shaved away the stubble, and finally a lean fresh-scrubbed face had looked back at him from the glass. But it had been the face of a stranger – looking ten years older than Mark imagined himself to be. Once upon a time, before the madness of Tír had entered his life, he had needed spectacles. But in this reincarnation, complete with the black triangle in his brow, he no longer needed them. Slicked down, his fair hair was shoulder length, but he hadn't attempted to cut it. His blue eyes looked like the eyes of a man who had already seen too much of life ever to accept things at face value again. The triangle in his brow had been quiescent, a flinty black. It had moulded itself so closely to his skull that, had it not been for the crystal gloss, it could have been a birthmark. But he knew that when called for, sparks of life would appear within it, pulsing with his heart-beat. And now, on the wintry bank of an unknown river, Mark felt those sparks awaken. That was what had signalled danger up ahead. Not the danger of a normal skirmish, but a deeper, more threatening danger, the sort of danger he and his three friends had encountered, and feared, just about every day of their lives since first arriving on Tír.

A few nights ago, as they had made their final arrangements for the return trip to London, Mark and Tajh had walked together towards the Mamma Pig, which had been illuminated by the sparks of some last-minute welding. Mark had liked the Scot since their first meeting and he still liked her company. He'd moved round to study the huge blade that was fixed to the front of the Pig. Earlier, he had seen Cal running a big grindstone up and down the bevelled surface and so he'd squatted down to feel the sharpness of it. It was a magnificent vee-shaped cutting tool as sharp as a blade. They'd been joined at the Pig by Cal and Brett. It had been a relief for Mark to find Cal's ire directed at the American rather than himself.

'You know that we don't fancy the return trip, but you don't give a shit, do you? All you care about is doing a bit of nosing around.'

'You're right about that, buddy.' Brett had lit a cigar and offered Cal one from the pack, but he'd refused.

'You know this is a suicide mission. We've only just managed to get out of there. What is it? If at first you don't succeed in getting yourself killed, try and try again?'

Brett had straightened his back to his full six foot three, looked down at Cal, and laughed.

'Heading back to London, it isn't a joke,' Cal had said.

Mark and Tajh had gone and stood by Cal. Brett was something of a puzzle to the crew and they'd wanted to know who, or what, Brett really was, and what he was up to. Mark said: 'Cal's right. It's stupid to expect us to take you down there. At the very least we deserve a better explanation than you've given us.'

'Guys – I'm bound by secrecy.'

Some wooden crates were loaded into the Pig under Brett's direction. Two of them looked large enough to contain weapons, but others were too small and they were being handled so carefully they probably contained delicate electronics, or even some sensitive explosives.

Cal became madder by the second. 'What's really going on here? Don't give me no bullshit about security.'

'In good time I'll level with you, but here and now all you need to know is that I'm here to help you win your war.'

'We're not idiots. We don't want some machine gun groupie getting us into some suicide bullshit.'

Brett lifted his hands, palms outstretched. 'Wouldn't think of it. There's no deception. You'll see soon enough why the security is there.'

While Cal stormed off to have it out with General Chatwyn, Mark had taken advantage of finding himself alone with Brett. 'Why can't you explain to us here and now?'

'The boxes contain my own weaponry, and some special electronics.'

'Why couldn't you say that to Cal?'

'Because he's a hothead. And he's beginning to bug me.'

'You can trust Cal.'

'Oh, I know he's a ballsy guy, the sort you can trust in the field. I heard nothing but praise for Cal from the General himself.' Brett had taken a contented puff on his cigar, watching the men load more crates into the belly of the Pig. By the time Cal had returned, Bull, who was still bandaged, was moving the crew's own machine guns and vast quantities of ammunition into the Mamma Pig. From time to time, Cal's eyes met Mark's questioningly, as if to ask if Mark had managed to squeeze more information from the American.

Mark had shrugged.

Cal said: 'I've spoken to the CO. We're not going to wait for dawn. We're going to take advantage of the dark and set out as soon as the stuff is stowed. We aim to get somewhere near 50 miles outside of London by first light and hope the camouflage will keep us out of trouble with the Paramilitaries. But just let them try to stop us and we'll show them the meaning of road rage.' With a humourless smile Cal had turned on his heel and headed back to gather the rest of the crew.

Mark had turned to Brett. 'You see – it's a mistake to get on the wrong side of Mr Angry.'

'Buddy, I reckon it'd be a bigger mistake to get on the wrong side of you.'

'Why's that?'

Brett's face crinkled into a toothy grin. 'I'm what you might call a spiritual guy myself.'

'The only spirits I've seen you communicate with have come from a bottle of Bourbon.'

Brett let out a single *ha*. 'You got that right.'

'Now that we're setting out, we need to trust one another. Why don't you tell us what's really going on?'

'Logistics is the name of the game.'

'Logistics?'

'That's right.' In that moment, Brett's face had adopted a harder look. He'd puffed on his cigar, his craggy features thrown into a rubicund glow as he took a deep drag. 'Let me tell you, Mark, this ain't the first hostile situation I've been called to fight in. Wars are won and lost on the logistics.'

During their journey southwards they had encountered people fleeing north, even in the dark. But the crew knew that the notion of safety in the north was a delusion. The big industrial northern cities were following the same dystopic pattern as London: Razzers were invading the streets, which gave Seebox's people the excuse to use emergency powers. And where Seebox's forces moved in, they were inevitably aided and abetted by the irregulars, the brutal Paramilitaries and the Skulls. At the same time, things were still in a state of flux and confusion. They were relying on the fact that the camouflaged exterior might make it easier for the Mamma Pig to return to the hot zone around London. Hidden, as it were, in plain sight.

And now, here by the riverside, Brett and Sharkey were dispatched to fetch the Mamma Pig, while Mark, Cal and Nan made their way across a muddy field, then climbed over a barred gate to emerge onto the road leading into another small town in flames. They inched closer, keeping to the brush-lined verges, to get a closer look at the inevitable roadblock. Adrenaline coursed through Mark's body. His skin felt as if it were burning in spite of the cold.

The roadblock comprised at least one armoured PC, but with such a dense river mist, and the obscuring snow, which was still falling, it was almost impossible to make out any more detail. The roadblock was on the far side of a two-lane road that crossed the river over a triple-arched stone bridge. Cal used binoculars to try to see past the roadblock, but he wasn't very successful. There was no sign to announce the town's name. The snow thickened as they waited for the Pig to arrive, exhaling steamy breath into the freezing air.

Cal glanced back over his shoulder, waving the approaching Pig to halt under a tunnel of trees. The bulky vehicle would have been hidden from the roadblock by a bend in the approach road, but it was unlikely to stay hidden for long. Cal had another look at what he could see of the town. 'I can't make out much at all. No sign of life.'

Where is everybody? Mark wondered.

They backtracked a hundred yards to rejoin the stationary Pig. Bull helped Brett to haul a few of the mysterious crates out of the belly of the vehicle, laying them out by the side of the road. Mark and Nan took advantage of the few minutes' break to look in on Padraig, finding him sitting back against the forward bulkhead with a mug of hot tea cradled in his hands.

'How are you?'

Those glowing blue eyes stared back at them, looking somewhat dazed. Padraig's lips moved, as if he had questions in mind of his own, but Cal grabbed Mark's shoulder and hauled him away.

'You'll get plenty of time to talk later. We need to keep tabs on Brett.'

Tajh and Nan stood point to the front and rear with the

Minimis, but they kept turning back to see what the great secret of the boxes was all about. They saw a computer console emerge, to be fitted with a screen.

'What the heck?'

'Attack window,' Brett cackled.

An even bigger surprise emerged from another crate. 'Man alive,' Cal muttered, 'I can't fucking believe this.'

Mark was equally astonished to watch Brett put together an unmistakable silvery outline with a wing span of about six feet from an assemblage of parts.

'It's a drone.'

'To be accurate,' Brett quipped, 'this here baby is a UAV – an unmanned aerial vehicle.'

'It's a bleeding drone,' Cal insisted.

'Ain't like no drone you ever seen,' Brett whispered back. He motioned to Bull to help him carry it clear of the Pig so it stood bang in the middle of the road.

'What are you up to?' Cal asked.

'The latest stealth tech, buddy.'

'A spy drone?' Cal's voice sounded deeply sceptical.

'The best eye in the sky there is. Now, I want you fellas to stand well back and let her do her thing.'

They watched as, with a buzz no louder than an electric shaver, the UAV took off and, within seconds, disappeared into the mist.

'Ain't no radar gonna pick up this baby.'

'So, what's the idea?'

Brett hauled the computer console up onto the bonnet

of the Pig, swivelling the screen round so they could all see it. 'You wanted to find out what we face up ahead.' With his six foot three frame, he was tall enough to operate the controls from a standing position. In a few minutes they had a crystal clear aerial reconnaissance of the town up ahead.

'How does it get a clear picture through the mist?'

'Technology, like I told you.'

They saw figures in grey camouflage moving through buildings, many of which were in flames.

'Paramilitaries!'

'Looks like a whole platoon.'

They also had a clear view of the barrier on the other side of the stone bridge. Two APCs, one armed with a cannon, pointing straight down the approach road. The second APC sported a heavy gauge machine gun.

'Shit!' Cal muttered.

'Shit, for sure,' Brett agreed, 'but useful shit to know.' He waved Sharkey nearer. 'Can you work with Cogwheel, connect me to your console in the Pig?'

'Already working on it,' Cogwheel said from inside the cab. 'Sharkey, you getting the connection?'

'I think so. I'm getting a good strong signal.'

Mark said, 'Let's see what's going on in the streets.'

They watched people in obvious distress.

'Can we move in closer, Brett?'

Brett twiddled with the console and the camera in the drone focused down. The picture was still crystal clear.

People were being lined up against a wall. They looked like ordinary folk, some of them in what might be coats or dressing gowns thrown over what they had slept in. They saw the flares of gun muzzles, the people falling.

Cal's eyes were popping: 'Bloody hell! You see that?'

Tajh clasped his arm. 'They're killing people.'

Bull said, 'We're going in.'

'But we'll be cut to pieces on that approach road.'

'No, fellas, we won't. Not if I can help it. But you better get back on board the Pig.'

'Right, everybody. Do what the man says.'

'All but me – not just yet,' Brett muttered.

Brett instructed Bull to dig out another of the long narrow crates. When he opened it, it contained what looked like another silvery drone assemblage. Brett and Bull hauled it twenty yards clear of the Mamma Pig.

'Another of your UAVs?' Mark muttered.

'Not this baby.' Brett stepped back as the drone-like thing became airborne.

'What is it?'

'Battlefield weapon.' Brett hefted the console off the Pig and cradled it in one of his arms while typing instructions with the other. 'Cogwheel – get ready to roll. Sharkey, keep the connection alive. I'll join you at the very last moment.'

There was a pandemonium of activity as Bull and Cal armed up the two machine guns and the Mamma Pig inched forwards out of the tunnel of trees.

'Cogwheel, Sharkey?'

'We got it. We're seeing what Brett is seeing.'

They were now visible from the barrier on the far side of the bridge. Cal muttered: 'Keep inching her slow and steady, Cogwheel. We should be able to confuse them with our camouflage until we get as close as we can.'

'Roger that,' Sharkey responded with his Biggles voice, sitting shotgun with Cogwheel up front.

Mark was leaning over Cogwheel's shoulder, looking ahead, watching through his eyes and through his oraculum for signs of activity.

'Brett!'

The American was running alongside the Pig, looking down at the console in the crook of his arm, keeping pace with Cogwheel's driving. 'Hellfire and damnation! Keep that dang connection as long as you can!'

Bull's enormous arm grabbed the back of Brett's jacket and hauled him in through the port.

'Right – Cogwheel! Put your bloody foot down.'

'What foot?'

'Put your bloody thumb on it, you shithouse. I can only hope this crazy American knows what he's doing.'

'They've clocked us. The cannon's swivelling.'

The Pig was trundling faster, the engines screaming. Up ahead they saw that the gun had stopped swivelling. It was trained right up their nostrils. Any moment now they'd see the flash . . .

They saw the flash, but it wasn't the cannon. The road-block had disappeared. It was there one second, and in the next it was gone. They saw a cloud of roiling smoke and flame a split second before they saw bits and pieces rising high into the sky, and then the thunder of the explosion. They were riding into a fifty-foot wall of flame.

Cogwheel yelled, 'What the fuck . . .?'

'We go in, lads – all guns blazing.'

The Daemon Furnace

Stop! Look! Listen!

Gully felt so frightened he was recanting the mantra with his eyes squeezed shut. There was no way he dared to investigate his surroundings. He was trembling so much that he felt a faint coming on.

Darkness!

The darkness was back.

He began to pant. He was panting his breath, in and out, trying not to faint. He was back in the darkness, where things could wake him from sleep and hurt him. He was back in the darkness where nobody cared for him, the darkness before his Nan had come to rescue him. He was back in the darkness of being cursed and sworn at, in the darkness of being slapped and shoved into cupboards. He was back in the deepest darkness in which oily rainbows glittered amid the distant splatter of lights – lights that glinted and gambolled over shapes of things that terrified him.

No!

A sudden crunch of what sounded like devastatingly heavy machinery drove the memories from his mind. It was so gargantuan and violent that it made his breath catch in his throat. Then, the thunderous hammering began again. It seemed to Gully that he had fallen into the forge of one of them old giant gods, with a hammer the size of a truck thundering down onto an anvil the size of a row of shops. The deep, ear-splitting sounds reverberated through the iron floor under his feet. Then, when his ears felt wrecked with it, the thunder stopped, leaving him with a ringing that echoed within the vault of his skull.

Gully waited for the thunder to start up again, his heart pounding inside his chest.

This horrible place! *Strewth, like . . . like some kind of a huge airplane hanger . . . and deep underground.*

He had lived in London all of his life and he had never seen no place like this. It was chock-a-block full of giant machines. He could hear the things now, all a whirring, pounding, pumping, clanking. *Maybe I shouldn't be afraid of just the pounding of machines? But it ain't just the machines, is it? It's the people – them wot's operating the machines. Like the giant robot wot ain't no robot at all but a daemon wot calls itself Bad Day.*

Gully's stomach felt like it had jumped up into his throat, so he was choking. He counted to twenty, patting his pockets: the five that remained to him. He breathed in and out of his open mouth. *Piss'n'shit!* He patted the place where the 'Keys' pocket had been. He missed it, the lost pocket, even though he had no use for no keys anymore.

He thought about all of it: *Nah – it can't be – it can't possibly be real.*

He waited a little while and then he told himself that none of this was real. And if it wasn't real then it didn't mean shit.

Stop, look, listen . . . Think again . . .

Even if it wasn't real the fact was he was deep in shit. So deep Penny's caution wasn't going to save him.

Strewth! It's just words, Penny. Words wot don't mean noffink. Not here. Not here, in the darkness.

He began to count out another beat of twenty. He wasn't entirely sure it wasn't real. That was the trouble. And he hated to go against Penny's mantra. She was so clever in her thinking. So maybe the mantra was still true? He didn't know what to think.

I don't know noffink about wot's wot no more.

The huge, thunderous hammering burst upon him again. Gully was back to panting in gasps from his *pffing* lips. His thoughts, his mind, was stopped dead by the thunderous clanking that was coming out of the pit. He crawled down into the lowest hole he could find and put his hands over his head. What kind of a hell was this? The hammering was followed by what could have been lightning strikes, and this in turn was followed by hailstorms of sparks. The sparks burned like nettle stings where they came down into the hidey hole where he was squatting, and made hissing contact with his skin. It took him several minutes to recognise that there was some kind of background humming. The humming was as disturbing as the massive noise and the lightning flashes. It made Gully put his hands over his ears and to rock backwards and forwards.

Oh, Penny – *Penny, Penny, Penny!*

Nothing that Bad Day had told him convinced Gully that he wasn't trapped: a prisoner of the giant robot. The robot was no more than strung together bits of junk, but there was no consolation in that; it was terrifying to know that there was something else inside of the bot that was the real Bad Day. A daemon bot – that was what he had called himself. He was trapped here by a daemon bot, called Bad Day, who was the slave of somebody even more terrifying that he called the Master.

Them was the facts.

Oh, Penny! This is real serious stuff. This is . . . I don't know wot the bleedin' 'eck this is.

Gully put his hands up to his face. He scratched at his chin, then turned his head to one side and hissed through his teeth. This was worse than anything he could possibly have imagined. This was . . . like . . . kinda like maybe the end of the world serious. He felt tears squeezing out of his eyes.

But it didn't do no good – no good bawling like some baby! It didn't help. Didn't do noffink, no way, no how.

I'm done for.

He tried counting slowly to a hundred, tapping on each of his five pockets in sequence, again and again. He tried his best to calm down. He tried to stamp down on his reeling thoughts. Might be there was something good to come out of this.

'Yeah,' he whispered to himself.

Might be that Bad Day had carried him all the way to where he had wanted to be, anyhow. He was back in London. And London was where Penny had to be, provided she hadn't left it at the same time he had.

You got to get a grip, Gully!

He did his utmost to get a grip. *I been captured, Penny. I got no idea wot captured me, or why. It really don't feel so very good. It feels like maybe I made some kind of horrible mistake in my calculations. I ain't got to expect . . . I reckon I ain't got to expect noffink . . .*

Gully clasped his head in his hands again. He just didn't know what to do or where to go no more.

The great clangs of a hammer, the banging and sawing continued at intermittent intervals but he felt too fragged with worry to figure it.

Then he was dreaming. He knew that he was wandering through a panoramic despoiled landscape, with tottering buildings, flames roaring through rafters, smoke rising into the wheeling grey sky . . .

<We must be patient, bwai.>

The voice came into his head from outside. He vaguely recognised it: it sounded like that Jamaican-sounding women, Henriette. There had been something really weird about her. Now he came to think about it, he thought that she was the weirdest woman he'd ever met. Gully had no idea how her voice could come into his head like that. *I know it ain't somefink I imagined up outta thin air, because I'd never ever have thought of her in a million years.*

<Weh, de good Lord forgive you, Gully.>

'Forgive my arse!'

His resentment was so strong, and immediate, he woke up. He was sitting in the dark, with his back against a towering wall of rusting iron.

<Do some'ting to help yousel!>

'Like wot?'

The prevailing darkness squeezed his mind shut. That and the hammering, and the showers of livid sparks. What was he supposed to do in a place like this? He was bruised all over and his elbow still throbbed. He pressed his head back against the hard metal and the rust and he clenched his eyes shut.

<Go find out what's goin' on', Dahlin'.>

That weird voice! It really sounded like Henriette.

'Wot for?'

<Because Penny's dependin' on you.>

That wasn't fair. It wasn't fair at all.

'No!'

<You gotta do it, bwai!>

'Why – why do I gotta do it?'

<Because she be needin' you.>

'Penny don't care noffink for me. She left me.'

<She couldn't help it, Gully. She was hurtin'. She was hurtin' so much she no t'ink clearly.>

'I don't understand.'

<Dahlin', she be needin' you.>

'Then why'd she leave me?'

<You got to put de anger out you' heart, Gully Doughty. Penny love you in her way, like you love her too. De Sword took a hold of Penny, jus' like it took a hold of dem Razzers settin' fire to dem streets.>

'Why you telling me these fings?'

<Oh, Gully. You and Penny – you both in de most terrible danger. Dere are such t'ings come into de world! Dere are such powers, Dahlin'.>

Gully's head dropped.

He wasn't altogether sure that he had ever really heard Henriette's voice at all. But the conversation left him feeling more afraid than ever. He fiddled with the collar of his denim jacket, which felt slick with oil. *If I'm gonna die, who cares? Nobody – nobody in the whole bleedin' world'll even notice.*

But then, in another kind of a sense, it meant, like maybe, he could do whatever he wanted.

<Dey's light up ahead, Dahlin'.>

What was that supposed to mean? There's light up ahead? All the light he could see was down there, in the distance, where all the hammering was going on and the sparks was flying. You got to be bonkers to go there. Every instinct told him that. Whatever was going on there, he didn't want to know about it.

Stop, look, listen, Gully.

He peered into the distance, between the towering walls of iron. He tried to appraise his surroundings, which was far from easy in the near dark, and the flaring sparks and the thunder of hammering. His legs didn't feel like his own as he began to move, shuffling stiffly through oily patches glistening with reflections of the flaring fireworks, and past great jutting shoulders of rusting iron, through a gloom so dense it was like wading through water. The air grew hotter with every step. Yet, step by step, he forced himself forwards. The noise of the hammering climbed through his bones from his feet to his spine, and from his spine right up into his skull.

Whatever it was, the furnace of thunder and fire was just around the corner. Sweat was now soaking Gully's clothes so that even his denim jacket was stuck to his T-shirt, which in turn was stuck to his skin. His ears were deafened by the thunder, his heart failing with fright at whatever lay ahead.

<Gully!>

Henriette's voice again – Henriette calling to him inside his head.

It wasn't fair. It just wasn't fair. It made him take another reluctant step, then another . . . another.

Then he saw it and terror consumed him.

'No!'

A gigantic figure was working the forge: its head was

horned, its face covered in what might have been black crocodile scales. The eye sockets blazed, and the molten-red of the volcanic flames glowed, spilling in flares through every junction and crevice of the armoured body. Its hands were massive claws covered in the same black scales, and a glowing molten lava was crackling out of every finger joint. Over its shoulders and back was a shell-like casing, maybe like that of a lobster. But then he noticed the shape of the casing. And it wasn't like no lobster at all. It was two huge wings extending from above its head and right down to its horny feet. The wings was a glittering black. That great horned head was turning round, the blazing eyes rotating as if suddenly aware of his intrusion. Gully wanted to back away, but his legs wouldn't carry him. He tumbled onto his knees before it.

'I had planned it to be a surprise.'

The voice was the deep gentlemanly voice of Bad Day, but this monster was far more frightening than the walking robot. The hammer, every bit as gigantic as Gully had feared, was in its gauntleted fist.

'Wot . . . are you?'

'I am the servant of the Master.'

Even as the monster's words entered Gully's mind, a huge flare of orange-red flames and a wheeling storm of sparks emerged from the furnace. Only then did Gully notice what lay at the heart of the flames: a minuscule face. Gully was beginning to make out a ghostly outline, in fire and molten metal. A familiar outline . . .

'Oh, shiiitttt!'

'I saw your loneliness. I thought you needed a companion.'

'Oh, my word!'

Gully turned from the tiny object at the heart of the furnace to stare up into the monstrous face of the blacksmith. He looked around the smithy and saw familiar pieces: a mudguard still retaining tiny shreds of red paint; two sprocket wheels; the springs from what had once been a saddle.

'Me Raleigh bike!'

When the monster opened its mouth to smile, a current of choking heat emerged. 'It was of convenient dimensions. The spokes proved readily amenable to the fine lacework of feathers.'

Gully was only just beginning to understand: Bad Day had hammered steel to sheets as fine as paper over a smaller core – a core of fire, like Bad Day's own.

'Wot's in there? Wot's inside of it?'

'Even a slave bot must have a soul spirit.'

'A soul spirit?'

'The essence of being.'

Now that the hammering had stopped, there was a new sound: a buzzing like a wasp, only deeper and louder. The buzzing was coming from the thing at the heart of the furnace. Gully looked at it again and slumped down among the rusting ironwork. He watched in silence as Bad Day hauled himself erect, shuddered, and then reassembled himself, changing from the demonic blacksmith to the clanking robot with the roomy mouth.

The buzzing thing was alive. It was fluttering wings of delicately-wrought iron that were still glowing a shade of furnace red. The bones of its wings had been made out of the spokes of Gully's bicycle. He spoke, in shock, in wonderment:

'Wot you just said – about me being lonely.'

Bad Day laughed, but the sound was a hollow thunder. The furnace heat was subsiding at its core. 'I cannot permit you to leave, yet I am conscious that such confinement might provoke unhappiness. So I constructed a companion.'

Sweat was dripping off Gully's face like rain. He rubbed at his right elbow, the pain making him aware of it once more.

'Wot is this place?'

'A nest of sorts. We daemon bots are nesting beings.'

Gully heard the buzzing as the newly emergent slave bot rose out of the cooling crater. It stretched its wings and then fluttered a foot or two higher, however clumsily, then it began to fall back into the furnace, as if the exertion had exhausted it.

Bad Day reached out its left hand, allowing the bird creature to land on it rather than plummet back into the furnace.

'It is gauche, not yet complete. The delicacy of feathers were surely a test of my lore. It will, no doubt, improve – learn is perhaps the expression – as it acquires experience.'

Ghork Mega

Alan's onkkh came to a fidgety halt on a small tor above an unexpected vista of grasses and wild flowers. The beast stretched its long neck in an evident desire to taste the stream of fresh water that gushed over a bed of blue-grey pebbles some thirty feet below. In the distance, easily visible now even with the naked eye, soared the curtain walls of Ghork Mega, two hundred feet high and, reputedly, fifty feet thick. Gatehouse towers, studded with cannon-bedecked rows, soared into the sky. The gargantuan fortification occupied an entire black granite mountain. As Alan studied it through his telescope, he saw how the geography of the city had adopted the natural terrain, making use of the slopes to enhance its own formidable defences.

Alan alighted from the troublesome beast that had borne him through vast distances, and dangers, and across the Flamestruck Mountains. He watched as, honking loudly, it descended stream-wards in a flutter of feathers and a clatter of taloned feet before fighting a path against a rush of others to the stream. When Alan glanced back over his shoulder, he caught sight of Qwenqwo, who had alighted nearby, landing even more badly than Alan had. Alan laughed as the dwarf mage almost upended himself, eventually landing on his rump. He could hear Qwenqwo cursing as he made his way up the slope to flop down onto the dense growth of grasses and flowers by the side of his friend.

'This march must have been the most blistering torture ever inflicted on the hide of a warrior.'

Alan had to admit that he had never become used to riding such a vile beast. Every bone in his back, bum, and thighs was aching. He had to envy the Shee, who had covered most of the march on their own clawed feet. Alan just allowed himself to fall back into the cool mattress of the sweet scented flowers and grasses, tempted to close his eyes and grab some sleep.

'I never ever want to see an onkkh again.'

'You and me both,' growled Qwenqwo, delving into his pockets to find his trusty pipe and his baccy. 'A bowl for you?'

Alan shook his head. 'But I wouldn't say no to the flagon, when you manage to find it. That's if there's a drop left after all that philosophising.'

'What philosophising?'

'The whinging that you have subjected all and sundry to for the last twenty leagues.'

'Ah! That philosophising!'

They laughed together.

Alan muttered, with his eyes closed: 'Oh for a whole twenty-four hours of rest with the lovely mind-numbing ecstasy of that burning comfort sliding slowly down my throat.'

'Desist. I am persuaded.'

But still the dwarf mage took his time in tamping down the baccy in his bowl, and then lighting the thing with a stroke of flint, and then inhaling the aromatic vapours of several deep puffs, before he gave his consideration to the flagon. But then, with a rueful grin, he had the grace to toss it to Alan before partaking himself.

'Not a lot left in this!'

'I'm looking forward to a refill when I meet up with Siam, who is somewhere out there in the fleet. I saw to that essential requirement before we set out from the Garg's City of a Thousand Islands.'

Alan took a swig and almost gagged – his dry throat felt like it was on fire. He coughed, wiping his mouth, then passed the flagon back to Qwenqwo, who swigged what was left in it. Alan groaned aloud as he forced himself back into a sitting position, then took a lengthy view of the yawning panorama that confronted them. 'People warned me that Ghork Mega was a colossus, but the sheer size of it still comes as a shock.'

'Indeed.' Qwenqwo groaned, rubbing at his aching back.

'Man – it must be what, thirty miles in circumference?'

Qwenqwo put his hand out for the telescope and took a long hard look at the mountain city for himself before returning the scope. 'Did you notice the Tyrant's Citadel: a fortification within a fortification?'

'I noticed.'

'The Black Citadel was built on the very apex of the mountain. So high it gathers its own nimbus of clouds.'

Alan looked through the telescope again at the eerie fortification of the citadel, which looked about half a mile higher than the bulk of the city, with numerous spike-shaped towers among a labyrinth of adamantine black walls. He couldn't make out a single window to soften the foreboding darkness.

'It looks pretty impregnable to me.'

'No city was ever built that bested the Fir Bolg.'

It was reassuring to have such an indomitable friend. Alan folded away telescope, stuffing its brass bulk into his sealskin pocket. 'Even so, it will take some powerful weapons to break through those fortifications.'

'Ebrit's warships have mighty cannons.'

'We'll see soon enough!'

Out there in the bay, the prince's fleet was already manoeuvring into place. Looking out over the formidable walls that confronted them, Alan reflected how the cannons of Prince Ebrit's warships, which had looked so mighty when he had first inspected them, now seemed less formidable. It was hard to imagine any bombardment that would level this terrible structure. And the threat extended beyond the walls. Within them lurked an enemy more dreadful still.

The mountain that had underpinned the Tyrant's capital had extensive rocky foothills arising out of the great sweep of the bay. For a landwards attack on the city, such as the Shee were about to begin, they would have to climb a series of steep escarpments. There was tricky ground at every step, with razor-like flint outcrops, and then a final approach that wound, like a writhing snake, up to the massive bulwark of the south gate. All the while the attacking army would be under bombardment from the bronze cannons poking, like the bristles of a porcupine, from the topmost half of the massive curtain walls. And even if they made it to the south gate, which was the only logical approach from where they'd stopped, they had to get past its secondary fortress, which was recessed into a granite cliff and flanked by two massive hexagonal towers, also housing cannons.

There were lamps aglow within the towers, even now in the light of morning, which suggested a prevailing gloom within those heavy walls. They could only worry any potential attacker all the more. Alan wasn't immune to their fearsome aspect. It was awesome to think that these formidable defences would be the setting for a battle that would soon determine the fate of Tír.

Alan had no need to look for Kate. He sensed her approach through his oraculum as readily as she must have sensed him, and he climbed to his feet, ready to help her alight from her onkkh's back. When they hugged, it was inevitably an awkward embrace: too many aches and pains. Yet they still gazed into one another's eyes for a joyous moment.

'Oh, Lord!' Kate exclaimed, looking seaward.

Alan followed her gaze to where a break in the clouds illuminated the fleet in a brilliant arc of sunlight.

'Spectacular, isn't it!'

The great sweep of bay was dense with the colourful sails and decorated woodwork of what, back on Earth, would have been the equivalent of medieval battleships. But they differed in many respects from any pictures Alan recalled. They were much larger than his admittedly vague memory of sailing ships, more angular, and, to his vision, more complex. It was a mistake ever to think of this world as Earth.

Kate said: 'Sorry – I stink!'

'Who doesn't, after that ride?'

They looked, as one, in the direction of the young Kyra, some hundred yards or so seaward of their position, as she metamorphosed to human form surrounded by dozens of aides.

'They're already marking out their encampment on the shore.'

'It's fortunate the bay is miles wide.'

The Shee were commandeering a sizeable section of it to accommodate not only the warriors who had shared the hazardous journey north with him, but also the multitude who were coming to shore from the carriers out there in the crowded bay. Alan's eyes searched in vain through the masses of great cats for the smaller, darker figure of Bétaald, who would be so important in advising Ainé during the coming siege. Alan would meet up with them both soon to plan the opening strategy. He was also looking forward to meeting Siam and Kehloke again when the Olhyiu chief was released from navigating Prince Ebrit's fleet. From what Qwenqwo had intimated, he too was looking forward to some rest and relaxation with the chief. Alan could imagine the consumption of baccy and flagons.

'Maybe we need an area to ourselves,' Alan said.

Kate smiled. 'Good thinking.'

'Count me in,' Qwenqwo said.

Alan looked about them. 'And Mo, where is she?'

'With Turkeya, most likely,' Kate replied. 'They seem close again.'

'I'm glad to hear it.'

'I worry about her, Alan.'

Alan also worried about Mo. He knew that he hadn't given enough time to her concerns on the last occasion they had spoken, but the truth was he didn't really know what to think. He wasn't sure he understood what was alarming her, and the distractions had been such he had never found the time to chat further – and from the look of what they faced here, he doubted there would be much time in the future either.

'We must help her, Alan.'

'I know, but I don't understand what's going on with her and I'm worried I'll give her unhelpful advice.'

'I don't know either, but I aim to find out.'

She hugged him then, a full body hug, ignoring the fact that they both stank.

He said: 'Do you think it's something to do with Mark – the fact we don't know what happened to him?'

'I suspect it's part of it. She misses him, and the Temple Ship.'

'I miss him too, Kate. I miss our friendship. I miss all four of us doing things together.'

'Me too!'

Alan was aware of Qwenqwo, his pipe now smoked, allowing them the courtesy of leaving them to it. He sensed that the Kyra and Bétaald were also allowing him and Kate the same courtesy. He kissed her, then made an apologetic face. 'See you later, Kate. Right now I need to talk strategy with Qwenqwo, Iyezzz, the Kyra, Bétaald . . . But you're welcome to join us.'

'I think I'd prefer to wash the dust out of my pores!'

He held onto her hand for a moment or two before freeing her to head towards the growing city of tents.

But he was already wondering if, now they were here, he should routinely include Magtokk in their war council meetings. Magtokk knew the Tyrant better than any of them. Who better to prepare them for surprises – unknowns? His tip about the eclipse had made all the difference, encouraging the Gargs to join their cause.

'Signals of welcoming?' Qwenqwo interrupted his ruminations, the dwarf mage sidling in to join him now Kate was gone.

Alan's attentions were directed to the sky, which crackled with exploding rockets, erupting into fireworks, some originating from the aides on land, but most of them coming from the ships in the encroaching ocean. As if in response to a signal, Bétaald and the Kyra joined Alan and Qwenqwo. All four of them stood, inhaling the fresh scents of the wind-swept prairie as they watched the vast fleet of galleons pull slowly closer to the coast, perhaps still three miles distant from the breakwaters below.

Alan asked Bétaald: 'What happens now?'

'The remaining warriors will arrive to join us and the siege weapons will be unloaded.'

Alan's eyes moved back to the enormous walls that confronted them, and within them the spires and towers of the vast proliferation of city buildings, streets, squares and citadel.

The Kyra read his mind: 'Giant walls harbour predictable weaknesses.'

'Such as?'

'The size of the army necessary to defend them: it would have to be vast to be so widely spread.'

'How vast, do you reckon?'

'A good half a million troops. And that is merely foot soldiers. There will be forces ranged against us that we cannot yet imagine.'

Alan glanced across to see that Qwenqwo was nodding, as if the Kyra's words confirmed his own thoughts. 'How is that a weakness?' he asked.

Bétaald said, 'Its vastness provokes logistical difficulties in strategy and coherence. Those logistical difficulties will become ever more difficult as attrition bites.'

Alan didn't like the idea of a war of attrition, but that was exactly what a siege called for. It was beyond his experience. Even as he mused on it, there was a thundering sound from a row of vessels that had arrived within firing range. They were broadsiding the walls of the city. Snatching the telescope, Alan could get a much clearer view of what was happening: a cluster of a dozen or so of the smaller warships in Prince Ebrit's fleet must be softening up the target by testing the curtain walls with their cannons. Further out in the bay were the really big ships that would soon come into play: the enormous warships the Carfonese called their Leviathans. Alan studied the complex sequence of firing, which followed an alternating pattern. Even then, the ships heeled over some twenty degrees with each cannonade.

'But they're missing the walls. They're firing right over them.'

Qwenqwo shook his head. 'These cannons are too light to do damage to the walls.' He lifted his pipe from his mouth and spat out some tobacco-coloured saliva. 'It's a risky trick that Ebrit's sailors explained to me: they make the iron cannonballs a mite smaller to allow for expansion, then they heat them in bellowed forges until they are red hot and fire them from their cannons. The heavy bronze cannon are able to fire blazing cannon balls without exploding. These cannonballs are not required to break down walls. What they bear is fire. Their aim is to set the roofs of buildings ablaze.'

Alan thought about that. 'Why risky?'

'The forges burn on ships built of wood.'

Alan turned his telescope onto the city beyond the walls. Smoke was beginning to curl into the sky.

'I see: it's working.'

Qwenqwo brought out his runestone from a pocket. 'Fire is a brutal weapon. But it is also a most potent weapon in a siege.'

'War is war,' the Kyra spoke.

Qwenqwo gazed down at his runestone within the cradle of his two hands. Alan saw it flicker into life. The runes within it started to glow. 'But we may confidently assume that our enemy is resourceful enough to counter with some strategies of his own.'

Alan looked at the Kyra, and Bétaald. He realised that between the army that had marched here and the reinforcements coming to land off the cargo ships, something close to the entire army of Shee were here. 'You're risking everything.'

Neither Kyra nor Bétaald replied.

'I'm sorry – have I said something wrong?'

'You must understand, Mage Lord . . .' Qwenqwo checked

himself and looked up at Alan askance. 'This is a day so many of our world have prayed for. Many, many indeed were those who never lived to see it finally arrive.'

'Yet, you seem troubled?'

'Only a fool would be other than troubled. We are fighting the most dangerous enemy this world has ever known. You think the worst is over in our march to this spot, but here real fortitude will be called for.'

The Kyra and Bétaald excused themselves. Meanwhile, Alan waited for the thunder of another broadside to pass.

'What sort of peril are you thinking about, Qwenqwo?'

'The mind of the Tyrant is surely impervious to the likes of me. I am a fighter, not a thinker, and our enemy is known to be clever and perfidious beyond human ken.'

Alan looked out over the scene again. The huge bay was already becoming crowded and busy. The Kyra and Bétaald were heading towards what was evolving into the Shee encampment. Here, the commanders had already begun the process of distributing troops; some to assist the disembarkation of still more reinforcements, others unloading the siege machinery at the beaches below; still others were deployed to construct a defensive perimeter around the encampment itself: working with the aides to dig out a deep defensive ditch, and using the dirt and rock to deepen it on the inside lip. Shee were already patrolling the barrier. Elsewhere, fires were springing up to cook the food necessary to feed the multitude of Ebrit's army and navy. The Shee and Olhyiu did not cook their meat. They were more than capable of devouring what they needed fresh and bloody from the hunt or the fishermen's nets.

There was a lot Alan needed to think about. From his memories of the Battle of Ossierel, he knew that the aides would play a more important role than might be assumed. They had so many different qualities when it came to warfare that they amounted to an additional layer of knowledge and expertise. Some were very closely involved with the Shee warriors; helping them through their rapid metamorphoses, dressing them for battle, supporting them, perhaps in ways he knew little about; others were experts in tactics, or forging weapons. It occurred to Alan that the aides were as secretive as the Shee, and that secrecy interested him. Assuming that, unlike the Shee, they did not breed from mother-sister to daughter-sister, they must have men-folk back home, but he had never heard them talk of it. How, Alan now wondered, did the two very different races live together back in their Guhttan homeland?

His relationship with the young Kyra would be very important in the days to come. They felt a lot closer than when she had first arrived to take her mother-sister's place. Since he had restored her mother-sister's memory, they had truly grown to trust one another. How important might those recovered memories of the mother-sister prove in the coming war?

Alan took another deep breath.

Even while he had been musing, a series of tents were being erected at the heart of the Shee encampment. Alan assumed that he, Kate and Mo would be included with the Shee. Kate must have retired to this encampment to wash herself clean. Would Mo see things that way? Was she somewhere out there beyond the Shee encampment, very likely with Turkeya, with the camp followers that would include the Olhyiu?

Somehow, he knew he must find the time to talk to Mo. They must all get together: he, Kate, Mo and Turkeya, to spend an hour or two chatting. Maybe then he might even get the chance to understand her.

Goya's Nightmares

Mark leaned the RPG on the near side of the Mamma Pig and fired on a butcher's shop that was already ablaze. They had no idea if there were Paramilitaries inside, but the shop's window looked out onto a bottleneck where the two-lane entrance road was constricted to a single lane – the perfect place for a trap – and they couldn't afford to take the chance. The front wall of the shop blew out and the roof collapsed in on it. They might have heard screaming from inside, but it was difficult to be sure against the roar of falling debris and flames and they didn't wait to find out. While Bull slammed the porthole shut, Cogwheel rammed the Pig through the shell of a burned-out lorry, the side of which had a triple infinity spray-painted on it in glaring orange. They emerged through blazing rubble into what had been the high street.

The central part of the town showed the typical rural

English pattern of new build sprawl around the rambling, original streets.

Tajh said: 'Slow down a mite, Cogwheel. And hush, everyone.'

Cogwheel slowed and they hushed.

'Open up the flaps on the screen a little more.'

Cogwheel opened the flaps.

'Now listen.'

They could hear people screaming.

'Can anybody tell where it's coming from?'

'Seems to be coming from close up ahead – maybe to the left.'

'I believe,' Nan said, 'it's coming from more than one direction.'

'Mark?'

Mark stared ahead. It was close to two in the afternoon with a winter sun barely above the horizon. The forward view beyond thirty yards was lost in the misty air tinted by snow, but he could see black smoke pouring out of blazing terrace cottages.

'Let's try opening the flaps a bit more.'

They all looked forward again through the snow that was melting onto the windscreen. All they could make out was ruin and smoke.

'Where is everybody?'

'The Paramilitaries must be forcing people to gather together somewhere convenient.'

'Like where?'

'Some building. A school maybe – or a church.'

Cogwheel cursed between clenched teeth. 'Where to now?'

Tajh said: 'We look for the green.'

'What green?'

'These villages always have a green. It'll be right at the heart of the old part of the town. Just keep on driving until we come to it.'

Cogwheel revved again, the guillotine blades at the front of the Pig ramming aside the burning wreck of a Post Office delivery van. Mark sat beside Padraig, both leaning back against the offside porthole.

'How are you, Padraig?'

'I've felt better.'

'Even so, it's great to be able to talk to you again. There's so much we need to discuss.'

'Alan? Kate . . .?'

'They're alive. At least, they were the last time I saw them. We'll talk soon. We have a lot of catching up to do. And Nan and me, we need your advice.'

Everybody aboard the Pig slewed to the right as Cogwheel made a sharp left turn into a narrow lane. Another terrace of cottages was on their left and a white plastered nursery school to their right. The nursery had its own walled car park on the corner facing a crossroads.

Mark felt Padraig's hand on his shoulder. He felt the squeeze offering mute reassurance.

Cal was on his feet and bent over in the low space behind

the cab. He was pointing to something over Cogwheel's left shoulder.

'That's where they were shooting people – the green.'

'What's going on?'

'I can see bodies.'

'Bloody hell!'

'Back up, Cogwheel. See if you can get us under the cover of the car park.'

Cogwheel reversed twenty yards at speed, then pulled up inside the vee of two tall car park walls. The top of the cab just reached over the walls and allowed them to see into the triangular green across the junction.

A hail of shots rattled the front nearside of the Pig. Cogwheel said: 'I can see where the firing is coming from – the upstairs window in that gable on the other side of the green.'

'Okay,' Cal barked. 'We split into three: Cogwheel – you, Sharkey and Brett, stay back and guard the Pig. Team 1 – that's me, Bull, and Tajh – we'll deal with the shooter. Team 2 – that's the rest of you, other than Padraig – stay put until we've done that and then check out the green.'

'Roger that.'

But as soon as Team 1 had exited, Mark felt a tug on his right sleeve. He turned to see Brett grinning back at him. 'You can count me in Team 2. I ain't for hanging around while you guys have all the fun.' He hefted a pump action shotgun into view. 'Best shooter in the world at close quarters!'

They waited until they heard the thud of the RPG and looked out to see smoke issuing from the upstairs gable window. 'Okay,' Mark tapped Brett's shoulder. 'Let's you, me and Nan go check out the green.'

Wordlessly, all three of them slid out of the offside porthole, then made a dash around the edges of the wall and across the junction. They took up a new position behind a big standing stone that poked out of the grass on the northwest corner of the triangle. Looking out from behind this stone, Mark could see scattered bodies lying in the snowy grass. He could see the bodies of several dozen men and women, but no children. It looked as if the adults had been herded here before being executed. Mark and Nan also detected the presence of living people in the houses nearby. Terrified families – people hiding.

He spoke to Nan, mind-to-mind: <You spot the enemy?>

<No.>

They heard the chatter of a Minimi in the distance. Cal and Bull had encountered the shooter. Brett was staring at the carnage with a bemused expression.

Mark spoke to him: 'So, what's our military strategist thinking?'

'I know Cal has a theory about evil being a kind of seed that just needs the right soil to grow. Looking at this slaughter, I think maybe he has a point.'

'I'm not sure if it's that simple.'

'What's your point?'

Mark aimed a kick at a couple of magpies that were

making patterns in the snow and cawing at him. 'You notice, there are no kids.'

Brett nodded. 'What do you reckon?'

'I think it may be more organised than you think. And maybe the missing kids might be the whole point of it.'

'Yeah? Where do you reckon we'll find 'em?'

'Thinking back to the Scalpie in London, maybe a church.'

'Yeah?'

'I'm also beginning to think that that's where we're going to find the presence that Nan and I sensed through our oracula.'

'You got yourself an idea of what's going on?'

'I think it could be a similar presence to what we sensed back in that burning Bedfordshire town on our way out of London. Nan and I think it could be a Scalpie. Perhaps converting the children to adoration of the Tyrant of the Wastelands.'

'Goddam!'

'My guess is that the Earth is destined to become another wasteland – like Nan would tell you about, from the history of Tír.'

'That what you reckon, Nan?'

Nan nodded. 'There is always a purpose behind the Tyrant's malice. He plays games with wars, terror, cruelty, but there is always some ulterior purpose behind it.'

'We back to magic here?'

Mark shrugged. 'Nan knows the Tyrant a lot better than

I do, and I witnessed strange and terrible things back on Tír.'

Nan spoke thoughtfully: 'I think the Fáil is at the heart of everything. The Fáil and now the Black Rose. I think it is all part of the Tyrant's strategy.'

'Then help me, you and the crew. Y'all got to help me find out what that strategy really is. That's the only way we're going to win this war.'

Mark lifted his arm and waved back towards the Pig. There was the sound of the heavy engine starting up, then Cogwheel backed out onto the narrow road and came up behind them over the small junction. Brett climbed in through the offside porthole, leaving Mark and Nan to straddle the steps on either side of the cab. Cogwheel reversed off the green before swinging through a bone-jarring arc, heading away from the massacre and towards the visible steeple of a small church, surrounded by a walled off graveyard. There was a lych-gate in the low stone wall surrounding the graveyard, capped by a wooden arch that was much too narrow for the Pig.

'Cogwheel!'

'Okay – gotcha!'

Cogwheel rammed the ten ton vehicle through the gate, disintegrating the wooden structure and tumbling the stone wall, then barged through the graveyard, tumbling gravestones everywhere as they barrelled towards the stone church that lay at the heart of it all. There was no hiding their approach. Any enemy in a two-hundred-yard radius would have heard them, but nobody on board the Pig cared anymore. They all sensed it now, even those without an oraculum: evil radiated from the tiny church.

'Hold it, Cogwheel!'

'What?'

'Drop me and Nan off here.'

'Are you mad? You've got to wait for the others before you even think of going in there.'

'We don't have time!' Mark dropped down onto the paved surface outside the arched entrance. Nan followed him. 'Call up Cal and Bull and tell them what we're doing. Then close off the entrance with the bulk of the Pig. Be very careful. Whatever we sense knows we're coming, but it won't know about our oracula. Tell Cal and Bull we need their help.'

Brett hopped down out of the belly of the Pig. 'Hold on, fellas. I'm coming with you.' He pumped the first round into the barrel of his shotgun. 'Okay, let's roll.'

As soon as they entered, the door slammed shut behind them. They hadn't expected the chapel interior to be so dark. Blackout blinds obscured the windows of both the nave and chancel, but the dark wouldn't matter to a Scalpie. He would see through the goblin eyes of the protective swarm of Grimlings, which had perfect night vision. But Mark could see no glowing eyes, moving and swirling in the attack patterns they had experienced before. The complete dark and the utter silence were unnerving. Had they guessed wrong that the children would be here? If they were here, he and Nan should easily be able to detect their minds, though they had refrained from using their oracula outside in case they alerted the enemy to their use of magic. They scanned the interior of the chapel, greenish-black lightning flaring from their oracula. All of the furniture had been removed, but the children were present, perhaps as many as forty. They were lying prostrate on the tiled floor, their legs and arms akimbo. Their minds were frozen with terror, as well they might be given that they were surrounded by spectres.

Mark whispered, 'Nan – you seeing?'

'Yes.'

Brett was staring at what must have looked like an empty chapel to him. 'What is it – what can you guys see?'

'Phantoms . . . apparitions . . . wraiths,' Mark muttered. 'They're the same horrible things I saw creeping up out of the ground when I was walking through the streets of London with Henriette.'

'Can you do something to let me take a gander at them?'

Mark sent the visions in his and Nan's minds to Brett's. 'Lord almighty! It's Goya's nightmares.'

'What are you talking about?'

'The Spanish artist – he painted nightmares.'

Mark said, 'I can see green lines, like snail slime, running over the architectural lines of the walls and buildings, just as I saw in London. It's as if another world were leaching into our structures.'

'What's it mean?'

'I don't have a clue, but now I'm thinking about those murals Penny drew on the ceiling of the squat she shared with Gully. The City Below invading the City Above.'

Limned in the eerie phosphorescent light of Mark and Nan's oracula, the chapel was congested by transparent beings with the same shining eyes Mark recalled from his walk with Henriette; the same insane look; the same smoke-like hair. The spectres were creeping up out of the floor and in through the green snail-tracks in the walls, and once inside, they were darting everywhere. It was as if they were guided not by the solid walls, but the etched lines of the underworld. Mark recalled Henriette's actual words: *'Like de boll weevil lookin' for a home.'* He spoke them aloud.

Brett muttered: 'A boll weevil's a parasite.'

'Yeah, I know.' He stared again, at the wheeling storm of wraiths. 'Henriette said they were . . . hunting. She told me they had many appetites. I think what she was implying is that they were infesting the Razzers – the people who were setting fire to everything.'

'You think the same thing's going on right here? These wraiths are looking to take over the minds of the kids?'

'I think it could be.'

But where was the Scalpie with its protective swarm of Grimlings? Mark could sense it still within the chapel. A malicious presence was in here with them, so why had they not seen it? For a moment he was overcome by a creeping sense of fright.

Nan whispered: 'Oh, Mark – I sense it too.'

'But where . . .?'

Both of them span round to look at the door through which they had entered the chapel. There was a slow movement, as if part of the floor were rising and detaching.

Nan and Mark focused both their oracula onto the area. In the green-black light, a rising cloud – a seething monstrosity – metamorphosed as they beheld it. The figure was shrouded from head to feet in a cloak of black, and its face was contained within a cowl of the same colour. It had been on its knees, with the cowl fallen, which explained why they hadn't seen it. Its voice was little above a whisper, yet clearly enunciated, a soft, plummy voice:

'You must not interrupt the ceremony. The veneration is not yet complete.'

Brett joined Mark and Nan in staring as the cowl was withdrawn. The face emerging from its shadow was a gentle one, with kindly avuncular eyes. As more of the figure was revealed, they saw the white religious dog collar around the base of a curiously long and gangly throat.

Brett took a step towards the figure. 'I beg your pardon, Reverend! We were under the impression that the children were in danger.'

'The little ones are quite safe with me.' He *tsskk*ed. 'Those scoundrels, with their tanks and guns, why, not even they would intrude upon the house of the Lord.'

Mark grabbed hold of Brett's right shoulder. 'Brett, step back.'

'What the blazes?'

'He – it – is not human.'

'No,' Nan agreed.

'Hold on – you telling me this is the Scalpie?'

Mark said: 'It isn't a Scalpie.'

Nan added: 'It's much worse.'

Even in the few seconds they conversed, the face within the cowl had changed. Its eyes had become dark circles within whites that were blood red orbits. The face leered at them. The cowled head dropped again and the figure returned to its posture of prostration before the intended sacrifice. Even as they took a step back from it, transfixed with horror, its form *melted*, and the face of the minister was replaced by the head of a fox, its amber eyes aglow.

Brett groaned: 'Sweet Jesus!'

The cloud around it expanded rapidly, and lines of force within it boiled and seethed. Two additional faces appeared next to the fox's: one was the long face of a man with a glowing cigarette between its lips.

The man's face addressed the fox: 'What you up to, dearie? Come for a little nibble?'

A third face appeared in the cloud; a woman with purple dyed hair, her mouth open wide in a horrified scream. The cloud metamorphosed once more, and many more faces appeared; faces with frightened eyes wide open, mouths attempting to speak, and mouths gaping wide in a scream. All around the nave, surrounding the prostrate children, spectres writhed and wheeled in a buzzing swarm. There was no escape for the children, Mark, Nan, or Brett, since the monstrous being blocked the single arched door that was both entrance and exit.

Mark heard the shotgun blasts as Brett fired and pumped repeatedly. The blasts had no effect on the expanding threat. The monster began to flow over the wall behind it, extending over both the side walls and up to the ceiling. It was going to engulf the entire nave, devouring all within it.

Brett muttered: 'Darn! I'm out of shells!'

Mark saw rancid feelers reaching out for them. Nan was screaming at him, mind-to-mind: <There must be no contact. The slightest contact and it will consume us.>

He shouted back: <We've got to separate. Put distance between us. Confuse it with the choice of attack.>

Mark and Nan were now working as a single unit through both oracula. They moved as far apart as they could, so the hissing fury couldn't attempt to catch them both in a single vaporous sweep. But the little church was too confined to allow them to move very far apart and the unconscious children would soon be exposed to attack. The vile being reached out further and further, its amoeba-like protrusions extending to cover everything. Mark and Nan directed their twin torrents of blue-black lightning against the darting, flowing danger, but even as the lightning poured over the spectral heads and pod like spidery arms, the being ensheathed itself in a force of his own; a green glow that insulated it against the attacking force of the Third Power. Even death was powerless against it.

Mark heard Nan cry out in pain.

He risked a glance in her direction. He sensed a wound to her forearm. She had managed to twist to avoid the penetration to her heart, but her teeth were bared in a rictus of agony as she forced herself to stay standing, still sending a torrent of the Third Power against the terrible spectacle.

Mark heard an alien whisper of seduction in Nan's mind, overwhelming her senses, willing her to become one with it. The horrific thought entered his mind: even if he and Nan were dead already, was it possible – a horrifying thought – that they could be absorbed by this vile, indestructible being? Would their *power* be absorbed by this creature?

The shock of this thought awakened a new determination in Mark. Even though he shared Nan's pain, he redoubled the force of his oraculum against the cloud. He deluged the figure with blue-black lightning. He felt its hold on Nan weaken, but his attack wasn't powerful enough to kill it. It had taken so much out of him that the strength was now draining from his body, and all resistance with it.

There was an explosion next to Mark's right ear; Brett had reloaded the shotgun and had fired it point blank into the leering fox's face. That shotgun blast appeared to hurt the thing more than any other blow had so far; dark blood leached out of the animal snout, its left eye reduced to a pit of gore.

Mark's voice sounded husky, croaky, as he spoke to Brett: 'I think, maybe, the fox is more special to it than the other faces.'

In those few moments, Mark was aware that Brett was pumping the gun, getting ready to fire again. It bought Mark a tiny respite, sufficient to let him take a step backwards. He had to do something to protect the children, but he was dizzy – the senses he still shared with Nan were becoming confused. And he had forgotten how closely packed the children were on the floor. He tripped and fell backwards onto the huddled bodies. But his eyes never left the single functioning eye of the fox's head, which blinked once, a closure in slow-motion, then re-opened: a dark pit within a crater of blood. Mark read the resolve there. It would ignore Brett's shotgun and any danger to itself: it reached out a cloud-like limb, ready to extend it into Mark's heart.

Mark raised his left arm to block the attack. He saw the pod-like tentacle rise, in a blur of anticipation, like the strike of a rattlesnake . . .

Then he heard a new crackling, and the air around him was consumed with a new flame, thunderous and echoing. At the same moment, he witnessed a look of shock in the rancid fox's eye. And then that same eye performed a ballet, turning around in an impossible circle so the veined white back of the eyeball was directed towards him. He realised that the thing was attempting to look behind it, to where a glowing runed blade, curved as a scimitar, was cleaving through the smoky flesh of its being. The cutting edge of the blade ignited the flesh of the monster as it cleaved and cleaved again, burning through flesh and green-glowing protection as if through beeswax.

Mark was looking at a Fir Bolg battleaxe, its runes ablaze with a throbbing power he had only ever seen wielded in the fist of his friend, Qwenqwo Cuatzel, dwarf mage of the Fir Bolg.

But Qwenqwo couldn't possibly be here.

Beyond the falling monster, a tall, emaciated figure filled the silhouette of the now wide-open door. It was Padraig, his fist clasped around the central hilt of the sigmoid bladed battleaxe. He had eschewed casting the weapon, choosing to spin it about the fulcrum of his fist to make it into an executioner's blade. The twin blades tore into the monstrous cloud, extinguishing face after face, a havoc of destruction until not a single one remained amid the stinking morass of putrescent flesh.

It took the crew hours to rescue the children from the despoiled nave of the church; time enough for Cal and Bull to join them after clearing the last of the Paramilitaries from the town. Now, the Pig had ferried the crew back to the green, where survivors from the town's population were gathering around their dead. Brett was standing at the crossroads, a cigar clamped between his teeth, his shotgun thrown over his left shoulder. The air was full of smoke and ash, and many of the town's buildings were still burning, their rafters crashing downwards, sending out flares of sparks even in the near distance. The crew were doing what they could to help the survivors – making sure the terrified kids had adults to take care of them. They were also making sure the survivors understood the importance of abandoning the town.

'Don't you get it?' Brett remonstrated with an elderly couple who were resistant to leaving their home. 'The bad guys will come back. They'll come looking for what went wrong with their plans here. You sure don't want to be around when they do.'

Mark passed the couple a loaf of bread and some cans from the Pig's stores. Behind them, Tajh and Sharkey were helping those who were identifying the dead. All the while the snow fell without cease. Mark watched as the surviving townspeople gathered the bodies into family groups. It was heartbreaking to watch and he wanted to help, but the light would be gone in three quarters of an hour and the crew needed to head out. Cal and Bull rode up to them on two captured BMWs. Cal took Mark to one side.

'We got us some captured uniforms – and a package that could prove a useful distraction. As a matter of fact, it's given me an idea about how we might get through Seebox's cordon.'

'Yeah?'

'We'll need two outriders from here on in. Given Bull and Sharkey's injuries, that's got to be you and me,' he said to Mark.

'Okay, but I'll need to warn Nan.' Mark looked around and spotted her close to the Pig, helping Brett. A father, with a frightened family in tow, was baulking at the advice that they might have to flee the town in such wintry weather.

'Where can we possibly go to?'

Brett advised him. 'Take what you need to keep warm and rig up a makeshift shelter. Head north, but make sure you keep off the major roads and avoid any towns and cities.'

Mark walked up to them, Cal following, and nodded agreement. 'We've sent a message to HQ about what we've found here. They're getting ready to fight back against Seebox and his forces. Hide in the woods. Tell everybody you meet to do the same. In time, somebody will get to you. The Resistance is coming.'

Mark explained to Nan that he would be taking one of the bikes and acting as an outrider, but he wanted to talk to Padraig before they parted. They found him leaning on the big standing stone on the Green. Mark insisted on shaking his hand.

'You saved our lives.'

'I owe you my own.'

'What happened to the battleaxe?'

'Back with Brett – stowed in the Pig.'

Mark smiled a rueful smile. He recalled the last time he had shaken Padraig's hand. It had been inside the old forge at the back of the sawmill, in Clonmel, when Padraig had agreed to let Mark help him forge the blade of Alan's spear – the Spear of Lug. It all seemed so long ago. Today, Padraig's handshake was a lot frailer than Mark remembered it.

'Sorry it took me so long to get to you. Even then I almost didn't have the strength to use the battleaxe. It's such a heavy blade.'

'It was lucky for us that you were here,' Mark replied.

Brett came over to join them, still smoking what was now the stogie of his cigar. He took a last puff on it before squashing it into the snow at his feet. 'I guess we're about ready to head out?'

Nan said: 'First, tell me – there was something you said, back in the church, about an artist?'

Brett scratched at the dark stubble over his cheek. 'You mean Goya and his nightmares? You never heard of Goya?'

'No,' she said.

'Well now! I gather that Mark here is taking one of the bikes, so maybe I can accompany you back to the Pig?' He patted his arm, indicating she could link it to accompany him. 'What Goya did, he painted a whole series of nightmare cartoons: Witches and goblins, mad gods, demons. But every one of them with human faces.'

'Ah!'

'But these pictures – the witches and demons and things – people called them Goya's demons. Some thought he was mad, driven insane by the cruelties he witnessed during the Napoleonic wars, but others think there's something deep in human nature that he recognised – something like those spectres back there in the church.'

They heard a child scream nearby – some little one frightened out of his or her wits, becoming hysterical before an adult's arms had time to comfort it.

Nan said: 'I think I understand. There are things that we sense, perhaps in our dreams – our nightmares. Things we can't pretend to understand, or explain, in the cold light of day.'

Brett hesitated outside the nearside porthole. 'Goya blamed the sleep of reason. When reason sleeps, that's when the nightmares come flooding in.'

Cal, who was already seated on one of the two BMW bikes, said: 'Can we all get a move on. Cogwheel's waiting.'

Mark watched Nan climb in through the porthole, where she huddled down along with Brett and Padraig. Then he headed for the second of the heavy bikes, slipped on the Paramilitary jacket and helmet he found on the seat, and powered up to ride point with Cal.

Owly Gizmo

The thing fluttered clumsily through the air to land, with a tinkling sound, on Gully's left shoulder. He had half expected it to weigh a ton because it was made out of steel, but it was astonishingly light. He could feel its claws, the size of a baby's fist, take a sharp grip of his skin through the jacket. The head spun through ninety degrees to look at him with ball bearing eyes. Its pupils were steely black enclosed by irises of gold. At the dead centre a pinpoint of the purest, fiercest red pulsated, as if the pyre of the daemon bot illuminated its inner spirit.

The slave bot seemed every bit as shocked to meet Gully as he was to meet it.

'It is customary to speak a word or two of welcome when a slave bot is introduced to its master.'

'I don't rightly know wot to say.'

'Hello, might be appropriate.'

'Hi ya!' he ventured.

It hooted back at him.

A thrill exploded through Gully. 'It's a tawny! I know because tawny owls is 'ooters!'

'Does this please you?'

'It's perfick!'

'I am flattered.'

'I can't believe you made it in that furnace.'

'Her?'

'But you told me daemon bots don't have no his nor her.'

'That is true, but I've changed my mind. Surely we can allow some flexibility – the circumstances may be taken into account.'

'Wot circumstances?'

'The companion you pine for is female. I paid heed to your requirements in her new figure – in her plumage. I confess that I also took liberties with her eyes.'

'Wif 'er eyes?'

Gully didn't know what those liberties might be any more that he knew the difference between a male and female owl's eyes.

As if reading his mind, Bad Day said: 'The females are bigger.'

'Wicked!'

'Might I encourage you to address the bot directly? Establish a working rapport.'

Gully's eyes widened still further. 'Like I got to fink up some name for it?'

'For her. And please address her directly rather than

through me. She has a daemon spirit. And where I come from—'

'Daemon bots is polite – I know.'

'Hmph!' The exclamation was as deep as a roll of thunder.

The slave bot fluttered her wings. Gully stared at this strange being perched on his shoulder – this newborn juvenile what was still looking back at him.

'I reckon I'll call you Owly Gizmo!'

Bad Day sighed. The bucket jaw wagged in a clanking rhythm that might have been a chuckle.

Gully couldn't get over the fact there was an owl perched on his shoulder. He whispered: 'You're my perfick Owly Gizmo.'

The slave bot hooted again. When Gully held out his two hands, cradled together in a bowl, she hopped down onto them, continuing to stare up into his face from her new perch.

'Look at you! You got two bushy eyebrows wot meet in the middle – an' a whiskery little beard, like some old army colonel!'

'Do I observe the manifestations of affection?'

'I like 'er, if that's wot you mean.' Gully was looking to see if the bot had ears. He couldn't see none, but she could hear him. He was sure of that. 'I know wot it means to me that she's a girl owl, but wot's it mean to 'er?'

'The donning of sexuality is complex with daemon bots. I could tell you some amusing stories.'

But Gully wasn't listening. Owly Gizmo was stretching

out her wings. The wingspan was huge, at least two feet. 'Oh, wow!' Gully preened. 'Just look at them feathers. Every single feather is perfick.'

Owly pulled in her wings and fidgeted for several moments, shuffling from foot to foot. He felt her claws digging into his skin. He could see the feathers slide over one another as she puffed up her chest. It was like – oh, wow – she was really breathing.

'You didn't, you know, put some kind of an 'eart inside of her?'

'That would be telling.'

Gully was entranced by it: a heart of fire beating inside that puffed up chest! He didn't dare to pinch himself for fear he might wake up and spoil the dream. He studied the wings, the body, the speckled plumage. He brushed his fingers down over her stocky little head, her shoulders, her wings and tail, thrilling at the finish of her ivory and chocolate brown beauty. He lifted her up close, only inches from his eyes, to admire her beak and big eyes, set wide in the almost human face.

'You're amazing – you know that? You came out of all that bangin' an' clankin' an' all them lightning sparks.'

Owly Gizmo just looked back at him fiercely, then she climbed up his body to get back onto his shoulder and, with a shove of her claws, took off, flapping up into the air and soaring around the enclosed space like a glider wheeling on a draught of air.

'She's a real good learner.'

'A chip off the old block.'

She landed on a rusty rail and then, with the tottering balance of a tight-rope walker, she waddled along the rail, her body rolling from side to side as she placed one foot determinedly after another.

'Look at you! Gorgeous – that's wot you are. You're my gorgeous Owly Gizmo marching along like some old colonel.'

She cocked her head at him, from a distance of ten feet away and opened her beak and hooted.

Gully cheered.

The owl took off again in wobbly flight, her wings beating a fraction too slowly for her weight, and headed away from him down one of the gargantuan shady tunnels.

'Hey – wot you up to?'

'I think she wants to play.'

'Like 'ide an' seek?'

When Gully climbed back onto his feet he almost fainted. The shock of the arrival of Owly Gizmo had made him forget that he was starving. He hadn't eaten in what must be days. If he stayed on here, in Bad Day's lair, he was going to starve to death, but still he wanted to follow the bot.

'Hey, you leadin' me someplace?' he called into the tunnel. He put his fingers in his mouth and blew an ear-shattering whistle.

Owly caught on and returned to hover a few feet from Gully. He pointed at his open mouth and performed an eating action. Then he aped a drinking movement and made swallowing noises.

'You get the idea? I could do wiv a bite to eat and a cuppa rosy lee?'

Those raptor eyes beheld his own.

He added: 'In case you don't get it, being some kind of a foreigner, that's Cockney slang for "tea".'

Owly Gizmo performed another swivelling motion with her head, but this time she looked at Bad Day as if to question him. Then she fluttered upwards, beating heavily against the air, before coming to a rest on a protuberance jutting out of one of the giant pillars. Gully stared up at her, a good fifty or sixty feet overhead, those eyes now tiny in the distance, but still blinking down at him from a jumble of mechanical oddments, glistening with blue and green oily sheens.

Was she expecting Gully to fly up there and join her?

'No way, gel!'

Owly Gizmo blinked.

Gully reached out and touched the surface of the pillar. 'Ouch!' He retracted his hand with shock. The pillar wasn't made out of steel at all, as he had imagined. It felt more fibrous, like the surface of a lump of coal. And there was a charge in it, like it was carrying perilous currents of energy.

'Come back down 'ere!' he shouted.

Even as he was shaking his fist at the distant bot, Gully felt himself yanked off his feet and tossed into the metallic maw of the giant. He barely had time to slither across the rough iron floor and shove his back up against the wall before Bad Day lifted an arm up, took a grip of the pillar and hoisted himself upwards some thirty feet in a single pull.

'Hey, you can't haul your weight up there!'

But the daemon bot wasn't listening. Giant hand over giant hand, he began to hoist them up in a series of huge and jarring elevations.

Pain lanced through Gully's elbow as he rolled around in Bad Day's head again. He didn't dare to keep his eyes open – the distance down to the furnace chamber was already a hundred feet. Then, for some reason, they arrived at a halt. Wincing, Gully peered out of the open jaw to see a junction. The pillar they were ascending had joining up with a second, like a fork in the roots of a colossal tree. And the direction of ascent was changing. Instead of vertical, the angle was now distinctly off true.

Realisation flooded Gully's mind. *These ain't no pillars. These must be the roots of the Black Rose!* The realisation terrified him.

Owly Gizmo was somewhere nearby. Gully could hear the tinkling chime of her wings beating. Then, for some reason, Bad Day stopped climbing and lowered his jaw, as if in an invitation for Gully to emerge. He clambered out, cradling his injured elbow and staring around at a roomy place filled with grey opalescent light. He couldn't make it out clearly because his glasses were caked with oily smudges.

'Where are we?'

Bad Day declined to answer.

Gully took his glasses off, spat on the lenses, wiped them clean with a rag from his pocket, then shoved them back up the slope of his nose.

Now he could see silky light flooding in from a giant cavern over to his right, and from a source below the level where he stood. A boulder, glowing with turquoise radiance, rose out of the depths immediately in front of him. A small tree sprouted from its apex, like them Chinese trees you saw on old Willow pattern plates. The trunk, branches, leaves and even the delicate blossom was pure white. It looked like it was made out of crystal. And now Gully looked harder, he could see that the background was a forest of gnarly roots with thorny projections, all writhing around one another even as they rose into the glimmering sky. Gully squinted – that couldn't possibly be the sky; they was still deep underground. It had to be . . . what would Penny call it? An 'allucination? As he continued to look into the light and clouds, he saw figures flying through the air. They looked like very big birds with stretched out bodies and wings.

The thought occurred to Gully: *maybe they ain't really birds at all?*

He thought about them monstrous things Penny had painted on the ceiling back at Our Place. These looked a lot like them – what Penny called free spirits of the wind. They wheeled and soared like angels come down out of heaven to take a gander at this subterranean world. And now he noticed them, Gully thought that maybe they had also noticed him. They was wheeling down in spirals. Gully had barely time to notice the huge stretches of diaphanous wings, the down-stretched feet, with raptor claws, the protruding mouths lined by fangs.

'Quickly!' he heard Bad Day's urgent shout.

The giant hand grabbed Gully and flung him back into the bucket mouth. Owly Gizmo followed him in, shrieking in outrage. Gully heard the squeal of joints as Bad Day shut his mouth, then they were bouncing all over the place. Even as Bad Day rocked back onto his feet and hurled himself into a new climb, the attack began.

'Wot are they?' Gully asked.

'Daemon bots of another kind.'

'Wot they want?'

'You.'

'Shit!'

'They would possess your spirit, devour your soul.'

Gully trembled with fright, hunkering down inside the mouth of Bad Day, holding on for dear life as the fliers overtook the ascending daemon bot and battered against the metal walls. The fury of the attack came from every direction. He heard their screams amid the gale of their malice.

Interloper . . .

Violator of the Sacred Skies . . .

Open the gate, fellow daemon, and let us in . . .

But Bad Day hauled them up, higher and higher, until the glittering dome of the false sky was all around them, flooding the chamber of the mouth with shafts of light.

Come – open your mind to the wonders of the Master . . .

Come join us and know the Mysteries . . .

Outside the rising giant the winged daemons still hammered and whispered. They invaded Gully's mind with sighs and moans. He caught glimpses of angular faces and pale eyes in which a horrible hunger danced and writhed.

Throw-back!

Puny earthling!

Unwanted street urchin!

The tips of their icy claws found their way into the cracks and fissures between Bad Day's giant teeth. The metalwork inside of the mouth sprouted a spider's web of frost. Gully heard the creak and squeal of tormented metal as they ripped and tugged at the hinges of the jaws, attempting to wrench them apart. With a screech, Owly Gizmo buried herself in Gully's arms.

Penny is calling you, Gully!

Penny waits for you out here with us.

Penny loves you.

Penny lusts after you.

Up and up, the giant daemon bot climbed against what was now a fearsome weight of icy bodies, their rage a thunder of hammer blows on every inch of Bad Day's armour. The light dimmed as the daemons' bodies covered Bad Day and his climb slowed. There were longer and longer delays in between each pull and the voices of the daemons came together in a single thunderous hiss.

We would consume it.

It will become one with us.

Then, abruptly, their motion changed. Gully wondered if Bad Day had let go his grip on the root. Maybe they was approaching the surface? Maybe there was some kind of a ceiling at the top of the false daylight? A sudden, dizzying leap . . .

Strewth!

Was the daemon horde through? Was they falling into the abyss?

Gully whimpered in fright.

There was a tremendous bang. Gully climbed painfully to his feet and ran to a crack; Bad Day had punched a massive hole in a mouldy brick wall. Gully could see no evidence of the daemon horde.

'Hooray – we done it! We escaped.'

The jaw clanked open. With a screech, Owly Gizmo was past him and through. Gully followed her lead, hopping off the teeth on the edge of the bucket to find himself in a pitch black space. He searched through his pockets – left middle – torch. His hands were shaking so badly he dropped it and he had to scramble around his feet to feel for its plastic shape. He switched it on.

They were in some big room with a vaulted red brick ceiling. There were broken bricks and debris all around them, though that was mainly due to Bad Day breaking through. Something was gleaming – a pyramid shape against a wall that was black with damp. Gully turned his torch on aluminium kegs of beer. It looked like the cellar of some hotel or pub, under the streets of the City.

'Yee-hah!' Gully pumped the air with his fists.

Then he winced. 'Ow – ow, ow, ow!' He had forgotten that sore elbow!

But he explored here and there and confirmed it was a cellar; there was racks of wine bottles. It made him laugh like an idiot. If only there was people up there and a market hereabouts, he'd have set up a stall and made a packet.

Bad Day was sitting on the stone-flagged floor. Even with his neck bent and his head in his hands, the top of his head was pressed against the arched ceiling.

'I must apologise for that experience. We daemon bots pride ourselves on civility.'

'Never mind! I'm still starvin'.'

Gully heard the tinkle as Owly Gizmo took off and exited through a door that stood half ajar. Meanwhile, he brushed some of the dust off his jacket before taking a closer look at the things in the room. There was a tube running out of one of the kegs. He yanked at the tap on the end of the tube, but it was stuck solid. Bad Day yanked the tube out for him, exposing Gully to a cascade of beer.

Gully sat on the wet floor and laughed, then downed enough beer to quench his thirst. He managed to wash the blood and other crud off his face and out of his hair with some bottles of gassy water. His swollen eye smarted, but at least it was open and working, and even though his head still ached and his elbow was stiff and painful, he was healing. He looked up to where the twin red beams of Bad Day's eyes shone down in sad reflection.

'Stop worrying about your stupid cousins. Fink about food. There's got to be food somewhere 'ereabouts. I'm off to take a gander.'

Gully soon discovered packets of crisps stuffed into crates. He crammed the entire contents of a packet of salt and vinegar flavour into his mouth and crunched on it as he dragged the cardboard box closer to the beer. Then he sat down in the mess and began to devour one packet after another.

Owly Gizmo flapped back in through the open cellar door, landing beside Gully with a flutter of her wings. She dropped something bloody from her beak. It was a dead pigeon. Its feathers looked mangled as if from an effort to pluck them.

Gully blinked. 'Wot you finking about, Gizmo? I'm supposed to eat it raw?'

'Forgive her! She has much to learn.'

Gully looked again at Bad Day, squeezed between floor and ceiling in that extremely uncomfortable position. 'You saved my life back there. Why'd you do it? Why'd you make Owly Gizmo for me?'

'The Master wishes that I keep you contented.'

'Why does he care about me?'

'To keep his promise to Mistress Penny.'

Gully's heart leaped.

Eternity

Penny whispered: 'I know you are here, Jeremiah – and I don't like it.'

<I have no desire to punish you.>

'I don't know what time of day it is – or even if it is day or night. I have lost all connection with time and place. I am . . . I am directionless.'

<You can demand all that you deem to lack.>

'Demand it from whom – from what?'

'From the world, the environment. If you will allow me to tutor you, from the very universe that surrounds you.'

'Oh, for goodness' sake!'

Penny wracked her brains to try to understand the bizarre possibilities that were being presented to her. Could she demand to be returned to the real world? To real consciousness?

She looked down at herself.

She pressed her fingers against her thumbs. She closed

her eyes and she opened them again. She sniffed, attempting to smell whatever might be in the air – if air truly surrounded her. She listened, though not for too long, for there was no sound whatsoever, other than the sound she made, stamping her feet a couple of times, clicking her fingers.

She clasped her hands to her face.

How was she ever going to understand this? Her life, her being had undergone such bewildering changes that it had become increasingly difficult to retain any sense of time and place. It was well nigh impossible to separate the worlds of her imagination from reality, so closely did imagination resemble and even merge with reality. If reality existed for her any more . . .

'What have I become?'

He spoke gently, calmly, without turning to face her: <Great power can be disorientating even as it is exhilarating.>

She felt something stirring, a faint vibration, as if a powerful machine were somewhere within the structure of the Rose. The vibration was coming to her through her bare feet. Penny hesitated, aware of veil after shimmering veil moving across her memories when she tried to focus on them. She couldn't bear the thought that Jeremiah was controlling her mind, her thoughts. She wanted to scream.

'You promised me free will. I will fight you if you try to control me.'

<I will not chastise you for your weakness. I am pleased

with your progress. You are a quick learner. Most important of all, you have a natural aptitude when it comes to the wielding of power.>

'I don't want the power of life and death over any other human being.'

<You have no choice, Penny Postlethwaite. I have gifted you with power beyond any that has ever been placed in the remit of a human. It is now an integral part of your being. To serve me you will make the maximum use of it.>

'I will oppose you if you try to force me to hurt people.'

<You are obstinate. How can I teach you the infinite possibilities of Dromenon if you persist in obstructing my will?>

'I will not help you to make war on Earth.'

Jeremiah manifested. He was looking at her reflection in what she now realised was the inner aspect of a petal of the Black Rose: in that same petal she saw reflected those twin orbs of darkness that were his eyes.

If only she could return to rationality and rediscover how to take control of her own ordinary thoughts, experiences, memories. 'You've tricked me – you're still manipulating me.'

He grew angry then and he turned to look at her. She felt the measure of those all black eyes focus on her, and the immense, unyielding force of his will brush against her mind.

'You swore to serve me.'

'I will not hurt people.'

'Your precious conscience – would you have me remove that useless relic of illogic in you?'

'No.'

He held her gaze, eye-to-eye. 'Have a care. There are limits to my magnanimity.'

Her teeth were clenched. In that moment of angry obstinacy on her part, and observing his reaction to it, she looked anew at him – a darkness in the form of an old man, yet a power beyond anything she could possibly imagine – one that had no need to barter with her to make her do what he wished.

She asked herself: *how dangerous is he?*

The answer came back: immensely so. More dangerous, perhaps, than she could possibly imagine. She wanted to oppose him. She wished, from the depths of her heart, to prevent him using her, taking over her will to hurt people, to wage his terrible war against her Earth.

'Penny Postlethwaite!'

Her name spoken by him now so softly, made her feel extraordinarily important to him. She felt admired, cherished, respected, something dangerously, desperately, close to what she had so longed for, moment by moment, minute by minute, year by year, from her father.

He spoke quietly, in hushed tones that emphasized his words: 'We are perilously close to a judgement in Dromenon.'

'What does that mean?'

'It means that time is pressing. My world is threatened.

Soon I shall call upon your service to assist me in my response to this threat. You must not disappoint me. You have much to learn in anticipation of such service. We must deepen your understanding with another lesson.'

Penny wilted at the thought. 'What lesson?'

She found herself looking into a terrifying pit. Its walls were hundreds of feet high, lined by iron plates, and pistons and the pumping thunder of machines. The lining walls of the pit gleamed and gurgled with oily reflection, coming from lamps of lurid red and pallid blue. She saw an extraordinary head, made up of huge blocks and fragments of industrial and agricultural machinery, with eyes that pulsed with turquoise light. The giant was hammering against an anvil the size of a truck within what might constitute a blazing forge of sorts, and the resulting noise was bedlam.

'Where is this? What's happening?'

'Look more carefully.'

She saw a small figure, minuscule when compared to the hammering giant. She recognised the awry spectacles on the sweating nose, the mop of dark curly hair . . . His face was bruised. He looked like a refugee from a war zone. 'Gully!' she shrieked his name aloud. 'Oh, Jeremiah – you promised you would not hurt him.'

'I have not hurt your urchin friend, although he is eminently capable of putting himself into harm's way all by himself. He suffered an accident while attempting to return to London. No doubt he was looking for you.'

Penny squeezed her eyes shut. She could believe that. Gully was so pig-headed when a notion took hold of him. 'Please don't punish me through him.'

'I sent my servant to save him from a perilous situation he had brought upon himself. I brought him here to safety.'

'What is that thing – the metal monster that's holding him?'

'Daemon bots have a fondness for metals. They cannot resist clothing their naked spirits.'

'That giant thing, it's hideous – terrifying. Please make it release him.'

'It is no gaoler, but a saviour. Would you have me return Gully to the danger he was rescued from?'

Penny's vision was transported to a blazing ruin, what might have once been a farm, built around an ancient building with leaded glass and mullioned windows. The buildings and compounds around them blazed and were littered with dead. She averted her eyes from this vision.

'He tried to find me?'

'He ran, but there was nowhere for him to run to. His injuries are not life-threatening. He is safe now, under the protection of my servant.'

He showed her other visions: streets, towns, cities, worlds – everything was burning, burning, burning . . .

'Why are you doing these terrible things?'

'I am at war with your world.'

Penny was struggling through a confusion of emotions,

horror, anguish, resentment, rage . . . She wanted to scream at him, but a tiny chip of ice in her heart warned her that it would achieve nothing. And then a fear began to grow in her, an inkling perhaps of a deeper understanding.

'You said that the Rose is some kind of machine?'

'Your world of science discovered nuclear power. You affected to own it, to control it. Yet is not the natural world already replete with such power?'

'What are you talking about?'

'The star that greens your planet.'

'You're talking about the sun? The Rose . . . it's linked to the sun?'

'What more natural and befitting than to construct a machine designed to feed off your source of life?'

Penny saw her horrified face reflected in those emotionless all black eyes.

<So now you understand that time is pressing. Your understanding must deepen.>

Penny wasn't listening. All she could think about was the fact that Jeremiah intended to destroy the Earth. That was the purpose of the Black Rose. The Black Rose was feeding off the sun, drawing energy from it to do something monumental, something terrible. She must discover a way of confounding Jeremiah's plans.

Penny wished she had Gully here to talk to about it. However stubborn, and pragmatic, he had always been sensible. What would Gully say about what was happening?

He would have reduced it to something ordinary. He would have called upon her common sense.

Stop, look, listen!

But it wasn't possible to fall back on what had been safe and simple in the past. Nothing was safe or simple anymore.

The Black Rose was at the heart of all that was happening. That terrible sight must be visible from anywhere still standing in London. It was probably visible for many miles outside London. It was metamorphosing from moment to moment. It infused the air about it with strange charges, colours, thunderous crackling sounds, to remind you that it was forever active, forever forming and reforming within itself, as if . . . as if it were strangely, terrifyingly alive. The utter alienness of it filled Penny's heart with dread.

'Oh, Gully!'

He was the only one, other than her parents, who had ever cared for her. He was the only one who had made it obvious that he loved her. She knew she had hurt him because she couldn't bear to be touched. What she had done to him was wrong. She so wished she hadn't run from him. She wished she could turn back time back and do things differently. She wished she could have spoken to Gully about what she had been thinking and feeling, and maybe then he would have talked her out of that final exploration of the City Below.

The City Below . . .

The City Below was dangerous. It was worse than dangerous. It was . . . monstrous. And Jeremiah was at the heart of it. He was inhuman. But did that mean that he was also wicked? He saw such moralising as meaningless. He had told her that morality was just a human invention. There was no morality in nature. Was he right? What was he really up to? Why had he come to London? Why did London have to be at the heart of it all?

Question after question queued for answers in her mind.

Still, Penny felt that she was making progress little by little in her examination of what was going on.

She had a flashback to something Jeremiah had told her, right at the very beginning, when they had talked about his impending war with Earth. She recalled his reply when she had asked him why he was here in London:

<What you sense is the coming war.>

War!

She focused her still slightly hazy, dreamy mind on that word. War was another relevant word – an altogether relevant fact.

<Your world has involved itself in a very ancient war in another world. It has taken sides against me. I attempted to be reasonable. I offered terms. But all appeals to reason failed.>

An ancient war in another world . . .?

It made no sense to Penny, this talk of a war in another world. Why was she important to his extending this war to Earth?

I must not dwell on imponderables. I must focus on facts.

She would have eaten and performed bodily functions over the days, and possibly weeks, of her time here, otherwise she would be dead. Yet, she had no memory of doing so. That meant Jeremiah had to be controlling her even when she was unaware of it.

He's controlling me. He's controlling every single aspect of my existence. He knows when I breathe, when I blink. He listens in to my heartbeat, my every thought, my every feeling. Even now, he knows how much I resent his controlling me. He will prevent any move I make to resist him.

But was that true? Was Jeremiah able to listen in to her every thought?

She had remembered something that now seemed important: Jeremiah's words. <*You only need to think it and it will be so*> he'd said.

Was it possible that she might discover something of Jeremiah's purpose through contact with the Akkharu? But how could she possibly communicate with the slug beasts? Up to now her only avenue of communication with them was through the mind-to-mind transmission of the metamorphosing images that Jeremiah had explained as blueprints.

Penny tried to clarify her thoughts. Then she thought, determinedly, clearly: *I would communicate with the Akkharu . . .*

She was standing within a very confusing landscape, half nightmare, half fairytale. Strange creatures peered out at her from behind an explosion of even stranger vegetation. The Akkharu were close. In her mind she saw the black discordant shapes that were their system of communication constantly changing against the ash white background.

Then, abruptly, she felt more at ease with the dark mystery of it. She began to interpret the message in their changing beauty.

The message was brilliantly colourful, like a proliferation of opulent flowers – but these were not flowers. There were no definable leaves, no petals. These were structures in a landscape, buildings that followed organic shapes. She watched the blueprints blend and change, and blend and change again. She knew now that she was within the common mind of the Akkharu, the creative womb where the ideas were thought up, toyed with, reshaped and altered until found to be satisfactory. And that made her wonder if she might be able to talk to the swarm.

Let me see the Akkharu.

In the blink of an eye, she was among the huge slug-beings, watching how their bodies moved through undulations within their amorphous forms. She looked more closely at their sideways mounted mouths, which were assembling crystals into fibrils that resembled silky blue-black wires. How could such lowly-looking creatures create such architectural wonders?

To communicate she would need to convert her spoken words to three-dimensional mathematical shapes in her mind. She would have to imagine the shapes even as she spoke the words aloud:

'Are you aware of me? Do you know who I am?'

<We sense you. You are the chosen.>

The response had been immediate and intelligent. Penny was so astonished she had to stop to think. 'I presume that you really are the Akkharu?'

<We are the weavers of the holy chardizz.>

'Chardizz?'

<What you call stardust.>

Penny hesitated again: 'What are you weaving the chardizz into?'

No reply.

She thought about the silence. Were the Akkharu forbidden to answer that question? If so, who had so forbidden them? It could only be Jeremiah. She rephrased her question: 'What is it you aspire to?'

Still no reply.

Perhaps in the silence there was useful information? Perhaps she was not failing to make contact, but asking the wrong questions. She rephrased her question: 'Do you dream?'

<We dream.>

Communication, again! Had she sensed a frisson of excitement in the otherwise placid beast?

'What do you dream of?'

<Eternity.>

The reply shocked her; it wasn't what she had

anticipated. On the one hand it was vague and abstract, but on the other hand it was tantalisingly interesting.

She wasn't sure what that answer really meant. *Eternity.* From what little she knew of it, eternity was a central aspiration of many of the major religions. Up to this moment, all she had ever seen of the Akkharu suggested that a common mind followed higher instructions like a machine; but a machine could never have formed that reply. It made Penny wonder if there was something else going on in their minds. Could it be that they concealed individual consciousness, higher intelligence, even, by hiding behind their swarm identity? People in factories did something similar. Penny knew this because she recalled a television programme – one of the very few Father had encouraged her to watch – that showed how workers on an assembly line communicated among themselves as they worked – nodding their heads, fashioning unspoken words on their lips, reading other's lips.

Was this instructive?

Looking at it from this angle, the jarring, mind-arresting images – the three dimensional, metamorphosing blueprints – might mean something quite different to what she had imagined. Not the wonderful language of mathematics that Jeremiah had beguiled her with, but overwhelming orders from their Master; brute instruction of such compulsion that they overwhelmed any individual consciousness?

The more Penny thought about it, the more she came to

question her previous assumptions about the Akkharu. Their slug shapes, devoid of eyes, and their rudimentary bodies, might have deceived her into thinking they weren't intelligent. What if the Akkharu were more complex and sensitive than she had assumed? What if they didn't need eyes, or ears, or the manipulative limbs of humans?

It startled her.

In the few books and films that she had seen, highly intelligent beings, whether godly or aliens from outer space, had been depicted as humans, often with film-star handsomeness. Artists from classical times had also painted or sculpted beautiful people to denote civilisation and intelligence. But what if that was a quintessentially human construct? What if the Akkharu were highly intelligent, however alien that intelligence might be?

To create the wonders they did using the crystals they called chardizz, they must be attuned to their environment through some alternative sensory organs. They must be capable not only of perceiving the world around them, but of being inspired by it. *How do the Akkharu sense the world around them?* Then she thought: *bats and cats!* Bats could detect the landscape about them even in the dark through their sonar. And cats could feel the proximity of their prey through their whiskers.

Penny examined the slug beast nearest to her more acutely. Its skin, which she had taken to be smooth, was not actually smooth at all. It was covered with scaly ridges. And wherever there was a scale, a tiny hair-like thing poked out. She was just beginning to appreciate how much further that realisation might take her. And what of emotions – was she assuming the Akkharu had a concept of human emotions, felt human emotions, when they might not?

But what, she now wondered, *if the Akkharu did feel emotions?*

What if they felt emotion as intensely as humans did? What if they resented Jeremiah's arrogant manipulation of their species, which, now that she considered it, amounted to a kind of enslavement, all the while being unable to express their frustration and rage?

Perhaps she was wrong? Perhaps the Akkharu did feel despair and anger, but had learned to hide their thoughts and feelings in the same way a human would at work? What if the Akkharu hid their real selves by keeping a system of communication at a private, altogether more intimate, level? The more she considered it, the more she became convinced that it was true. Tentatively, with delicacy and a lightness of mind-to-mind touch, she probed this extraordinary idea.

<How?>

The response appeared to be silence, but it was a silence like static in your ears wearing ear phones when a radio transmission had been switched off.

A secret place based on . . . static . . .? Silence? It seemed improbable, but Jeremiah was so incredibly clever at reading minds. Could it be that they kept their feelings below the radar by communicating with one another in a way that Jeremiah did not recognise?

Oh . . . oh, my!

Oh, if only it were possible to escape Jeremiah's control.

Penny thought again about those factory workers and their lip-read conversations. They performed quite complex, but repetitive tasks for the factory owner – for their controller – but at the same time they had this secret system of communication that they kept below the radar. They conversed among themselves by lip-reading. They read one another's facial expression. Humans were very good at reading one another's facial expression.

An idea crept into her mind, one that would be most unwelcome to Jeremiah if he knew of its presence. A dangerous idea.

What if I too can find a secret means of communication, a code that is below Jeremiah's radar? Could this be the first step in opposing what he is planning to do to Earth?

As if he had read her rebellious thoughts, Jeremiah manifested beside her. With a flick of a finger he opened up a vision of a world, and threat, altogether more tangible. Penny found herself hovering in space, in a place where darkness stretched in every direction.

Is he punishing me with a vision of eternity?

But then, with another flick of his finger, green lines, curves and parabolas appeared to fill the emptiness about her. Penny thought: he didn't read my wondering about a place to hide. He didn't read my wondering about a secret means of expression. She tucked this realisation away: it was her secret.

'Where is this place?'

'It is known as Dromenon.'

'But what does it mean?'

'Do not be frightened.' With another flick of his finger, pinpoints of green appeared, then began to spread, moving like cosmic nibs across the three dimensional darkness, etching as they moved.

Penny gasped: 'Oh!'

She recognised the familiar outline of St Paul's Cathedral, but now it was etched into the emptiness by the glowing green blueprint.

'Dromenon and reality co-exist. You might sketch your new city here – much as you captured the old on the ceiling of your hiding place. Such is the wonder of Dromenon, your creativity that might be translated into physical realisation in the new city.'

'The new city?'

'Your city, Penny – the new London.'

In spite of her fears of mere moments ago, Penny felt excited by the prospect. 'But how do I do it?'

'I will call upon another power to enable you. But first I need to free you from all constraints.'

'I—'

He dematerialised. She felt him invade her mind. He said: <I must show you how to think through to the minds

of the Akkharu. Let me guide you so that they become your pencils and brushes.>

Penny gave in to him and he became one with her, reaching deeper and deeper into her thoughts, her spirit, igniting a frenzy of creativity that burned like a furnace. With effortless ease her mind entered communication with the common mind of the Akkharu. In that communion Penny found that she was looking at the world as the Akkharu did; through a vision that was, as she had correctly figured, exquisitely sensitive to every nuance. But now she could also control that mind: she could recall with precision the cityscape of London; the monuments she had drawn again and again and the desolate spaces that now surrounded them. She could direct the Akkharu to follow her blueprints to make it whole again, to revive her beloved city, while at the same time blend old and new into a masterwork of creativity.

A pinpoint of glowing green grew and spread, creating curls and arches, helices and arabesques. Walls appeared, constructed of a three-dimensional lattice of overlapping circles; buildings of spectacularly organic shape, making use of space and the most fluid of lines allowed by the magical crystals. Buildings, devoid of flat planes, straight lines and the unpleasant sharpness of angles appeared to defy gravity, more still had transparent walls, or captured light in all of its prismatic colours. On and on the creativity stretched, so Penny became lost in the wonder of it, while all around her the new city of air streams and currents of visual movement flowed around, in and through her.

When, at last, it was finished, she felt exhaustion overwhelm her, body and spirit. She desperately needed to rest . . . to sleep. But within her mind he – Jeremiah – resisted it.

<Your task is not yet complete.>

'What more can I do?'

<You constructed within a dream. It is still no more than a dream, trapped in the timeless wastes of Dromenon. It must be taken out of Dromenon and given substance, transposed to real time and space.>

'I cannot do that.'

<You can and must, but it will involve an even deeper communion.>

'A communion with what?'

<You spoke to the Akkharu. You asked of their dreams.>

'They dream of eternity.'

<An impossibility for slug beasts, but through communion with me, Penny, such an aspiration might become possible.>

'Communion with you?'

<Would you spurn eternity?>

'What is eternity?'

<The Fáil is surely its root and direction.>

'The Fáil?'

<I mentioned another power. The Fáil is the ultimate repository of power in this universe. The Fáil is the eternity

the Akkharu dream of. It is power, Penny, such as the very greatest and most ambitious of minds dared to dream of!>

'I . . . I can't. I wouldn't dare—'

<You are still constrained by human fears and emotions.>

'I have disappointed you.'

<Far from it. In you, I have found a mind sufficiently unique to escape the limitations of your physical being.>

He chose this moment to withdraw from her mind and manifest again. His hands cradled her face. His figure, for all that he radiated power, now appeared so curiously frail – almost vulnerable. She watched him, every line and plane of his face, the slight smile about his lips, as he spoke:

'Would you share eternity with me, Penny?'

She wanted to deny it, but she wasn't strong enough. She dropped her head as she whispered: 'Yes.'

The Nature of Mo

Alan lay sleepless in his tent in the Shee encampment, but it wasn't Ghork Mega that kept him awake. He was thinking about Mo. He knew that Mo was changing. He also knew, without question, that Mo was important. She was different from the other three friends. Nothing he had experienced since his arrival on Tír was down to chance. Therefore, these differences in Mo – the changes that were so disturbing her – were not happenstance. They had to be important. He reflected on the strange, sometimes terrifying events they had experienced on their journey down the Snowmelt River. He revisited the moment Mo had been dashed overboard, during the attack by the Storm Wolves . . .

Mark's mind had been turned by a succubus. He had been told to push Kate overboard, yet it had been Mo who had ended up in the moiling spate of river. It had seemed an accident, a mistake – but had it really been a mistake?

At the time, Alan had assumed that Kate had been the target. Mark had described how he had resisted the succubus – there had been a battle within Mark for his own will – and yet it had been Mo who had been put in jeopardy. Alan had saved Mo's life, but then, in the confrontation with the Legun at Ossierel, it was also Mo who had put herself between Alan and the Legun and she had returned the favour, saving him. In his mind's eye, Alan was back at that horrifying confrontation.

The Legun reached out and picked up the still unconscious former Kyra, then extended two great talons towards her eyes . . .

Alan was struggling back onto shaky legs, challenging it, keeping its murderous focus upon himself. Then, he heard Mo's voice.

'Stay your malice, Septemvile!'

He recalled how she had stood, erect and fearless between them. She held her bog oak talisman aloft in her right hand. He heard her speak, but her lips did not move. He heard her voice through his oraculum, but the voice he heard was growly and deep – not Mo's voice at all. It was enough to switch the focus of the Legun to his friend.

Alan had sensed a powerful force behind Mo's words as he struggled to get to his feet. He had called out to her, his voice hoarse with exhaustion:

'Mo – get out of here! Save yourself!'

He thought, *This is crazy. How could Mo think she could deflect the rage of the Legun?* Then Alan heard the Legun speak, in a voice like the crackling of thunder:

'What pretty spoil are you?'

Through his oraculum, Alan glimpsed something dark and shadowy behind the slender figure of Mo – a triangular shadow that silhouetted her from behind. A figure, impenetrably dense and resolute, cowled in spider's web.

Granny Dew!

Even as Alan regained his feet, he saw Mo glowing with spectral light. Mo spoke again, in the same deep voice.

'Your master will know me by my true name. I am Mira, Léanov Fashakk – *The Heralded One.'*

The Heralded One . . .

Alan sat upright on his pallet, his face bathed in sweat. Mo . . . Mo was vitally important. Special. And now this business with the Akkharu in the Valley of the Pyramids . . .

It was hard to think logically about the situation, but the question that perturbed him most was: Who *is* Mo?

In the beginning she'd been just another of the four friends – strangeness aside – but now she had changed so much, Alan wasn't sure that he really knew her. Perhaps the question wasn't so much, who was Mo, but *what* was Mo?

An hour or so later, Alan was joined by the two friends he trusted most in the world: Kate and Qwenqwo Cuatzel. The air in the tent was already filled with the aromatic scent of Qwenqwo's pipe.

'So, tell me exactly what she said, Alan.' Kate sat in front of him and reached out to take his two hands in her own. 'What happened to her when she travelled as a soul spirit to the Valley of the Pyramids?'

'She told me there's a labyrinth, very complex and deep, under the valley floor. She told me she was discovering the fate that brought her through to Tír from Earth. She was terrified by what was expected of her.'

Alan thought back to the conversation with Mo. Magtokk had been there in an invisible form – a soul spirit. He remembered how pale she had been, and how fiercely she'd gripped his hand. 'She said that Magtokk had told her she needed to make another dream journey in the Valley of the Pyramids. She said she had to "become one with the minds of the Akkharu".'

Kate frowned. 'How would she do that?'

'Beats me.'

Qwenqwo asked: 'Are the Akkharu those winged creatures guarding the towers of skulls?'

'She told me that the skulls are those of dead Akkharu, but the winged creatures we saw are just guardians. The Akkharu live underground in the labyrinth. She also said that the Akkharu weren't just warning us, but urging Mo to act.'

'Act how – by going back to the valley?'

'What do you think, Qwenqwo?'

The dwarf mage pulled at his beard. 'Was Mo frightened of these Akkharu?'

'No. Not at all. She was more frightened by what was expected of her – her fate.'

Alan recalled Mo's look of fierce determination as she'd squeezed his hand. Her words . . . *'I have to do it, Alan. I came to Tír with a purpose, just like you. If I must face danger, then I have to find the courage to do it.'*

Kate said: 'Can't Magtokk help her?'

'That was what I suggested, but she told me that it was Magtokk who was advising her to do this. She also told me that Magtokk was a True Believer.'

Qwenqwo took the pipe from his mouth and looked down into the glowing embers within the bowl. 'Mo thinks it vital, this link to the Akkharu?'

'Yes.'

Qwenqwo mused: 'Then she believes wholly that her fate is inextricably linked to these beings, or she would not believe it to be so vital.'

Alan hesitated. He studied Qwenqwo's face, and waited for the dwarf mage to speak again.

'When I first met Magtokk, I assumed that he is, or perhaps was, a mage, but now I think he is more than that. I believe that he is a manifestation of a True Believer.'

'The True Believers have been helpful to us – they protected Mo and Kate from the rage of the demi-god, Fangorath, so should we trust Magtokk?'

'There are many different kinds of True Believer. And not all are benign.'

Alan sighed. He didn't know what to believe. What could he do?

Kate hugged his arm. 'Mo was always different.'

'I know that.'

'Do you remember how Padraig reacted to her?'

'Yeah!' Padraig had seen something different in Mo from the moment they first met. How had he known she was different? Was there some clue in those Ogham runes he had pointed out to them? Some lesson from the ancient history carved over the walls of the barrow tomb of Feimhin?

Kate hugged his arm again.

'Do you remember her gathering all those strange things around the den?'

'Her arcania.' That had been Mark's word for it.

'Padraig acted as though he had been expecting her.'

'He saw something in her notebook.'

'And Granny Dew – she treated Mo as if she were different.'

'And you too, Qwenqwo. You said she was different.'

Qwenqwo lifted the pipe from his mouth, and then he nodded. 'Indeed I did.'

The sky was illuminated by the glow of evening as Mo walked along the bay, returning from another exhausting day helping Turkeya treat the sick and injured. She had left him as he'd headed for the small encampment of the Olhyiu, where he was looking forward to meeting his parents, Siam and Kehloke. It had lifted Mo's heart to see her shaman friend so happy and excited. The Olhyiu were more useful as sailors than warriors in this dreadful battle, and

Mo wished them well. They had been driven so close to extinction by the Tyrant's ruthless tactics back in Monisle that it had taken the Shee and the indomitable courage of Alan, with his gift of the First Power, to save them. And now, as her tired limbs brought her closer to the camp of the Shee, she heard the ritual prayer of the spiritual leader, Bétaald, and the answering chorus of tens of thousands of purring voices.

Mo's eyes searched the shadow-strewn landscape, looking for the orang-utan manifestation of Magtokk, who might carry her in his long arms, but instead she caught the eyes of the dwarf mage, Qwenqwo. He had a puzzled look on his face. Was Qwenqwo, who had been her friend ever since her imprisonment in Isscan, a little jealous of her growing intimacy with the magician? Mo decided she would have it out with him.

But, upon approaching him she found herself confronted by those gentle emerald eyes in that redoubtable bearded face, and she changed her mind.

How could she ever offend Qwenqwo, who had been such a fearless and supportive friend to her? She felt ashamed of her impulse to rebuke him.

'Qwenqwo, I've neglected you.'

'So you have, young lady.'

Mo was discomforted to find herself on the receiving end of his rebuke. 'Please forgive me.'

'Only if you will let me advise you.'

'Of course.'

'You have become somewhat oblique in conversation of late.'

'Oblique?'

'Secretive, my princess.'

'Have I?'

'You know you have.'

Mo clasped his burly arm and they walked the short distance that would allow them to view the sunset over the ocean.

'You know that your friends are deeply concerned about you.'

'I know Alan is worried.'

'Should I be worried too?'

This unexpected kindness immediately reawakened her affection for him. She should have spoken to him more, and she wanted to speak to him now about what was happening to her, about her anxieties about her own courage and worthiness. 'I – I—'

'You fear what is expected of you?'

'Oh, Qwenqwo, I'm terrified I will let you all down.'

He placed his gnarled hands on her shoulders and looked up into her face, now a foot higher than his own. 'I have always had the utmost faith in you. You have the heart and spirit of a lioness.'

'Then,' she smiled back, 'perhaps I should have been a Shee?'

He squeezed her, gently. 'Be your own brave self.'

'You know who I am, don't you? You have always known

my true name? When you comforted me in the captivity of the false mage in Isscan. You told me the false mage was attempting to discover my secret.'

'Indeed I did.'

'You must have known that the eagle, Thesau, was not protecting you and your runestone, but me?'

'I suspected as much, though I did not know for certain.'

'But you never spoke of it?'

'You were so young, so very vulnerable. You were not ready yet for that burden. My self-appointed role then, as now, was to protect you.'

'I still feel so vulnerable and unready.'

'Let me assure you that I am still here, ever ready to protect you still. You may count on me no matter what the occasion or the threat.'

'I have always known that I could depend on you.'

'Here I am, Princess. Here I will stay!'

The Rose

Mark peered through a clinging fog to where Brett and Padraig were standing in huddled conversation before the Black Rose. They were still a good half mile away from the monstrosity, but even from this distance, its threat was overwhelmingly oppressive. Overhead, snow continued to fall out of a sky as heavy as lead. Mark observed Brett taking a measurement with an electronic instrument – most likely a GPS device. Brett looked up to where the towering structure disappeared into the fog, then moved about fifty paces nearer to it to repeat the measurement before pulling back again. His lilting Kentucky accent was audible even from fifty yards distant: 'My, it sure is awesome!'

'A fearful construction,' Padraig coughed in agreement. 'You feel the increasing cold as we drew nearer?'

'One could hardly miss it.'

'Like it's soaking up heat out of the air?'

Mark turned to glance back towards the Mamma Pig, its bulk a pallid shadow within a misty world of shadows.

When, on impulse, he put an arm around Nan's shoulders, he felt her shivering even under several layers of clothing. Brett was right. There was something unnatural about the cold air around the Rose.

Mark thought it was extraordinary that they'd made it here at all, and the fact that Padraig was now well enough to be studying the ominous structure with them made the situation all the more remarkable.

He and Nan had spent hours explaining what they knew to Padraig last night. He had wanted to know everything that had happened to the four friends after their arrival on Tír. He had been very relieved when Mark had assured him that, as far as he was aware, the other three were all alive: Kate and Mo, as well as Padraig's grandson, Alan. Now, watching Brett and Padraig examine the Rose, Mark wondered if he'd know if the situation were otherwise, and the others were dead. Was their friendship really so deep he'd have sensed it even though they were a world away? Would the Third Power really help him in this? He didn't know the answer to that vitally important question.

'What's Brett up to?' Tajh's voice came softly from the open cabin door of the Pig.

'I'm not altogether sure. My guess is they're making a tactical assessment.'

Now he recalled, it had been the intensity of Padraig's eyes – the purest, most disturbing blue that Mark had ever seen – that had warned him that there was something unusual about Padraig. Padraig's grandson, Alan, also had strikingly blue eyes, but Padraig's were like searchlights – you had the impression that when you became their focus, Padraig could see right down into your soul.

Mark's feelings must have shown because Tajh climbed down from the cab to join him and Nan. She said: 'Oh, my god – what a journey! I don't know how we made it this far.'

Mark nodded. 'Just what I was thinking.'

It had been pitch black, maybe a little after 4.00 a.m., when Mark and Cal had pulled up before a roadblock on a small arterial road inside the blocked-off London outer circular, the M25. Snow had been wheeling hard through the cones of their bike headlights, illuminating a background of ruined buildings and streets. Although the plan to get them through the cordon had been Cal's, Mark was instructed to do most of the talking, since he could read the guards' minds. That, and the package of war spoils they were carrying, was key. It was a decidedly risky plan. Mark took small comfort in the fact that Nan would also be listening to the conversation and relaying the gist of it to the others in the Pig. Even as he'd waited for the nearest of half a dozen Uzi-toting Skulls to challenge him, he'd received a message mind-to-mind from Nan.

<There's somebody asleep in the black vehicle behind the road block.>

<Yeah – I've got a fix on it.>

Mark hadn't had a great deal of confidence in Cal's plan, but they'd had no option. He'd lifted the visor of his helmet to spit out the gum he had been chewing, then he'd entered the mind of the man snoring in the back passenger seat of the black limousine. The passenger had been disturbed by a guard rapping on the glass. Mark decided that he would heighten the sense of confusion in the waking mind.

'What the fuck's going on?' one of the nearest of the Skulls had demanded, whilst aiming his Uzi at Mark. Mark had to switch his focus from the guy in the cab. He shook his head: 'Special D.'

'Special D my arse!'

'Rations,' he winked at the guard. 'A present for the coming occasion from the big man's friends up north.'

The Skull shifted on his feet. 'Wot occasion?'

Mark looked from the Skull to the limo, and then at the Skull again. He entered the guard's mind and planted a notion: *Them markings on that truck is ours. Look at that fucking armoured thing – it's a fucking safe on wheels!*

The guard spoke by radio to the waking man in the limousine. 'You coming out, or you want us to deal with this?'

The limo man now sitting up, only half awake. Mark entered his mind and he enhanced the hangover he found in that mind. He spiked the rage. He impressed the response: 'I'm coming out.'

'Let's have a look at them, then – the rations,' said the Skull.

Cal spoke then: 'You shouldn't – you really wouldn't want to spoil the big man's party.'

The Skull switched attention from Mark to Cal. It gave Mark a few more seconds to focus on the mind of the man in the limo; he sensed the withdrawal shivers. Mark took control of the man's shaky right hand and doodled with a fat index finger in the heavy condensation on the passenger door:

KILLERBLADE

The Skull fired his Uzi over Cal's head. 'I won't ask again, arsehole. Show us the rations.'

Several of the other Skulls had closed in on the convoy. The nearside passenger window of the Pig slid open and Bull leaned his massive left forearm out of the window, letting himself be seen, though he kept the belted Minimi out of sight.

Cal said: 'I told you – these goods ain't for you.'

'We'll see about that.'

Mark watched the man climb out of the limo.

Cal said: 'I don't want to name names. If I do, you'll wish I hadn't. We got orders to bring this shit here. No fault of ours you got your wires crossed.'

The Skull glanced back in the direction of the limo, sweating heavily despite the cold. A huge man stood just next to the passenger door having just climbed out. He swayed as if dizzy. Mark looked out through the big man's eyes and saw what those eyes saw: the scrawled word on the glass. Mark watched as the man turned round to take in all three vehicles at the roadblock: the two BMWs with their bikers wearing Paramilitary uniforms, and the heavily armoured Pig in Paramilitary camouflage colours.

Cal was lifting his arms in resignation: 'On your own stupid heads . . .!'

The big man shouted, 'No!' He began to push the guards aside to deal with the situation himself. Mark noticed the absence of a uniform; instead he wore a creased grey open-necked shirt over creased grey suit pants: a Grimstone high-ranker. One of the Church's secret police. He came close to examine the bikes, his puffy eyes slitted with suspicion. Mark re-entered his mind and enhanced the paranoia.

The ogre looked at Cal and said: 'What the fuck's going on?'

The Skull spoke: 'Claim to be bringing in a special delivery.'

The big man turned, grabbed the Skull's coat, slapped his face hard. 'Not you! I'm talking to them.' The big man had kept a hold of the Skull as he'd turned to look at Mark through narrowed eyes.

The Skull squeaked: 'They could be lying.'

The big man gripped the Skull's scalp, then brought the Skull's face down and rammed it into his knee. 'You call me Sir.'

'Sir – I'm sorry, Sir. They're lying, Sir.'

'Give me your gun.'

'What . . .?'

'What, Sir!' The ogre rammed the Skull's face into his knee again. Blood was dripping off the Skull's face like a tap. 'Your gun!'

The Skull pressed the Uzi into the big man's one free hand. Then the ogre rammed his knee into that face again and again and again before tossing the bleeding Skull aside. Then he aimed the Uzi at Cal's head.

'If there was a delivery I would know about it.'

'So you should, Sir.'

'Shoot them.'

The other Skulls looked uncertain. 'Sir, I think they're claiming it's for the Field Marshall himself, Sir – some special occasion.'

'Bollocks!'

Mark said: 'Sir! May I speak with you in private?'

'Shut your fucking mouth.'

Mark nodded to Cal. He said: 'This here is Jarman – Jarman from Manchester.'

The big man hissed: 'I told you to shut your mouth.'

'Well, somebody was expecting us,' Cal said with a sneer. 'Special D. Maybe you just weren't invited to the party.'

Mark sensed the man's paranoia soar. The ogre rapped the Uzi barrel against Cal's brow.

'Sir,' Mark whispered, 'there's a codeword.'

'I told you both to shut it.'

Mark put the picture of the fogged up door and the

spelled out word, KILLERBLADE, back into the ogre's mind. He inserted the thought: *What if I'm so fucked up with this hangover, I forgot something?*

Mark watched the ogre's head turn back towards the Limo. The word was still visible, though now inside-out. It was melting away as the condensation dribbled down the window.

Paranoia screamed through his mind.

'Kill them!'

One of the other Skulls hurled himself at Mark. He grabbed him by his hair and tried to smash the Uzi into his face. But Bull had climbed out of the Pig and now he ran between them. Bull picked up the Skull like a rag doll and impaled him on the spiked rail of the roadblock. The impact triggered the barrier to lift and the impaled guard was hoisted up into the air with it.

The confrontation was now down to two Minimis facing half a dozen Uzis.

Cal had a mobile in his hand. He shouted: 'I've had enough of you morons. I'm going to fuckingwell call up the Field Marshall himself.'

Mark sensed the wave of panic in the ogre. 'Okay – we'll talk. You two, and me – nobody else. Inside the Portakabin. Now!'

The standoff continued for several more seconds before Cal nodded to Bull. Cal took the package of war spoils from the blazing town out of the pannier of his bike and nodded towards the Portakabin.

The big man kicked the door shut behind them as all three of them squeezed into a confined space that was largely taken up by a cluttered desk. Mark and Cal were pressed back against the wall inside, while the big man sat on the corner of the desk.

'This so-called codeword?'

'Killerblade.'

The ogre blinked twice, then growled: 'Okay, let's see it.'

Cal tossed the package onto the desk.

'So you're dealing. Who's buying?'

'Figure it out for yourself.'

The ogre poked a fingernail through the polythene wrapping on the package. He shoved the tip of his little finger through the hole, then withdrew it and sniffed at the white powder before rubbing on his gums.

'Must be four ounces of pure.'

Mark was inside his mind and knew what the ogre was thinking: *kill them both and keep the gear.* But Mark reminded that mind of the codeword the ogre's own finger had written in the condensation on the car window.

'Nobody's gatherin' no brownie points here. I'll ask again, who's trading?'

'We told you the truth: there's a coming celebration, a big one. Word at our end is it's the man himself.'

Mark saw the fear enter the ogre's grey eyes. He no longer needed the oraculum, the man's fright had grown of its own accord.

Cal spoke calmly. 'As it stands there's no harm done. But

if the man gets to know you stopped us, you're dead. We're all fucking dead.'

The ogre took a snort of the cocaine. 'Four ounces, straight off the block. I could take it and fry you.'

'You going to shoot all those witnesses outside?'

'Now you listen to me, dickheads. Maybe you're a bit slow to see an opportunity: there's a packet to be made here. We can lay our hands on some serious money; more than you could possibly imagine.'

Mark shrugged. He looked at Cal, who said, 'I reckon we're dead already.'

'What the fuck you talking about?'

Cal spoke resignedly. 'We're already running late; people have been expecting us for half the night.'

'If I were you,' Mark added, 'I wouldn't want the brass to know that I had anything to do with this.'

'What you ranting about?'

Mark fell silent, but he entered the mind of the ogre and he placed a false memory there. He showed the ogre Grimstone's own hand closing on the ogre's grey suit lapel and Grimstone's own lips whispering the all important codeword: KILLERBLADE.

A look of panic now crossed the ogre's face. He hurried out of the Portakabin and back to the limo, then flopped down into the back row passenger seat. The word was still there, however much of it had dribbled down the window. He swatted it away with his hand, made sure it was utterly erased by wiping it with his sleeve.

He staggered more than ever when he climbing back out of the limo. He aimed a furious kick at the unconscious guard, bleeding into the snow. 'Let them go,' he growled.

The four surviving guards were staring back at him: 'Sir?'

'Let them go!' He hurried back into the Portakabin and scrabbled through the contents of the drawers. He wiped an oversize hand over his sweating brow, dripping big drops of oily sweat onto the forms he was signing. 'Gentlemen – please don't let this disturb the equanimity of the Field Marshall.'

Mark had to suppress his smile as the ogre pressed the security clearance papers into his hands.

'Go on! Get the fuck out of here before I change my mind. I promise you that I'll deal with these incompetent bastards myself.'

Those papers had proved invaluable as they'd made their way through the dense ring of defences around London, passing by squadrons of tanks, missile launchers and attack choppers, encountering devastation and ruin everywhere.

Mark's train of thought broke off as Tajh passed him a plate of fried bacon and egg with a side bowl of baked beans. They were well embedded by now in a new hideout in what had been a backstreet garage. They were only about a mile away from the Black Rose.

Mark nodded his thanks to Tajh, glancing over to where Sharkey, in his element, was cooking the food with one hand. Tajh sat next to Mark, leaning against the oil-blackened brick wall: 'Looks like we're here for a bit. I wouldn't want to risk heading back out.'

'Me neither!'

Mark dipped a piece of toast into the yolk of his egg and looked at Nan, who was chatting to the returned Padraig and Brett.

The rickety garage was one of very few surviving buildings in the hinterland this close to the Rose.

Tajh couldn't help shivering. 'We certainly rode our luck.'

'Mmm!' Mark acknowledged, as Nan came over to sit on Mark's other side.

'What's Brett really up to?' she asked.

'You really asking me?' whispered Mark.

Everybody in the building tensed as the thunder of attack choppers passed low over their heads. There was a common sigh of relief as the noise receded. Mark smiled at Tajh.

'I'm ashamed to say I've never been to Scotland.'

'You've missed a treat.'

He laughed. 'Tell me more about you.'

'Born in Edinburgh. Then got fatally attracted to London's bright lights.'

Mark glanced at Tajh's hair, now clotted with dust and sweat. He tried to imagine her younger, her grey eyes dazzled by the bright lights. 'Is that where you met Cal?'

'Fated,' she said, lighting a cigarette. 'We shared a taste in music. Or maybe it was music and the sexual healing that went with it?' She laughed openly, blowing out smoke. 'I was nineteen, Cal was twenty-six. At least, that was what he was in years – claimed he was twice as old in experience. My first impression – I thought he was half crazy. But craziness can be attractive when you're of a certain age. Seven years difference between us – seven was my lucky number.'

'How did you come to meet?'

'At an underground club, where Sharkey was DJing. You've no idea how brilliant he was at it. He and Cal already knew one another. Bull was around too, somewhere in the background – those were the days.'

Tajh looked at him, and took a drag. Then Cal interrupted their conversation. Mark hadn't noticed him getting closer. He joined them, with his own plate of food. He said: 'You haven't finished your story, Tajh. Tell him what he really wants to hear.'

'Hey, give it up!'

'Tell him how we used to spend our nights after the gigs, in your flat or my boat on the river. Tell him how good the shagging was.'

'Be patient with him,' Tajh said. It reminded Mark of the tension he had felt when they'd first met, in the barn where Cal had been welding the blade of the Mamma Pig. Now, just as back then, Mark had seen her focus on the oraculum in his brow.

Cal flopped down on the other side of Tajh, who draped her left arm around his neck. 'Oh, Mark, would you like me to tell you about the shagging? I'm beginning to think that Cal won't be happy until I do.'

Mark laughed. 'I think you should treasure that memory all to yourselves.'

Attack on the South Gate

'If the Mage Lord pleases!' The aides' group leader said.

The request did not please him – and it was the second time the aides had used sarcasm to convey discontent in just a few days. Alan lifted both his arms, bent at the elbows, so they could manoeuvre the heavy breastplate, with its fastening straps, into position.

'The Shee,' he grumbled, 'do not wear armour.'

'The Shee,' she retorted, 'can afford to die on the battlefield. Through their daughter-sisters, they are resurrected. But you will not be resurrected. And think you not that you will prove a prime target for the gunners yonder as you get within range of the fortified gate?'

The aides was right. Alan grimaced as he felt the additional weight pull on his shoulders. 'I'm sorry to be so disagreeable.'

'We would prefer that you be safe rather than sorry, Mage Lord,' she pressed on with ordering the group who were dressing him in battlefield armour, while two more held his onkkh at the ready.

Qwenqwo had no more sympathy for his friend than they did. The dwarf mage was already fully decked out in the bronze and doubtless heavier battlefield armour of the Fir Bolg, and he was already mounted on his onkkh. Right now he was ignoring his grumbling friend to look seawards to where the thunder of a new cannonade was erupting from the assembled fleet. It echoed in the space between the waiting Shee army and the city walls.

'Can somebody please hold the spear for me while I climb aboard the vile beast?'

Kate accepted the heavy spear from Alan and, as soon as he was mounted on his onkkh, passed the telescope up. Even his attempt to look through it was made clumsy by the gauntlets and the restless movements of the beast beneath him. Eventually he managed to see past the dense clouds of drifting smoke to make out the dozen towering battleships Ebrit called his Leviathans. The Leviathans were the most menacing warships Alan had ever seen. Though the hulls were built of oak, they were armoured with overlapping scales of iron, like the hide of a reptile, to help deflect the enemies' cannonballs. This in turn allowed the Leviathans to get in close enough to do serious damage with their broadsides. They had three gunnery decks; deck two would wait for deck one to fire before firing themselves, then deck three would fire in suit after the roll back from deck two. The guns themselves were big enough to throw a sixty pound ball a distance of two miles. Even at a distance of what must have been three miles from him, Alan was deafened by the cannon fire; the thunder of the discharge echoing from the rocky headland. The cracking disintegration of the granite walls as the hundreds of heavy balls tore into it produced a storm of debris, which billowed into the sky and deluged the slopes and choppy ocean with ruin.

Qwenqwo dug his heels in to control his restless mount. 'Do you recall, you thought these walls impregnable?'

Alan could not fail to be impressed. The city walls were said to be fifty feet deep, but no wall could withstand such carnage, round after round – and there had been something close to forty broadsides since first light. He scanned over the triple-masted Shee warships, equipped with batteries of oars that enabled them to manoeuvre even in the absence of wind. The Shee army probably numbered a quarter of a million now, not counting aides. And there were about eighty-thousand soldiers and grenadiers from Prince Ebrit's army, most of them lightly armoured with chainmail over a thick pleated coat of sheep's wool, their heads and hearts protected with helmets and breast plates.

Alan spoke his thoughts aloud: 'Still no direct reaction from the Tyrant?'

'None.'

Alan knew that the Kyra was as puzzled about this as he was. Up to now there had been no counterattack from the city other than the returning fusillade of the cannons that lined the walls. Prince Ebrit was winning the artillery battle. It was just too easy considering their wily enemy.

'Perhaps,' he said, 'Magtokk might have an idea as to how the Tyrant will react to this threat?'

The orang-utan manifested, as Alan had expected him to. He looked at Alan, his expression deeply thoughtful. 'Up to now, the Tyrant had shown himself to be calculating and resourceful. I see no reason to anticipate anything other than the same resolve. He will bide his time. All too soon, I fear, we will face new deadly games.'

Alan turned back to Qwenqwo.

The fact that they were both weighed down with armour, and back once more on the bone-jarring onkkhs, had no effect on the dwarf mage's determination. He passed a pipe, brimful of tobacco, down to Magtokk, before tamping down one for himself. 'I think,' he opined, 'that Magtokk has the truth of it. The real games will emerge soon enough.'

Magtokk joined Qwenqwo in lighting his pipe, the two of them adding the scent of tobacco smoke to the stink of cordite from the cannonades. The mage looked downslope to the beaches, where the Shee army, assisted by vast numbers of aides, were assembling siege machinery. The ground beyond cannon reach was a carnival of tents and braziers. Blacksmiths were working in pairs; heavily muscled men and women hammering iron for the stirrups of Ebrit's cavalry, or the bolts for the heavy crossbows favoured by their archers. Others boiled a stinking glue made out of the bladders of fishes for the fletchers. Traders, who would normally conceal the techniques of their trade so much so they were called the 'mysteries', were doing their best to maintain their secrets under the watchful eyes of the aides, who were no doubt looking to pick up new tricks.

Alan looked at the huge siege towers, borne on the largest wagons he had ever seen, their wooden wheels some twenty feet high. The unwieldy towers were tall enough to breach the curtain walls. Other wagons bore trebuchets, their throwing masts almost as tall as the siege towers, but as yet unused, since they needed to be much closer to the walls to be useful. A hundred or more braziers were blazing under huge cauldrons of tar, ready to coat the fireballs that would be hurled over the walls into the city when the trebuchets got close enough. But that series of razerine slopes up ahead made Alan wonder if they would ever get close enough make a contribution. More wagons bore field cannon capable of discharging multiple lead balls, or chains armed with a hundred deadly spikes. These would be useful when they broke through into the city. And there was more weaponry lying in wait for when they broke through the south gate, including blunderbuss-like cannons with barrels a foot wide, capable of clearing a street with a single discharge. Added to this was Prince Ebrit's cavalry: four thousand troops, fully armoured and mounted on chargers, equipped with muzzle-loading musketry, halberds, mace and longswords.

Alan nodded to Kate, who passed him the Spear of Lug.

Kate hated the fighting. He saw how her eyes were full of anxiety. He took a firm grip of the shaft, looking up for a moment at the lengthy rune-incised spiral head.

Thank you, grandfather! He closed his eyes wondering if he would ever see Padraig again.

Kate called out to him: 'They're waiting for you.'

He opened his eyes again to look to where the Kyra, and Bétaald, were standing at the head of a spearhead of Shee. Alan and Qwenqwo spurred their onkkhs horizontally across the hillside to meet up with them. He lifted his forearm, to conduct the Shee greeting with the Kyra.

'Ready when you are!'

Bétaald looked at him: a direct confrontation, eye-to-eye. 'We are ready to attack the south gate of the city. I salute you, Mage Lord, who thus risk your life though you are a stranger to this conflict. Many indeed have been the years we have prayed for this day. We would restore the light to our world!'

Alan bowed his head, in concert with the Kyra, Qwenqwo, Kate, Mo and Turkeya, as Bétaald intoned a prayer for success in their assault on the city. He waited for the prayer to end before he asked the obvious question:

'What danger can we expect?'

'We will be confronted by the usual defences one might anticipate in the siege of any fortress city. But this is no normal city. There will be darker perils that we should anticipate.'

Qwenqwo nodded. 'The Septemviles.'

'What do we know about the ones who are left?'

It was the Kyra who answered him. 'As I have said previously, our knowledge is scant. All are said to be immortal, but, as we have discovered to our joy, immortality does not mean invincibility.'

Alan looked at Magtokk. 'What do you know?'

'I'm familiar with a few of them through legend. There is one that is known as Lightbane, another as Stormbane and yet another as Firebane. None who has encountered them has ever lived to illuminate history with adequate description – or the means to defeat them.'

Kate reached up to grip Alan's armoured left hand. He bent to kiss her hand before releasing it, then looked at the Kyra. 'So now we know why the Tyrant has only offered a token resistance so far. He's looking to draw us in.'

Alan sat erect on his onkkh, his eyes closed for a moment or two while he took a firm grip of the Spear of Lug in his right hand, its shaft rammed against the rocky ground. When he opened them again, Qwenqwo was tamping out his pipe against his brass-covered knee. Alan felt the tingling sensation of the First Power run through him. Kate reached up and Alan took the final opportunity to kiss her on the lips before his helm was passed up to him. He slipped it over his head. The aides who had ministered to him now stood aside.

He nodded to the Kyra, who told the trumpeters to sound out the signal for the assault to begin. She metamorphosed to the shape of a giant snow tigress. He spoke to her, oraculum-to-oraculum: <From now on, we should communicate mind-to-mind. We should proceed cautiously. Stay alert for any reaction from the city.>

<My thoughts entirely.>

They began slowly, ascending the grit-strewn slope that led to the first of the rocky ridges. Ledge after ledge of the same black granite criss-crossed their approach, their edges sharp as blades and their sloping surfaces slippery as ball bearings. All around them, the Shee had metamorphosed to great cats, their claws extended to grip the rocky slopes. Alan looked up, searching for a useful break or cleft in the crags that would provide a path up the rising slope. His every instinct bade caution. As they rose, the landscape became ever more brooding, as if daring them to proceed. Alan's onkkh had its own way of dealing with the treacherous ground and so he allowed it to plod forward at its own pace.

The attacking army reached the first ledge, pouring through the narrow and twisting pass, but within minutes, began a new zigzagging ascent. The Shee widened their forces in order to try out several different passes up to the second ledge.

Alan planned to attack the gate with the First Power, but first he needed to get a clear view of it, and this was difficult from the position he was in, with scarp after scarp rising before him and blotting out any clear view of the more distant fortifications. A shadow moved across the ground as something gradually covered the sun. Glancing overhead through the visor slit, he saw thunderheads moving at an unnatural speed.

Alan addressed the nearby Kyra.

<Have you looked at the sky?>

<I think we are observing the work of a Septemvile. Perhaps the one described by Magtokk as Stormbane.>

Even as Alan lowered his head again to face the direction of the south gate, the first forking trails of lightning crackled down out of the thunderheads, disintegrating a rocky outcrop and the squadron of Shee that had been bounding over it.

'Shit!'

Alan racked his brains in an attempt to think through this new threat. How could he use the First Power against something that was so similar? Even as he struggled to think of a strategy, a trumpeting sounded from all around him: a new order from the Kyra.

The Shee were fanning out to reduce the risk of lightning strikes hitting them. They were also speeding up their ascent, passing by him on either side. There was a deafening fusillade from the naval artillery in the bay below them: Prince Ebrit following their progress and doing what he could to help them. Meanwhile the darkness was rapidly deepening. Alan dug his heels into the flank of the onkkh thinking that speed of ascent might compensate for the onkkh slipping as it clawed through the rubble-strewn ascent.

Then he heard Kate's voice: <The fleet is coming under a new attack. The Leviathans . . . they're burning. Magtokk says it's another Septemvile – the one known as Firebane.>

The communication faded. Alan turned to his left, attempting to look out to sea. His normal vision was useless in the obscuring dark, but when he used the oraculum, he saw that Kate was right and the Leviathans were consumed with flames. Even through the oraculum he could only glimpse it poorly. It alarmed him that the encroaching darkness was capable of obscuring not only his vision, but his senses through the oraculum.

He redoubled his efforts with it.

<Kate – Mo – I'm seeing something running under the sea.>

It was Mo, and not Kate, who answered him:

<I can see them through the Torus: wraiths of fire moving under the waves. Many of them, perhaps hundreds, even thousands. They are attacking the fleet from under the water.>

Alan had to turn away from the horror of what was happening to the fleet. He had to focus on a single objective: the most important contribution he could make was to destroy the south gate. He must do this at any cost, otherwise the Shee would be stuck on these unfriendly slopes. There would be nowhere for them to go and the walls above would direct their firepower down onto their unprotected bodies. Through the thickening gloom, he glimpsed something within the formidable bulk of the walls: the twin towers of the fortress surrounding the south gate.

He spurred the flanks of his onkkh in an attempt to catch up with the advancing Shee, though they were now a hundred yards ahead of him. He sensed rather than saw Qwenqwo following his lead, his armoured bulk close to Alan's heels.

But they were still not much higher than the lower slopes, and the south gate loomed higher and more threatening as they drew closer.

Ahead, the boom of cannons roared from the walls. A glowing ball swept by him, no more than a few feet away, to explode somewhere behind him. He felt the heat of the explosion on the back of his neck. A hideous green glare permeated the inky light. The cannon balls were hollow, filled with the nacreous green luminescence of the Tyrant's poison he remembered from the Battle of Ossierel. Even minor wounds inflicted with that vile poison would turn to gangrene. With a cry of defiance, he spurred his onkkh into a still faster climb, ignoring the twisting and turning of the track ahead and heading into a direct confrontation with the monolith ahead. Explosions and violence surrounded him, much of it lost in the dense black smoke, until he found himself three quarters of the way up the slope – close enough at last to see the arched silhouette of the south gate, which looked relatively small in proportion to the flanking towers. There was a strange illumination from within the arched gate. It took Alan a moment or two to realise what this meant: the south gate had been flung wide open.

Alan warned Ainé, <Do you see?>

<I see!>

Alan probed the opening with his oraculum, but his view of it remained hazy. It occurred to him that he was being restricted by the helm covering his brow; the heavy iron was blinkering his oraculum.

He tore off his helmet and cast it aside. He felt better and stronger immediately. He closed his eyes and examined the view of the gate through his liberated oraculum. Something was standing within it, half as tall as the opening. Assuming that the gates were forty feet high, it could not possibly be human. He saw a figure pallid as wax, a face as still as a sculpture. The eyes within the face were black, as if a soul of darkness were looking at him. The cold indifference in that face was challenging.

<Ainé!>

<A Septemvile – the Legun known as the Lightbane.>

<Perhaps we should retreat – reconsider our strategy?>

<We cannot retreat. Our unguarded backs would brook annihilation.>

Alan returned his focus to the Septemvile. He had to defeat it with the First Power. He began to charge the Spear of Lug with it, keeping his focus on the enemy. He saw no sign of fear on that waxy face.

The Legun floated forwards to the top of the slope ahead – confronting him. Alan lowered the Spear of Lug and fired a thunderbolt of glowing red lightning at the Legun. The thunderbolt struck home and the figure dissolved, but in its place he saw a spreading mist. The mist billowed and widened, flowing like a heavy vapour over the edge of the uppermost slope, then tumbling down, scarp by scarp, like a stepped waterfall.

<Ainé!>

<I see!>

The cannons in the walls were still raining down a catastrophic fusillade. With his onkkh now halted, and with the spreading vapour descending towards the attacking army, it could only be moments before the leading Shee came into contact with it.

Mo's cry, mind-to-mind: <It blinds, Alan. The slightest touch upon the eyes and it blinds its victims, leaving them defenceless.>

A Strategy

Mark and Nan's conversation around a makeshift table in the abandoned garage was interrupted by a signal from HQ, picked up by the radio rigged to the Mamma Pig. It was evening, and would have been pitch dark in here had it not been for the lights running off the Pig's generator. They'd put blackout blinds on the windows to prevent the light seeping out. The garage had become a field station of sorts, with the hidden Pig sprouting a proliferation of electrical and electronic leads to an adjoining ad-hoc video-conference centre, based around the same table. Tajh spoke into the microphone: 'Roger – receiving!'

She played the conversation with a comms tech through a speaker so everybody could listen in to a conversation with Resistance HQ: 'General Chatwyn is taking part in a conference call with a spokesperson for the joint Chiefs of Staff at the Pentagon. We need to speak to Mr Travis urgently.'

Tajh said: 'What's going on?'

The tech's voice asked: 'Who am I speaking to?'

'Tajh Madine – one of the crew.'

'Is Mr Travis available?'

'He's outside. It will take us a few minutes to get hold of him. In the meantime, could I have a word with Jo Derby, if she's available?'

A few seconds later, Jo's voice came on the line. 'Hello, Tajh. How are things where you are?'

'Tense. We're all wondering what's going on?'

'If you're referring to the Pentagon, I have no idea. But globally the situation is worsening.'

Tajh glanced at the others around the table. Everybody was interested in news from HQ. Then she said: 'There's nothing here except the Rose. No Razzers. Just a devastated landscape and the threat of discovery by Seebox's air and ground patrols. What's Grimstone up to in America?'

'The same as he was here: provoking chaos. He's been conducting monster evangelical meetings.'

'I presume he has the Sword?'

'Is that you, Mark?'

'Yeah.'

'He has the Sword.'

'Then the Americans have a big problem.'

'President Harvey has declared a state of emergency.'

A newly-arrived Brett plonked himself down in a free chair and listened in. He muttered: 'Oh, shit!'

They also shuffled to make room for Padraig around the ad-hoc conference table.

The tech voice cut across the conversation to tell them: 'I'm now handing you over to General Chatwyn.'

Brett accepted the microphone from Tajh. He said: 'General?'

'Brett, you making any progress?'

'From what I can determine, the Black Rose is a massive power sump. That central pillar – the dang thing two miles high – looks like a receiver. It gets increasingly cold as you approach it. And you can feel the ground vibrating in slow but incredibly powerful waves when you get really close.'

'The Pentagon is becoming understandably prickly, given Grimstone's presence over there. I've been trying to explain what little I understood from talking to Mark and Nan – about the Tyrant and this other world called Tír.'

'General, I can confirm that I've seen some very strange things on the road to here. Everything Mark and Nan have been telling us appears to fit. Seems to me we're dealing with an enemy, and resources, that are way out of the ordinary.'

'Put Mark on, Brett.'

Brett passed the microphone to Mark.

'Mark, you have any thoughts?'

'General, Nan and I have had a good look at the Rose. We've looked at it through our oracula, which give us a better view than through ordinary eyes. We both agree with Brett. It's soaking up energy.'

'Makes one curious as to what it's doing with all that energy?'

'We've talked it over with Padraig. All three of us are convinced that the Black Rose is somehow linked to the Fáil.'

'Ah – the Fáil?'

'Do you remember what we told you about that?'

'I recall your speaking about it, but I can't really say that I understood. I'm not sure what we're talking about here, Mark. Are we talking about magic?'

'The people on Tír talk about portals, which are like gateways, to the Fáil. The Tyrant has been attempting to take possession of one. If he succeeds, that would allow him to control the Fáil.'

'Even though I don't understand a word you are saying, you're still managing to disturb me.'

'Sir, we also think that Grimstone's church is a distraction. This has nothing to do with religion. It's to do with power.'

'Well, at least that's something we do understand. I can well believe that the social upheaval, the violence and the anarchy are being orchestrated by this Tyrant you speak of as a means to power. And I can also believe that his purpose is very much contrary to our interests.'

'Then we share the same goal, Sir. We need to stop him. So, the only question is: how do we stop him?'

'I've talked to our friends in America. The weight of opinion is that the answer lies in London. We have to destroy the Black Rose.'

Mark said, 'I'd better pass you back to Brett.'

'Brett – you with me?'

'Yes, Sir.'

'Brett, we're opening up an encrypted line. You should already have the codes.'

Brett now accepted a keyboard from Tajh. He looked at the screen, his fingers typing in a series of sequential codes. When he was finished, the screen filled with the image of a grey-haired officer in an American uniform. There was a brief conversation between Brett and the officer and then the crew were looking at the face of Adam Wilberforce Harvey, the President of America.

'Mr President!' Brett said.

'Can I speak to you alone?'

'Sir, these people have risked their lives to get me here. They know things that I don't know, things that might be relevant to this discussion. I would prefer to keep them in the loop.'

'This is FEMA, Brett.'

'I know, Sir.'

'We have a very important decision to make.'

'Yes, Sir.'

'Very well! I don't think I am revealing any state secrets showing you this.'

Mark, like everybody in the crew, stared at scenes of anarchy and chaos in New York, Washington, LA and many other American cities.

'You, or your buddies over there, have any real explanation for what makes folks burn down their own cities?'

'Sir, can I ask if General Chatwyn is still privy to this conversation?'

Chatwyn's voice arrived through the laptop, though he remained invisible from the screen. 'Yes, Brett, I'm here.'

'Right, Sir! Over here they call these basket cases Razzamatazzers – Razzers for short.'

'Brett, I want you to see this. This is Central Park, right now.'

The screen showed vast numbers of Razzers gathering in the park. They appeared to be milling around a specific focus, next to a pond. As the camera focused in on individual faces, they saw hundreds of thousands of men and women milling in dense crowds around what looked like a raised bandstand.

'Look at their expressions, their eyes!'

The camera focused on face after face, showing the same blank looks, the same repetitive chanting on their lips.

'Brett, you have any idea what's going on?'

'It's a kind of mind control, Sir.'

'You mean they're drugged – stoned?'

'Some may be stoned. But from what I've been gathering here, Grimstone doesn't need drugs to control folks. He can do it through the effects of a talisman, a kind of magical sword. They call it the Sword of Feimhin.'

'Now, you know as well as I do how that sounds.'

'Yes, Sir. But I've seen Padraig here wield a magical battleaxe. He saved all our lives with it. Crazy things appear to be happening.'

'Up to now, these guys – the Razzamatazzers as you call them – have been indulging in criminal behaviour. I've sent in the National Guard in support of the police, and not just in New York but in Chicago, Washington, LA, and other cities. But the size of the problem is overwhelming our resources and we've failed to stop them. They've already burned out entire cities. And the madness is spreading.'

'Following the same pattern as here, Sir.'

'We've called up every reserve. They take no notice of warnings. They don't appear to care if they're shot.'

'I gather you've come across this guy, Grimstone?'

'He's everywhere.' The President glanced to his left, where somebody was muttering something to him in a soft voice. President Harvey turned to face them on screen again. 'I've just been informed that he's making an appearance in Central Park. He's what these flakes have been waiting for.'

'What's he doing?'

'Talking to them – sermonising, as far as I can see.'

'Can I have a look, Sir?'

'Okay! They're uploading pictures right now. Hold on a moment. I can make out his face. This your guy?'

Brett turned to Mark, who nodded.

'It's him, Sir, the Reverend Grimstone.'

Mark cut in, 'He's no Reverend.'

'You hear that, Mr President?'

'I heard.'

'That's from his adoptive son.'

Mark said: 'See if he's carrying a sword.'

The President spoke: 'He's sure as hell hefting something. Whatever it is, it's getting the crowds excited. But it looks more like a cross than a sword.'

Mark said, 'Could we see it in close-up?'

'Okay, you guys!' The President's voice muted, as if addressing somebody off screen. 'Maybe the camera in the chopper . . .'

Mark and Nan craned in to get a closer look at what Grimstone was holding aloft. 'Yeah, it's the Sword of Feimhin – but he's holding it upside down so the hilt and crosspiece resemble a cross.'

'You getting this, Sir?'

'I'm with you. But what does it mean?'

Mark looked to Brett: 'May I explain?'

'Go ahead.' Brett spoke to the President, 'I'm going to ask Grimstone's adoptive son, Mark, to explain, Sir.'

'Go ahead, Mark.'

'Sir, I'd also like to rope in my friend, Nan. She knows far more about the Tyrant than I do. I'm afraid that Grimstone has long been the servant of the Tyrant of the Wastelands. We believe that the Sword links Grimstone to both the Tyrant and the Black Rose.'

The President hesitated a moment or two, as if to consider what Mark had told him. 'Mark – I should explain that there are some very sceptical people this end. You need to take that on board.'

'Yes, Sir.'

'Very well then, Mark and Nan, the floor is yours.'

'Sir, as far as Nan and I have been able to observe, America is following a very similar pattern to what we saw in London. We believe that the Tyrant of the Wastelands has declared war on Earth. If, as we now assume, Grimstone has been his servant all along, he's been preparing for this war for many years, decades even. So the groundwork has been laid down during this time. It's all about power, really. Taking control on Tír to start with, and now Earth. Grimstone has been spreading a false religion, aimed at mind control. Several years ago, he took me and my adoptive sister, Mo, to Clonmel, in Ireland, but he was after the Sword even back then. He must have known that Padraig was its custodian. And he wanted to get his hands on it.'

'This is the same sword Grimstone is lofting in the Park?'

'Yes, Sir.'

'My word, Mark, I'm looking at that sea of faces! They're mesmerised by it.'

'Sir, we believe that the Sword is a repository of enormous power. We think it is capable of drawing power from the Fáil.'

'But you claim this Sword has been hidden in Ireland for thousands of years?'

'Sir, the war on Tír has been going on for thousands of years. We believe it extended into Earth right at the beginning. And it was only ended here when an army known the Fir Bolg crossed from Tír into Earth and killed Feimhin, a Bronze Age prince who wielded the Sword back then.'

'You're talking thousands of years ago?'

'Yes, Sir. I would like to ask Padraig to speak to you. He and his family have been custodians of the Sword for all those thousands of years. It was hidden in a barrow grave in Padraig's woods, on the foothills of the Comeragh Mountains.'

'Is Padraig prepared to speak to us?'

Mark looked across to Padraig. The old man nodded.

The President studied Padraig's face. 'Would you care to add to what Mark has been telling us?'

'I concur with all that Mark and Nan have told you, Sir. Nan in particular knows far more about Earth's sister world, Tír, than I do. Grimstone is the Tyrant's servant. The Sword, which, alas, we now see wielded in Central Park, is the repository of dark power. It is also likely to be the key to the mind control we heard discussed in this conference. But Grimstone is not the main threat, even when wielding the Sword. The real threat, and I believe it to be a very great threat indeed, is the arrival of the Black Rose in central London.'

'But why is the Earth so important to this Tyrant? From what you say, he's an alien being from an alien world?'

'This is a very important question, Sir, and one I have given much thought to in the last day or two. I can only conclude that the arrival of Mark and his three Earth-born friends into Tír has threatened the Tyrant's plans in that world.'

'But you claimed that Grimstone has been paving the

way for the present catastrophe for decades. From what information General Chatwyn has been sending us, the four friends only entered Tír a few years ago. Why would the Tyrant have made preparations to extend his war here a generation before there was any threat to his plans from any incursion into his world from Earth?'

Mark interrupted. 'Sir, if I might interrupt. I think that perhaps Nan might be best able to answer that question.'

'Nan, can you throw any light on this?'

'Sir, it is understandable that you still do not understand the Fáil and the power it wields over life, and over worlds.'

'Can you explain it, then, in words we might understand?'

'The four friends, Mark, his adoptive sister, Mo, Alan and Kate, were seduced into entering Tír by the powers of the Holy Trídédana – these goddesses are immensely powerful back on Tír. I would presume that their powers also derive from the Fáil. In attempting to gain access to, and thus control, the Fáil, the Tyrant of the Wastelands threatens the goddesses. The goddesses are his rival for power, and thus his ultimate enemy.'

'But that would assume that the Tyrant – and perhaps these so-called goddesses – anticipated the future? That would imply that the Tyrant must have known, in ages past, that the friends from Earth would, in the future, threaten his plans?'

'Yes, Sir.'

'He can predict the future?'

'There can be only one of two explanations. Either he anticipated the seduction by the goddesses of the four friends – or the Earth has always been an important conquest in his plans.'

'Go on.'

'The Black Rose must have taken years to effect. We met a girl called Penny, who sensed its presence long before it made an appearance. She painted a fresco over an entire ceiling of what she called the City Below. We think that Penny's City Below came from the growing roots of the Black Rose underneath the city of London, which she called the City Above. This was going on long before we travelled into Tír. It suggest years of planning and preparation on the part of the Tyrant.'

Mark added: 'And Grimstone has been preparing his false church for decades.'

The President nodded on screen: 'So what might this imply?'

'The Black Rose must be central to the Tyrant's ambitions to control the Fáil.'

'Which also implies that the Black Rose is the key to this war?'

'That is what Mark and I believe, Sir.'

Attack on the Rose

'This place,' Tajh muttered, 'is freaking me out.'

Mark glanced down at his observation partner, who was curled up within the horseshoe of bricks and rubble they had cobbled together in an attempt to keep warm. He and Tajh were one of three observation posts based around the location of the Pig, though they remained close enough to keep in touch through hand signals. As Seebox was operating a fleet of surveillance and attack drones, it would have been suicide to transmit any kind of radio or electronic communication.

Although Mark liked Tajh, he wished they had teamed him up with Nan. But Cal and Brett had said that the oracula were too valuable to put in one place; divided, he and Nan could cover more ground.

Tajh moaned: 'I'm wearing two vests under my shirt and two thick pullovers over it. And I'm still *freezing*.'

Mark shivered.

The ruins they had chosen as their shelter still bore the remnants of pea-green paint on the rubble, but all that was left of the front façade of a former restaurant was three feet of powdered brick.

'Shit!' Tajh continued to grumble. 'Look at that sky. Is that pretending to be daylight?'

Proximity to the Rose had put all of the crew under tremendous strain. The vast, alien nature of that soaring deadwall was unnerving, all the more so when you could feel the vibrations coming from it through the ground. The dread of it leached into your consciousness, as if you had woken up into a nightmare that refused to let you go.

Mark rubbed his hands together: *Focus on the present!*

By now Seebox was probably aware that his perimeter blockade had been breached. The crew had camouflaged the garage walls with heaped rubble to hide their den from the drones with their infrared scanners, but they couldn't avoid detection forever.

Tajh's voice fell to a whisper: 'Hisst – out there!'

'What is it?'

'Thought I heard something.'

Mark peered out into the grey murk. In the distance, he saw the ruins of a six-storey warehouse with its concrete roof caved in, its broken walls flecked with a rust-grimed tangle of ironwork.

Then he also heard something. After a second or two it faded again. It had sounded like an engine.

'What do we do?'

'We keep our heads down.'

The snow continued to fall onto the ruined landscape like a leprous confetti, creating a horrifying vista in which the tormented cityscape seemed upside down, with the ground lighter than the lowering sky.

'Try to think about something pleasant.'

'I can't bring to mind a single blessed thing,' Tajh grumbled.

'Think about green fields.'

'You're talking to a city girl, Mark. No rosy-hued dream of growing things or keeping chickens. I get claustrophobic if I don't see houses.'

Mark grunted: there weren't many houses round here any more.

'Try thinking about drinking cold pure water out of your cupped hands from a mountain stream.'

'Don't push it.' But she managed a grin.

'Then what?' Mark asked.

'There was one thing.'

'Yeah?'

'A little cock robin – when I was eight or nine years old.'

'A cock robin?'

'With his little puffed out chest. He was always in our yard, even when the snow was a couple of feet deep. I got the little sod through some hard winters.'

Mark returned the smile. 'You fed him?'

'Yeah. Every time I peeped out into that yard, there he was, cheeky laddie, always up to something.'

'No cheeky robins around here, huh?'

'Not a one,' Tajh paused. 'Mark, you really believe that Brett knows what he's doing?'

'We have to believe so.'

Tajh snorted. She paused for another second or two, then climbed to her feet having spotted a signal from Cal, whose head was poking out of a foxhole fifty yards away. Cal had been paired with Nan. Now Tajh got out the binoculars to interpret his gestures.

'Vehicle incoming.'

'Shit!'

They ducked back down into the horseshoe, peering now and then over the snow-capped sill of what had been a street level window. Within a minute or two they spotted the ghostly shape of an armoured car, its outline slightly darker than the grey murk, its exhaust billowing smoke. They could make out the silhouette of it more clearly as it drew abreast of them; it had the flat top of the gun turret at the front and the long aerial dangling from the rear. By the time it was thirty yards away, Mark could make out the helmet of the driver poking out of the front of the cab. The vehicle sported a heavy cannon and had a dish on its roof.

'What now, Marky boy?'

She had only begun to call him that with this present assignment. Mark put it down to her growing nervousness. He said: 'I need to think.'

The dish was scanning through 360 degrees:

eavesdropping for electronic signals. Tajh muttered: 'What if those blasted drones have picked up on Brett's satellite comms?'

Mark shrugged. There was nothing they could do about that if they had, but even if they hadn't, it wouldn't be too long before they did. When that happened the garage would stand out like a painted target . . . and it was the only place to hide in the surrounding square mile.

'That cannon could do some damage.'

Mark flashed a mind-to-mind picture of what he was seeing, and thinking, to Nan.

'We have to destroy it,' Tajh said.

'That could bring even more attention down on our heads,' Mark whispered.

But then they saw that the circling dish on the top of the vehicle had stopped – and was pointing straight at the garage. The cannon rotated in the same direction.

'Do it! Do it now!' Tajh shouted.

Mark focused his oraculum on the squat grey outline and incinerated the occupants of the armoured car in blue-black lightning. He did his best to dampen the flare, but he couldn't guarantee it hadn't been spotted from overhead.

'Jesus – glad to have you on our side!'

'Sorry Tajh. One of us is going to have to check they're dead.'

'Meaning me?'

He watched her scurry over on the crouch to the ruin of

the vehicle. While she was checking the bodies, Mark used his oraculum to reconnoitre the surrounding environment: ground and sky. As far as he could determine there were no responding drones, but Seebox's people were bound to investigate the missing patrol. Within a few minutes, Tajh was back in their foxhole and signalling to Cal – thumb and finger in a circle: threat dealt with. Something he signalled back excited her. She looked a lot more cheerful when she signalled Cal back: *copy that.*

Mark said: 'Copy what?'

'The strike on the Rose – it's on!'

From the moment they had first arrived, it had become obvious that the Rose had been Brett's primary assignment. He had been sent there to find out what it was, what it was capable of doing and how to eliminate it. Upon arrival, he had fired a series of three separate drones into the inky blackness of the night sky, aiming for a point high above the Rose. These had enabled him to make some key observations on the positioning and size of the Rose, and now they were providing readings that might reveal much more to his team in the USA.

Right now, in his foxhole, Mark knew that Resistance HQ and America were analysing the data Brett had sent them. The confirmation of the impending strike would please the crew. It meant their mission had achieved its end. But, as they were so close to the Rose, it also meant they were in danger of friendly fire. Yet, they had no option but to stay: the fate of London and perhaps the world at large depended on them continuing to monitor the Rose and the effectiveness of the strike.

Figuring this out, Mark muttered, 'Shit!'

Tajh's voice betrayed her shivering: 'C'mon, Marky boy! Get down here and huddle up. Keep us warm.'

'D'you reckon Cal is keeping an eye on us?'

'You know he is – just like you're keeping an eye on Nan.'

Mark grinned, stepping down and huddling up. He thought back to President Harvey's tired face on the monitor: a shot of him sitting at the centre of an oval table, surrounded by the Chiefs of Staff . . .

'You still in there with us, Brett?' the President had said.

'Yes, Sir, I'm here,' Brett replied.

'Our scientists tell us that in the short time the Black Rose has been with us the mean atmospheric temperature over the Earth has risen two degrees.'

'Sir – how does this fit with whatever else has been going on?'

'I'm going to pass you on to FEMA's scientific coordinator, Professor Jess Harding, who will explain.'

An angular white-haired woman occupied the screen. 'We don't pretend to understand the object in question.' The object in question, or the OIQ, was what they were now calling the Black Rose. 'It resembles nothing we have ever seen previously, in terms of weaponry or anything else. However, there is plenty to suggest that it is threatening.'

Brett said: 'How so, Professor?'

'It is absorbing energy.'

'Can you be more specific?'

'We believe that it is drawing its energy from the sun.'

The crew around their makeshift table stared up into the comm screen with open astonishment.

Brett said: 'What the hell does that mean?'

'You must have considered its shape: plants soak up the energy of the sun to photosynthesise. Think of radio receivers – we use the same dish-like shapes. We believe that that's why the OIQ looks like it does: it's a vast receiver directed at the sun.'

'But why? What's it need all that energy for?'

'This we don't know. But we've been studying the sun and examining the arc of its surface as we turn to face it at midday, GMT. A large solar flare now occupies that vicinity; a huge flare that wasn't there before the OIQ appeared.'

'So, that's what's raising the atmospheric temperature?'

'We think so.'

'Mr President, if this is true—'

'We're gathering more evidence from various other scientific groups, both in the States and globally. The world's climate is undergoing some serious upheavals.'

'Shee-it,' Brett breathed.

'We are effectively at war with an unknown threat from an unknown and alien world. We have no choice here but to attack.'

'This is London we are talking about, Sir.'

The President sighed, his eyes scanning the ranks of the senior officers around the table. 'Which means we have to contain the strike, as best we can. And that also means we must ask you to monitor the success or otherwise of the strike and report back to us.'

Sitting in his freezing foxhole, Mark acknowledged that order with a clenched jaw. They were the sacrificial grunts.

A Bargain with Death

Alan's onkkh was refusing to advance. Its nostrils were streaming puss from the acrid mist that eddied and flowed down the slopes from the welling source at the south gate. On contact with eyes and skin, it burned like acid. Alan looked downslope to his left, to where the ocean was on fire. He could hear faint screams from the sailors aboard the Leviathans as the giant battleships were annihilated by the Septemvile Firebane. He hoped that the remainder of the fleet, including the warships of the Shee, had been able to withdraw. The menace was every bit as bad on the landward approach, but here the screams of the dying were fully audible, though it was impossible to see the way ahead because of a dense ground-hugging mist. He switched to his oraculum, knowing that something worse than mechanical weaponry, the Septemvile Lightbane, confronted him.

Attack by a Septemvile was deadly, but Alan didn't care about his own risk. He asked himself what it implied.

The Septemviles were said to be immortal. Was this really true or was it merely a reflection of the awe and terror they put into the hearts of their enemies?

Alan was inclined to question it. He wondered if all it meant was that none had ever been beaten in battle. But those who had fought them in ages past had not been armed with the magical powers of oracula. Recently Earthbane had been defeated by Kate and Mo. So they were, potentially, defeatable. Alan had previously confronted the skull-faced Captain. He had fought this terrible being in the Battle of Ossierel. The Legun had appeared indomitable then, proving impervious to Alan's Spear of Lug, even though it was infused with all of the power of his oraculum. It had also shrugged off the former Kyra, when in a final desperation she had amplified her own power with Alan's First Power, to make her dying self into a weapon. But the Captain had been forced to flee the battlefield by the army of the dead Fir Bolg. Two Leguns: and both had been defeated, even though their defeat had required magic, exceptional knowledge and power.

All this swept through Alan's mind as he made ready to attack the enemy forces that confronted them at the south gate.

Lifting his gaze above the mist-covered approaches, he took in the panorama of the slopes and the two hundred foot high walls that rose from them, and highest of all, the reinforced fortress that enclosed the south gate. Surely this Septemvile, Lightbane, would prove to be equally defeatable?

Alan began to climb again when he heard a warning cry from Iyezzz, high in the air above him. The Garg prince had spotted something new up ahead. Alan called, mind-to-mind, to the Kyra and warned her. His senses were on high alert as he spurred his resistant mount upwards. The onkkh beneath him reared. Its clawed legs were slipping and sliding. It was beginning to topple over. Alan's grip on the beast was slipping, his body toppling forwards, over its lowered shoulders. He leaned all of his weight back, hauling the beast back into its stride.

He heard the Kyra roar ahead and to his right. He contacted her urgently, oraculum-to-oraculum.

<What is it, Ainé?>

<My sisters-in-arms are facing annihilation!>

<What's happening to them?>

<Blinded by the miasma of the Septemvile, the forward thrust is leading into a multitude of traps. The ground, under the irritating mist, is constantly changing. A quicksand appears without warning taking all who had previously assumed it to be solid ground. A pit of spikes rears up out of the ground, impaling all who stand upon it. Whirling blades of razor sharp iron cut through what would appear open air, severing neck and limbs of the Shee, reducing warriors to mincemeat. Meanwhile the Death Legion is issuing in large numbers through the gate.>

<Damnation! How can we stop them?>

<We must find a way through the traps to engage them hand-to-hand.>

The onkkh all around Alan were honking madly, reacting to the uncertain footing. His mount swayed violently from side to side, shifting from one clawed paw to another. At any moment it would throw him and flee the battlefield.

What was he to do?

Alan stared anew into the foggy scene ahead. He could make out nothing that would possibly help him command the attack. His nostrils retracted from the acrid stink of the blinding mist. He must surely be closer to the Legun, Lightbane. He had to challenge it – kill it.

'Qwenqwo?' he shouted.

'By your right flank!'

'Your advice – quickly?'

'We are losing this war of attrition. We should throw caution to the wind. Charge forward immediately. At close quarters we might get to grips with it.'

Alan spurred the onkkh ahead, the Spear of Lug pressed before him.

There was a scream from Kate inside his head. She was calling out to him:

<Ebrit's Leviathans are destroyed. Magtokk fears that the battlefield has been lost. He has fled the scene, taking Mo with him.>

Alan understood now why the Tyrant had played with them on their march to this confrontation: Ghork Mega was itself the trap. Never had he anticipated such ferociously opposing power. His senses were overwhelmed with the violence of attack.

Still, the blinded Shee continued to fight using their other senses and their acute sense of smell, to battle on. For a single extraordinary moment he was one with them, sharing the common heart and mind of the Kyra that spurred them onwards. Their vanguard was within a hundred yards of the south gate. They ripped with their claws and snapped with their fangs at the nets and spears that were hurled upon them, refusing to be defeated. But they were fighting overwhelming odds and Alan sensed thousands falling as the mist reached them, their flesh boiling, their bodies reduced to living skeletons before death.

Damnation!

The losses he sensed were enormous. He saw, through his oraculum, that as they died, their soul spirits rose into the air, wailing – pining for the unbroken circle. He tried to communicate with them, but their dying spirits could not see him, their eyes blank, opened onto darkness. Despair rose inside him. He didn't know what to do to halt it.

Alan reminded himself: *Think of Mom and Dad.*

The need for action overtook him. 'Qwenqwo – quickly – loft your runestone!'

'To what purpose? There are no Fir Bolg on this battlefield. All lie dead and buried in the Vale of Tazan, a thousand leagues to the west of here.'

'Qwenqwo, please, for my sake – do what I ask!'

'The Powers preserve us!'

Qwenqwo's words struck Alan like a physical blow. They

echoed in his mind, provoking an extraordinary, maybe outrageous, idea. He recalled a terrifying experience right at the beginning of their journey into this war-ravaged world. They had made their way to the summit of Slievenamon, the so-called magic mountain, where they had discovered an Ogham-inscribed stone bowl in the cumulus of stones on the summit. Here they did what had been suggested to them by Alan's grandfather, Padraig: they had gathered the waters of the three rivers that flowed into the estuary of Waterford, the Suir, the Nore and the Barrow. The rivers were sacred to the Trídédana of Celtic legend – Mab, who together with her daughters, had cured Mo after she was spiritually damaged by the Legun known as the Captain; Bave, the goddess of the land and elements, whose ruby oraculum Alan still bore in his brow; and Mórígán . . . Mórígán, the dreaded goddess of death . . . death and the battlefield . . .

The goddess of the battlefield!

Alan recalled how, in a moment of terrifying threat on the summit of Slievenamon, he had been consumed by the impulse to incant the name of the goddess of death . . .

Alan wheeled his onkkh around to discover the Kyra nearby. He shouted to her: 'Ainé! Have the Shee form up in a new triple-pronged attack.'

'It will be done.'

Alan took a firm grip of his agitated mount. He turned his face skywards, where the air was being poisoned by Lightbane.

He allowed the oraculum to turn inwards, invading his

flesh to glow fiercely within the core of his being. With every last ounce of his strength, Alan hurled a name into the sky: *'Mó-rí-gáááán!'*

He sensed the name condense into a point of utter darkness, which became the focus of his own oraculum.

<Our purpose in coming to this world is under the gravest threat. If we lose this battle, you lose this world . . .>

Alan did not know if she could hear him, but he issued the words through his oraculum anyway.

Then he saw the pinpoint of black expanding. He was one with the darkness as it proliferated and took form: a gigantic triangle of black consuming the light. He was one with the mountainous skull with its cavernous pits for eyes – one with the slow beating of the leviathan wings. He was one with the almighty raven that expanded until it circumscribed the heavens.

<There will be no battlefield bargain with this one!>

Who was speaking?

Pain exploded in Alan's head. He was flung off the back of the rearing onkkh to crash against the rocky ground, the breath ripped from his lungs, his thoughts a confusion of rage and need.

Before him, a great force assuming the form of a pillar manifested. Within the pillar he saw a cowled figure. The Tyrant! He probed it through his oraculum, discovering a spiritual being, a blazing storm of power, a face that was a matrix of dark and light.

<Mórígán . . . help me!>

<Cha-teh-teh-teh-teh-teh.>

A new voice, more friendly, inside his head, one he recognised from what now seemed half a lifetime ago. The growling cadences of Granny Dew!

<Duuuvaaalll – daaannngerrr!>

<What am I to do?>

<Would you embrace death?>

<Yes!>

Alan's spirit was torn from the battlefield to wheel through caverns bedecked with stalactites and stalagmites as fine as hair, their crystals glittering like diamonds. He entered a circle of petrified trees. In the centre was a single stone figure, cowled and shawled. As he grew nearer, he saw that it was blue-black and flickering with light. He could smell something like incense, oils . . . Grimy taloned fingers grasped his shoulders and propelled him forward, into the maelstrom of power. The deep voice he recognised as Granny Dew's growled another warning, but it was also a demand for veneration:

<Cha-teh-teh-teh-teh-teh!>

Danger . . .

A face manifested in the head of the stone figure: a skull that was only half emerged from terrifying shadow. Its teeth were bared in a dreadful smile . . .

He was unable to resist the impulse to touch the skull. He brushed the ivory teeth, which felt colder than ice. There was an overwhelming instinct to withdraw, to run . . . but he fought against it.

A new impulse compelled him to bring his brow against the rounded bone. He could smell herbs and oils. He could feel the area of contact condense to follow the triangular shape of the oraculum. He felt a new overwhelming compulsion to kiss the smiling mouth, the rictus of teeth. Lacking the strength to hold back any longer, he kissed the teeth that passed for its mouth, tasting earth, the cloyingly sweet taste of aromatic oils . . .

A new shock of union rippled through him like an electrical discharge, thrilling to the very tips of his fingers and toes. A deep, animal part of him exulted. He was back on the battlefield, but he felt different. His heart, his spirit, felt indomitable.

There was no time to think. He raised his right arm, the Spear of Lug blazing with the ruby glow of his oraculum. 'Now let Death take force in me. Let Death become me. Let me kill them all – all that remains of the Tyrant's Septemviles – every last one of them in this city.'

Death moved through him like a hurricane, robbing him of thought and feeling. Blue-black lightning rose out of his arm into the Spear of Lug, then struck out from the blade in all directions. He could see the Septemvile, Lightbane, up close ahead – pallid as wax, with eyes that were all black – restored to its waxy glowing figure within the towering arch of the south gate. A sneer of triumph stretched its pallid lips. Focusing all of his rage, Alan hurled the Spear of Lug at the approaching Legun. The force of the throw threw him backwards through the air. But he had no care for his own safety. As he landed, he felt an expanding wave of darkness strike his target and heard the dying roar of the Legun. He curled up as the blast hit him; his hair and skin burned inside his armour, as if a furnace had suddenly opened its gates before him.

He lay on the ground in a maelstrom of fire and lightning. He was losing consciousness, but he still registered the changes taking place around him and the Kyra's roar: 'Forward – through the broken gate!'

Voices calling . . . Alien voices . . . Voices shrieking things he did not understand. He had visited this place of terror and pain before.

Something was moving inside him; trying to break free. It made him wonder if he was dying. At the same time his consciousness was being probed by an external force: a vast impersonal matrix. There was an awakening agony in which his limbs felt as if they were being torn from their sockets. The suffering deepened. It became so agonising he would have welcomed the liberation of death. It was simply unbearable, as if he were a mote of concentrated agony utterly lost.

Then, a new voice . . . a kind voice. More voices . . . Among them a voice of love . . .

<Oh, Alan – please don't die on me!>

Kate . . . Kate's thoughts: he was hearing her thoughts enter his mind.

A kiss on his feverish lips.

The return of his sight began with a cooling aura of green as Kate healed him, beginning at his brow and then expanding her power down through his head and neck and out into his chest, his arms, then further into his abdomen, his legs, to the tips of his fingers, the tips of his toes.

'He's coming to.'

'What ails him?'

'He embraced Death.'

'Why in the name of the Powers?'

'To destroy the Septemviles.'

'Are they gone?'

'I think so – I very much hope so.'

'But at what terrible cost?'

That was his thought, too.

He recognised the voices as Kate's and Qwenqwo's: 'The Shee are pouring into the city through the breached gate.'

'Qwenqwo,' he whispered. 'Help me up!'

He could no longer make out Qwenqwo's reply in the rising babble of a great many raised voices.

For some reason he could not understand, he was gazing out onto an ocean. He was looking at gentle waves coming and going, and he had no idea what it meant. But it was a very restful vision. He tried to speak.

Kate's voice: 'Hush now – rest! You have exhausted yourself. The aides are coming with healwell. In the meantime, let me help your body and spirit recover.'

He tried to tell her he loved her. But his whisper was inaudible.

'Hush now!'

Mo's Fate

<Mira!>

Mo heard the voice inside her mind. It came from the Torus. She knew that it was the voice of one of the True Believers: <The singularity is approaching. You must make ready for the ceremony of judgement.>

This time it felt different from any previous visitation. She looked across at the sleeping form of her guardian Shee. Usrua would normally wake at the slightest noise, even a tiny change in the pattern of Mo's breathing, but she slept on. Mo looked down at her hands, sensing their solidity as she lifted them to brush the skin of her face.

'Where are we going?'

<Would you know your destiny?>

'Yes.'

<Then come!>

Mo hesitated: 'Will Magtokk be accompanying me?'

<If so you desire.>

'I do.'

It was deeply reassuring to know that Magtokk would be with her.

<Do you need more time to prepare?>

'No. I am ready.'

She had deliberately avoided discussing her previous journeys in advance with Alan or Kate. This time she wouldn't even have the opportunity of explaining. She wondered if Alan in particular would disapprove. Alan didn't want her to take any risks while he placed himself in huge danger and bore huge responsibilities all by himself. But she was no longer the 'Little Mo' who had arrived here on Tír those few, eventful years ago. She wasn't some cosseted female who must be protected at all costs. She had been preparing for this journey since they had first arrived.

Mo climbed to her feet and dressed, as if she were preparing for an ordinary journey into the cold night air. She whispered: 'Magtokk – are you here with me?'

<I am here.>

'I presume, from what I've been told, that we are returning to the labyrinth beneath the Valley of the Pyramids.'

<Indeed.>

'Will we need Thesau?'

<There is no need. Your journey will be empowered by your talisman.>

Mo gripped the Torus with both her hands. She closed

her eyes tight. She felt a wave of communication flow around her, like the fluttering of silken wings.

<Come!> The voice in her head whispered.

It was the familiar voice – the voice that had addressed her when she had stood on the roof of the Comeragh Mountains, at the very beginning of the adventure. A magical voice, an enchantment . . .

She felt the song rise to her lips from the spirit being within her.

Mira sang, as she had sung that morning on the Comeraghs. There were no words to the song, just the melody of the enchantment. And already she was back, without even noticing the journey, in the Valley of the Pyramids. Only recently, when she had last come to this arid, unsettling valley with its haunted landscape of despoliation and its towers of skulls, she had allowed her fears to overwhelm her. Tonight she no longer feared it. She saw a glow rising like a mist of fireflies up out of the stony floor and recalled the wonder of its cause. She saw the wasp-goblins fluttering out of their stone-capped holes in the ground, their wings catching the starlight. She saw the proliferation of millions, perhaps billions, of glistening filaments, like silken threads, streaming out of the pyramids until they filled the entire valley floor.

She recalled Magtokk's explanation from the last time she had come here: '*The eye of the weave is woven from crystals of stardust.*'

She looked down and saw, where one would expect

shadows, that crystals cast shadows of glowing light on the ground. She remembered Magtokk's explanation: *'The weave of nets . . . designed to monitor the cosmos.'*

'Oh, Magtokk – it's wonderful!'

Still, she welcomed his manifestation, the heavy arm that wrapped itself around her shoulders. His breath was soft against her ear: 'It is time for you to embrace your destiny.'

'What is my destiny?'

'I cannot explain. You must discover it for yourself.'

Mo struggled to swallow the lump in her throat. The Torus was pulsing steadily, powerfully, as if something wonderful was about to happen. In anticipation, Mo wrapped both her hands around it, looking down at the pulses of light illuminating the cradle of her fingers. She couldn't stop herself shivering in the cold. Her mind was full of black clots, wheeling and changing against a harsh white background. The Akkharu were calling out to one another – and to her.

Magtokk spoke, gently, into her ear: 'Mind-to-mind from this point on.'

'Mind-to-mind,' she whispered back.

<They are waiting for you.>

<Who are?>

<All from the lowliest Akkharu apprentice to the most senior of the elect.>

<The elect?>

<The beings you know as True Believers. Take heart. On

the last occasion you came here, things were somewhat disorganised. Today all is in readiness for your coming. There will be celebration. You will be welcomed.>

They drifted through the underground passageways and caverns, weightless. Crowds lined the byways eager to welcome her. The air was filled with the petals of blossoms and flowers like motes of pollen caught in a glade of sunlight.

<Oh, Magtokk!>

Mira accepted showers of kisses on her hands and feet from a flock of tiny creatures that looked like the flower fairies. They were incredibly delicate, and their flesh was semi-transparent with a moiré sheen that made it look like silk.

<You must now open your mind.>

<*Why?*>

<To free your spirit. Take a deep breath with me. When you exhale, feel all the resistance flow from your mind to your limbs, and out of your limbs. Feel the liberation that comes with it.>

Mira's body, back in the tent, took a deep breath. She allowed the breath to drain from her, exhaling not merely from her lungs, but allowing her the resistance, born from her fears, to flow out through every organ and limb.

<Every part of me is tingling.>

She felt her senses expand. Her mind delighted in the most intense curiosity, a need to know everything about everything, no matter how trivial as they drifted through the underground labyrinth.

<I need to look more deeply. I need to follow the logic . . . I need to understand how the fabric of this strange world works.>

She sensed, without needing to see it, Magtokk's smile.

Mira noticed that the thoughts of the Akkharu flowed from one to another as they shared experiences.

<Chardizz, in their language> he explained, <means stardust.>

Mira nodded.

<The same substance of magic is found in the legends of many peoples in many worlds: in shoel, which means life; in réaltan, which means the stars; in sheeriochtan, in the Garg tongue, which means the longing for eternity.>

Eternity: Mira held onto that word. She sensed the potency of it and the allusion to her fate.

She was learning, very rapidly, about the blind underground goblin-beings who called themselves the Myrrh. They buzzed by her, aware of, but nevertheless ignoring her presence. The Myrrh darted around in clusters; in groups that had shape and purpose that she now recognised, and with recognition, she understood: their purpose was to protect the Akkharu so the Akkharu could focus on creation. With the delicacy of a spider's spinneret, the Akkharu wove the weightless crystals of chardizz into beautiful shapes and structures. Underground, the assembled shapes were constrained by their surroundings, but out there in the cool night air of the valley they floated, impervious to gravity, weightless. The skulls of the Myrrh were somewhat insectile in shape, but as large as a human baby's. There were other wingless forms that were tall and angular, which Mira now understood to be the Myrrh females. They inhabited egg chambers. The flesh of the females was more delicate than the winged males, with distinctly different mouth parts that comprised both vertical and horizontal jaws. These chewed a pulpy mass into honeycombs in alternate bites. The etiolated females had smoky blue eyes. It was these females who cultivated the fungi underground in gloriously colourful mushroom gardens.

Right then, in the middle of satisfying her curiosity about the Myrrh, Mira was startled to discover that they were also telepathic. She listened to their conversations, which involved, for the most part, a communication of needs and urges, the organisation within a group mind. Then she discovered a commonality that startled her out of her reverie. They were communicating the direction and pace of a single invader, whose passage was noted and spread throughout the common mind. She discovered the name of the invader, and with it their name for her: Star Weaver.

<Magtokk – did you hear it too?>

He said: <You push against the boundaries of creation within your mind and bit by bit, your understanding expands and changes. This is how creativity functions, whether you are a child drawing the crude picture of his parent's faces or a great artist or composer – or indeed a magician weaving a spell.>

Was this what she was doing? Was she a magician weaving a new spell?

How curious that she should be discovering more about herself by applying her new, insatiable curiosity about others.

The female Myrrh chewed on root fibres to make bedding and clothes for the young, which were incredibly ugly in their nakedness. They cannibalised their own dead. In this way all was recycled, the dead continuing to contribute to the living. In such an ungiving landscape nothing was wasted. The Myrrh saw the Akkharu as deities working amongst them. In the giant caverns they venerated grottoes of Akkharu skulls, thus the construction of the pyramids above ground was a religious instinct and a veneration.

Mira and Magtokk had descended into the deepest layers of the labyrinth, where the metamorphosing black clots filled one's mind, and the Akkharu laboured over the chardizz crystals.

<At this point we must tread gently> Magtokk said. <The Akkharu communicate in concepts rather than words.>

<What does Akkharu mean?>

<In your language, the closest concept might be dream catcher. But it might also be dream stealers, or dream weavers. So many meanings are wrapped up in this single word.>.

To Mira, the notion of a dream stealer was frightening. It reminded her of the ravenous monsters that had preyed upon them as they had approached the Witch's Tower of Bones.

<Why are these crystals so important?>

<They are imbued with the forces that gave rise to the initial creation of the universe and the property inherent in that same creativity is immortality.>

Magtokk's words stunned her. These black crystals were linked right back to the forces of creation? How could this be true? How could they be so important?

She was entering the strange, enchanting cavern she likened to a hall of mirrors and she had the same impression of it that she had experienced on her last visit to the labyrinth: it was as if her spirit were passing through veil after veil of twinkling barriers, but this time, her senses were no longer clouded with fear. Mira realised that the barriers were stages of transformation; and it was she who was transforming. With every transformation, she felt increasingly powerful as she gained understanding that was profound, electrifying and disturbing at once.

<Stay aware, Mira! Do not be overwhelmed. It is important that you keep a close control on your senses at this point. Let your mind expand – but you must remain in control.>

<What's happening?>

<We are about to enter Dromenon.>

<What is Dromenon?>

<It is a creation of the Arinn; a bridge between the finite and infinity.>

<Oh, my! So the True Believers . . .>

<Are capable of crossing the bridge between the immensities.>

Mo had to focus on what Magtokk was explaining. She remembered his caution: do not allow yourself to be overwhelmed.

<It is no accident that the Akkharu are the Tyrant's most closely guarded secret. Our journey from this point may prove alarming as well as enlightening.>

<In what way?>

<You must take nothing for granted – there will be no certainty of place, or time, no certainty of being alive. What you formerly assumed to be realities are abstractions here.>

<I don't understand.>

<All that you take for granted can be gambled, utterly changed, or even utterly lost, in the creative weave of being.>

<Oh!>

<Now do you understand the skill of the Akkharu?>

<I . . . I think I do.>

<You must engage with them. Quickly now. We must close our spirit eyes . . .>

Even with her eyes tightly closed, Mira was temporally blinded by the blaze of white light as they entered a new chamber, where the filaments all converged into a dome that blazed with light, like the surface of the sun.

<This is the cynosure> said Magtokk.

<I don't know if I will get used to the brightness. Oh,

goodness, but I don't even know where to begin. Is what you ask of me humanly possible?>

<You will be guided.>

<Who—?>

<Here they come. They are rising out of Dromenon to welcome you.>

Mo was giddy with excitement as she saw the starry beings who called themselves True Believers emerge from the blazing floor. They flowed into her, and yet again, just as she had encountered in the hall of mirrors, the communion felt strangely natural and empowering.

<What is happening to me? What am I becoming?>

<The Heralded One.>

As her eyes and senses became more accustomed to the proximity of Dromenon, it no longer felt threatening or alien to her. She whirled around and around, examining the chamber's vast stellate composition, its ceiling of intricate cones through which the weave rose towards the valley floor.

<It's so beautiful – so glorious.>

<Yes.>

<What are we waiting for?>

<The first ripples of the Great Cycle.>

Mira heard the song of the Akkharu, and the blueprint of the song took shape from the metamorphosing black shapes. As if taken up in a dance of magic, the Akkharu began to shape gossamer structures from the crystals with their elongated teeth and claws. On and on they spun the magical weave, so the filaments soared all around them until she and Magtokk found themselves at the centre within a bubble of filaments. This coalesced with other bubbles until a glistening spindle shape was made. The spindle established contact with the meniscus of Dromenon and then it began to move through it, trailing a passage of light that was still connected to the filaments of stardust covering the valley floor.

The girl Mo had not been ready for it then: but the new woman, Mira, was ready for it now.

<No more riddles.>

<The cycle of being is everywhere. A human child is born, matures to adult, lives, reproduces, then dies. Then the offspring repeat the cycle. Water falls as rain, enters the rivers, flow to the sea, evaporates to the skies and then falls as rain again. The seasons rotate, the death of winter wakes to the birth of spring, the maturity of summer and then dies to winter again. All is a cycle. Even in the very cosmos, great stars are born, mature and ultimately die, to be reborn. The cosmos is a weave of cycles. Its great cycle can be observed, not with the temporary eyes of the living, but through the weave of the Akkharu, a weave that you are now capable of understanding. And thus are you capable of predicting the moment we call the singularity.>

<That was why I had to be born?>

<Yes.>

<It's the True Believers who are monitoring the change? They're directing the Akkharu through the eye of the weave, aren't they?>

<Yes.>

<It will be a wonder to behold; the end of one cosmic cycle and the birth of another.>

Mira thrilled with the wonder of it.

She heard a song – a very beautiful song. She realised that it was her own song, but it was being returned to her on the lips of something that could not be human. It was that same voice that had called her on the summit of the mountain. She heard its enchanted whisper beckon her, mind-to-mind . . .

Looming Questions

'I beg the counsel of my Lord and Master.' The Preceptress' face was a mask of agitation, her voice drowned out by another thunderous cannonade from the massed fleet, which had mysteriously recovered from the earlier oceanic conflagration. 'I beg and beg and yet He ignores my pleas.'

Snakoil Kawkaw bowed to hide his sneer. How soothing to witness her disarray, her dress rent from her agitation, her dirt-encrusted feet bare. Now, in the moment his ears were still ringing from the thunder of the cannons, he took comfort in the thought that her desperation might imply a golden opportunity for him.

'His venerated city is burning. Doesn't He care that the situation has become desperate – grievous!' she said.

'A dreadful dilemma, indeed, beloved Mistress.'

She whirled in a fury. 'Would you mock me?'

'Would I be so devoid of pity?'

'Pity? Is pity what you would offer me, you snivelling cur? When I can see how gleeful you are at my despair.'

'Noble Lady—'

'Shut your snout, you stinking bear.'

He had to bury a wide grin – a toothsome bear grin – by looking at the floor. 'Perhaps I should go back out? See if I can find some useful morsel of information?'

'So you can gloat over the appalling spectacle of the ruined city? Is that your perfidious intention?'

He didn't need to lift his gaze to know that she would be caressing her dagger – hoping for a sign. Oh, sweet fate! Kawkaw was attuned to his new opportunity.

'Go on! Get out of here! Take your rancorous stink out of my nostrils, you loathsome fish gutter.'

He threw on his sealskin, and slipped a dagger into the deep pocket under his surviving left arm. But even as he slouched out through the entrance slit, her contempt trailed him into the din of battle.

'You scum! When my Master wins this war, as He most assuredly will, He will cleanse this world of you fish gutters.' Even as she spoke, the Preceptress' face changed. Her lips twisted into a scowl of pleasure as if she were savouring this picture.

What had changed? Had she received a message from her master? He couldn't help but notice how her left hand – the hand that held the dagger – was trembling. But was it trembling with panic or excitement?

There was another possibility still, a more worrisome

one. Had her Master cast the dice on some new gamble? Was that why the city was burning? Had the Tyrant of the Wastelands always followed an altogether different plan, one in which such losses were irrelevant? In emerging from the cloying tent, Kawkaw's mind was already in torment. But, he couldn't afford to worry about the Preceptress' threats, not when there was a more pressing situation. Everywhere the Shee witches, and Ebrit's mailed army, were in the ascendant.

He was careful to avoid the vast proliferation of tents, banners and pennants of the prince's army. Less worrisome were the giant siege towers of the Shee witches – no longer needed now that the city was fallen. Still, he gave their ditched and patrolled enclosure a wide berth. Those cattish nostrils could sniff him out in a trice. Instead, he struck south, distancing himself from the blazing city and the vast encampments of one sort or another that filled the air with the smoke and smells of a thousand cooking fires. His compass, as ever, drew him towards the poorer and less guarded warrens of the Olhyiu. Here ramshackle bars proliferated.

Here Kawkaw managed to distract a youthful assistant chef with filthy jokes, giving him the opportunity to slip half a roasted duck inside his coat. The rising aroma of the roasted flesh caused his mouth to water before he had put a hundred paces between himself and the bar. He was so hungry he devoured his entire prize in a few hungry crunches, the bones, sinews, and fat dribbling flesh.

O powers who dare!

Not a single guard, Shee or Carfonese, had confronted him. None was interested in a solitary feral.

Ho, then! Am I invisible?

He strode to the summit of a hillock, a vantage which overlooked the entire battlefield from the ship-clogged ocean to the blazing inferno of the Tyrant's city. From this high point, Kawkaw could see a black pall of smoke, which created a vast cloud that wheeled and battened over the wide bay. Soot fell from it like black snow. The fleet, which only a day or two before, had retreated with fire licking at their sterns, had returned to crowd against the walls of the city. Kawkaw could make out the blackened ruins of most of Ebrit's Leviathans poking out of the shallow waters near the shore, but now, all around them, the ocean was solid with hundreds of lesser craft endlessly spitting cannon fire, no matter that they were pounding ruins.

What a sight was the burning Ghork Mega! From this elevation, Kawkaw could glimpse the continuing battle within the city walls. He could make out ant-sized figures still fighting within the vast labyrinth of streets and squares despite the billowing flames and the clouds of black smoke, determined to fight their way to the Tyrant's own lair, the adamantine citadel that crowned the summit. An acid of consternation burned in his belly to witness how the great city – perhaps the greatest gem of architecture and wonder in the whole of Tír – was being reduced to havoc and ruin. What was to gain from such plunder? More pertinently, who was to gain?

Not him – not Snakoil Kawkaw, who had suffered such privations in the journey hither. Not the witch warriors, who had no empathy for architectural grandeur, any more than they had for gold and jewels. They would destroy it all. Never in his life had he had the pleasure of entering the outskirts of Ghork Mega, nor the pleasure of viewing the vast metropolis from within. Even the hinterlands had been so warded and threatening that they had excluded all but the Tyrant's pets from enjoying its pleasures.

And just look at how the mighty were fallen!

How had things come to this? What did it signify? More pertinently, what did it signify to Snakoil Kawkaw?

These questions whirled in his mind. He had long admired Ghork Mega's wealth. No city, not even Carfon, with its treasures of architecture, could hold a candle to this – this overwhelming abundance. All the jewels and pleasures of the flesh the greediest heart could desire. Or so the mealy-mouthed poets had proclaimed. It was rumoured that within the high citadel, at the heart of the city, the buildings were lined in tapestries spun from golden thread. And the slaves within were said to be beauties of every race and pedigree, so comely in voluptuousness that man or woman would find them impossible to resist.

How natural that he had dreamed of being granted access to such overweening wealth, and pleasure. Why else had he accepted the burden of spying for that weasel, Feltzvan, back in Carfon? *Have I not braved danger after danger, because at the heart of it all I fostered a dream of love? Did*

I not accept the dreadful burden of that talisman of doom that killed poor Porky Lard, my best friend? Was it all an impossible dream? Did I not steal for no reason other than to bestow jewels upon the woman I loved? The woman I adored with a passion worthy of the fireside legends?

What privations had he suffered! And all for nothing! At every step of the way, his finer feelings had been spurned – pissed and shat on – until the gentle heart within him had been turned to stone.

Surrounded as he was by perfidious enemies, Kawkaw saw there, in the burning city, a metaphor for himself. Now, looking down through the moist eyes of endless hurt, he beheld the spreading plague of fire and its insatiable destruction of the city's splendour.

How could this be happening? How could the almighty Tyrant of the Wastelands, whose Black Citadel rose into the very clouds, permit the scum of Shee witches and Ebrit's callow troops to destroy such wonder? Why would a being as powerful as the gods allow these scum to destroy his city and with it Kawkaw's most treasured dream?

Man Down

'I'm bloody petrified,' Tajh said to Mark.

'You and me both.' Mark blew into his cupped hands to try to warm his fingers. 'I never imagined we'd be out here this long.'

Tajh looked across at him from a distance of a few feet. She was smoking a cigarette with shaky fingers. She had offered him one, but he'd refused. 'That great monstrosity – I know it's doing something, I can feel the vibrations. But why does it need all that energy?'

'I really don't know, Tajh.'

'This Tyrant you talk about, if he's the one behind it do you think he might be in the Rose right now?'

Mark paused within the foxhole of the ruined café and thought about the Tyrant of the Wastelands. 'All of my childhood,' he said, 'and my sister, Mo's, too, was warped by Grimstone. And now we know he was the agent of the Tyrant all along.'

'But who, or what, is this Tyrant?'

Mark blew into his hands again. 'What more like? He can't be human. According to Nan, he's been waging war on Tír for thousands of their years.'

'I just can't get my head around it. We're under attack by a being of magic from an alien world?'

'I'm afraid there are many things about Tír that wouldn't make sense to someone from Earth.'

'Like the thing in your brow.'

'My oraculum is empowered by a goddess you wouldn't care to meet. Mórígán is literally Death.'

'Where did the Tyrant come from? How did he get his powers?'

'I have no idea. But a dying ruler, called Ussha De Danaan, told us that he had gained a partial access to one of the portals to the Fáil.'

Tajh shook her head, no wiser. She couldn't stop herself shivering despite the fact she was wrapped up in numerous layers of clothes.

Mark looked in the direction of the Black Rose, barely visible in the grey misty light as a shadowy leviathan. 'On Tír, magic is as familiar to the inhabitants as technology is to us. And the Fáil is at the heart of it. I think that whatever game the Tyrant is playing, it all revolves around it.'

'And Padraig understands this magic?'

'I wouldn't go so far as to say he understands it, but he knows more about it than anybody else here on Earth.'

Mark thought back to the barrow grave, when Padraig

had taken him and his friends to see it. He recalled the ancient writing that ran around the walls; horizontal lines in which strange verticals and slanted inserts went above and below the lines, a system known as Ogham that was perfect for rapid inscription in stone. Padraig had read a little of it to the friends. He had explained how the Ogham – ancient as it was – captured an oral history that was more ancient still: knowledge that had been handed down by Padraig's druidic ancestors, which stretched back into the Bronze Age.

'Padraig is knowledgeable, but what I'd really like to know is how my friends are getting on with the war on Tír. That war must be important to our battle here. Earth and Tír are closely linked.'

'Do you feel guilty that you've returned to Earth?'

'I do feel guilty, but if Nan and I hadn't come back we wouldn't be helping you fight the Tyrant here.'

At that moment the oraculum in Mark's brow flared. Abruptly he grabbed hold of Tajh, and pressed her down, shielding her body with his own.

Tajh cried: 'What is it?'

'Stay down!'

At that moment something large, streamlined and utterly silent tore overhead at extraordinary velocity. When the roar of its passing followed it a split second later, it coincided with the explosive detonation of the missile as it struck the great cliff face of the Black Rose. The explosion blew apart Mark's foxhole like a sandcastle caught up in a tidal wave. It lifted him off the ground and tossed him twenty yards through the air to land amid broken pieces of brick and debris. Mark stared at the conflagration of flames and smoke that had become the entire horizon.

'Oh, god . . . shit!'

He felt overwhelming pain. He was half blinded, deafened, lost in the confusion of the explosion. His mind was blank, fading . . . He called out in a husky whisper, 'Tajh! Are you all right?'

There was no answer.

Groaning, Mark struggled to bring his feet under him. He moved his head agonisingly slowly to try to find Tajh in the dust-filled devastation. He could find no sign of her. It was an agony just to breathe. There was something grossly wrong with his right leg. When he looked at it he saw that a rusting steel rod had torn through his buttock and passed through bone, muscle and tissues to emerge half way down his thigh. Pain was beginning to register there, coming in sickening waves.

'Fuck!'

For a while the agony overwhelmed his ability to think. Mark screamed. A thunderous symphony erupted in his ears, blotting out his rational mind. It was as if it wasn't him that was screaming, but the entire world around him.

Then a voice he did not recognise spoke to him, mind-to-mind: <The oraculum . . .>

The oraculum!

<Use it!>

Mark wept and grabbed hold of the steel bar with trembling hands. What should he do? Should he pull it or push it?

There were stars in the air around where he lay. One of the stars was speaking to him. <There is little time. You must make use of your oraculum.>

'What in the name of . . .?'

<You cannot tarry, despite your wounds. On Tír the gates of Ghork Mega have been breached. The singularity is approaching.>

The Gates of what?

<You are chosen. Now you must hurry!>

He took a firmer grip on the metal bar . . . and pulled. His scream filled his skull, almost rendering him senseless. He slumped back, his eyes shut.

<The oraculum – it will heal you.>

'What?' He was stupid with pain – he couldn't figure out what the voice wanted. Perhaps he had fainted? He looked around and saw a nearby bundle of rags. *Tajh* . . .

Tajh wasn't moving.

<Your companion is dead.>

'Oh, god!'

<There will come a time for grief. But this is not that time. Momentous events are coming into play. You must rejoin your friends in Dromenon.>

Mark stared at the bundle of rags, tears filling his eyes. He attempted to climb to his feet, but his right leg was useless.

<Look!>

He looked up, aware that the pain in his thigh was

lessening. He tried to interpret what was happening around him. At first all he saw was flames: gargantuan flames, as if gas towers a mile or more high had exploded into blazing disintegration. Then he saw further moiling clouds. They grew and squeezed against one another, as if there were insufficient space for them to fill it.

'The Rose—'

<The Black Rose is changing.>

He could see that now. In its place was an explosive conflagration that swelled and grew. Mark took advantage of the light from the firestorm to crawl across the debris to Tajh.

She looked horribly broken. She was covered in blood and bits of her were missing: one leg from the knee down, the other from mid-calf. There were injuries that were too much for him to absorb . . .

Dragging his injured leg behind him, trailing his own bright red blood, Mark leaned on his functioning left knee. He tried to manoeuvre Tajh's body into the crook of his arm. He tried to hold her to him.

'Tajh,' he called to her, brushing his fingers over her brow, her cheeks.

Think – *think!*

Her head felt wrong.

Mark had never really felt anyone's bones before, but now he brushed his fingers over the dome of Tajh's head, and around the back; it was crunchy, like the broken shell of a coconut.

<Your companion is dead, Mark.>

'No. I was injured, but now my injuries are healing. My oraculum – my oraculum did that. So, why shouldn't it heal her?'

<You must abandon her.>

'No – *no!*'

He remained squatting in that uncomfortable position for a while, his entire body wracked with shivers. Through an ocean of pain, Mark forced himself back onto his feet. His wounded leg no longer gave way under him. He forced his thoughts to enter the oraculum, and he forced it to pulse with power. He stood there, in the whirling dust and debris, amidst a conflagration of his own blue-black lightning. He forced it to shine harder and more brilliantly until he became a tiny sun of cascading lightning bolts. By the time his rage settled he had burned away the tatters of his clothing. He stood naked in the debris and dirt, gazing at a fireball of lava-red force.

Overhead, something extraordinary was happening. Splinters of strange light were invading the landscape. The fireball had a life of its own, aggregating into patterns that might have meaning to one who knew how to read them. The sky overhead was streaked with flame-red, purples and violets. Cycles of fire intersected one another. The world was consumed in a frenzy of wild energy, out of which intermittent discharges of lightning struck the ground.

'The Rose?' he asked.

<I'm afraid it is not destroyed.>

A prickling, expanding terror rose as he witnessed the truth of those words: a leviathan reconstruction was happening at the heart of the Rose.

'What is it? What's happening to it?'

<A metamorphosis . . .>

'Oh, no!'

<It is being reborn.>

'Shit!'

Mark stumbled on through a landscape illuminated by the metamorphosis of the Rose. In places it resembled a blacksmith's forge, with cracks of red heat showing through the charcoal-black surface. In other places it shimmered, as if remaking itself from pure energy. He reached the foxhole where Nan and Cal had been observing the attack. Both were injured. Cal was unconscious but breathing. Nan's eyes were blinking, watching him in a stunned silence. He knelt by her side and cradled her in his arms.

He would have to get help and come back for Cal and Tajh. The blood soaking Nan's body was making it slippery, but she understood what he was trying to do. Her eyes were looking into his. Mark got his arms under her armpits and adjusted his grip so he wouldn't let her slip. He picked her up and began to walk with Nan in his embrace; on tottering steps he headed back in the direction of the derelict garage and the Mamma Pig.

His bare feet left footprints through the livid red sparks that were showering down out of the air.

The Communion

'You must awaken!'

The voice was Jeremiah's, but it was injected with an unusual urgency. When Penny opened her eyes, she found herself back in the garden at her parent's house. It was late spring, with the scents, the colours, the whirring of bird wings amid the blossoming apple and cherry trees.

'Oh, it's so lovely to be back.'

'It is appropriate that you should feel rested in spirit.'

'Why?'

'There has been an event.'

'What event?'

'An attack on the Rose. I sheltered you in Dromenon, desiring that you should be untroubled.'

'What sort of attack?'

'Three machines of war approaching with mathematical precision from equidistant angles.'

'Were you hurt?'

'I was not hurt. Such weapons are incapable of hurting me. But I was concerned that you were safe.'

'What happened to the Rose – to London?'

'There is no cause for alarm. The attack was anticipated. I reconstructed your beloved garden here in Dromenon.'

'In Dromenon?'

'As you see.'

Penny felt increasingly troubled by the implications of this conversation. But then Jeremiah reached out and touched her brow, after which her eyes drifted closed. Tranquillity invaded her being.

'I don't want to sleep.'

'As you wish.'

She opened wide her eyes, fearful he had spirited away the garden. But she still found herself in the familiar and joyful surroundings.

'Thank you!'

The saturnine lips in the face smiled. The eyelids parted, then opened wide to reveal those iris-less, all black eyes. Penny heard a host of tiny voices.

'Who are they?'

'See for yourself.'

Hunting gleefully through the tunnels in the wilderness, she discovered children, unwashed faces, hair awry, clothing torn and stained.

'They look like human children.'

'They are.'

'They look uncared for.'

The black eyes looked directly into Penny's. 'They are the lost children.'

'What do you mean?'

'As once you were lost, Penny Postlethwaite. And now they have joined you. All lost in this same garden.'

She looked around, astonished to find more and more children appearing from every direction. They gathered around her. Already there were dozens of them, perhaps as many as a hundred.

'Why are they here?'

'I recognised your need. You refuse to hurt, to punish. You express the desire to help the weak.'

Penny inhaled deeply and stood in the dappled sunlight and stared at them all. It seemed miraculous that all of these children should appear in the garden she remembered. Their unwashed faces gazed up at her. Were they expecting something of her? Were they expecting her to take care of them? But how could she possibly help so many children?

She said, 'What do I know about lost children?'

The light darkened.

She called out: 'Jeremiah!'

A voice she didn't recognise spoke, as if directly into her ear, or possibly her mind: 'The Master cannot be disturbed at present. He will speak to you soon. But now I must take you deeper into this new experience.'

'Who are you?'

'A servant of the Master.'

'Why am I being taken here? What purpose will it serve?'

'The Master has urgent business elsewhere. It will offer a new experience.'

Penny was led into a decrepit building. No such building had been part of her family garden.

'I don't want to go here.'

'It is necessary.'

The building stank of bodies, cigarettes, alcohol, toilets. A big man, completely bald and dressed in a sweat-soiled cotton gown sat beside a rickety table upon which were various glasses, bottles of alcohol, cigarettes, cigars, and an extraordinary medley of vials, loaded syringes, and powders laid out in scraps of foil. He beckoned with a ring-bedecked hand for her to choose anything she wanted from the table and then enter through a door behind him.

Penny refused. 'I don't feel comfortable here.'

'It is not necessary that you feel comfortable.'

In the background was a rumble of conversation, many voices, all shouting rather than speaking, none of it in English.

'I don't want to be here.'

The voice suggested: 'I would ask for your patience. There is one who might benefit from your indulgence.'

The big man shoved the door half ajar. Penny stared into a room of semi-darkness. 'What is this place?'

'I will leave it to your imagination.'

She was gazing down onto the bald man's coal black eyes. His perspiring face grew pale as her mind confronted his.

'Who is he?'

'Merely a gatekeeper.'

'What is within the room?'

'You must enter to see for yourself.'

Penny moved through the door to inspect what the gatekeeper was guarding. There were many women within, in various stages of undress. They were all young, mostly girls even younger than herself.

'This is a brothel?'

'Yes.'

'Why bring me here?'

'So you can discover your true self.'

'Is that what Jeremiah thinks of me? I belong in a place like this?'

'Quite the contrary!'

Penny moved deeper into the room with its horrible, cloying medley of smells. She arrived at a door in a blank section of wall, locked with a sliding bolt. On impulse, she undid the bolt. In the cell was a naked young woman, much the same age as herself. Her hands were tethered with irons behind her back. In spite of the chains, she tottered to her feet to confront Penny on her arrival.

'Who are you?'

Now she was standing, the young woman was a good six inches taller than Penny. She stank, as if she had not bathed in a long time. Her face was smudged with dirt and sweat and her skin criss-crossed with red wheals of flagellation. Yet still her face, and her eyes, were defiant.

'Who are you?' Penny demanded again.

The young woman stared. She made no attempt to speak.

Coming closer, Penny saw that her hair was long and lank, a natural mahogany but streaked with darker and lighter shades. Her eyes were the same shade of mahogany as the bulk of hair. Her lips were the colour of blackberry juice. Their eyes met. The dark brown eyes of the enslaved young woman: the silvery grey of Penny. They stared into one another's eyes.

She whispered into Penny's ear, 'How can I pleasure you, Mistress?'

'I am not here to use you. Please tell me your name?'

'Those who pay for my services buy the right to name me.'

'Have you no shame?'

'I have none, Mistress. But if you will pay to be pleasured, you will be allowed to shame me.'

'You must have a name.'

'I was never allowed a name. Am I to be your hand maiden?'

'If I can free you – would you be my friend?'

'The Mistress will decide on her pleasure.'

'Then my pleasure is to ask you not to call me Mistress. My name is Penny. And though I don't yet know how, I want to help you.' Penny hesitated at the sound of screams from elsewhere in the establishment. 'I assume that you have no name because you were sold into slavery as a child.'

The tormented face stared back at Penny. The young

woman's hair was dangling over her face in sweat-congealed straggles. Penny remembered her own imprisonment in a helmet of glittering jewels. But this girl's mask was made of iron pins, with black heads, which were embedded in her flesh, forming a bridge over her eyebrows, and trailing down over her cheeks. Tiny rivulets of blood trailed from several of the pins, suggesting a recent torment.

'Do they treat you as some wild animal? Is that supposed to be your special attraction – your ferality?'

The young woman's eyes, so dark a shade of brown they now appeared almost black, glittered back at her.

Penny entered the young woman's mind. She probed deep, looking beyond the wall of hurt, beyond the vast litany of desecration she had suffered here, to the beginning of her experience. She discovered no loving, no mothering, no comforting experience at all. The desecration had begun so soon after birth.

Her fingers trembled in reaching out and touching the hurt face. Penny was astonished to find the face retracting from her touch. One by one she removed the pins that were buried in the woman's flesh. Their eyes met again.

Penny commanded: 'Remove the irons that bind her.'

The irons slipped off the young woman's wrists, leaving bracelets of scarred and ulcerated skin.

Penny scanned the woman's body from head to foot, registering signs of what was probably disease. Parasites boring into skin. Bacteria and viruses in the organs and inner flesh.

'Jeremiah – I know you're watching this. I want you to cure her – cure her of every illness that afflicts her!'

A plane of crackling light moved over the figure of the young woman, scouring her body of every parasite.

'Now clothe her – make her decent.'

A dress of pale blue silk clothed the girl's body. Sandals of doe-soft leather enclosed her feet. Only then did Penny pause to gather her thoughts. 'The bald-headed man, he owns you?'

The woman nodded.

'I cannot conceive the horror of your life, how you have suffered. Yet I sense that you never surrendered. You fought for dignity when there seemed no hope.' Penny shook her head, led her out through one door and then the second, into the refreshing spring air of her parent's garden. 'You're going to need a great deal of healing.'

The woman stared at her.

'Jeremiah, I must see you. I must talk to you.'

He materialised beside Penny, who studied his implacable face, the all black eyes that simply returned her gaze.

'Why are you doing this? Why have you brought me here?'

'To measure the need in you.'

'You don't really care about lost children – or women.'

'I reward loyalty.'

'But I have already agreed to your terms.'

'I have looked into your heart. I discovered a weakness there. Humans are slaves to passion. They fall victim to discontent.'

'You discovered that I cannot abide cruelty. You saw this as a weakness in me that you could exploit?'

'You would save the lost, the hurt.'

'Why would you care about that?'

'I care nothing about it. But I am sensitive to your needs.'

Penny stared back at this strange dark being, unable to believe a word he was telling her. She considered her reaction: had she really, like she suspected of the Akkharu, found a secret place within her mind, a place that Jeremiah could not read? If so, how could she use this to her maximum advantage?

She said: 'Please take me back to London and the Black Rose. Stop hiding the truth from me. Stop treating me like some wanton child. I need to know everything that is happening.'

Penny felt herself wrenched from a domain of relative peace to witness a vision of apocalypse. Fires blazed through a vast landscape. The sky above had become a furnace. Jeremiah gazed out over the ruined world, his all black eyes reflecting the flames.

'It's horrible – awful!'

'You demanded to witness.' His voice was softly gloating.

'What is it? What am I looking at?'

'Is it not obvious? You are gazing at the region you designate the Eurasian landmass.'

'It's burning.'

He said nothing.

'Why is it burning?'

'It combusts spontaneously because the temperature of the atmosphere has increased.'

'Why are you doing such terrible things?'

'They are consequences of the growing war. The Rose gathered the power of your sun in preparation for the coming singularity.'

'Are there other such . . . consequences?'

'Many.'

'Show me!'

Penny was plunged into the dark, her vision being forced to accommodate near darkness in which moiling spurts of lava erupted from a landscape made up of numerous volcanoes. Rivers of molten rock ran down the mountainsides for hundreds of miles.

'Where are we?'

'The region you call the Indian Ocean.'

'There must have been people here?'

'No doubt there were. Soon there will be similar catastrophes in the regions known to you as the central European forests, North America, Asia, the great island you call Australia.'

'You don't care about hurting all those people?'

Again he held to silence.

'Please, Jeremiah – show concern for people.'

'Is this your new demand of me?'

'Please show people respect. You are responsible for all of this?'

'I planned the Rose – and it demanded empowerment. What you see is the fruit of my planning though I did not weigh the manifold secondary consequences.'

'Why do you so hate us?'

'We are repeating a conversation we had already.'

'There is more – isn't there? There must be more.'

'Yes.'

'Please show me.'

'Your star was a convenient source of energy for the metamorphosis. I have been drawing on its plentiful resources from the moment of my arrival.'

'Heedless of the fact you were damaging the Earth.'

'Uncaring – but hardly heedless.'

Penny entered the secret place she had created within herself, using the example of the Akkharu. How very dangerous he was. And how she hated him for what he was doing. She hesitated, waited to see if he had read those thoughts.

'What about all of the people, the life forms – biodiversity.'

'Have you learned nothing from our conversations? There is no morality in the cosmos. What happens to one small planet is of no consequence.'

'I can't believe what you are saying.'

'Perhaps you are unaware that stars breathe?'

'What?'

'As your sun moves through time and space, it emits energy and entities that you could regard as a breath – you know it as the heliosphere.'

'Why does that matter?'

'The modest star, which you so jealously call your sun, controls many aspects of your planet, including your climate.'

Penny's heart was sinking.

'You clearly do not understand what you call the solar wind.'

'How can there possibly be a wind from the sun?'

'It is not a wind. It is something else entirely. The critical aspect, in my calculations, is that it undergoes cycles.'

'Please – Jeremiah. Stop! I don't want to know any more. I can't bear the thought that you are deliberately hurting the Earth.'

'Another cycle is nearing its turning point. A very great cycle! We must be perfect in timing the communion.'

'Communion with what?'

'We are not alone in our ambitions. I have enemies. And you have a rival in discovering the moment.'

'What rival?'

'An immensely powerful one.'

Penny was startled into silence.

'You would save your Earth? You would help the lost children?'

'Yes.'

'Then do not fail me.'

The Lip of Darkness

Mark sat with his back to the crumbling wall of the building that concealed the Mamma Pig. He was staring at the sheer cliff wall of the Black Rose, which pulsed with a fiery light. Padraig, who was sitting next to him, interrupted his thoughts. 'You and Nan – you have remarkable powers of recovery.'

'Perhaps because we're dead already.'

Padraig hesitated, as if considering his reply. 'Others among the crew were not so resilient.'

Poor Tajh was dead. Mark closed his eyes. He didn't want to revisit the scene when he and Bull had carried Tajh's body back to the Pig.

Padraig said: 'At least Cal is alive. He'll recover – given time.'

Would he recover? Mark questioned that. Cal had been concussed in the blast. And then, on coming to back in the garage, he had been faced with the death of Tajh. Padraig interrupted his thoughts once again. 'You must pull yourself together, Mark. I'm afraid we don't have time to feel sorry for ourselves.'

Mark had been glad of the opportunity just to sit and talk about what had happened with Padraig. His right thigh still throbbed with pain. He rubbed at it distractedly. 'What do you mean? Do you know something I don't about what's really going on out there?'

'I'm far from sure.'

'If you know something, anything, please tell me. How could that thing have survived the missile attack? It just swallowed it all up. The missiles didn't even dent it.'

'You and Nan are not alone in your resilience.'

'What does that mean?'

'They didn't harm the Rose but I believe they changed it.'

'How?'

'Do you not sense the changes? Not even through your oraculum?'

Mark stared at the monstrosity that had evolved out of the Black Rose. Its curtain wall glittered, as if it were a colossal gemstone, its surface a scaly web of diamonds. If he closed his eyes and examined it through his oraculum, he could see its surface was a metamorphosing pageantry of colours and patterns, like light shifting over water on which some oily substance, like paraffin, excited rainbow patterns. Even now he could smell it, a hot furnace stink, a noxious sulphurous smell. And it growled – a continuous thunderous roar, as you might expect of a waterfall a mile high.

'I – both Nan and I – we do sense changes in it.'

'What do you sense?'

Mark couldn't easily put it into words. 'Some sort of evolution. Maybe some cranking up of the level of danger.'

'Have you noticed the changes in the weather since the missile attack?'

'What changes?'

Padraig grunted. 'The weather is not natural. It changes from day to day, even from moment to moment.' His eyes lifted into the foggy dawn in a scary sky.

'Is that important?'

'That's the question I ask myself.'

'You think it might explain the satellite interference?'

Another unwelcome consequence of the missile attack was that satellite communication was no longer possible between Brett and President Harvey, though Sharkey and Brett were still attempting to make contact through the intermediary at HQ.

'What's the Tyrant up to?'

'Has it occurred to you that the Rose might be purposeful?'

'Like part of an attack on the Earth?'

'That certainly. But perhaps there might be an additional, more subtle, purpose?'

'Like what?'

'Like an end game strategy.'

Mark fell silent. He stared at the monstrosity once more and thought about Padraig's words. *An end game strategy?* The thought provoked a shiver that ran through him from his brow to his toes. If that were true, how could Padraig remain so calm? Mark felt so restless that for the first time in what seemed ages, he retrieved the battered harmonica from his jacket pocket. How long since he had last played a tune on it? Once he had played it every day – he and Mo had danced to its tune. It had travelled between worlds with him. But he had stopped playing it after the Battle of Ossierel.

Padraig smiled. 'It's been a long time since I heard you play a tune.'

Mark sighed. He doubted he would ever play his harmonica again. The last time he had played it was engrained on his memory – the tune, *Cajun Girl*. He recalled the setting as if it were yesterday: a snowy embankment during the journey down the Snowmelt River on board the Temple Ship. It had been a time of great danger for the company, as well as great hunger. It had also been a time of personal darkness for Mark, when he had been under the influence of a succubus called Siri. She had pretended to love him. He had hated himself for his weakness even while he could not bring himself to confess his deceit to his friends. A group of Olhyiu children had been delighted with the tune, laughing and dancing while he played it. Their delight had been a ray of sunshine for Mark in that time of tormenting guilt.

In particular he recalled a little Olhyiu girl called Amoté, who had bright red poppies painted on her cheeks. She had screeched with laughter as she ran her fingers through Kate's auburn hair. She and her friends danced to Mark's harmonica tune. Then, during the fighting at Ossierel Mark had been guarding the cellar where the children, including Amoté, were hiding. He had killed the succubus who had attempted to divert him. He had also killed a Garg, but not before the Garg had poisoned him with its wing talon. Then, as he attempted to stop them entering the cellar, he had been stabbed a second time by a preceptor's poisoned blade. He would have died there had it not been for the battleaxe of Qwenqwo Cuatzel.

That had been the end game of his former life.

He had been instructed by Qwenqwo to climb the Rath of the Dark Queen, to fulfil his destiny. It had been a horrible struggle for him, suffering from two poisoned wounds. At the summit he had collapsed under the statue of the so-called Dark Queen, Nantosueta. In his dying breath, he had become one with her – but he had since discovered that she was no dark queen. She was a young woman, confused by the circumstances of battle, as he was confused in the company of Padraig right now. She became his beloved Nan, a girl whose life, and soul spirit, had been taken and enslaved, as had his own, by Mórígán, the goddess of death.

Mark took a deep breath to control his palpitating heart.

Since then neither he nor Nan had known for certain if they were alive or dead, manifesting bodily and spiritually at the forbearance of the dark goddess. Even Mark's repeated recovery from serious wounds was not as comforting as it might appear. It might be the confirmation that both he and Nan were already dead.

In his mind he heard a familiar voice call out his name: <Mark!>

Mo's voice . . .

Mark jerked back to the present. He had been day-dreaming, his eyes gritty with tiredness.

Mo's voice – but Mo was not here. He had left Mo behind on Tír. Mark experienced a feeling close to panic. What had he heard? Had he merely dreamed the voice of his adoptive sister?

He pressed the thought abroad through his oraculum: <I worry about you, Mo.>

<As I do you.>

Was he dreaming this strange conversation?

Adoptive sister – was that how he really felt about Mo? He didn't think so. Mo was closer, if anything, than a sister. But even as he realised it, he felt the dream withdraw, and Mo's mind with it. He resisted the withdrawal. He wanted the dream to persist. There was so much he wanted to ask her about what was happening, so much he wanted to tell her.

<I'm losing you, Mo.>

<We're losing each other.>

His heart missed a beat with her words. And then she was gone. He felt her absence like a wound to his spirit.

Confusion upon confusion! Had he just experienced a real communication with Mo? If so, how? Mo had no oraculum. She had never even been given a crystal. But perhaps she hadn't needed one? He had needed the oraculum, just as he had needed the crystal, which had been born in the hands of Granny Dew. All three of them had needed crystals: Alan, Kate and he. Their crystals had been fashioned by Granny Dew from their mobile phones: communication. But Mo had hated mobile phones, just as she had hated all thing mechanical all of her life. What did it mean? Mark had no idea.

Just what level of communication was his oraculum really capable of? The oraculum had not been given to him by Granny Dew. The oraculum had been given to him – and to Nan, who shared it with him – by Mórígán.

Mark spoke to Padraig: 'I think I just had communication from Mo.'

Padraig stiffened.

'You recognised something in Mo. You felt something from the moment you first met her.'

'I did.'

'What was it?'

'I couldn't be sure she was the one, but I saw the signs – those remarkable drawings in her notebook – and sensed the power in her. But I was just one of many generations of guardians. I couldn't be sure that the time of prophecy had arrived.'

'What prophecy?'

'A story, a legend, purportedly passed down from the great mage of the Fir Bolg, Urox Zel. Something written down a thousand or more years later in the Ogham you saw in the chamber.'

'What was it?'

'A prediction of doom and terror that would threaten the entire world. The Sword of Feimhin would rise again. All hope would depend on the coming of The Heralded One. In the Ogham, this saviour was called the *Léanov Fashakk.*'

Mark shut his eyes. It all sounded so very unlikely. Legends from an age of ignorance.

'You are unconvinced?'

'I'm too exhausted to think clearly.'

With a sigh, Mark ceased his daydreaming and toyed once more with the harmonica that was the only connection he had ever had to the man he believed to be his biological father.

'Go ahead! There's a tune demanding to come out.'

'Would you put your arm around me, Padraig?'

The old man chuckled, then reached out his long bony arm, and encircled Mark's shoulders as he played the tune that was demanding to come out: he played the tune *Little Red Rooster*, tears rising into his eyes. He played it with feeling, looking out at the sheer wall of the rose that soared into the misty heights in the distance, with what appeared to be strange, deeply menacing furnaces within its crystals.

'I'm terrified that I'll never see Mo again.'

'You don't know that. Perhaps you will?'

'I can't imagine how.'

Padraig hugged him a little closer.

Holding Hands

'Strewth!' Gully wiped his nose on his sleeve. He was too frazzled to look for a rag. 'We ain't never gonna find Penny.'

'Would you abandon hope, now that you are close?'

Gully didn't reckon they was close. He didn't reckon so at all. He found himself looking at his reflection in a pool of oil. He felt wearier than he had ever felt in his life. What an outfit they amounted to: his ragamuffin self, Bad Day and Owly Gizmo. They was climbing up a sloping strut as thick as the girders of Tower Bridge. Right there, in the middle of nowhere, they'd had to make way for an army of slug beasts the size of single-decker buses, standing aside to watch their undulating progress as they slithered by surrounded by buzzing Grimlings.

Gully flopped down on his bum, exhausted. He rubbed at his throbbing elbow. At least it was getting better in the sense that it only hurt when he used it. In the air overhead, Owly Gizmo was making a racket because a Grimling had come too close. That was what the hooting was about. Owly saw off the Grimling with a fury of pecking and fluttering.

'I just want to find Penny.'

'You will not find her by pulling faces and sighing.'

From the looks of it, they were wandering into yet another valley with high rocky cliffs all covered with spiders' webs. The webs was aglow with the same greenish slime as the rocks.

'All this wanderin' about, it ain't never comin' to an end.'

Bad Day laughed, a deep booming laugh, though to Gully it sounded suspiciously half-hearted. 'Surely our exploration has hardly begun.'

'Give it up. You ain't foolin' nobody.'

Owly alighted on Gully's shoulder. She was staring at him like it was a conspiracy between the two of them. 'That's it. I'm downing tools.'

'What tools?'

'Me fagged out legs is wot.'

Gully caught a glimpse of multifaceted eyes in a nearby spider's web. 'Gawd in 'eaven, them fings is vicious.'

A memory inside his head whispered: *All drawn to de Sword.*

They moved on to find a rubble-strewn path that ran along a sheer cliff face. Wraiths and spectres peeped out at them from the cracks as they plodded along the path, their weird little heads wobbling to and fro, like weeds moved by the currents under water. With a flutter of its metallic wings Owly pounced on one of them, yanking it out of its hole, and she laid it at Gully's feet as an offering.

'Get outta here!'

Owly screeched and fluttered up onto the wall immediately above Gully's head. She was pecking wildly at things, provoking a storm of writhing movements.

'Tell 'er to bring me a pigeon or somefink.'

Bad Day took no notice of him. The daemon bot had reached the plateau at the top of the cliff where it was pacing around, provoking clouds of dust as it rooted through the rubble of some fallen walls. Gully wondered if maybe it was sniffing. It sure was making a weird mechanical snuffling through them grilles that passed for a nose.

Looked like something odd up ahead.

Owly flapped down to within a few feet of Gully. She hooted, then clawed her way up to his left shoulder.

'Wot's up, little birdie?'

Even Bad Day had fallen silent.

Gully peered into the gloom. Something was approaching them, floating through the air. It looked like a star wrapped up in wobbly rings of colour. Rays of coloured lights were coming out of it; yellow and orange and a muddy jade, then some shade of plum purple, and then bright blood red.

Gully's eyes sprang wide open as he felt it sneak into his mind. He began to count to twenty. His hands was patting down the pockets.

<About time, Gully bwai. You an' you frien's been leadin me a merry dance.>

The voice was coming from inside his head.

'I know you ain't no daemon bot. How'd you do that?'

<Daemon bots – dey ain't de smartest banana in de bunch.>

Gully wondered if he was so exhausted he had fallen asleep and was dreaming. He knew who he was talking to, that voice inside his head. It was the mad old bat, Henriette, who had met him in the caravan with the rags all over the floor.

'I got noffink to say to you.'

<Me come to help you, Gully.>

He very much doubted it.

Gully looked ahead to where Bad Day looked like it had run out of oil.

'Shit! Shit, shit, shit!'

<To find your true love you got to leave de world of de flesh.>

Gully began to laugh.

<She done it for you.>

'Wot game you up to now?'

<Your t'ink you know more'n a pipsqueak knows. You t'ink you figure it out. But you no capable of knowing.>

'You're talkin' riddles.'

<Penny Postlethwaite – she can no afford de risk. Jeremiah is too dangerous for her to do dat.>

'Wot do you know about Penny?'

<I know you come here to save de girl.>

His heart was beating twice as fast as it had a moment ago. 'You know where Penny is? Take me to her.'

<She no want to see you, bwai. You make t'ings worse. Forces gathering. A time of reckonin'. Dis t'ing is beyond you an me both. But de girl, Penny, she knows.>

'Wot does she know?'

<Be patient, Gully.>

'Wot do you know – you know noffink?'

<You gotta be patient, Dahlin'.>

He heard her voice inside him. But she wasn't really there. It was a star talking to him inside his head. Nothing made sense no more.

<If you want to see her, close dem sceptic eyes!>

Gully didn't want to close his eyes. But he didn't dare not to close them.

<Look, Gully. Look with you mind's eye in Dromenon!>

He was looking at some kind of a vision of Penny. She was standing in the middle of a bunch of kids, a bunch of ragamuffins whose faces was all painted up in charcoal and coloured pigments. Their bodies was wrapped in white feathers and leaves. On their brows was tiaras of yellow flowers.

'Penny!' he shouted.

<Gully – how did you find me?>

'I ain't got a clue. But I really want to see you.'

<I want to see you too. But not now – not here.>

He didn't get it. What was going on with Penny? He didn't like the fact that her face, her head, was in the air above some bizarre drawing of a city, like a dream of wheeling lines and soaring shapes. He didn't like the fact everything had gone crazy and slug beasts was taking pieces of the dream out of her head and weaving it into streets and buildings that looked like a fairytale.

'I miss you, Penny.'

<I miss you too.>

Penny hesitated. She had to be some kind of ghostly 'allucination, but still it felt like Penny. And she was saying the kind of crazy things Penny would say.

<I have learned a lot of lessons, Gully.>

'Like wot, for instance?'

<Like how cruelly I treated you.>

'Yeah?'

<Will you ever forgive me, Gully?>

'You know I will. But only if you mean it this time.'

Her voice filled with emotion as she replied: <I do.>

'So wot you learned then?'

<I'm beginning to understand things here. It's incredibly complicated, but there is a kind of logic running through it – if one utterly different from our normal logic.>

'Uh-huh?'

<I've been learning a kind of knowledge that can't be understood except by . . . Oh, I don't know . . . by observing it, by experiencing it, by sharing it with things who have accumulated creativity of a very different kind.>

Gully shook his head. 'I ain't got a bleedin' clue wot you're on about, gel.'

<I want you to come and join me.>

'Come where?'

<To St Paul's Cathedral.>

'How the 'eck . . .?'

<I have things to do. I might have to leave you there

for a while. But you'll be safe there – at least for the moment.>

'Oh, yeah?'

Penny just reached out and, spirit to spirit, they touched hands. Ghost or spirit, or whatever exactly they were, it was the most wonderful feeling Gully had ever experienced.

<We can touch one another more deeply if you like, mind-to-mind. We can be close, just like you wanted.>

Gully couldn't believe that there were tears in Penny's eyes – ghost tears in her ghost eyes.

<There are problems I need to solve. I don't quite know yet whether we might have to die and be reborn.>

'Bleedin' Norah!'

<Gully – nothing, absolutely nothing – is quite as it seems.>

'Now you're talking bullshit. You can't just spend your life scribblin' up there on the ceiling no more, gel.'

<These days I scribble in time and space, Gully.>

Gully felt Penny squeeze his hand. It felt real. The shock of it caused him to tremble. He went close to fainting, even as his world became dark.

<I feel it too.>

'You do?'

There was a thrill running through him, from his head to his toes, to his arms and legs, right to the tips of his fingers and toes.

<Wait for me, Gully, in St Paul's Cathedral. I'll come for you – I promise. Everything will be all right.>

Rage

'Get out – out! Find me some useful information.' The Preceptress discharged her rage at Snakoil Kawkaw. It came out of her eyes, wide and bloodshot; out of her face, aflame with a passion close to insanity. 'The time is approaching. The Master commands it. He must control what is happening! It's imperative!'

'What am I? A mind reader?'

She was becoming more unravelled by the minute, pressing her already blackened and fissured lips so frequently against the sigil in the dagger that they were openly bleeding. What was her confounded Master's will? Was he to kill the huloima brat called Alan? Or would it serve Him better if he were to disembowel the auburn-haired witch called Kate? What did it matter to Snakoil Kawkaw? Why should he be interested in spying in the wastelands out there? What was the point? The metropolis, with all of its fabled power and riches, was reduced to cinders. If rumour among the camp followers were true, the witch warriors were scouring its very bowels, to annihilate the remaining sewer rats.

'Out!'

'I'll go when I please.'

'Out now you perfidious wastrel and liar! I will follow the Master's last desire. What must be done . . .'

He spun around to glare at her, fingering the blade deep in his right pocket. 'What then must be done?'

She wasn't listening to him. He watched, appalled, as she pressed another bloody kiss upon the glowing hilt, a kiss so passionate and violent that he could smell the burning flesh of her lips.

Suffering hogspiss!

Dark days! Oh, such ruinous days in which anguish wheeled through the tormented soul of Snakoil Kawkaw! The unfairness of it was unbearable. What new frustration loomed over his plans to humiliate Siam the stupid? What cruel blow to his yearning for the love of Kehloke? He was so buried under a blanket of despair he no longer cared about the Preceptress' rages. He said: 'Do you have no idea what is happening? You keep imagining you're getting some message through that execrable dagger. But the truth is that he's abandoned you.'

She tried to strike at him, to claw at him, with the dagger. A scratch would surely be the end of him, since the blade was death.

'Desist – desist most wonderful Mistress! Though my

heart is broken, I go. I will fight the hopeless fight for you out there in the quagmire of defeat.'

'No,' she said.

'No, most lovely . . .? You no longer want me to go?'

She wasn't listening to him. She was talking to one other than him. Her lips were pressed again to the sigil. He would have sworn he saw sparks, a tiny flame at the point of contact. Then she gave a cry that was part wail and part screech of triumph.

She wept the words at him: 'I have it! I have the command!'

'What command?'

'Yes – oh yes – my beloved Master!'

With her descent into sobbing, and caterwauling, he sensed a change from the directionless rage. But was this news of the same interest to Kawkaw? 'Would you send me out there, Mistress, into that beer-sotted celebration of our common woe?'

'Scheming you are! Adept with excuses, fish gutter. I shall indeed send you out, but with a most specific purpose. I require you to locate the holoima you once failed to deal with when you had the chance.'

'What do you now command?'

Tears flowed over her burning cheeks. 'My ultimate mission, a mission most sacred to His purpose. And you feral scum will have the undeserved honour of assisting me with its success.'

At that moment a thunderous detonation from the

blazing city distracted them both. It gave Kawkaw a moment to think. What plan, in this time of loss and despair, did her master offer to change the tide of battle? Such hubris! Only she, with her vaunted adoration of the Tyrant, could see it as anything other than pissing into the face of a cyclone. He couldn't bring himself to look in her direction.

'You – you!' She prodded the poisonous black spiral of a blade against his breast bone. 'You misbegotten wretch!'

He was forced to retreat from the stinging point. 'What?'

'You had her and failed to kill her.'

He slapped the vicious blade away with his hook. 'What in the plague-rotted fantasy of a whorehound are you babbling about?'

'The brat of a girl who made a fool of you.'

What was she talking about? A time when his senses had been clouded by the pain of his recently amputated arm . . . *What brat?*

'The brat you sold to the Mage at Isscan.'

'She's the one?'

'She is the nemesis the Master fears.'

He was taken aback by surprise. *The huloima called Mo!* The dreaded Tyrant of the Wastelands feared a huloima brat?

Kawkaw abandoned the tent with his mind in a quandary. Surely he had to think this through this? He was being asked not merely to creep and spy, but to find a way to destroy one of the strangers. And not just one at random but the strangest of them – the witch urchin he had once held in his capture. An alien female shadowed by a fearsome guardian such that even to approach her was likely to prove suicidal? Was the Preceptress telling him the truth? Was it even remotely possible that the Tyrant feared this girl?

If so how might the Tyrant reward the person who brought her death? What if he, Snakoil Kawkaw, saved the day for the great lord? Saved the day when all appeared hopeless? How might such loyalty be rewarded?

Was he being stupid? Was her madness catching?

Everything around Kawkaw – the inferno now consuming the city, the air out here that filled one's nostrils with the soot and the cinders of towering defeat – suggested the idiocy of such a plan.

You should run. You should lose yourself. Make yourself invisible in some hidey hole where none will find you.

Yet . . . Oh, glory of glories, were not the fates perfidious? Did the histories not speak of great battles turned on the loss of a horse, or a change of wind or tide?

To have even the slightest hope for his dreams to be resurrected, Snakoil Kawkaw had to stay alive. To do so he must keep the closest possible watch on the Preceptress herself, venturing out for short periods at a time, and returning ostensibly to give her the latest news, but in reality looking for the opportunity, any opportunity, to save his own skin. He still had the snotty-nosed urchins out there spying for him, but what hope could he expect from that miserable quarter? His nostrils provided a better source of information in such times. The lip-smacking odour of hops marked the increase in beer brewing in anticipation of some final celebration. The drink was being provided in plentiful quantities to the victorious troops of Prince Ebrit, whose navy was still pounding away at the ruins and flames.

Cautiously does it in such perilous circumstances!

He ignored those merrily singing to themselves, and those swaying with drunkenness having a piss in the dirt, searching for one of suitable size in suitable shadows, who had lapsed into a vomit-scented stupor. It was a shaking hand that inserted the blade between the drunk's vertebrae at the point where the neck formally left the curve that joined it to the sweat-soaked head. A professional execution, quick and silent, the issue of blood controlled with a press of the thumb, and then a modicum of patience to wait for the heart to stop.

The leather jerkin he quietly appropriated, then the pleated gambeson that reached to his knees. Ignoring the stink of piss and vomit, he dressed the body in his old clothes, so as to suggest a nobody, one whose death would cause no ripples. The implications for his own death were not lost on Snakoil Kawkaw. He held up his own trousers with the trooper's belt, re-attaching sword and dagger. His hook would provoke no suspicion in a battle-scarred old warrior. So attired he swaggered out of the shadows, heading towards the lamp-lit benches.

Run, you hopeless dreamer, run . . . !

A cyclone of confusion, of humiliation and raging hurt, rose in his mind. *Darkness, darkness, darkness . . . Here I am, now committed to the ultimate stupidity.* He couldn't think, he couldn't see, or hear, for several moments. Then he realised that a plump young Olhyiu barmaid was staring up at him from the other side of the make-shift bar, made up of a single wide plank atop two barrels. She was brown-haired and, perhaps, even younger than his first impressions had suggested. She had a bonnet on her head that made her resemble a startled rabbit in the soft light of a nearby lantern. He blinked, his mind only half emerged from confusion. Why, in the name of sweet adversity, was she smiling at him as if she knew him, her rubicund cheeks a rash of pimples.

'What are you staring at?'

'A warrior – a hero, if I am not mistaken.'

He realised that he was snarling. He brought his rage back under control and lowered his head to think. He watched her place the gratuitous flagon of beer on the board in front of him. He wiped his nose with the sleeve of his hook.

'Oh, my!' She reached out and touched the hook as if it had feeling in its rusting steel coil. 'What tales you might tell.'

He squinted his calculating eyes at her. 'I might, may-haps, be the devil himself, and you would not know it.'

The Creative Weave

Time was a stream running through Penny's consciousness with a flow and direction all of its own. Unfamiliar mathematical concepts were expanding in her mind. As she considered a concept, an event, a place, a time, the thought became real and she found herself within it; there was no separation between the stream in her mind and the external world – she was making a new reality. And this new reality then became intrinsic to the next step in her tentative exploration.

She was aware of how clumsy she was compared to the Akkharu. The key thing she must now grasp was the concept of control – to begin with, control over her own creativity. *How strange*, she thought, as she absorbed this simple necessity, *that the link between my own being and mind should be an obstacle*. It felt as if she were learning how to use a remote control on a detached robot. She knew she must practice and practice to make this preliminary step perfect before attempting the next stage: control over the common mind of the Akkharu.

Jeremiah's voice was little above a whisper in her mind: <What do you see?>

'A white glow that extends to infinity.'

<What you see before you is Dromenon. You might regard it as the blank new canvas for your art.>

Penny thought about this. 'But what I am seeing in my mind is three dimensional – it extends everywhere.'

<So will it be in Dromenon. Now, imagine what you want to create – just as you did when you reconstructed your beloved city.>

'But the Akkharu are not here.'

<No, but there is a new source of creativity present that you cannot yet sense. One rather more powerful than the Akkharu.>

'What is it?'

<It is called the Fáil.>

'What does it do?'

<It has infinite capability.>

Penny was startled. 'No – that cannot be.'

<It is true.>

Penny hesitated. What he was saying intrigued her. It also frightened her. She still wasn't sure she understood what he meant.

<All you need do is think back . . .>

Penny recalled the creation she had asked the Akkharu to build – a liquidly flowing mother of pearl wonderland, with walls smooth as glass displaying an exotic variation of hues and degrees of opacity. It had curving walkways and glancing alleyways intersecting the walls, all illuminated from within their crystalline lattices. A mental brush upon the walls, as light as a kiss, would change illumination, build a new passageway, construct a place of rest, even construct a mysterious labyrinth that contained a thousand offices, or a single utterly magical bedroom.

<Simply construct it here.>

'Place my thoughts here in Dromenon?'

<Exactly.>

She thought about what he was asking of her. 'I know we have talked about this wonderful place, Dromenon, but I don't really understand it.'

<It is beyond definition.>

'How then—?'

<Do not your artists, your composers, enter a kind of Dromenon of the senses in order to create? Are their creations definable?>

The idea Jeremiah was placing within her mind was lovely – beyond definition. She thought about her joy in her family's abandoned garden. Could she explain the wonder, the tranquillity she felt in the garden by defining the colours of flowers, of butterflies? Could she define the feeling of joy?

'I am ready to begin.'

<Do not attempt to analyse – simply create.>

She decided that she would begin with something out

of her memories, something as serene as the landscape with which she had repaired London. But this time she took her inspiration from the garden. She constructed a tree – an enormous tree, shaped like the baobab tree. She loved the story of those trees – they were said to have been planted upside down in the Arabian desert by the devil to stop their eternal wandering during the dark of night. This tree, with its enormous cylindrical trunk, bore thick fleshy branches that reached up into the sky. She watched it grow and grow so that the trunk, against which she now pressed her palms, became a hundred feet or more in diameter.

<Why so big?>

'I was testing the limits.'

<There are no limits.>

'But the tree, the emerging garden in my mind, is still black and white.'

<Because you willed it so.>

She willed it to become colourful.

The landscape was now perfused by brilliant sunshine. The sky was a deep cerulean with banks of cloud over the dome. The sea – where had the sea come from? – was Prussian blue, shimmering with light over and beneath its surface.

'It's just a lovely illusion?'

<Then make it real.>

'How?'

<Believe it is possible. The Fáil will empower it.>

'But if I can't see, or feel, or even sense its presence, how do I know that I am interacting with the Fáil?'

<All of Dromenon is infused with it.>

'Are you saying that this . . . this creative essence . . . is, for want of a better word for it, essentially magical?'

<Think of it as such, if it helps.>

Penny experimented. She willed her tree to grow to three hundred feet high, its foliage to adopt the shape of an old-fashioned kettle. She constructed another giant tree to the shape of a stag's horns, its gigantic antlers some three hundred feet about the ground.

'How amazing – enchanting!'

<You see now that there is no limit to your creativity here. Your imagination sets the only limits.>

Penny tested it again. In her mind she created what artists in the nineteenth century would have called a fairy picture. She imagined fairies appearing in the garden of the lost souls painted by Hieronymus Bosch. She watched it evolve moment to moment, become ever more complex and real. She gasped at the horror of the empty husks of human souls who were infested with a perversity of bird's beaks and fishes' heads, while in the near darkness towns were erupting into flame. Then she tempered the horror of it with brightly coloured foliage and buried everything in a rapid proliferation of plants and flowers, roots and leaves – a massive brilliant floral exuberance – until the entire view became a melee of leaves and petals, a screen to hide the abominations.

<Have you toyed enough to convince yourself?>

'Yes.'

<You know now that there are no limits to it – none other than the creativity in the mind of the True Believer.>

'Am I a True Believer?'

<It is through learning of and then accepting the creativity of Dromenon that one becomes a True Believer.>

'Why have you given me this gift?'

<So that you will serve my purpose.>

Penny saw him manifest before her, his face in profile. She saw his face turn to confront her own, those all black eyes devouring her.

She said: 'What do you want me to do for you?'

'There is a doorway – a portal – I must enter. Your creativity in this place of unlimited potential will allow me entry into that portal.'

'And then what will happen?'

'I will become a god.'

The Black Citadel

Alan pushed away the dead body of a Centurion he had killed with the Spear of Lug, streaking his armour and mail in yet more gore. He had to pause for breath within a circle of protective Shee, relieved to have recovered both the Spear and his strength of mind and purpose after the terrible battle with the Septemviles at the south gate. But the battle was not yet won. The burly legionary had managed to break through the Shee shield in an attempt to get at him. Suicidal attacks of this kind were becoming more common as the Tyrant's legionaries fought a desperate rearguard action to block off their approach to the Citadel. Sweat ran in rivulets down Alan's face, running underneath his armour to add to the itching. Everyone around him was haggard with fatigue. After Kate had healed him, the fighting had continued unabated for two whole days with night making no difference. By day the sun was blocked out by the billowing smoke that blanketed the sky. By night the battlefield was illuminated by the inferno of the blazing streets. Trumpet calls were rallying the Shee and Ebrit's troops to his side. They fought for a total victory and until that was achieved, there would be no end – it was a war to the death and this, the heights surrounding the Black Citadel, was the final stretch of the battlefield.

Alan realised that in defeating the Septemviles including Lightbane, he had declared undying fealty to Mórígán as well as the First Power. He didn't quite know what this might imply in time, but he sensed that it had changed him. He had discovered a way of turning his oraculum inwards as a source of replenishing his energy. He had learned of the possibility of doing this from the mother-sister of the present Kyra in that terrible confrontation with the Legun incarnate at Ossierel.

He assessed the situation anew while Ebrit's cannons and the dual arrays of Shee archers and Ebrit's naval assault crews rained fire arrows and heavy armour-piercing bolts into the massed ranks of the legionaries, whose numbers were being squeezed into smaller and smaller spaces. Bétaald had estimated that the city was defended by something like half a million troops, but the slaughter had been dreadful. Briefly, in breaks in the smoke, Alan caught glimpses of the towering architecture ahead. The Citadel capped the central tip of the mountain on which Ghork Mega had been built, a complex of tall buildings, black as obsidian. They couldn't be more than half a mile distant by now. But that half mile promised to be perilous.

He studied the vast palatial complex – its adamantine walls carved from the solid granite of the original mountain top. How strange that he could make out no windows or internal illumination within the spiky towers or the surrounding labyrinth. He spoke to Iyezzz high overhead:

<What can you make out of the defences of the Citadel? Can you see past the smoke and flames?>

<My view is impeded, Mage Lord. I can see little more than a peak of darkness, surrounded by some strange encircling moat.>

<A moat this high up?>

<I have to admit, a strange moat indeed. It would appear as if a third fosse takes the form of a river of nothingness.>

Alan could not see what Iyezzz had described from this distance, but as they pushed forwards again, fighting for every yard, he began to make out more details of the Citadel, acknowledging that, in spite of its bleak darkness, it possessed its own dark beauty. Closer to, he realised that he had been mistaken in assuming that it had been carved from a natural granite peak. He could now see that it had been cast out of some dark multihued crystal. Here and there he glimpsed architectural details of such intricacy that it was hard to imagine any human hand capable of carving them. The joins flowed seamlessly from building to building, which were all strangely iridescent. So tall were the central spikes he had to crane his neck to gaze up at them. And, in glimpses through the palls of smoke, he saw something of what Iyezzz had described: there was a strange circle of clouds whirling about the periphery of the Citadel.

There was something very odd going on; a dark magic that Alan felt too tired to understand, yet he knew it could prove to be the ultimate threat. Mo might understand it, the way she had understood the dark shapes that had been invading his mind during the journey here. But Mo was not by his side.

Perhaps something the Tyrant himself had hinted at . . .

Alan was reminded of the time he had been threatened by the golden robot. He had witnessed visions of galaxies and nebulas moving around him, and explosions of what he took to be supernovae giving rise to oceans of light and fire more brilliant than any rainbow. Places where new stars were coming into existence . . .

He had demanded an explanation from the Tyrant.

'The witches saw fit to criticise the harnessing of such a wonder. Small minds terrified of the ultimate ambition – infinite power!'

Now he witnessed the Citadel close to, Alan wondered again just what lesson he had been taught in that frightening encounter.

'You're talking about the Arinn?'

'Of all the beings on all the worlds, the Arinn alone had the knowledge and the courage to embrace infinity. Such was their vision, they constructed a malengin capable of harnessing the root of existence. They became one with it.'

The Tyrant had always been several steps ahead of them. And now a thrill of fear ran through Alan's heart as he gazed up at the bizarre moat of clouds. Were they approaching the third fosse of Ghork Mega?

A new message from Iyezzz interrupted his musings:

<I can make out a single point of crossing. There is a bridge that straddles the emptiness of the moat. You should soon be within sight of it.>

The Garg prince had been forced to fly very high, out of reach of the heavy crossbows of the enemy, who had the advantage of enormous height when firing from the upper reaches of the Citadel. But the eagle-like visual acuity of the Garg had overcome the disadvantage.

'You heard?' Alan spoke to the Kyra.

'Yes.'

Then Alan had his first glimpse of the bridge. It was illuminated by flames at least fifty feet high in the neighbouring buildings.

'That looks really weird! What do you make of it, Ainé?'

The Shee replied: 'All is blurred and strange. I can make out little beyond the clouds.'

Alan studied the crossing, which consisted of a bridge running through the wheeling barrier of nothingness. There was an indication of what could be stone walls at its entrance, but then the distant half of the bridge was lost in shadow. The shadow itself appeared to be a living thing that oozed and crept out of the Citadel, as if feeding the encircling emptiness with its dark stream. Looking more closely at where the bridge led, he couldn't see beyond the shadows.

The Kyra called the Shee to form a spearhead, its point now having a specific focus. As if sensing their purpose, two platoons of black-armoured enemy cavalry appeared out of the surrounding streets to take up formation between them and the bridge. The cavalry charged into the Shee with lances and tridents, spurring their heavy steeds, covered in battle mail, into the advancing front line. Alan watched the Shee's metamorphosis to great cats in a spreading ripple.

The Shee trumpets sounded faint and tinny in the elevated air. The fighting entered a new ferocity. Alan felt peculiarly distant from the new roars of the Shee and the screams of the injured and dying. The cobbled road beneath his feet was running with blood, making it difficult to keep his feet.

Ainé's sibilant purr interrupted his thoughts: 'Do you not sense it?'

'What?'

'The Legun Incarnate.'

A new roar, deeper by far than any tigress, sounded from horribly close. Alan shivered in apprehension. A spectre reared out of the confusion of battle no more than thirty yards ahead. Its huge skull-like countenance turned from side to side, as if searching, until the furnace pits of its eyes detected him. Then the fanged maw gaped as it roared its challenge anew – a challenge directed at Alan personally. There was no mistaking the Legun called the Captain. It reared, colossal and deadly against the wall of flames. Dark power crackled and streamed around its arm as it struck with a huge flailing mace, scattering dozens of Shee in that single blow as if they were skittles.

Ainé purred again: 'It is forming the apex of a wedge – attracting the Death Legion's warriors to its side.' She hesitated, looking to Bétaald, whose eyes met the Kyra's. 'There is no time to be lost. We must attack before they build up an unstoppable momentum.'

Alan shook his head. 'I think I should deal with this.'

'You are not yet fully recovered from the last confrontation.'

Sweat stung in the tired corners of his eyes as he looked to Bétaald for support. 'This monster killed the Kyra's mother-sister in the Battle of Ossierel. And in the arena of this city it also killed her grandmother-sister. The present Kyra is of the same pedigree as those brave ancestors. If she confronts it, it will kill her.'

'What then? You would confront it by yourself. You who were equally powerless to destroy it at Ossierel?'

'I'll find a way.'

The Kyra stared at him, with those huge blue eyes. 'If I die, I will be born again. But not so you.'

'Neither of you will die,' Bétaald declared. 'The Fir Bolg defeated it with battleaxes. We will do the same with arrows and javelins.'

The Legun was smashing his way towards them at the apex of a dense wedge of emboldened defenders. The Kyra transmitted a new command through her oraculum. The

Legun became the focus of a thousand arrows and javelins. But something was wrong. The weapons struck the monster, but bounced off, as if encountering a shield wall.

'There is some kind of protective force.'

Bétaald nodded. 'The Tyrant has learned from the defeat at Ossierel.'

The Legun roared again and executed a forward thrust, one huge arm still wielding the giant spike-covered mace, the other arm wielding talons a foot long and sharp as daggers. It smashed through the wall of Shee that stood between it and Alan. A voice that hissed, like lava polluting a lake of ice, battered Alan's mind:

<Brat seduced by the Witch of Ossierel – you would declare war on the beloved Master. Again do I challenge you to mortal combat.>

Alan's oraculum blazed in his brow. 'I call upon the Trídédana to strengthen me!' Assuming the First Power, he held aloft the Spear of Lug, so that the weapon forged by his grandfather, Padraig, shone with runes, like a rubicund sun.

In a huge leap, the Legun was before him, the arm wielding the giant mace drawn back to destroy him. Alan drove the spiral blade, incandescent with the First Power, into the throat of the Legun. But the thrust encountered some strange defensive force there, with the Spear rebounding as if from a pillar of steel. Then the defensive force struck back at Alan, weakening his spear arm, and extinguishing his oraculum. He was thrown down onto his back before the massed ranks of Shee. As if in one streamlined action, the Legun's arm reared back, the ball, with its terrible spikes descending towards his head . . .

'Stay your malice, you ugly brute!'

It was Qwenqwo's voice. The shadow of his friend, the dwarf mage, fell over Alan's eyes, the runestone cascading light in his left hand, the Fir Bolg battleaxe aloft.

'No!' Alan cried out with shock.

No – no – no! Alan's mind was unable to accept what was happening. The killing blow tore through Qwenqwo, the malice too great for runestone or battleaxe. A miasma of grief invaded Alan's heart, the unbearable anguish of loss . . .

'Quickly, Alan!'

'No!' His flailing mind was filling up with those metamorphosing spectres of black, they were invading every part of him . . .

An arm curled around his shoulder. He knew, without turning, that it was Mo's. As he turned to face Mo he sensed the difference in her. Then he saw it in her eyes. Mo was talking to him, but it didn't sound like Mo's voice. It sounded like the beauty of music, but at the same time a voice of enchantment:

'They call them weaves.'

'What . . .?'

'The black things that so tormented your mind.'

He wanted to lose himself in his friend's embrace, but nothing was capable of curing his pain. His friend Qwenqwo Cuatzel was dead.

Alan turned and glimpsed the Monster crowing with triumph, hoisting the shattered remains of their bravest warrior – their greatest hero – aloft.

'You cannot fight the Legun. You're exhausted and outmatched, just as you were at Ossierel.'

'Then we've lost the battle, Mo.'

'Not yet. Magtokk and I will help you.'

'Magtokk?'

'You must trust me.'

'Oh, Mo . . .'

'Rest . . . Let me help you.'

Alan felt tears fill his eyes. 'I failed them, Mo. I failed my mom and dad.'

'No.'

'How can I die, knowing I failed them?'

'It isn't over.'

Alan was suddenly immersed in a strange sense of peace. Time hovered, suspended here in this unreal world of drifting light and shadow.

<Mo?>

<I'm here.>

He sensed her friendship, her love for him, through their communion. His mind, still confused by grief at the death of his friend, drifted. He was surrounded by creatures resembling angels: ethereal beings who existed in a perfect harmony.

<Are you one of them, Mo?>

<Yes.>

He saw her then, as a figure detached from the others, a being of gentleness and light, one who knew neither malice nor selfishness. He couldn't believe what he was seeing. He was dumbstruck for several moments.

<What are you, Mo?>

<My birth name is Mira.>

<The Heralded One!>

<You remember . . .>

<From Ossierel – yes!> Then Alan felt a wave of panic sweep over him. <The Legun! It will kill them all!>

<The Legun is no more. It has been destroyed as you slept. The last of the Septemviles is gone.>

<How?>

<The True Believers. They destroyed the Legun as they destroyed the demi-god, Fangorath. You slept then too.>

<I'm sorry. Oh, Mo. I'm sorry I couldn't do more.>

<You need not apologise. The Citadel was intended to draw you in. It was a trap that would have ended your quest.>

<Where are they all? What's happened to the armies – the Shee?>

<The war is over. With the loss of the Legun, the Death Legion threw down their arms and surrendered.>

Alan felt his spirits rise. <Is it truly over then, Mo?>

<The war is over. But our purpose is not yet completed.>

<Our purpose . . .?>

<The purpose for which we were chosen.>

The importance of that slowly dawned on Alan. <Where is this place?>

<Dromenon.>

How comfortable she seemed in this strange world. Stars wheeled and spiraled about them. Nearby Alan saw a shining disc of whirling energy. It reminded him of the black holes that the cosmologists talked about being at the centre of galaxies. But this was a mirror image of that: black was white and white was black. And the hole was a disc of utter darkness that ran around the rim of a brightly shining hole.

Mo said: <It's the projection of the Black Citadel into Dromenon.>

<I don't even pretend to understand all that you are telling me, Mo. Was this what you discovered in the Valley of the Pyramids?>

<This and more. At first when my soul spirit entered there, I was so afraid. I couldn't face what I was seeing there – what was expected of me.>

<What is expected of you?>

<It's all right. I'm not scared of it anymore.>

<What are you not scared of? What's happening to you, Mo?>

<I am fulfilling my fate.>

<Your fate?>

<We – all four friends – were brought to Tír, each with his or her individual fate. I've been delaying mine.> She shivered. <Maybe I've been trying to avoid coming to terms

with my own destiny. I admit that I was frightened of it, the human part of me.>

<For pity's sake, Mo.>

<I know. It has been difficult for each of us in turn to accept. My fate, as Magtokk has known all along, is to direct the singularity. It's so difficult to explain – our human language is inadequate. Suffice to say, the Arinn created the Fáil. Only the Arinn can deal with the anomaly.>

He stood, or at least it felt as if his spirit stood, and he took hold of her slim shoulders. <I'm worried about you.>

Mo gazed back calmly into his eyes.

<There's no need.>

Alan hesitated, confused by what he sensed in that simple communication.

<My soul spirit can move through the weave of the Akkharu at will. The Akkharu use crystals of stardust they call chardizz – what was left from the creation of the universe – and weave them into patterns of force, including, if they are so guided, forces of creation. Maybe there are many universes. I still don't understand it all really. I am learning from moment to moment. I see things and feel things differently from how I used to. I might have to show you, instead of explaining.>

<Show me?>

<What still needs to be done . . . What will be . . .>

Mo looked down at the Torus and the bog oak figurine dangling around her neck. She had kept the figurine safe since Padraig had given it to her, all the way back in

Clonmel. The Torus was glowing brightly, pulsating with Mo's heartbeat.

He asked her: <How will it be done?>

<I must construct a new weave of chardizz using the Akkharu – an alternative route.>

<I don't understand.>

<I'm not sure that I understand myself, but I can see it clearly in my mind. I must weave a new pathway through space and time. Please don't worry about me. The True Believers will guide me.> Mo spoke softly, <Our quest must be completed.>

Alan awoke to the sight of a blazing Ghork Mega. He looked around, aware that Ainé and Bétaald were supporting him. They were helping him to his feet, as if he were only now recovering from the shock of the annulling of his power. He confirmed that the noise and violence of battle had ended, but the Black Citadel still towered above them, surrounded by its river of nowhere. The single bridge had disappeared.

'Is the battle really over?'

'There is some residual fighting in distant streets, but it is mainly the legionaries attempting to flee.'

'Thank goodness!' Alan turned around to search in vain for his friend. 'Mo? I hope you're still here with me? I've got some more questions to ask. And I doubt that I'll like the answers – if I even begin to understand them.'

<Don't worry, Alan. I'm still here.>

A Tactical Inbound

Mark roused himself within the rickety garage to one more dawn in a world that had gone insane. The death of Tajh had thrown the crew into a pall of gloom. Bull and Sharkey hadn't slept at all throughout the night. They were still singing rowdily to themselves, drunk as skunks on the lavish supplies of Bourbon that Brett was doling out to anybody who wanted it. The singing was drowned out by another cyclone of wind that hurled bricks and debris against the increasingly precarious walls and roof. New holes were appearing all over the place, letting in the smoky morning light. The pulsations were coming more and more frequently, heralded by a whistling noise, like a monstrous kettle coming to the boil. Then there would be a huge throb, a battening red glow and a thunderous rumble that would shake the ground before an explosion of heat that would illuminate the inside of the garage as if it were a blacksmith's forge.

The news, what little of it they had managed to glean from a patchily recovered line of communication with HQ, was hardly comforting. The Rose was drawing out a huge flare from the sun. Scientific advisers to the American president blamed the flare for the climatic disturbance that was wracking the globe with earthquakes, tsunamis, cyclone winds and ferocious storms. The scientists had provided the President with charts and graphs, and increasingly gloomy prognostications: the bottom line was that Earth was heading for a global disaster in no more than days.

'Anyone for a Havana?'

An unwashed heavily stubble-faced Brett broke the panicky silence following the latest pulsation. He had spent the night in the passenger seat of the cabin of the Pig, exchanging jokes with an equally dishevelled Cogwheel. Overnight they had just about finished a bottle of whiskey between them.

Cogwheel hiccupped before a carefully enunciated reply: 'I'll have a couple, if you don't think me presumptuous.'

'Help yourself, buddy.'

Cogwheel slid one of the cigars into the pocket of the driver's side door, then allowed Brett to cut the head of the second for him, before putting it between his lips and sucking against the flame of the lighter. When Brett himself lit up, the cab filled up with smoke. Brett looked through a single squinting eye into a three-quarters empty bottle before taking a swig. He passed the bottle to Cogwheel. 'So, Buddy, what's the plan?'

Cogwheel finished the bottle before slinging it out onto the concrete floor through the open driver's window. 'Folks, seeing as the darned place is about to fall in on us,' he did a slurring imitation of Brett's Kentucky accent, 'I reckon it's time we moved out.' He puffed some more on his cigar before abandoning the accent. 'Problem is we got nowhere to bloodywell go. We head east, we hit the Rose. We head north, west or south, we hit Seebox's cordon.'

Brett puffed contentedly on his cigar. 'Well – I guess it's been a privilege getting to know you, Cogwheel.'

'Reciprocated with bells on,' Cogwheel hiccupped.

'Aw – what the heck! You want me to open another bottle?'

'Sounds like an idea.'

Brett reached back so Bull could pass him one of the two bottles remaining in the crate. He laid it in his lap for a moment while he took a thoughtful drag on his cigar, held the smoke in for too long and ended up coughing smoke out of both nostrils. His eyes watered as he uncapped the new bottle and took a swig. 'Don't know about you guys, but I sure as hell didn't figure we'd end up here.'

Cogwheel shook his head. 'We can head out, if that's what you chaps want. All we have to do is decide a direction.'

'What do you say – we toss a dollar?'

'We don't have a dollar.'

Bull's slurring voice from the belly of the Pig: 'Would a button do?'

'Sure! Why not – but we got to decide which is heads and which is tails.'

Cogwheel said: 'Flat versus curved?'

'Sounds good to me. You call it, buddy.'

Cogwheel sneezed, then wiped his nose with his sleeve. 'Curved is the Rose. Flat we hit the smoky blue distance!'

The button spun.

Brett looked at it: 'Smoky blue it is!'

Sharkey's voice singing to the Bob Marley tune: 'Don't worry about a t'ing. One more pulse and de roof's coming in.'

This provoked laughter from Bull. 'Hey, Brett, don't forget me and Sharkey back here when you're doling out them cigars.'

'Wouldn't dream of it, fellas.' Brett passed a handful of cigars back into the gloom. 'We got all we need of whiskey up front, so the last bottle is yours.'

'Cheers!'

Brett passed Cogwheel the new bottle for a final swig before starting up the heavy engines. He spoke thoughtfully: 'You heard about the famous Roman philosopher, Seneca – what happened when he was coming back into Rome out of retirement in the country, and he heard that Nero had given him the death sentence?'

Cogwheel hesitated, the bottle to his lips. 'No – what happened?'

'He hugged his wife and friends and told them to moderate their grief by giving some thought to the lessons of philosophy.'

Cogwheel choked with laughter on his swig.

'You okay there, buddy?'

'Yeah – that's a great story. I'll tell you what, Brett. When this is over, I'm heading for the life of a busker.'

'No change there,' muttered Cal, accepting the bottle tossed his way by Sharkey. He spurned the cigars, opting for his usual self-roll.

Nan and Mark waved away both bottle and cigars. Nan was complaining aloud to anybody who cared to listen: 'You men realise that the atmosphere in this vehicle is lethal.'

Her words provoked several belly laughs. Cogwheel said: 'There was something additional and utterly profound I meant to say. But in the excitement of thinking about it I've forgotten what it was.'

Cal said, 'Good!'

They were moving out of the dilapidated garage. Cogwheel's erratic driving snagged the near-side door jamb, collapsing the entrance arch on his way out of it. This brought about a slow-motion implosion of the entire rickety building, which provoked another round of belly laughs and cheering.

The Rose's wall of radiant heat hit them as they emerged and they argued whether it would be best to open or close every window. A perspiring Cogwheel leaned his cigar-holding arm on the frame of the fully lowered driver's window. 'I've worked it out in my mind. There are things going for me, man.'

'Cogwheel, shut the fuck up.' Cal's eyes wandered to where Tajh's remains were wrapped up in a tarpaulin.

They were putting some distance now between them and the collapsed garage. But since the drunken Cogwheel had no real sense of direction to aim for, they might have been driving around in circles. Nobody really cared. Cogwheel looked over his shoulder at Cal, who was staring out of the nearside wide open porthole at the looming monstrosity. 'Fuck you,' he said. 'The way I see it, you could look upon the busking as a political statement. You're not really asking people to give you money. You just sit there next to this cloth cap wearing an intelligent look on your face and the interaction invites a conversation. What passer-by wouldn't want to engage by tossing a donation into the cap?'

'Cut the crap!'

The heat, and the polluted atmosphere, was making a number of people cough. Cogwheel sniffed. 'All I'm saying is that it has surreal possibilities.'

Cal muttered: 'You haven't got a cap.'

'I'll fuckingwell knit one then. So there's me busking alongside my gorgeous knitted cap.'

'You can't knit.'

'I'll learn how to. I'll teach myself the knitting. I'll pick a good pattern too. Design, colour – lots of colour. I'll knit it to the shape of a cloth cap. Then I'll take care placing it on the floor facing up. I can think of a dozen metaphors for that upended knitted cap with its big mouth wide open. It will suggest the need to feed it, but at the same time there's no obligation to feed it. The decision – whether or not to feed it – is the prerogative of the passer-by. That's the surreal twist of the situation. Though conversation would be welcome, no words need to be spoken. The art would function just as well at the level of an ambiguous silence.'

The cigars and whiskey had made the rounds back to the ambiguously silent Padraig. He took a swig out of the bottle, which caused his eyes to water. Outside the vehicle the whistling of a new pulse began. The cyclone of wind was rising, whipping up dirt, bricks and rubble, rattling the bodywork. They argued all over again whether or not they should close the flaps and portholes – but this would probably bake them with the heat.

Brett warned Cogwheel: 'Head thataway. You're wandering too close to the thing.'

'Okay, boss!'

Mark stared out of the portside porthole at the flaring monstrosity that had become of the Rose. The missile attack that had killed Tajh had failed to destroy it. If anything, it had made the situation worse. The monstrosity had swallowed up the explosion, and that suggested that any further missile attacks would be counterproductive. But no-one among the crew thought the military leaders would share that opinion.

Mark accepted the bottle from Padraig and took a modest swig. He had no real liking for neat whiskey, but he shared the despair that was eating at the crew.

From those fragmented communications overnight they

knew that President Harvey was in touch with other world leaders. Parts of Moscow, Paris, Berlin and Rome had already been destroyed by fire. The chaos had invaded Asia, provoking Australia and New Zealand to offer military cooperation with China, India, Japan and a wide raft of other countries. There had been a continuing series of meetings at the UN. Everybody throughout the world was watching what was happening in London. The experts all agreed that the Black Rose was the root cause of the cataclysm. The solar flare was the visible manifestation of its threat. Even as Mark stared at the monolith, building up towards a new gargantuan pulse, he knew, as did every other member of the crew, that a new attack was inevitable.

'Hey, Sharkey,' Cogwheel called back over his shoulder, 'you dextrous with those Celtic style armband tattoos?'

Cal swore at Cogwheel and told him to button it. 'Brett, can you see if you can open some line of communication with Resistance HQ?'

Cogwheel asked him: 'What's the point?'

'We need to know what the fuck is happening.'

Brett tried his luck with a console resting on his lap. 'No luck for now, Cal. We're too close to the Rose to pick up anything but static.'

'Cogwheel – put your foot on it,' Cal growled. 'And Brett, keep on trying.'

The vehicle shook with the rumble of the new wave from the Rose. Mark squeezed Nan's hand. A crackling flame ran over the face of the Rose, provoking a static electricity that raised the hairs on their heads even at a distance of more than a mile. The cyclone erupted and the debris slammed into the Pig again. Mark rammed the porthole shut, then put his arm around Nan, waiting for the pulse to abate. They sped on as another thunderous detonation shook the ground under the vehicle. Brett's crates tumbled around the interior while outside large chunks of rubble battered against the walls and roof of the Pig.

Cal shouted: 'That one – that wasn't a pulse.'

They threw open the flaps and portholes to witness a screaming volley of missiles pass overhead and slam into the Rose. They heard the distant thundering of what sounded like heavy artillery.

Cal shouted: 'That can't be Seebox. It's General Chatwyn! The Resistance is attacking the Rose.'

Cogwheel hesitated, looking back over his shoulder at Cal: 'What do we do?'

'We bloodywell join them,' Cal whooped.

The crew broke out into a wild burst of cheering.

Brett was looking up at the huge monolith where numerous different explosions marked the impact of high explosive shells. Brett whooped: 'C'mon Cogwheel. Speed it up. We've got to see if we can get a message through to them.'

Cogwheel threw his stogie out of the window. 'Oh, dear. I suspect I'm a little above the drink drive limit.'

As Cogwheel spun the wheel, directing the Pig

westwards, the horizon ahead of them became a mass of explosions and flames. It had to be a battle between the Resistance and Seebox's cordon. Brett howled, 'Yee-hah! We're gonna hit those S.O.B.'s from behind.' He was still fiddling with a digital console on his knee when a voice broke through the static. A voice but no picture . . .

'This is Brett Lee Travis speaking for the crew of the Mamma Pig. We're asking for battle instructions from General Chatwyn.'

'Caution . . . Mamma Pig. I repeat, caution – tactical incoming!'

'What the fuck . . .!'

Everybody was shouting at once, including a bewildered Cogwheel, who was tugging at Brett's arm. 'What was that?'

Brett was slapping at sparks running over the console and onto his lap from where he had dropped the lit cigar out of his lips. 'Holy shit!'

The vehicle was still thundering towards the blazing western horizon.

'What is it?'

'Whoooaaaaa! Cogwheel – you got to slow her down! Get us down into that there dip!'

'What's going on?'

'Get down into it – and then swing the Pig around.'

'Why?'

'We got a minute or two, as I figure it. We gotta put the guillotine in the path of the expanding wave.'

'What?'

'Do it, buddy! We're maybe two miles away from a tactical nuclear strike.'

People were falling over crates, and one another, as they dived for the floor in the wheeling vehicle. Everybody was shouting or screaming at once, slamming the shutters closed on every window. There was a vision of Brett reaching forward to close the windscreen flaps ahead of him. Then the flash . . . so brilliant it turned everything into a negative, white to black, black to white, with a blood red halo outlining every pallid face. Then the shockwave and the colossal impact of a tsunami of expanding force. It lifted the front of the pig a foot off the ground, then dumped it back with a shattering crash, then it shoved it careening backwards. They screeched in a zig-zag, with Cogwheel fighting to regain control of the wheel. They heard the gearbox disintegrate. And still the expanding wave drove them backwards, slewing the vehicle a distance of something like fifty yards through debris, broken walls, wrecked vehicles, until at last they came to a jolting halt against something immovable. But the noise didn't stop. Their ears were still shredded by a pandemonium of thunder.

Mark heard people cursing and groaning. Cal's shout: 'Anybody seriously injured?'

Cogwheel wheezing: 'One suspected dead – me!'

They were too shocked to move for several minutes. Then, when they opened the flaps and portholes they could see nothing because of the dust storm. Mark was the first to exit a porthole, falling out of it at a crazy angle onto the wind-whipped stony ground. His vision was blurred and blotchy, as if he had stared into the noonday sun. There was a high-pitched ringing in his ears, a dizziness within his head. The ground below him was spinning. It was a struggle to get to his feet in the battering cyclone of wind, which was ripping at his clothes. He glanced over to where the rear of the Pig was impaled on a girder sticking out of the concrete of a ruined silo. He realised: *I can't hear a thing!*

'Oh, god!' he panted for breath.

He forced himself to look back in through the porthole. The steel was too hot to keep his hands pressed against it.

'Nan – you and Padraig all right?'

He thought he heard some reply, though it might have been his imagination. Then Nan's face appeared at the open porthole and the long bony hands of Padraig assisted her out into Mark's own hands. He whispered: 'Thank goodness!' He helped her down and then back to her feet. They supported one another.

She spoke to him, mind-to-mind: <I can see stars.>

<I'm not surprised.>

But she was shaking her head. Her finger was pointing to the sky. There he too saw stars, stars spiralling and wheeling around them in the gale-torn sky.

They turned as one to face the Black Rose. Where it had been, a gigantic sphere made up of myriad bolts of lightning now expanded: reds, purples, ultramarine, blues, greens and yellows extended and metamorphosed across the sphere moment by moment. There was a wall of solid lightning several miles in diameter and it continued to thunder and crackle without cease. It was the most terrifying vision Mark had ever witnessed.

He was beginning to hear the wind now, a howling of a thousand banshees that he would have preferred to have remained deaf to. Brett was helping Cogwheel down out of the driver's side of the cab. The hoist of the Pig was clearly broken.

'Why aren't we dead?' Mark was looking to Nan, who looked as confused and uncertain as he did.

'I don't know.'

Padraig was also emerging from the ruined Pig, helped by Bull and Sharkey. But he was too shattered to stand. They helped him sit in the dirt against one of the wheels, his breath emerging in slow long sighs. Mark and Nan sat down beside him and comforted him. Padraig was attempting to speak, his voice breathless and little above a whisper, but Mark had to put his ear close to Padraig's mouth to hear him:

'They made a mistake . . . attacking it with a nuclear missile. It fed on it. The Tyrant must have predicted they would do so. It was a . . . a trap.'

'Cal – did you hear?'

'Why?' Cal's teeth were gritted with anger. 'Why the hell would anybody want to be attacked with a tactical nuclear weapon?'

'I think, for some reason, it must have needed the energy.'

'For what purpose?'

Nan looked up into the expanding sphere of lightning. Prongs were reaching out into the air around it, as if it were consuming everything about it. 'Perhaps,' she said, 'to gain entry to the Fáil.'

A cowled figure manifested a short distance away from the apex of the guillotine blade of the Mamma Pig. It was kneeling, with its head lowered, facing the monstrosity that had evolved from the Rose.

'What the fuck . . .?' Cal breathed huskily.

Nobody answered.

'Is that thing real?'

Mark stumbled out onto the wind-blown ground, his head reeling with dizziness as he approached the kneeling figure. He stared down into its shrouded face, which was grey in colour, with eyes closed.

'Who – or what – are you?'

<A Keeper of Night and Day.>

The whispered reply, mind-to-mind, startled Mark. He was even more startled when those eyes opened to meet his own, confronting him with reflecting mirrors. 'Why are you here?'

<We observe the beginnings and ends of worlds.>

The reply took Mark's breath away. He looked at Nan, who must have heard the exchange oraculum-to-oraculum. 'Does that mean that our world is about to end?'

<I observe but do not prophesise. The Great Cycle is now

due. I must observe the end of the Old and the beginning of the New.>

Mark heard cries of astonishment from behind him. When he turned around, his head still spinning with shock, he saw that still more stars were descending out of the sky. He stood there, transfixed, as a stream of knowledge expanded in his brain. He felt a presence calling him. Nan was running forward to join him, throwing herself into his arms, her own arms around his neck, hugging him close.

She said: 'The Temple Ship is calling us.'

'The Ship?'

'Yes!'

He had only seconds to bid goodbye to Cal and the others. He didn't know what words to say to them. He didn't know if the Earth would survive the calamity of the expanding monstrosity that had grown out of the Black Rose.

Even as he hesitated a shadow fell on him. The Temple Ship had descended to no more than a hundred feet above them, colossal, in its great raptor manifestation. Mark spoke to Nan: 'Somehow we have to find a way to make contact with the others. We must join Mo and Alan and Kate.'

'Through the Ship?'

'Yes – through the Ship!'

Time was running out for them. Cal and the crew were staring at him, open-mouthed.

'Padraig,' Mark called out to him. He saw the elderly

head rise, the lips in the lined face were smiling back. 'Come with us.'

The hoary old head shook. 'No, thank you all the same. My work is not yet done.'

Mark felt a void expand in his chest. The emptiness was so great it felt as if a universe would not fill it. A mind was enfolding his, enfolding both his and Nan's. They were drowning in the prescience. No time to think anymore.

Padraig lifted his hand and waved: 'Goodbye Mark – Nan!'

Mark's lips formed the word he was no longer capable of speaking: *Goodbye!* But what was in a word that could not be expressed in a final exchange of glances.

Cal's face was the last image to fix itself into Mark's vision, into his memory: Cal's need meeting his, pain for pain, anger for anger. Mark activated his power through the triangle in his brow. In that moment he heard the enclosing mind, demanding of him and of Nan both:

<Come now! Be one with me!>

For Kehloke

A plague on her! A plague on the pox-faced harridan!

Snakoil Kawkaw scratched obsessively at his chin with the hook, gazing down onto the two urchins squatting in the sand.

Fish-gutter!

The Preceptress' derogatory dismissal of him! Was that what he amounted to? Was it all that he, in his wild and adventurous life, added up to? A piece of flotsam to be abandoned to the cesspit of history?

His heart palpitated. He was lost in rage for a moment or two, his breath huffing and puffing through his clenched jaws. Again and again had he found himself harking back to that conversation he had overheard from outside the slit opening of his irascible mistress' tent, this priestess to the great loser, Tyrant of the Wastelands, since waste was what his vaunted capital had been reduced to.

'This witch-urchin from another world? Beloved Master! It will be my heart's desire to see her dead!'

How closely he had listened, even though he had heard nothing of the other side of the conversation. But it had proved easy to read it from her sycophantic replies. The black dagger would see the huloima, the one called Mo, dead.

'You would kill the huloima? When she has an amulet of power she wears on a thong around her throat? When she is guarded by a most ferocious Shee-witch, who sticks closer to her than a shadow?'

'You had better find a way.'

She would take all the credit for it: meanwhile Kawkaw would take all the risk. He had spat the words at her: 'What about me? My life?'

'What matters your miserable self against the Master's interest!'

She thought herself so clever. That execrable bitch with her red-veined eyes! That sycophantic venerator, with her obsessive kissing of the sigil!

Formidable lady? Formidable my arse!

And yet her words, and their insinuation, continued to haunt him: 'A power that is not for your hairy ears, bear-man!'

Me she threatens, when I would rip her black heart out!

He must somehow calm himself. *Have a care for oneself, Snakoil Kawkaw, in such a perilous situation!*

Appraising the pair of urchins, he was still struggled to

control his rage and think clearly. The girl must have read the rage in his eyes.

'Please, Mister – we does wot you says!'

Kawkaw panted again, thinking back. Oh, she might look very different these days but he remembered everything of that brat called Mo. She had always been so strange. He recalled his agony, the very day the Storm Wolves had severed his arm. He rememberd how, driven to distraction with her whining, he had kicked out at her. But he had felt no weight at all on the end of his boot. There had also been that devilish cowl of spider's web about her, that same covering that had cloaked all four of the huloimas when they had appeared out of the wilderness at the ice-bound lake. Siam had failed to recognise the danger they bore. Siam the stupid, who had stolen his lovely Kehloke, provoking her into rejecting him – condemning poor Snakoil Kawkaw to a lifetime of loveless wandering.

'A plague on the bitch! May it rot her conspiring heart!'

'Please, Mister? Don't be angry wiv us!'

'Shut your gob and let me think. There is something you can do for me. You must do it exactly as I tell you.'

'Yeah, Mister. We does it, honest!'

What else was the weasel going to say? He could make out a scar on her eyelid where her stye had been. The huloima brat, Mo – what trouble she had taken over this urchin! He had to make sure the urchin didn't betray him out of gratitude. He slapped her, hard, knocking her to the sandy ground, next to her bawling brother. Even so, her dazed eyes looked up at her brother, protectively. Oh, without doubt, the mute was the weakness he must fix on here!

'Him – this piece of shite – he must fall down and look like he's dying.'

She was snivelling from the blow. 'I'll tell 'im. 'E will, Mister. Honest, 'e will.'

'And you will draw the attention of the huloima to your distress – the one called Mo, who has been looking after you.'

A hesitation now in those miserable eyes. A quiver in her voice, 'Yes.'

He reached out with his hook and he brought it up under the chin of the mute. He pressed it in hard, drawing blood. 'Your sister better not let me down.'

The girl answered for him. 'We won't. We does like you said, Mister. Me brudder falls down an' I screams and screams.'

He rammed the hook deeper for a moment, taking pleasure in the way even a mute could moan. Hah! The blood that now ran down his chin would help.

He hissed, through teeth clenched so hard he heard one crack. But it was of no matter. He had no time to care about a broken tooth. 'I'll be very close behind you. I'll be watching every move you make.'

Confound her! Confound Siam the Stupid! Confound them all! *Oh, my poor broken love, my poor lost dreams!* Yet was the sweetness of revenge still possible? Could it be that he might yet triumph? Old Snakoil Kawkaw, the outcast, the accursed one?

'Hellfire and abomination!' He loomed over the brats, bloody spit dripping from his broken tooth. He growled: 'Remember my instructions. Your brother will gobble my blade if you let me down.'

She nodded, too terrified now even to speak. Kawkaw saw the snot run down over the sister's lip. That was how to control the brats. That was how to make sure they did what you wanted them to.

Yet still Kawkaw's heart raged. He couldn't stop himself scratching distractedly at his own chin with the point of the hook, drawing still more blood. Spit rose in his throat at the memory the Preceptress' insults. Bear-man, fish-gutter, feral, sub-human! That was him. But it was also Siam the Stupid, and . . . and his beloved Kehloke!

A plague on her black heart and soul . . .

Within her tent on the sea shore before the vast blazing canker of Ghork Mega, Mira waited. Sleep had been impossible through the night. She had spent it squatting within the enfolding arc of her Shee guardian, Usrua, her legs crossed at the ankles, her arms drawn up to support her head where it was nestled down onto her chest. Above Mira's head the guardian star of Magtokk, the True Believer, hovered in a second protective vigil. Beyond the tent, and hovering higher still, yet in a perfect alignment with girl and star, the great eagle, Thesau, hovered. All waited in a perfect repose for the Great Cycle to begin.

That she was changing, had already changed, no longer frightened Mira. She accepted her metamorphosis. Quite what that would finally entail she wasn't altogether sure. When she was small, Mark had told her a story he had invented in which they were birds of prey. Instead of being hunted, they were the hunters. Mira recalled the feeling of changing from hunted to hunter. But it wasn't the fierce cruelty of the hunter that had impressed her then. It had been the notion of change. Metamorphosis, as she was now experiencing it, overwhelming, all-embracing. It could not be explained in words. It had to be experienced.

Mo heard the voice of the True Believer, tinkling like a bell inside her mind: *You must make ready for the ceremony . . .*

She took a tight hold of the twin powers that dangled on the thong around her neck, the talisman, given to her by Padraig and the Torus that was the legacy of her birth mother, Mala.

Would you know your destiny?

She whispered: 'Yes.'

Lifting her head, she was aware of the looming forces that linked her with the omens in the heavens above the encampment, next to the dying city.

What was light would become dark: what was dark would become light. It would manifest in the crystals of chardizz. The Great Event: the omega becoming alpha. The cycle was necessary for the Universe to exist. It was what enabled all to come from nothing. There would be an instant in which time, and with it creation, would stand still, as the old cycle ended and the new cycle began. That critical moment was fast approaching. Her place was not here but in a perfect communion with the power that was dawning deep underground, in the Valley of the Pyramids. The immensity of it, the awful implications of it, flooded her being. Thesau, the eagle, sensed it and stiffened in its cruciate shape high above. The star above her head sensed it and issued a single pulse. And then there was a scream – a dreadful scream, the high-pitched shriek of terror that could only emanate from a child.

Moonrise was screaming.

Mo heard her scream even as the gimlet eyes of Thesau pinpointed its source, within the scrabble of boxes and shanties of the camp followers.

Moonrise needs me!

Mo fingered the Torus on its chord. She saw a cluster of figures in the crepuscular shadows just before the dawn.

Moonrise screamed again.

Mo opened her mind to the needful child. In the mind of Moonrise Mo saw her own face. She searched further, quickly, urgently. Through the eyes of Thesau she saw the limp figure of the small boy, Moonrise's brother, Hsst. There was blood spilling down from his throat and onto his chest.

It is too close to the moment.

Mo sensed Magtokk's warning, but Moonrise's scream

had carried such terror with it that it evoked memories of Mo's own tormented childhood. There was no question of her ignoring Moonrise's need.

She thought: *I am following the vision in the mind of the eagle. I am there already.* She manifested within a cluster of three figures, the two children and a bedraggled wretch of a woman, perhaps a camp follower. The woman was kneeling by the side of the children, comforting them. She was also calling for help.

'The little boy is badly hurt. Oh, the poor little mite!'

Mira reflected: *I am no longer Mo Grimstone.*

Even so, even though the immensity was summoning her to the Valley of the Pyramids, she was unable to refuse Moonrise's call for help.

Kawkaw hung back within the shadows, seething with anger and resentment. He could make out the group of them through the feeble light of dawn – the brats and the priestess – heightened by the glitter of the sigil in the hilt of the harridan's dagger. The act of killing the huloima was sure to have repercussions. The Shee guardian would kill them both. It confirmed her stupidity. The stupid prostrated themselves before the gods, but in his experience the gods did not listen. *Go, now, Snakoil Kawkaw. Flee this doomed situation. Let her get on with it. Let her pay the price. Let them both die.* What did it matter to him now? But then the rage rose in him again. It appalled him that there would be no recompense for the tribulations he had undergone. None whatsoever!

What piece of shit have I become?

An instrument, stupid Kawkaw, of her beloved Master . . .

The huloima called Mo was approaching the trap. She had appeared out of nowhere. How strange she truly was, stranger even than he remembered her! So tall now – taller than most women. Perhaps even as tall as Kawkaw himself. And how her face had changed, become elongated and delicate, with those hazel eyes aglow, like an elfin princess.

He heard her words: 'Oh, Moonrise – is Hsst injured?'

Look into the brat's eyes, stupid. Kawkaw reeled at the stupidity of women. *See the terror there, you moronic girl!*

The Preceptress was playing her part with concealed glee. 'Oh, Mistress – thank goodness you are here. The poor mite – I fear there is no hope.'

Kawkaw heard her wheedling voice masking the shifting of her black-bladed dagger underneath the rags. *No hope indeed!*

He glanced around. Where was the Shee guardian who never left the huloima's side? Were they so stupid they didn't realise that she would kill the huloima, Mo, and then she would strike out at everyone within her vicinity?

In his dreams, night after night, he had relished the thought of killing his tormentor. He had enacted the killing in such perfect slow detail that when he wakened, he was surprised she was still alive.

You must kill her now.

Why – why would I kill her?

You know. You know why all is lost. You know why all is confusion.

It was that thing he had overheard, confirming what she had said to him on so many other occasions, something so wicked he hardly dared to think through to the implications. It was during that final conversation between the Preceptress and her beloved Master. She had turned to glare at him, her dagger charged with a terrible new malice, such a look of triumph on her face before she pressed the dagger to her lips. He had seen in that look that she was no longer interested in his arguments. And somewhere in the argument that had raged anew between them her fateful words . . .

'This pathetic world will be replaced by a more perfect one. Why do you think the Master has allowed His city to fall? Do you think there will be a place for fish gutters like you in that perfect world?'

No place for fish gutters like you . . .

No place for the Olhyiu – the Children of the Sea!

He was shaking.

No place for his beloved Kehloke . . . the woman he loved. He knew she was here, somewhere in the vast conglomerations of camps on the beach. She was close again, so nearly approachable. He had dreamed of proving himself worthy of her. He had dreamed of taking her out of the arms of the stupid Siam and making her his bride, of covering her with jewels to make her his princess.

No! No! Noooooooo!

He saw the Preceptress begin to move, that cunning face made grimy with charcoal to play the part of an Olhyiu beggar. The hand under the rags tensed around the hilt of the dagger . . .

Rage drove him. She was so preoccupied with timing that she had forgotten old Snakoil Kawkaw. She was unaware of him until she felt his right fist close around her hair from behind and his hook rip into her throat. He cut deep, to the grinding core of bone, and he tore out all in between, blood and cartilage, muscle and sinew, with savagery. But she had an endurance that went beyond the grave. Her head spun on the exposed bones of her neck, and like the strike of a snake, she thrust the black-bladed dagger into Kawkaw's heart.

The Shee witch had arrived too late, the tigress snatching the head of the Preceptress from her neck with a single bite. In his dying moments he watched the tigress shake the headless Preceptress from side to side, as if she were a rag doll, before those terrible claws began to rip and sunder her body, reducing it to blood and shreds.

As if floating, Kawkaw fell to the ground and felt the rage leak out of him. There was consolation in the fact that the Preceptress was dead. He could see the huloima brats being hurried away by the giant monkey. No one was concerned about him. No one gave a damn that it was Snakoil Kawkaw who had confounded the Tyrant's malice. Even as the darkness closed about him, there was no glance at him in any of their eyes. Not even when he was dying here in the dirt, like a dog . . . Like a tinker's cur . . .

*

As the giant eagle descended out of the twilight, Alan rushed towards it with the Spear of Lug blazing with runes in his right hand. Magtokk also headed towards its swooping form, carrying two small children in his arms. 'Have no fear. It is a True Believer. Its name is Thesau.'

Kate had joined Alan. 'What's happening?'

Magtokk called out: 'Look upon the scene not through your human eyes but through your oracula.'

They did so.

Myriad stars were descending out of the dawn sky. They wheeled and spun around the eagle as it beat its great wings in order to make a landing. Then the stars began to form a spiral around it.

Alan pressed Magtokk: 'What's happening?'

That enormous face, with its huge plates of cheeks and the deep mahogany eyes turned from the sky to smile at Alan and Kate. 'The True Believers are coming for Mira, and you too, Alan and Kate. But first, Kate, if you could spare a moment. There's a little one who might benefit from your healing powers.'

The Spindle

Mira looked around her with wonder at an indigo sky holding thousands – perhaps tens, or even hundreds of thousands – of wheeling and spiralling stars. She thought: *I have entered the weave of the Akkharu.*

She felt the comfort of Magtokk's voice and the presence of Thesau as stars on either side of her. <As before the Torus will be your guide.>

She thought: *I know. I must close my eyes, close all of my senses.*

<With your senses closed you will be less likely to be overwhelmed.>

Mo had found herself back in the enormous chamber below the labyrinth in the Valley of the Pyramids. It had taken her several moments to acclimatise to the dazzling light that shone from the floor, as if it were the up-curved circumference of a sun.

What must I do?

<Allow yourself to become one with it.>

She had been thrilled by the experience of consummation, and then communion. The vast weave of black crystalline filaments became one with her senses, so she flowed with them through the vastness of space.

I feel it, the first ripple of the Change . . . the Great Cycle . . . What happens now? What am I to do?

<Nidhoggr has been released. The Tyrant of the Wastelands will now take control of the Third Portal. The future is chaos. We must await the judgement.>

What judgement?

<This will be yours to determine.>

Alan attempted to wake up but he failed to do so. His failure infuriated him, but no matter how hard he tried to overcome it, he continued to fail. The experience made him suspect that his consciousness, his will, was being manipulated.

What's going on?

He was obliged to think it rather than speak it: the muscles of his throat felt useless here.

<Oh, Alan!>

Kate! He was startled by her voice inside his head. <Kate – is that really you? Are you here with me?>

<Yes!>

They weren't there bodily, so they had to be there as soul spirits. Alan tried opening his eyes. His vision widened, as if a huge window was opening within his consciousness. He knew instinctively what the wrenching feeling in his eyes implied: his pupils had opened beyond iris or the whites. He was streaming through an exploding cloud of gaseous matter in the vastness of space.

This can't be happening.

<I must apologise for the shock of the change. The seed of chaos has now entered flower. You are approaching the focus of change. The True Believers are gathering . . .>

<Who are you?>

<I am the dragon Kate knows as Driftwood.>

Kate's voice again: <Driftwood – is it truly you?>

<Have you forgotten that I am also a god?>

Alan felt Kate's soul spirit reach out to touch him. He sensed her hand enclose his. He struggled to understand.

Alan heard Kate question Driftwood: <What's happening to us?>

<You are being led to the spindle.>

<What spindle?>

<Look around you, Green Eyes!>

<We're drowning in an ocean of stars.>

Alan saw that they were moving through billions of stars. He felt a tremor sweep through him. Mentally, he clutched tightly at Kate's hand, drawing her spirit being closer to him, hugging her.

The dragon's voice spoke to them again, mind-to-mind: <Do not be afraid. You have friends here to guide you.>

<Guide us where?>

<To where the spindle will form.>

Kate asked him: <What does that mean?>

<We must rendezvous at the eye of the spindle where the Fates have ever been taking you.>

What did any of this mean? Events of monumental importance were being decided. But as ever they were buried in riddles. What had anything really meant since their arrival into this baffling world of Tír? Perhaps, as Mo had said, there was no explaining it in human terms? Perhaps they would understand it only by experiencing it.

Alan felt so very exposed. He tested his oraculum and felt nothing happen.

<Please – no more riddles!>

The dragon flooded their consciousness with light. They entered a fairytale landscape populated by elfin beings. Their spirits were filled with wonder.

Kate's voice whispering in his mind: <Oh, Alan – they're the Arinn.>

<What does it mean, Kate?>

<The Arinn created a world of perfect harmony devoid of mortal needs and desires. Their soul spirits knew only gentleness and light, and in consequence they had no understanding of malice.>

<How do you know all this, Kate?>

<Because Driftwood showed it to me. He explained that was how the Fáil was created. The Arinn were beings of grace that made it possible to enable every wish or desire to come true. But in their innocence, they assumed all such wishes and desires would be pure.>

Alan witnessed the passing of aeons: the arrival on Tír

of more primitive beings; hunter-gatherer people wandering the landscape, desperate for food, clothing, shelter. Simple folk whose needs and understanding were basic. Shamans among them prayed to the powers they imagined ruled – powers they saw as supernatural. He saw how the Fáil made real the objects of their prayers, their elemental ideas, their superstitions. Superstitions that grew into beliefs – made gods and goddesses.

He thought: *Oh, wow – the Trídédana!*

The voice of Magtokk confirmed his suspicions. <So were gods born. Such deities you know and were empowered by: of the land, birth, healing, death. But so too were more cruel forces, the aspirations of darkness.>

< The Tyrant?>

<No. Such evil could never have come into being through the work of the Arinn. The Tyrant came from beyond this world, drawn by avarice.>

<I have met the Tyrant – more than once. He attempted to bargain with me.> That horrible memory had not faded. <He seemed so powerful, infinitely so, in his malice. Why did he bargain with me?>

<Soon you shall discover the answer.>

<Something to do with the De Danaan. She chose us. She even chose the circumstances in which she called us.>

<You have not thought it through.>

<What do you mean?>

<Who really brought you to Tír – and why?>

Alan struggled to see what Magtokk meant.

<We have discussed this before. When we walked by the River of Bones.>

Alan thought back. He recalled Magtokk's words.

<The Trídédana and the Tyrant, they're rivals for power?>

<Of course.>

<Oh, man!>

<Do you at last understand?>

<We've been manipulated all along. We've been manipulated by both sides, including the Trídédana. We've been their pawns . . .>

<Enlightenment can be painful.>

<I can't believe it. What about the Shee? The Gargs? The Olhyiu? My friend, Qwenqwo, and the brave Fir Bolg?>

<Think about it.>

<Help me to understand.>

<Were not all of them born under the influence of the Fáil?>

<So they weren't capable of . . . Of acting beyond it?>

<Thus was the birth of Mira necessary.>

<What?>

<Do you still imagine your friend to be human?>

Kate's mental voice and her overwhelming sense of shock flooded Alan's mind: <Oh, no! Oh, god in heaven – Mo!>

<Yet even to think such a trajectory was anathema – blasphemy to many. Only a single great mind, one gifted with profound knowledge and understanding, dared to think beyond the blasphemy.>

<Ussha De Danaan?>

Alan thought back to that horrifying scene, the conversation below her crucifixion, her precise words: '*You who were born outside the influence of the Fáil . . .*' But who had she really been talking to on that terrible occasion? Had she been talking to Alan and Kate, the oraculum-bearers born on Earth, or had she been talking specifically to Mo, their friend, who had never really been quite the person she appeared to be?

Kate was staring at the kneeling figures of the cowled Keepers, beings she recognised from the final days of Ulla Quemar. One of them lifted its head to regard her. She wanted to question them, but whom could she trust?

<I don't know what your priorities are, but I need to understand. I apologise if that is forbidden here.>

<What would you understand?>

Kate hesitated. She wished she knew what she needed to understand. She said, with a faltering heartbeat: <I do not understand what will happen here. I hope I am not being too stupid to ask such simple questions.>

<I cannot explain the judgement. I can only observe it.>

Something profound was about to happen. She struggled to think through what any of this might imply. There was a rising feeling that the trivial things she was considering might have almighty implications. She asked a daunting question: <Is it possible that, through the altruism of the Arinn, all subsequent battles and wars for supremacy arose?>

<It is.>

A sense of growing danger, like sirens screaming through her mind, was urging her to refrain from further analysis.

There were vast forces at work here with little interest in her and against which she was of no importance. She attempted to examine what was happening through her oraculum. There was something very like an explosion: a moment in time in which she had no idea if she were alive or dead, followed by extraordinary visions. She felt that she was moving through a cosmos, with great blowing geographies of gas and violent forces.

<I am truly lost.>

The kneeling figure spoke: <You are not lost – you are needed.>

She found herself within a peculiar void in which a great star loomed close.

<You know – or at least you should now understand – that the Tyrant will demand deification?>

Kate hesitated, thinking about what the Keeper had just told her. <I sense that there will be terrible implications if he succeeds?>

<Terrible implications, indeed!>

In Dromenon, through the heightened senses that had been nurtured by Jeremiah, Penny saw the wheeling heavens, nebulae nestling in their beds of gases, in all the colours of the rainbow. She saw where new stars were being born. She felt herself drawn to the conflict of titanic forces, converging on a focus of extraordinary change. She allowed her senses to lose themselves in the wonder of it all, only refocusing her mind and wits upon the arrival of a great ship, a condensation of living energy, in the form of a raptor bird. It touched her mind-to-mind to reveal a being so powerful and strange that she witnessed ripples in the fabric of Dromenon provoked by its passage. From within its golden heart she witnessed two discrete soul spirits emerge. She recognised them as the alien beings, Mark and Nan, who bore the black triangles in their brows. As she continued to observe, the raptor bird fragmented into a billion scintillating motes, which transformed into a vast spindle entirely comprised of the black crystals of stardust. Poles appeared at either extremity and an equator condensed about its centre. Penny was drawn to take up a position at one of the poles. She saw a rival being, a spirit of shimmering light in the shape of an elfin female, take up the opposite pole.

Penny whispered: <Jeremiah?>

<I am here.>

She saw the spindle gather soul spirits to its equator: the alien beings, Mark and Nan, their eyes all black, radiating a force that was the opposite of light. Two others, alien to Penny, arrived at the equator, one male and one female, in whose brows triangles of ruby and emerald pulsed with power. Jeremiah whispered their names into her mind: <The Earth-born Alan Duval and Kate Shaunessy.> Along the outer crescents of the spindle a gathering appeared, made up of thousands of kneeling figures, their fallen heads shrouded within cowls. <The Keepers of Night and Day> Jeremiah informed her, though the implications were as obscure as ever. She saw a selected group of stars take up positions along many fibrils of the spindle. <Confounded True Believers> Jeremiah informed her. Penny was enchanted by their starry lights contrasting with the dark crystal of the fibrils that were made of pure stardust. The entire spindle glowed with light. A multitude of presences filled the surrounding voids of space, some wearing the masks of lesser gods, some mere shapes devoid of faces, and among this miscellany, two enormous beings that, from their forms and titanic wings, could only be dragons. Jeremiah explained:

<The King of Dragons, Qwenuncqweqwatenzian-Phaetentiatzen. The other is Nidhoggr, harbinger of chaos.>

While Penny's mind reeled with astonishment at what she was witnessing, a strange voice spoke within her head. The voice was coming from a single representative of the Keepers: <What is your name?>

<My name is Penny Postlethwaite.>

<Whom do you represent?>

Penny hesitated. She spoke the words as they were placed by Jeremiah in her mind: <I represent the god-in-waiting known to me as Jeremiah.>

The voice of the Keeper addressed the elfin being at the opposite pole: <What is your name?>

The elfin being spoke:

<I am Mira, The Heralded One.>

<Whom do you represent?>

<I am the Arinn reborn.>

Gasps of astonishment came from the lips of Mark and Nan, and Alan and Kate. The same astonishment rippled through the True Believers. Penny heard the shockwave echo from mind-to-mind throughout the ocean: <The Heralded One . . . The Arinn reborn . . . The Makers of the sacred Fáil . . .>

Penny whispered: <Jeremiah – what does it mean?>

<The Universe must be renewed. It is known as the Great Cycle. The cyclical nature of being, what you term reality, is fundamental to how the Universe was formed. The Fáil was created in the very moment of such universal change. Only by taking advantage of the pivotal moment could the Arinn capture the mystery of creation.>

<I still don't understand why we are here. Must the Fáil itself be renewed?>

<That is the entire point of it: its renewal is integral to the judgement to be made. Only at such a pivotal moment can the Fáil be remade – or unmade.>

Penny had many more questions to ask, but their conversation was interrupted by a fast-encroaching darkness. She heard a cry from one of the oraculum bearers on the equator of the spindle – the young woman, Kate: <Mo – if we can still call you Mo – what is expected of us? We have lost the powers of our oracula. I don't even know if you can hear my voice calling out to you.>

<I hear you, Kate.>

<Can we still be friends?>

<We shall always be friends.>

Penny thought that Kate was lost for words, but then she rallied. <You must tell us what is happening.>

<I'm afraid that a great burden has been placed upon your shoulders. You were given powers to serve a purpose, one that prepared you for a duty of judgement. The Fáil could only be renewed at the turn of the same great cycle that created it long ago. My birth was calculated to coincide with the present cycle. In the moment of change, the force that created the universe is manifest, however briefly. Only in such a moment can the Fáil be uncreated. That is the judgement that must now be made.>

<Who are the judges?>

<You are – you, Alan, and Mark.>

<Oh, god, Mo – why us?>

<It was why you were chosen by the last High Architect, Ussha De Danaan. She searched and found you, three children from a world other than Tír, three born without the influence of the Fáil, three whose hearts were pure.>

Kate had fallen silent. But Alan took up the challenge: <Go ahead, Mo. Tell us what we are supposed to do.>

<The judgement must be made in due clarity before the True Believers and it must be witnessed by the Keepers of Night and Day.>

<What depends on this judgement?>

<The Tyrant of the Wastelands is making ready to force

entry to a portal of the Fáil. If he succeeds, he will wrest control from the Arinn. But he must do so at the pivotal moment in between the existence that was and the existence that will be. The High Architect anticipated this moment. She feared that were he to succeed, all would be corrupted to darkness.>

Mira waited for the import of her words to sink in with the three friends. It was Alan again who spoke for them: <And if we decide against the Fáil?>

<The Tyrant will fail in his ambitions.>

<Well then, we have little option, do we?>

But now Kate spoke: <But what will be the price for Tír?>

<Tír will lose its magic.>

<The Trídédana?>

<They will be no more.>

Kate bowed her head. <What of you, Mo? The Arinn . . .?>

<There will be no Arinn.>

The hushed silence that fell upon the gathering was shattered by a thunderous roar, words hurled into the universe in the language of beginnings:

<THERE WE HEAR IT – THE BLASPHEMY!>

A great raven shape appeared, casting an immense shadow over the entire spindle.

A second great roar thundered through the multitude. A second and equal darkness fell over the gathering and clashed with the first.

<IN THEIR JEALOUSY OF MY APOTHEOSIS, THE WITCH
GODDESSES HAVE CREATED THEIR OWN GRAVES.
TÍR WILL BECOME AS EARTH,
A WORLD EXTOLLING THE LOGIC OF HUMANS,
A WORLD GIVEN OVER TO MACHINES.>

Darkness thundered against darkness.

<YOUR PRESENCE IS LOATHSOME TO ALL THAT IS JUST.
YOUR AMBITIONS ARE AN ABOMINATION.
THE CHOSEN WILL DECIDE.>

Vast forces clashed around Penny, blotting out the wonderful vistas of stars and nebulae. Then in the darkness that had spoken with Jeremiah's voice, she glimpsed an outline – a being larger than any living thing she had ever witnessed with an enormous dome of a head covered in coarse black fibres. Enormous wings sprouted from the region of its spine, wings as large and diaphanous as mountain tarns. Its eyes were fixed with a terrible intensity upon her, two enormous black orbs above four smaller eyes in a row. They bulged with a dreadful intelligence. The monstrous thing glared, reaching out to her with antennae-like forelimbs, causing her spirit to shriek with terror.

She thought: *I've seen him – I've seen the real Jeremiah.*

<I WILL NOT RISK ETERNITY ON THE WHIMS
OF THREE PUPS.

I WOULD MAKE A GRAVE OF THE UNIVERSE
BEFORE I ALLOW YOU WITCHES TO RULE AGAIN.>

Penny saw legions of stars rise from the spindle to populate the darkness, wheeling and attacking. But other legions, stars of darkness, manifested in equal masses and fought back. The space around the spindle was a maelstrom of fury.

The Keepers intoned in one voice:

<THE MOMENT FAST APPROACHES.
LET NOW THE JUDGEMENT BE MADE!>

Penny's head spun. A medley of voices hurled themselves against her ears. But rising louder, more insistent and urgent than any other, she heard Jeremiah's shout overwhelm her senses:

<PENNY POSTLETHWAITE!
FULFIL YOUR PLEDGE!
BE ONE WITH ME FOR ETERNITY!>

The Arinn Reborn

Penny heard her thoughts expressed aloud:

<What is a world devoid of magic? Is a world of logic preferable to such a wonder? Morality is fundamental to reason and what we, on Earth, treasure as human. But for morality to exist, we must face choices of good and evil, light versus darkness. How can you value light without its counterbalancing darkness? Life without the possibility of death? Truth without the possibility of lies?>

Her words provoked a stunned silence, not merely in her audience but within Penny herself. There was something deeply wrong about them. Penny had no memory of thinking the words. Jeremiah had somehow spoken through her as if . . . as if he were becoming an integral part of her mind. The realisation shocked her to the core. Penny tried to force her mouth open. She attempted to speak the truth, to contradict Jeremiah. But no words emerged.

The Keepers were already intoning:

<LET ALAN SPEAK.>

Alan spoke his thoughts aloud:

<Are we supposed to abandon all the good that has come from scientific knowledge to go for a world where everything is at the whim of gods and goddesses? That isn't a world I care to live in. Are we forgetting how we came to be here? Are we forgetting our murdered parents, yours Kate, and yours Mark – and yours too Mo, your mother Mala? So that a murderous scumbag can preen himself as a god? The De Danaan was right. We have to stop that happening.>

The Keepers intoned:

<LET THE ARINN SPEAK.>

Penny saw Mira's face appear above the spindle as a gigantic mask of bright glowing jade. It comforted Penny to see such a wonder of light. The eyes in the mask were closed in repose, like those of an embryo. The face of the mask was serene with grace. Around the periphery of the spindle, the Keepers eyes turned up towards the mask to become crescents of reflection. In that moment, Penny felt a change in her. She felt an expansion of knowledge. She saw with amazing clarity the mathematical precision of creation, the gravity driven cycles, the greater spirals, the lines of force, and the chaos that was an integral part of the whole: the chaos that would accompany the end of the old world and the birth of the new . . .

She was receiving a communication . . . but not in words. What could it possibly mean?

A communication at odds with mundane reality, like the wordless communication she had sensed with, and between, the Akkharu . . .

In what seemed a mere fraction of a second later Mira spoke to the assembled multitude:

<I WILL NOT ARGUE FOR EITHER EXTREME.
MY PURPOSE IS TO CARRY OUT THE JUDGEMENT.>

The gathering of Keepers, as a single choir, intoned:

<THEN LET THE JUDGEMENT COMMENCE!>

In Penny's mind, she heard Alan speak, his voice caustic with condemnation: <I vote to end the Fáil.>

In Kate's mind she recalled the dragon's tale, as Driftwood was ferrying her back from the Cill children to rejoin Alan. She recalled the terrifying vision in which the golden ring of Nimue the Naïve was held within the grasp of a clawed hand. She recalled her lack of courage then, the decision she had been too timid to make. Was the ring captured within the claws of menace, or was it being offered up by the friendly hand of a dragon, helping to return the power of Ree Nashee's magic to his queen, Nimue? If she voted with Alan the magic would die, and with it her beloved

Driftwood. This time she had no hesitation. In her mind she felt herself dive into the cold dark pool within the cavern and she felt her fingers close about the ring.

Her voice was equally determined: <I vote for the Fáil to be renewed.>

The Keepers intoned:

<LET MARK SPEAK.>

Mark heard the chaos of voices address him mind-to-mind. He recognised among them the furious warnings of the Trídédana: Mab, Bave and Mórígán. They addressed him in the ancient language of power, a strange mixture of Mórígán's fury with the mother-soft pleading of Bave and the melodious seduction of Mab and her daughters:

<WOULD YOU END OUR EXISTENCE,
WE WHO HAVE CHERISHED LIFE, BEAUTY,
AND DIGNITY OVER THE AEONS?
WOULD YOU FORGET WHO SAVED YOU FROM CERTAIN
DEATH ON THE RATH OF NANTOSUETA?>

He spoke his thoughts: <I understand your importance and acknowledge my debt, and that of Nan, to you, Mórígán. But I have a price in return.>

<WOULD YOU BARGAIN WITH US,
KNOWING WE OWN YOU, HEART AND SOUL?

WOULD YOU SACRIFICE IMMORTALITY,
FOR YOU AND YOUR BELOVED?>

He insisted: <I've thought about it and I still demand a price.>

<WHAT IS THIS PRICE?>

<You must free the Fir Bolg from their service to you. Mórígán must free them all, including my friend, Qwenqwo, from death.>

<WHERE WOULD THEY GO?
THEIR LANDS ARE LOST IN THE MISTS OF TIME.>

<Let them live in the land they have long protected – Ossierel.>

<WHERE WOULD THE QUEEN RULE?>

<Nantosueta and I – there is nothing for us on Earth. We will live in Ossierel as ordinary humans together with the Fir Bolg, in peace after all the tormented years.>

The great raven manifested over the spindle, as she had over so many battlefields.

<THIS IS THE BARGAIN YOU WOULD ASK OF ME?>

<These are my terms. Let us all live out our mortal lives in Nantosueta's fertile valley that is devoted to you.>

<YOU SPEAK FOR NANTOSUETA?
SHE, LIKE YOU, WOULD SPURN IMMORTALITY?>

Nan spoke for the first time: <Mark speaks for me. Slavery forever is still slavery. I would live out my mortal life and grow old, die, so that you can remain immortal, my Lady.>

<SO BE IT!>

Mark and Nan spoke in one voice: <Then we vote that the Fáil be renewed.>

The judgement was decidedly strange to Penny. She didn't understand what Mark and Nan were proposing. She had no idea who the Fir Bolg might be, or why Mark and Nan should sacrifice so much on their behalf. But surely it was the answer that Jeremiah had craved. Two of the three chosen had voted for the Fáil to be reborn. Yet she sensed a bridling uncertainty in him. And the gigantic face in glowing jade still hovered over the spindle, the Arinn in repose . . .

He's afraid of Mira. Jeremiah – the dreadful thing I glimpsed in that awful darkness – he hates the Arinn because he still fears her.

Moreover, the great shadow of Mórigán was also

unsettled, the shades within the darkness wheeling and moiling, a magma of implacable menace. What Penny had assumed all settled, it really wasn't settled at all.

A tidal wave of darkness was pouring out of the shadow that was Jeremiah and filling the space between the mask and the spindle. A fury was emerging from it, a colossal anomaly, exuding as if out of nothing and into being. Penny gazed upwards, eyes agog. She saw how lines of force followed a weird mathematical symmetry within it, fashioning spirals of great complexity, to create a maelstrom of what, to Penny, felt like wrath. She stared up at the ghastly phenomenon, which still appeared in the throes of its own evolution.

'What is it?'

<BEHOLD MY PORTAL.>

Penny shrunk from the vision. It resembled the spawn of a monster – a perversion of what might once have been functional and beautiful, reduced to a deformity of bones and flesh and organs.

<SACRILEGE!>

<BLASPHEMY!>

<PROFANITY>

The Trídédana cursed its appearance, threatening storms of violence. But the attack was constrained by the will of the Arinn.

<NOW!>

Jeremiah's shout was directed at Penny, a thunderous hiss, croaky with expectation inside her mind.

<FULFIL YOUR PROMISE TO ME.
OPEN WIDE THE PORTAL.>

Penny stared up into the monstrous spawn. This was his portal? She whispered: <I don't understand . . . I'm afraid . . .>

<REMEMBER WHAT I TAUGHT YOU!
MANIPULATE THE FÁIL!>

Penny's terrified eyes lifted beyond the spawn to the titanic mask of jade above it, the face of the Arinn, serene and terrible. Was she mistaken in sensing a split-second communication again. Another communication beyond words? Penny swallowed against what felt like a bone dry throat. She forced herself to recall Jeremiah's lesson, to imagine the stream of consciousness once again. She directed its flow towards the monstrous anomaly. Mathematical lines of force began to wheel around it, exploring it, discovering huge unknowns. She found herself within it. The latent power shocked her, disorientated her senses.

<It feels utterly wrong – different to how I imagined.>

<I DO NOT CARE HOW IT FEELS.
CLEAVE OPEN THE PORTAL!>

To Penny the violence of what he was suggesting was wrong.

<I . . . I cannot do it.>

She felt her mind, her spirit, penetrated by a blade sharper than a serpent's fang.

<DO YOU NO LONGER YEARN FOR ETERNITY?>

Penny wasn't sure that she did. There was that strange sense of communication again: a communication with the mask, without words.

<I . . . I sense that it is the Arinn that I should probe. I cannot force access to the portal without first entering her mind.>

<DO YOU THINK ME A FOOL?>

<I'm frightened I will fail you – that I will let you down.>

<THERE IS NO MORE TIME.
TOGETHER WE SHALL REAM ITS SECRETS!>

Penny screamed, a wail of terror, of abandonment, of fury, as the darkness enclosed her. She felt the overwhelming power of him. She was no more than a speck lost in the adamantine darkness of Jeremiah. He was hurling her, hurling them both, into the resistant monstrosity. It was like being sucked into a maelstrom. And only now did she observe that there was a presence waiting at the heart of Jeremiah's portal, a cold thing, with empty eyes.

She gasped with horror.

She saw a vision of apocalypse far worse than anything Hieronymus Bosch had ever imagined in his most tormented nightmare. Penny fought to hold herself together. She recalled the experience of her attempted rape. What horror could eclipse that? She felt a gentle power close down what was vulnerable in her mind, like a gardener, patiently putting the lids onto hives of bees. The gentle power was the source of the communications beyond words. She was reminded of the secret resistance of the Akkharu: the poor creatures of brilliant creativity who had been the slaves of Jeremiah for millenia. She sensed the secret communication beyond words:

<<Bear the pain for what will be but a moment.>>

She gritted her teeth in anticipation . . .

The moment fell, a vastness of stygian darkness, during which Penny's mouth was wide open in a soundless scream.

There was no time anymore, nothing . . .

The moment ended with another communication from

the Arinn, a communication that was visual, without need of words. The great eyes in the jade mask were opening wide. She felt an overwhelming desire to rise into them, to be comforted by them. Within them she saw, appearing, as if from darkness, the wonder of cosmic explosion, the birth of stars, the emerging galaxies . . .

Somewhere distant to her, Jeremiah was screaming, but already his scream was fading, had faded into nothing.

Then Mira spoke to Penny, a communication in words: <What the Tyrant failed to grasp is that, as part of the cycle, all must die and be born again. All! We Arinn – you the chosen – the Fáil . . . and its portals.>

<The portal was dying when he entered it?>

<All must die in order to be reborn.>

Penny shivered: <I glimpsed him – his true nature . . .>

<He came from a place where darkness rules. Drawn to the Fáil he discovered Tír and the weakness of its benevolent light, and, in his malice, he thought that, in creating a wonder that might make dreams become real, he – a destroyer of worlds – might readily pervert that wonder to selfish exploitation and darkness.>

<Thank you for saving me!>

The lips in the jade mask smiled even as they were in the act of gentle exhalation. Penny was liberated with what felt a gentle kiss on her brow.

<GO!>

The mask spoke gently in the language of beginnings, addressing all that had assembled, divines and mortals.

<GO NOW ALL WHO WITNESSED THE GREAT CYCLE.
GO TO WHERE YOUR HEARTS DIRECT YOU.
THE JUDGEMENT IS UPON US.
THE NEW UNIVERSE IS BORN.>

Earth Song

Kate wept into Alan's shoulder. Around them there was a snow-covered green and the white-capped distant Comeraghs. A cutting breeze whipped up the sluggish waters of the Suir, thick with river algae. She lifted her gaze up to the far bank and the sloping garden of the Doctor's House, partly obscured by bushes and trees.

'It's still there.'

'Yes.'

It was a little frightening how easily Magtokk had guided them here at what, judging from the cloud-blanketed sky, felt like dawn.

'Was any of it real?'

Alan hugged her in silence.

'I shall miss them, Mark and Mo.'

'Me too. But I've thought about it, Kate. I think Mark made the right decision to stay on Tír. There was nothing left for him here.'

'And Mo, she called herself Mira! Said she wasn't even human. I don't know what to make of it.'

'It's too soon to think. We're both exhausted.'

He continued to hug her until she had cried herself through, then he picked up the Spear of Lug, which he had dropped onto the snow-covered grass, before guiding her towards the path by the river by the side of the limestone wall of the Presentation Convent. They walked in silence, lost in memories both bitter and sweet, arriving at the curl of steps that took them up onto the second of the two stone bridges. To their right the road would take them to the sawmill and the wooded foothills. A moment's hesitation, but then they turned left. Kate linked her arm with Alan's left, his right leaned on the spear. They trailed footprints in the snow as they crossed the first of the bridges over the river tributary and then the road junction at the top of Irishtown. Left again and they arrived at the high twin gates to the Doctor's House.

Kate stood before the small door in the left hand gate. Her voice shook as she whispered: 'I don't dare to hope.'

They heard a furious barking coming from the other side of the door. Alan clicked the old-fashioned iron latch and the door swung open. A furry bundle of black and white erupted from the doorway, whining and running circles around them. Kate was blubbering all over again, and before they quite knew what was going on, Bridey had joined her in blubbering, before Kate's uncle, Fergal, was ushering the melee of humans and dog back into the strange old house, with its Georgian windows and corner turrets.

Bridey plumped down in one of the thick armchairs in the sitting room, a glass of whiskey clasped between her red-raw hands. A log fire blazed in the hearth. 'Sure I thought . . . Ah, mother of mercy! I don't want to go reminding myself of what I've been tormenting myself with!'

Kate, clutching Darkie fiercely to her breast, had collapsed in another of the chairs. 'I'm sorry, Bridey – and for you too Uncle Fergal. We never knew what we were letting ourselves in for.'

'Sir,' Alan had placed his glass on a small side table, untouched, 'is there any word of my grandfather, Padraig?'

'Don't you know about the fire at the sawmill?'

'What fire?'

'Mark and Nan didn't tell you about it?'

'Mark and Nan were here?'

Bridey's eyes were round with excitement. 'Yes, they came and told us some of what happened to you all. We thought they were spinning a yarn. But at the time they arrived London was troubled with them riots. Everywhere was burning.'

Alan pressed her: 'What about grandfather?'

Bridey shook her head, sniffed tears back into her nose. 'We don't know. There was nothing seen of him after the fire. He disappeared.'

'Disappeared?'

'We assumed he had died in the fire. But the fire brigade, the guards, they didn't find him in the ruins.'

'So you don't know what became of him?'

'Things have been very confused for some time,' Fergal added. 'The university in Cork has been closed for the duration. It's the same everywhere.'

'What's going on?'

'Don't you know about the riots in London? The monstrosity they call the Black Rose? The whole world has gone mad. Big cities everywhere have been razed – the madness, Razzamatazzers?'

Alan and Kate stared at him.

'I can show you the papers. You'll see what we're talkin' about.' Bridey was waved to sit down by Fergal. 'Young people losing their wits.'

Fergal sighed. 'I was away when Mark and Nan called round. Bridey told me what they told her. I could scarcely believe my ears. I thought she was mad to help them. Something about a Fir Bolg battleaxe.'

Alan and Kate jerked alert at the mention of Fir Bolg.

Bridey took a swig from her glass. 'A vicious looking thing! We had to smuggle it to them after they had left for London.'

Kate was stroking Darkie's head, gazing down at the grey hairs that had appeared over its muzzle in her absence.

Bridey looked from Kate to Alan, and back to Kate again, as if still unable to believe she was back with them. 'Did ye never meet up with Mark and Nan after they left here?'

'Yes, Bridey, we did.' Alan recalled the extraordinary judgement at the spindle. 'But there was no opportunity for explanations.'

'No time even for proper goodbyes,' Kate said, still close to tears.

Fergal said, 'Half of Dublin has been razed like London. Like the big cities everywhere. Belfast, Cork, Limerick . . .'

Bridey added, 'Nobody had the slightest notion of what was going on.'

'That's right. We don't know if the madness is settled, even now.'

Alan looked at Kate, then turned to Fergal, who was auburn-haired, like Kate, and sporting a close-cropped beard. 'Sir, this fire at the sawmill? Was anything left standing?'

'Only the old dairy.'

'Your little den,' Bridey nodded.

Mark and Nan stood within the wide breach in the walls of Ossierel and watched the Fir Bolg climb towards them through the many mountain trails. They looked weary, as well they might after thousands of years of enslavement. Mark and Nan felt weary themselves after climbing the many steps to the summit of the Rath, there to issue the command of liberation. Cataracts of blue-black lightning had arced once more throughout the Valley of Ossierel, exciting rainbows over the steep slopes throughout the wooded vales and crags. The lightning bolts had separated into myriad rivulets and streams as they struck the slopes, sundering one stone head after another. And everywhere, amid forest and rocks, rising out of the beds of streams and from meadow and the very roots of the trees, the reawakening had begun. Ensheathed in crackling spiderwebs of power, the horned heads of the war beasts tore open their former graves and the drum masters were beating out a new message of freedom.

It had been the last command to issue from the black triangles in Mark's and Nan's brows, the triangles dissolving as their powers faded. They embraced one another as the aftershocks took place.

But they could not complain. Mark had demanded it of Mórígán and she had kept her word. All were freed – alive again to experience the ups and downs of normality. They were free to live their lives, but also condemned in time to grow old and to die.

The first Fir Bolg to approach them was a drum master riding his massive war beast, the huge claw-footed animal horned and its body covered in a blanket of raw hide. The drum master continued to beat out the rhythm of a steady march on his semicircle of six great kettle drums, each producing a different note, the melody thundering out as he climbed through the breach in the inner fosse, and finally the steep ramp that opened onto the cobbled streets of the magnificent ruined city.

Mark and Nan clapped the drum master's arrival. He

turned his beast around to look back down over the slopes, the drum beat now thunderous in such close proximity. His call joined with the many other drum masters throughout the entire valley, to resurrect the life in every waking heart and mind, to liberate all, every family and every friend. Soon a gathering crowd of Fir Bolg were flocking around Mark and Nan, bowing and saluting them, some pressing their lips to their saviours' fingers.

If they recognised the figure before them as that of the former Dark Queen, they saw how her grim visage had been replaced with a more gentle face. But now Mark encountered another effect of the loss of his oraculum. He could not understand the speech of the Fir Bolg. Fortunately Nan spoke the language fluently.

Nan must have reassured them a thousand times already. 'I am no longer a goddess. Mark and I are just normal people. Be welcome to find a home here, in the city, or in the valley, for you and your families.'

It was mid-afternoon, and Mark and Nan were still watching the growing multitude that spilled over the slopes when they heard the great roar they had been waiting for. The burly figure breaking through the crowds of Fir Bolg was plain to see, his raised arm holding an upraised runestone. But then Mark saw that Qwenqwo was not alone. A stocky female with a determined jaw and a brush of wayward red hair walked beside him, together with a brood of red-haired youngsters.

'Qwenqwo – it's so good to see you!'

Mark tried to hug the dwarf mage, only to be lifted off his feet and spun in a circle like a child.

'Nan – tell him how glad we are to see him.'

'I think he knows. He wants you to meet his wife, Tegor, and his children Zurr and Orru.'

'I am honoured to meet you, Tegor,' Mark said, kissing her hand and causing her to blush and erupt into gales of laughter.

Mark and Nan were taken up by the entire robust family, tottering with the hugs and kisses. They found themselves bowled over by the enthusiastic crowds, then hoisted aloft and carried on shoulders to meet the king, Magcyn Ré, and the high shaman, Urox Zel, who were being carried on war beasts through the breach. It took a command from the king to stop the enthusiastic crowds parading him and Nan around the ruins of Ossierel.

The king asked Qwenqwo, 'Is the enemy truly vanquished, then?'

Qwenqwo harrumphed. 'I left the battlefield early. I think I had better leave it to Mark and his beautiful consort to explain.'

Magcyn Ré looked at Mark and Nan.

It was Nan who confirmed it: 'The two thousand year war is over. The Tyrant has yielded his kingdom in the Wastelands.'

The king was astonished. 'That is wonderful news. You must tell us how it became so.'

'Sire,' spoke Qwenqwo. 'There will be plenty of time for

rejoicing, and the telling of tales, but I humbly suggest this is not the time.'

'Indeed – if the son of Urox Zel so advises!'

Qwenqwo bowed. 'Your Majesty, this is the young Ironheart who, with support of his consort, Nantosueta, saved our people from eternal servitude.'

The king alighted from his war beast and embraced Mark and Nan in turn. 'We are most grateful to you, Mark Grimstone, and to you, Queen Nantosueta. Though there be painful history between us.'

Nan stood proud as a queen. 'Sire – alas the city is in ruins.'

The Fir Bolg king put his hand into a deep pocket and he plucked out a pipe, with an enormous bowl. He clicked his fingers and those about him supplied the baccy, and they struck a flint that supplied a flame. He puffed on it, scratching his head, then licked his lips. Hands passed a largish flagon from one to another, until it reached him. He took a hearty swig. It appeared that Qwenqwo's fondness for the baccy and flagon were shared with others of the Fir Bolg.

He announced: 'Madam, we are not merely a warrior race. We are builders. And though I may be accused of swanking, I think it is fair to say that, ahem, you will not discover any finer builders in this benighted world.'

He was in the process of passing the flagon to Urox Zel, who eschewed it, passing it with a knowing wink to his son, Qwenqwo.

'The economy of the island is sorely tried, Sire.'

The king puffed out his lips, his hand reaching out for the flagon, which arrived back to where it had begun.

'I will pass on your concerns to the stripling you appear to know already.'

Qwenqwo made his own pantomime of lighting his pipe. 'It will take a day or two, at most, to restore the pulleys to lift up stores from the fertile plains below.'

Mark said: 'Qwenqwo – where would we be without you!'

'I find myself remembering your trials, on board the Temple Ship – and then I look back at my own tribulations over two thousand years. And yet the wonder of it is that here I stand as if untouched by it all with my beloved Tegor and my two rascals, Zurr and Orru. All this do I owe to your courage and sacrifice in confronting Mórígán.'

There was a loud cheering and shouts of congratulations from the multitude that had been gathering around the meeting of friends. Then Qwenqwo's expression changed. He held the Fir Bolg runestone above his head. 'Ah – something interesting this way comes.'

A presence hovered over them for several moments, then alighted to the ground, and Mo, who was Mira, manifested in a ghostly form. She said, 'I could not leave you, Mark, without saying goodbye.'

'Oh, Mo, I'm missing you already. You're the only family I have.'

'I'll miss you too – and Kate and Alan.'

'I can't bear the thought of never seeing you again.

Please say you'll return, as time goes by, even if just for a minute or two.'

'I can make no promises. There is so much I have to learn. Can you remember how upsetting it was to you to feel uncertain if you lived or died? I now face a similar quandary – but in my case it's not about death but the price of immortality.'

'Then you truly are a goddess – an Arinn.'

Mo smiled. 'The Arinn are not deities. In our way, we are the very antithesis of goddesses or gods. We extol logic, civilisation.'

'Forgive me if I have difficulty coming to terms with that.' Mark laughed, but it was a hollow laugh, anticipating her loss.

'Goodbye then,' Mo's spirit kissed Mark's cheeks. Then she kissed the brow of Qwenqwo Cuatzel and lingered a moment, gazing at Mark before she faded.

Nobody spoke for a little while. Mark's eyes were moist as he turned to Qwenqwo. 'Are your adventures truly over?'

'I have a warrior's heart. But in truth, I confess that the thought of a farm, and seeing more of my family, an attraction. Nevertheless I suppose that in time I shall miss the cut and thrust of battle.'

Mark said: 'I won't.'

Nan added: 'Nor will I.'

'Ah, so you speak now. But such memories do we share. What tales will I tell your children . . . ahem . . . should I say my grandchildren, eh?'

Mark and Nan hesitated, but then they laughed. They

both hugged Qwenqwo at once. Then Qwenqwo also extended his burly arms about them. 'The thing to remember,' he said with a cackle, 'is that when a war ends all that matters is the tales you spin.'

Fergal had offered Alan the loan of his Landrover, but he had insisted on walking to the sawmill alone. Kate was more than upset enough already and her mood would not have been assuaged by these fire-blackened ruins.

He looked around the burned out main buildings, then at the dairy that had been their den, its roof covered with the virgin white snow.

He said: 'Grandfather!'

The star of a True Believer appeared before him.

<You knew?>

Alan's head fell. 'I didn't know for certain. But I wondered. And now I see it confirmed I don't want to believe it.'

<Why?>

'I wanted to find you still alive. So I could apologise for my behaviour before I set out for Tír.'

<There's no need for apology. I understood then – as now.>

'It's all a little confusing. We could have destroyed the Tyrant, but Kate and Mark didn't want to destroy the Fáil. So I was overruled. But then Mo sealed his fate anyway.'

<Then you succeeded. Mo destroyed the Tyrant and you also destroyed his armies, liberating Tír. I think that should count as a considerable success. I'm proud of you, as would be your parents.>

'You think so?'

<I know so.>

'Thank you.' Alan dipped his head. 'I heard that Mark and Nan came here. They talked to Bridey and went to London.'

<Yes. They rescued me there.>

'They did?'

<Thanks to Grimstone the city was in turmoil and ruin. I was intended as some kind of sacrificial victim.>

'What happened to him – to Grimstone?'

<Oh, I think the Americans will have taken care of him and his misbegotten church now their Master is gone.>

Alan looked at the star hovering amid the falling snow. It was hard to imagine that it was truly his grandfather. Hard to think he would never see him in the flesh again. 'I'm really glad to hear that they rescued you. I was mad at Mark because he took the Temple Ship away from us. But now I see he was fulfilling his destiny too.' He hesitated. 'I'm going to miss Mark and Mo.'

<What will you do, Alan?>

'I don't know. I haven't had enough time to think.'

<Come back to me, here, when you have sufficiently thought. There is an inheritance here, though you might feel it too great a burden.>

Alan thought about his grandfather's words and what they might imply.

<Promise me you'll think about it?>

Alan nodded. 'I promise.'

The Fate of the Rose

Gully looked around the soaring gloom inside St Paul's Cathedral in a panic. He had no memory of getting here. Even as he began patting at his pockets there was a thunderous eruption from all around the building. It had to be coming from the Black Rose. His eyes darted towards the doors. But he could see no sign of Razzers, or Paramilitaries or Skulls. There wasn't no sign of nobody.

'Strewth!'

It was nothing short of amazing. The whole place was intact – near enough undamaged. What was going on?

He could only recall bits of his journey here, which had begun on a bicycle. He had been wandering somewhere inside of the Rose with Bad Day and Owly Gizmo. He missed his perfick Owly Gizmo.

'Wot the 'eck is going on?'

Then he saw her up ahead – Penny! She was spinning around like a ballet dancer on her bare feet in the centre of a great tiled circle. Gully couldn't believe she really was here to meet him. He couldn't take his eyes off her, watching her dancing. She sort of glowed as she spun around. She looked so . . . happy. Like the sun was shining down on her especially.

But now she saw him and she stopped. She was just looking at him, staring at him, with those grey eyes glittering like they was mirrors.

He said: 'Hey, is it really you, Penny?'

'Of course I'm me.'

'Why you staring at me like that?'

'Oh, Gully, you look so battered and bruised. And you've grown. I can't believe how you've grown.'

'Yeah?'

'You must be three inches taller.' She reached out and touched his cheeks. 'And you're developing a fuzz.'

Gully felt at his chin and was shocked to find that she was right. 'I don't have a clue wot's been happening, Penny. I was lost in the roots of the Black Rose. I think I must've fallen asleep or somefink. And then I woke up 'ere. Don't ask me how that kind of a fing can 'appen. But we can't stay here. It ain't safe. The Rose is blowing apart.'

'With Jeremiah gone, it's become unstable with wild power. I've been instructing the Akkharu to uproot it, Gully. We've been working together.'

Her words made no sense to him. Yet she seemed so calm. There was another thunderous detonation from outside that shook the walls. It provoked a shower of plaster to fall like angel dust out of the dome. Gully felt the floor beneath him judder and he grabbed at Penny, his legs going from under him. He expected her to shake him off, but she made no effort to push him away. In fact she hugged him back.

'Gawd in 'eaven!'

'It's okay. We'll be fine. I'm just waiting for them to appear.'

'Who?'

'The True Believers.'

'Who the 'eck are they?'

'They're powerful spirit beings that inhabit Dromenon. You might think of them as . . . as you used to think of angels, Gully.'

'I never thought about no angels in my life, gel.'

Gully and Penny continued to hug one another as the world dissolved into light. It felt as if they were floating on nothingness, free-falling into nowhere.

She whispered: 'We've entered Dromenon.'

'Shit!'

She whispered, mind-to-mind: <I think they're coming, Gully.>

'Bleedin' Norah!'

She could hear him, counting to twenty, patting at his pockets. She said: 'I know it must be really scary. But you can open your eyes now.'

'What the . . .'

Penny just continued to hug Gully tight, as something manifested before them, taking the shape of a four-pointed star. She saw the corolla of light that surrounded and flowed out of the star like the penumbra of an eclipse, all the colours of the rainbow. A coursing river of stars followed. Then the leading star expanded into a ghostly figure, the spectral figure of an old man, so tall and willowy he looked like a plant that had been denied light. She saw that his eyes were the purest blue. He was bearing an upright column of white fire in the clasp of his hands. It bore a faint resemblance in shape to the hilt and blade of a great sword.

Gully exclaimed: 'It's the ghost of Padraig!'

The ghost spoke to her: <Who are you?>

'I'm Penny Postlethwaite.'

<Ah!> He nodded. <The girl who drew the City Below.>

'Yes. But who are you?'

<Your companion, Gully, is right. My name is Padraig.>

The ghost was speaking to her with an Irish accent. 'How do you know about us?'

<Mark and Nan talked about you.>

Ah! Penny thought about what he was saying. 'Are you human?'

<I was.>

'And now you're a ghost?' Gully asked.

<I don't pretend to know, Gully, but I believe that I've become a True Believer.>

Penny asked him: 'Why are you here?'

<I'm the keeper of the Sword of Feimhin.>

'Oh!'

<I'm afraid that we have very little time. I believe you know what must be done?>

'Yes!'

<Are the Akkharu ready?>

Penny closed her eyes. She re-entered the stream of creativity, as Jeremiah had taught her to, but this time she was more confident about it. She made open communication with the waiting Akkharu, who accepted her control. She became the lynchpin of a vast common mind, a mind she no longer regarded as an obstacle to be overcome, but one whose weave she shared and respected: the crystals of chardizz responded to her instruction.

Working step-by-step with the Akkharu, she expanded her consciousness until she encompassed the entirety of the roots of the Rose, its immense spread of attachment to the Earth, sensing and then detaching that attachment root-by-root, quenching the malice that Jeremiah had planted there.

When that task was complete she freed the Akkharu from all bounds of control.

Her consciousness returned to Dromenon, and the ghost of Padraig, who was waiting for her with the soul spirit of Gully.

She said: 'It's done!'

<Thank you, Penny Postlethwaite.>

She watched him elevate the column of white fire, high

above his head. She saw how its force extended to infinity, the stars wheeling and following its implacable trajectory. She knew that, back in London, that column of white fire had now pierced the moiling sphere of incandescence, ripping open a pathway of least resistance to the brightly welcoming sun far overhead.

Back beneath the dome of St Paul's, Gully and Penny detached themselves from one another's arms, although Gully's eyes were still clenched shut.

'You can open your eyes now, Gully. The Rose is gone. Listen, if you don't believe me. You won't hear it thundering anymore. Padraig sent it back to where it came from.'

Gully didn't ask her to explain. He opened his eyes to see her sprint forward and round the back of the altar. When he followed, he found her inspecting the stained glass windows of the American Chapel.

He heard her exclaim: 'Thank goodness – they're intact.'

He followed on after another sprint, to reach a side door to the right of the main altar that was ajar onto the garden. The wind was blowing snow in through the open door. She was staring out of it with such a forlorn look on her face that he put his arms around her again. Then he led her back to the tiled circle under the dome, where they both looked up at the light falling through the high windows.

She said: 'Do you know what date it is?'

'I got no idea, gel.'

'I was hoping it might be spring leading into summer.'

Gully shrugged. 'I don't fink so.'

'You know that Americans call autumn the fall. I like that. It seems such a perfect match for the spring. Spring and fall. They go together – don't you think?'

He just held her. It felt so good to be allowed to hold her at last, he never ever wanted to let her go again.

'Summer and winter are fine. They sound perfect as they are.'

She made him let her go so she could dance again, her bare feet spinning in the dust and her face turned up to the shower of light.

He said: 'Was it you wot saved St Paul's?'

'It was part of my bargain with Jeremiah. Oh, he tricked me, Gully. He wasn't what he pretended to be.' She closed her eyes, though he could see the lids fluttering with excitement. Then she opened them again to look at him, with a fierce, uncompromising gaze. 'But, still, he kept his side of the bargain.'

'Penny, you got to forget about him.'

'I don't think I'd be capable of forgetting. Jeremiah showed me how to do things.' She looked like she wanted to pirouette again but resisted the temptation. Her expression grew more serious. 'He showed me things.'

'Wot fings?'

'He explained the Akkharu to me – they helped me recreate the new city you are about to see. It was amazing to build something beautiful from the ruins. But it was just part of my learning curve as far as Jeremiah was concerned. Jeremiah showed me that there was no morality in nature. But he couldn't see that we humans aren't obliged to follow suit.'

Gully stared at her, ignoring her strange words. He felt lost in her, lost in the fact his Penny was here next to him.

She must have read his mind, because she laughed. 'Oh, Gully!' She looked wistful for a moment. But then she seemed to become altogether calm and collected again. 'I think you've grown into a man.'

Gully shrugged. 'There's no bleedin' food no more. An' no Our Place to hide.'

'We'll find a new Our Place.'

'Like where, exactly?'

'I've something to show you.'

Gully stared in open-mouthed disbelief as the great tiled circle, with its inner star, rose up out of the floor. Once standing perpendicular, it began to spin to form a giant sphere, which filled up with light.

Penny took him by the hand and she led him onto the sphere. 'Close your eyes again if you feel dizzy,' she said.

'We goin' someplace then?'

'Some place that can't be explained in words . . .'

Acknowledgements

As always throughout this series I owe my deeply felt thanks to my publisher, Jo Fletcher, who first commissioned The Three Powers, and has been a steadfast supporter throughout. I should also acknowledge the contribution of my editor, Nicola Budd, who has been invaluable in knocking my creative thoughts into the shape it finally took on the pages. It is a special pleasure to thank my agent of many years, Leslie Gardner, who became the all-important go-between from the beginning, and who supported and made helpful suggestions throughout. It was a wounding blow indeed when my mother, who had inspired my love for the magical landscapes and legends of my youth, did not survive to see the series come to this conclusion. But I still hear her songs in my head and am comforted, and ever inspired by them.